A Hard Woman to Kill

Alex Howard was born in London and educated at St Peter's College, Oxford and Edinburgh University where he studied Arabic and Islamic History. He worked in adult education for the British Council and other institutions in the Middle East and London. He is married with two children.

Find out more at www.alexhowardcrime.com

Also by Alex Howard

TIME TO DIE

COLD REVENGE

Alex
HOWARD

A Hard
Woman to Kill

HEAD
ZEUS

First published in the UK in 2015 by Head of Zeus Ltd

9 7 5 3 1 2 4 6 8

A catalogue record for this book is available
from the British Library.

ISBN (HB) 978178471083
ISBN (E) 978178471045

Typeset by Ben Cracknell Studios, Norwich

Printed and bound in Germany
by GGP Media GmbH, Pössneck

Head of Zeus Ltd
Clerkenwell House
45–47 Clerkenwell Green
London EC1R 0HT

WWW.HEADOFZEUS.COM

He who takes delight in the slaughter of men
cannot have his will done in the world.

Tao Te Ching

PROLOGUE

Claudia Liebig looked at the young boy's picture. Serg was frowning hard in concentration as he drew. In five years of teaching Claudia had never met such an intense child. Everything Serg did was coloured with the same remorseless focus.

Claudia had rebelled against the tenets of her art school, which was ultra-liberal, focused on the idea that theory was as important, or maybe more so, as technique. Claudia disagreed and here at the small, international private school near Alexanderplatz in central Berlin where she was the art teacher, figurative work featured highly. By all means, she said, be abstract, but before you do me a series of coloured rectangles or Cubist faces, or before you display an everyday object as art, show me you can paint like Mondrian, Picasso or Duchamp could.

Today her pupils were drawing their parents at work. Desks and rudimentary offices were the main themes – most of the parents worked in offices and some of the children's parents were in TV, so there was a smattering of cameras and monitors depicted in the paintings.

Serg was drawing some tanks; they looked scarily real. She admired them.

'T-80s,' said Serg. He spoke flawless German even though Russian was his mother tongue. He had an amazing vocabulary too, thought Claudia. Teachers shouldn't have favourites, but they do. Serg was hers. Despite being Russian. Not a popular thing to be in nineties Berlin.

'That's nice,' said Claudia. Serg bowed his head over his painting, colouring in the tanks battleship-grey. 'Are they good tanks?' Serg lifted his head and looked steadily at her with his startlingly green eyes. He was a child of almost unearthly beauty, thought Claudia, like his mother.

'My father says that remains to be seen.'

'Is that your father in the tank?' Claudia pointed to the picture.

Serg shook his head and indicated a figure in a jeep. It was astonishingly well drawn. Claudia had met Serg's dad once, rumoured to be head of the FSB, the former KGB, at the Russian Berlin embassy, the Stalinist-style palace in the Unter den Linden, in the heart of the city. She could recognize his powerful bull-like neck and physique, the angry energy that the hunched figure seemed to radiate.

'That's him,' Serg said.

'Get that machine gun up here now,' barked the colonel. Captain Kamenev ducked as more clods of heavy Chechen mud rained down on them from the remains of the park they were sheltering in. The colonel in his filthy uniform, some medal ribbons sewn on to the breast pocket – Kamenev recognized a couple from Afghanistan and, taking pride of place, the red ribbon of the Hero of the Soviet Union, from way back in the glory days, before the USSR fragmented – picked up an AK74 rifle and fired a dozen shots at a third-floor window a couple of hundred metres away on the other side of the park. He put the gun down, turned and directed the reinforcements trickling up from the ragged lines behind them. They were confused and scared conscripts, some of whom had received only a few hours' training and were now up against seasoned Chechen troops, battle-hardened in Afghanistan, and fighting for their religion, their soil, their families and their lives. One of the colonel's sleeves was soaked in blood. Watery sleet fell from a dull, silvered sky. Three burnt-out T80 tanks lay like dead metal dinosaurs in the no man's land between the park and the three apartment blocks, pockmarked by shell fire, windows blown out, the grey concrete scorched here and there by fire. In huge, Cyrillic letters someone had painted the Chechen slogan, *Svoboda ili Smert*, freedom or death.

And the cold rain fell down from the leaden skies above.

Small-arms fire crackled menacingly from the buildings opposite alongside the heavier, meatier sound of a PK mach-ine gun. 'Why don't we blow those bastards up?' grumbled Kamenev to the colonel. He scratched at the lice under his rough battledress. Filthy Chechen lice, they itched like crazy. He peered through a jagged hole in the brickwork where a Mukha RPG shell had punched its way in, and looked at the park. There were three dead Chechens there, the colonel's handiwork. The colonel rolled his eyes, took out a Belomorkanal cigarette and lit it. The cheap, harsh tobacco seared his lungs comfortingly.

'Cos they're all underground in sewers and cellars and those dimwits in their tanks can't drive down a proper street in Grozny, let alone one full of rubble, and do you really want to provide more shelter for the *Dukhs*?' Learn from history, boy, thought the colonel. Learn from history or you're doomed to repeat it. My dad fought at Stalingrad; I was brought up on stories of fighting in ruined cities.

He got into a low crouch and rubbed his knees. I'm not as young as I was, he thought.

'Better get back to headquarters. I'm not supposed to even be here.' He shook Kamenev's hand, crushing the young man's fingers in his powerful paw, and was gone, relinquishing his temporary control of the forward position. The captain looked mournfully at his retreating figure. He wished to God the colonel was still here to take command and tell him what to do. He looked around him, saw the terrified faces of the conscripts around him. *Blyad*, he thought, I guess I'm in charge now.

Several hours later, the colonel was in the back of a UAZ 4x4 as it bounced along a rutted track through what seemed to be an endless forest about forty kilometres from Grozny. It was late afternoon but already dark. In the front was Cherkov, his FSB bodyguard who had been with him for twenty years, and in the back, next to him, Velnikov, a staff captain from 58th Army, based at Vladikavkaz in North Ossetia. The guy behind the wheel was a driver from a Group Vympel Spetsnatz Unit. The colonel didn't know the man, but he could do with losing a few kilos. The ruts were so deep, the earth impacted by the weight of heavy logging lorries, that the driver was keeping the UAZ at an almost forty-five degree angle, the offside wheels on the raised central soil, the nearside wheels in one of the troughs. Whoever the driver was, thought the colonel, he was doing a bloody good job. To keep up the speed he was doing in those conditions showed some skill and a cool head.

Grozny should have been surrounded, hermetically sealed, but there were gaping holes in the ring surrounding it. The colonel, with his knowledge of military tactics, practical, hard won fighting the Mujaheddin in Hazarajat in the central Afghani mountains, had been brought in specifically to identify these areas. He had discovered the biggest gap in the Old Sunzha sector and they were on their way to meet a Chechen informant who would supply the names of the Russians who were being bribed to let it happen.

'Hey, Cherkov,' said the colonel to the man in the front passenger seat. 'Is it true that woman cook at the base gave you that shiner?'

Cherkov turned and grinned, one hand cradling his KMP sub-machine gun. One eye was almost closed, a riot of blue and yellow. 'Yeah, she hit me with a soup ladle,' he said. 'I'd told her she had an arse like a badly packed parachute.' They all laughed. They were the last words he ever spoke.

The driver turned a corner, hissed under his breath, and slammed on the brakes to avoid hitting the tree that lay across the road. While the car skidded to a halt, the passenger window exploded in fragments of glass as three rifle bullets hit Cherkov. He died instantly. The colonel swore and grabbed his machine pistol from the seat next to him, pulling the trigger and firing blindly through the smashed window at the unseen attackers. He heard a scream and silence, and turned to Velnikov. The colonel was about to shout to follow him, and his hand reached for the door handle as he tried to take the fight to the enemy. The staff captain shot him in the face at point-blank range.

Velnikov opened the screw-topped vodka bottle of 80 per cent proof Ruskova vodka and took a swig.

'That was easy,' he said to Arkady Belanov. He had expected more from the dead man, knowing his reputation. He looked at the body of Colonel Surikov sitting next to him, his head resting against the rear window, covered now in gore. Blood from the bullet hole in the colonel's forehead had stained the neck of the white T-shirt he wore under his battledress the exact red as the colour in the medal ribbon of the Hero of the Soviet Union on his chest. He handed the vodka to Belanov. The fat man took the bottle with his left hand, nodded his thanks and casually shot the captain through the heart with his right.

'Yes,' he said to the corpse, sitting next to the dead colonel. 'Very.' He took another pull on the vodka bottle and put the Baikal pistol down on the seat next to him.

Claudia Liebig said to her class, 'Five minutes to finish, children.' She walked over to Serg Surikov. His picture was nearly finished. Claudia looked at the picture. Behind the tanks a city was burning. She could see red flames and black smoke. In the corner, in the sky, was a figure with wings,

'Is that an angel?' she asked.

Serg nodded.

'To protect your father?'

Serg nodded. His very green eyes were slightly slanted, an inheritance from his Siberian Tartar mother, then he added softly, 'Or to avenge him.'

Outside, the skies were darkening over Alexanderplatz and it started to snow.

CHAPTER ONE

'This is my husband. His name is Charlie Taverner.'

Oksana Taverner (née Oksana Ilyinichna Yegorov) looked across the desk at Hanlon. The policewoman's features, Oksana decided, were harshly pretty but not helped by a swollen and badly bruised left eye that was a purplish-black in colour. Oksana's eyes dropped to check for a wedding band on Hanlon's left hand, but the long, strong fingers were free of ornamentation. So, not done by her husband then, which had been Oksana's immediate thought. Yekaterinburg, Oksana's home city, like most of the Urals, most of Russia, most of Eastern Europe, had a poor record when it came to violence against women. If you saw a woman there looking like Hanlon you'd know who had done it.

Then their eyes met and Oksana decided that Hanlon would be nobody's pushover. Oksana thought they belonged less to those of a state official and more to those of a gangster, someone from the Uralmash mafia. They were disconcertingly chilling. The eyes were matched by a face whose expression was equally cold.

Oksana had grown used to the, in her eyes, overly friendly British. Where she came from, people didn't usually apologize, say please or thank you or smile in a self-deprecating way. It had taken her a while to realize that politeness didn't equal weakness. No chance of that happening with Hanlon's face, she thought. For a second or two Oksana wondered if maybe her English had let her down and she wasn't in Missing Persons but somewhere more sinister, or if Charlie's death (she was sure it was murder) was being handled by the British equivalent of the FSB, the Federal Security Bureau.

Hanlon looked back at Oksana Taverner and saw a tall, very attractive dark-haired woman in her late twenties with classic Slavic features, high cheekbones, large almond-shaped brown eyes. She was casually but expensively dressed in muted browns and greys, a vivid-coloured scarf artfully tied around her long, shapely neck.

Her eyes dropped to the glossy photo of Charlie Taverner that beamed at her through a see-through plastic wallet. Oksana, a veteran of Russian bureaucracy, had also appended photocopies of his passport, driving licence, security ID for the Home Office and their wedding certificate. She had even included a photocopy of her birth certificate, passport and her degree in metallurgy from USTU, the Urals State Technical University. Oksana had also gone to the bank and withdrawn a thousand pounds in nondescript twenties just in case a *vziatka* – a bung – was needed, as it would be back home. It was in her bag, in a manila envelope.

Hanlon looked at the photo of a chubby-faced amiable-looking man with glasses and a receding hairline, aged about fifty. Then up again at the beautiful Russian woman young enough to be his daughter.

And just what, she wondered cynically, could possibly have attracted you to the well-paid and securely pensioned Mr Charlie Taverner with his large detached house in Windsor, a spitting distance from the castle?

'How long has he been missing?' asked Hanlon wearily.

'Sunday night. Today is Thursday so four nights. He should have been with your Metropolitan Police for a meeting on Monday. He was not there either.' Oksana looked at Hanlon with a hint of disdain that implied the glamorous world of the Met was something that Hanlon could only dream of, here in Langley Police Station. Langley, thought Oksana dismissively. It wasn't even Slough.

The policewoman said nothing, but tugged at a loose strand of the coarse, dark hair that framed her face in a fringe of unruly corkscrews. Oksana would have straightened it before coming to work, even in a place as pointless as this. She began to regret taking Charlie's boss's advice to seek out this woman. She decided to emphasize Charlie's importance, his proximity to high-ranking officers that this lowly woman could never know, never have.

'He should have been presenting evidence to commission chaired by Assistant Commissioner Corrigan on Russian mafia in London.'

Now she had Hanlon's attention. Oksana's sharp glance noticed a slight stiffening of posture, a narrowing of the eyes in the woman opposite. Hanlon looked hard at her. Corrigan had sent Hanlon into this living exile in Berkshire. Was Charlie Taverner a lifeline back to her old job in some form of serious crime with the National Crime Agency?

Corrigan, thought Hanlon. The name had jolted her awake.

Until now, Hanlon had not been paying that much attention to the Russian. Everything came at a cost and Oksana was paying the price for her beauty. No one really took her seriously except when her exams had been marked without anyone knowing what she looked like. Hanlon herself was not immune. She had mentally dismissed Oksana as a mail-order bride and had more or less assumed that her husband was probably playing away with some other woman of doubtful virtue. Some other East European bimbo from an agency.

'May I ask what he was supposed to give evidence about at this inquiry?' she asked.

'Prostitution and their. . .' For a moment Oksana's mind went blank as she mentally searched for the English; she knew them as *soutiner*. Then it came to her. 'Pimps, particularly growing connections between Moscow and London, *lya, lya, lya*.' She shrugged. 'Russian population here is increasing. Five years ago, Charlie tells me, there were maybe forty thousand Russians here in London, now, who knows how many now. Some say two hundred thousand, some say four hundred thousand. V.V. says Russian oligarchs own Chelsea now.'

'Who's V.V.?' asked Hanlon, baffled.

'Vladimir Vladimirovitch. President Putin,' said Oksana, rolling her eyes and her 'r's.

'Oh,' said Hanlon.

'But is dangerous to lift up rocks and look underneath,' said Oksana. 'Sometimes you find more than you expect. That is what Charlie was doing, picking up rocks.'

'What do you think has happened to your husband?' asked Hanlon. She raised her voice slightly as another jet passed overhead. She was beginning to get used to the endless noise of the flightpath. Heathrow was only a couple of miles away. Both Mawson and McIntyre were out of the office and the place was silent apart from the roar above them. Absent-mindedly she touched the tender, bruised flesh around her eye, a sparring injury from her boxing training.

'Charlie is dead,' said Oksana flatly. There was a bleak acceptance in her voice that touched Hanlon, who was used to people being either in denial or more visibly shaken. The woman across the desk was calm and matter-of-fact. There was no 'I can't believe this could have happened'. She was just stating a fact. If there is one thing Russians are, Hanlon thought, it's tough. She'd met a few. Oksana's face was expressionless.

'What makes you say that?' she asked.

Oksana looked at her steadily. 'The people Charlie knew, particularly from Moscow, that is how they deal with problems. They eliminate people.'

'I see,' said Hanlon. Maybe in Russia, she thought, but not in Windsor, not tubby ex-civil servants like Charlie. Litvinenko, yes; Taverner, no. 'But you shouldn't really be talking to me about this. Your husband was a civil servant, ex-Foreign Office, an important man. You have a reasonably convincing story suggesting a crime has been committed. Go to Corrigan. He's surprisingly accessible.'

'No,' said Oksana.

Hanlon wasn't over-burdened with work but the Baranski disappearance was generating more than its fair share of paperwork and she had a meeting with Child Protection looming that she had to prepare for. Oksana's problem wasn't her problem.

Even if what she said was true, her husband's disappearance wouldn't fall under a Missing Persons remit. It would be Thames Valley's Serious and Organized Crimes' baby.

She also suspected that Mawson would not be happy at Hanlon taking it upon herself to bypass procedure. He'd made it clear that such things would not be tolerated.

'Look,' said Hanlon, leaning across her desk and pushing some hair from her forehead. The light through the window picked out several long, pale scars on her forearm. There was a slight kink to her nose that suggested it had been broken some time ago. Oksana noted the fine lines that time and pain had etched on Hanlon's forehead, the tiredness around her eyes. She had obviously known hardship and trouble in her life.

She also noted the ligaments moving elegantly under Hanlon's skin. Oksana, a former gymnast when younger, until she had become the wrong shape – too curved, too tall – could appreciate how strong Hanlon was. Her eyes now ran over the elegant musculature of Hanlon's frame. She could easily imagine her on a parallel bar or a beam.

'You need the National Crimes Agency. Maybe even MI5 or 6.'

If it's a threat to the country, which I doubt, she thought. I wish you'd go away.

'Not me. I'm Missing Persons, OK, Mrs Taverner,' said Hanlon wearily. 'I find errant husbands and sometimes I order reservoirs dragged for missing Polish junkies.'

As I am at the moment, she thought, thinking of Datchet Reservoir, Peter Baranski's probable resting place. She should be seeing the Specialist Search people really, rather than wasting time with this woman. She thought, You really don't need me, not unless Charlie is shacked up with his secretary in South Berkshire.

Oksana shook her head angrily. '*Nyet, nyet, nyet*, Hanlon. Sorry, I mean no. These other people. They are *nomenklatura*.' She virtually spat the word out. *Nomenklatura*, the high priests of the ruling caste. Every Russian's nightmare. There was no Party in the UK, but there was its equivalent, the civil service.

'They are officials, government officials. Charlie's killers have access to *obshchak*.' She hunted in her mind for the English word; the policewoman was looking baffled. She found it. 'To trough, like pigs. But a trough full of money. They will have someone to help them in government. They will have someone in police. We say in Russia, 'roof', a *krysha*. They have millions to spend. You cannot trust government.'

'I'm the government,' said Hanlon acidly. She had a certain amount of sympathy with Oksana's views but she didn't appreciate someone from the back of beyond, the Urals, telling her the score.

'Yes,' said Oksana. 'But you are different. I have seen your file.'

You have done what? thought Hanlon. Her thoughts – alarm, rage and wonder – were painfully transparent to the Russian opposite.

Oksana said simply, 'You cannot trust government. Like I said.'

'So you've read my file.' Hanlon's voice was low, menacing. Hanlon was a very private person and the idea that someone like Oksana could access it was as alarming as it was enraging. How the hell had that happened?

'Yes. Charlie's firm has many connections. It is think tank, it has many government connections.'

'Oh, does it now,' said Hanlon menacingly.

She had a mad desire to leap over the desk and smack the woman opposite hard across the face. What right have you to review my life? she thought. Not even my account of my life either, but that of some official. Presumably it went into detail as to why I'm stuck here, in Missing Persons, cleared of any serious charges but deemed unsuitable for front-line police work. Better deployed in back-office jobs, like this.

Oksana smiled. 'Yes. You are not corrupt, Hanlon, you are just crazy. I read your file. It is all there.'

'Is it?' asked Hanlon. I very much doubt that, she thought bitterly. My side of things won't be there. So much for data protection.

Taverner's widow nodded. 'But back to Charlie. In Russia we say *navomnye ubiistvi*. Contract killing. If I go to normal police, I think nothing will happen.' She paused and her long fingers with their shapely ox-blood nails played with her expensive

Hermès scarf. 'They know Charlie is missing, they will go through motions, that is all.' She frowned angrily. 'I have spoken to some policeman already. He asked me if I knew Charlie liked to go to see whores.' A contemptuous look flickered across her face. 'Yes, I say, is where his contact is. This policeman, he as good as told me that he was with some whore for sex, not information.' Oksana made an expansive gesture with her hands. The movement encompassed her incomparable body, her beautiful face. Look at me, it said, look at me.

Hanlon looked at her as Charlie had almost certainly done, five feet ten of unbelievable sex appeal. Oksana nodded at her. Look what Charlie got for free at home. No sex worker was going to compete with her, that was for sure.

'You can make things happen, I know this,' she said. 'I read your file. Facts are facts.'

I could help you, thought Hanlon, looking at her, but I'm not going to. I can't fight the world's battles. She thought of Mark Whiteside lying silently in the room in the hospital in his drug-induced coma. The sands of time were running out for him. Maybe Taverner was dead; she had the living to attend to. She had her own priorities and Oksana's husband was not one of them. Priorities. She shook her head.

'I'm sorry,' she said. Finality was in her voice. 'Speak to Corrigan. He'll help.'

Oksana leaned forward. 'Please, I beg you. Charlie is dead. I cannot bring him back. In Russia I cannot touch his killers. Here, you can. Please will you help me?'

'No,' said Hanlon simply.

The Russian woman's eyes narrowed. 'None of us can bring back dead, that I do not expect. What I was hoping for was justice, an eye for an eye, as they say. A life for a life.'

'I'm sorry.' Hanlon's voice was curt.

Oksana recognized the irrevocability in Hanlon's tone. She stood up, tall and elegant. Hanlon had rarely seen such a beautiful woman. She even smelled fantastic; some expensive light floral perfume that Hanlon didn't recognize. The Russian woman had a point. If you had Oksana to come home to, you wouldn't want to play away. She also revised her earlier opinion of Taverner. Oksana was not the kind of woman to just want a sugar daddy. And there was no doubt that she cared very much for her missing husband.

Her almond-shaped brown eyes rested contemptuously on Hanlon. 'So the *vor* and his *suki*, his bitch Belanov, have won then. Is nothing more to say.'

Hanlon stiffened behind her desk. Arkady Belanov. Now Oksana had her interest.

'Please sit down, Mrs Taverner. I think I've just changed my mind.'

Oksana Ilyinichna Taverner, née Yegorov, put her hand in her pocket and took out a memory stick.

'It is all here, if you want it.'

Vengeance is mine, saith the Lord. Shona McIntyre, her colleague, had told her that.

Hanlon nodded and took the memory stick. Oksana gave her a curt, formal smile and sat down.

'Why don't we begin at the beginning, Mrs Taverner?'

'Thank you, DCI Hanlon. Please call me Oksana.' She nodded at the stick in Hanlon's fingers. 'Time for you to meet the Butcher of Moscow. Charlie's killer.'

'And Arkady Belanov,' added Hanlon.

'Him too,' said Oksana.

Hello, Arkady, thought Hanlon, still hurting women then? It'll be nice to see you again.

CHAPTER TWO

Assistant Commissioner Corrigan of the Metropolitan Police, naked except for a small towel preserving his modesty, looked thoughtfully at the man, similarly attired, sitting opposite him in the steam room.

The hot, heavy damp air, like being inside a heated cloud, billowed around them, obscuring vision, deadening sound. The thick, grey marble walls, a century old, dripped and ran with condensed moisture.

Through the mist, Corrigan saw a heavily built man in his late twenties, early thirties. His body was muscular, not the overly defined, chiselled look of the gym but spectacularly solid. His waistline was beginning to carry a couple of folds of surplus fat, but he wasn't too far removed from the boxer he had once been. Corrigan, whose family had almost all to a man worked in construction, knew strength when he saw it. Enver Demirel was a powerful individual. He had a mournful face that bore the traces of the boxing ring, a heavy drooping moustache and sad, brown eyes like a seal's. Corrigan's gaze dropped momentarily to the man's right foot. There was a small, red puckered scar where DI Demirel had been shot a year or so ago in the line of duty.

DI Enver Demirel stared unhappily back at the assistant commissioner. Corrigan was a huge man, six feet five, and the towel wrapped around his waist looked like a face flannel against his massive bulk, a weightlifter run to seed. Generations of Corrigans had done nothing but heavy, manual labour, and in some kind of Darwinian way the results of centuries of coded musculature were there in the AC's body.

Enver averted his eyes. He hated public nakedness and was very uncomfortable in these surroundings. He was also uncomfortable with deviation from routine and he suspected that Corrigan had brought him here for some off-the-record discussion that he most certainly did not want to be having.

They were in the basement of Corrigan's club. Most of the members were military or businessmen who'd done time in the Guards, so it was old-school masculine, scuffed Chesterfields and deer heads on the wall. The walls were wood-panelled, the heavy pictures portraits of long-dead, long-forgotten generals or military events – *Rorke's Drift*, *Saving the Colours*, that kind of genre. A huge stuffed pike dominated the bar from above the fireplace. The club was open to women, but Enver had never seen one in there. He wondered what they would make of Hanlon.

Enver knew from office gossip that the AC had rented out his flat in Notting Hill for an astronomical sum and moved Mrs Corrigan to their cottage in Sussex. Corrigan had bought the flat when Notting Hill had been predominantly Irish and Afro-Caribbean. (*No blacks, no Irish, no dogs*, the signs in rented properties had often read in those days.) Now only the super-rich could afford to live there. If you'd forecast that at the time, people would have questioned your sanity. Thirty years ago, Corrigan's neighbours had been a squat full of dope-smoking hippies on one side and a West Indian drinking den on the other. Now he had a TV producer to the left and an alternative treatment centre for the extremely well-off worried-well on the other. Corrigan preferred the old days.

During the week Corrigan stayed in this club, which had cheap rooms for its members. When Corrigan had invited Enver there for a meeting he'd assumed it would be in the tranquil old-fashioned bar, not in the bowels of the building in this strangely accurate nineteenth-century reproduction of a Turkish steam room or hamam from the Ottoman Empire.

So now he sat uncomfortably on a marble slab – a marble banquette really. The whole room, with its high, vaulted ceiling, was a temple to marble and brass. Sweat trickled through the forest of black hair on his body, while Corrigan said, 'What I really like about this steam room, Demirel, is it's so hard to bug anyone. Look around you.' He waved a thick arm at the steam room. Through the swirls of vapour, pink blobs of people – rich, white, elderly and male, Corrigan's clubland colleagues – could be glimpsed, and a circular dais in the centre where two masseurs pummelled and kneaded their clients. There was no furniture, no nooks or crannies to embed microphones, and the watery atmosphere with its ninety-eight per cent humidity would destroy most electrics. And, with everyone being naked, there was nowhere to hide a recording device or a camera. Corrigan nodded his satisfaction. Being recorded was anathema to him. These days he had to assume everything would be made public, captured on a phone, photographed from a satellite or a car, and now there was the advent of smart glasses.

What he had to say was for Enver's ears only. He wanted no record – no email, no paperwork, no photographs, no witnesses – just nice simple deniability if things went wrong.

'Yes, sir,' Enver Demirel said. He wondered if Corrigan had a particular reason to feel paranoid or if all one-to-one briefings would, in future, be conducted in spas, plunge pools, showers. Maybe swimming pools. Hanlon would like that, he thought. He had seen her swim, elegantly, effortlessly, tirelessly. He floundered in water. He felt he looked ridiculous.

He hated being here. He looked down angrily at the swell of his stomach. It used to be flat; now it billowed out, straining his skin. I'm obese, he thought with self-loathing. Fat. I look pregnant.

'I take it you read my briefing notes on the people-trafficking debate we're having in London?' asked Corrigan.

'Yes, sir,' said Enver. He quoted, pleased to be able to take his mind off his body issues, paraphrasing freely, 'Conservative estimates would place the number of cases of trafficked sex workers in the UK in the thousand to two thousand mark. CEOPS reckon that there are about five hundred children trafficked for sex purposes and in London we're dealing with about a hundred cases, each on average involving about a dozen people.' Enver had a retentive memory for facts and figures and he could see Corrigan beaming at him through the steam, a teacher whose prize pupil had done well as usual.

'Yes,' Corrigan said. 'But what particularly concerns me at the moment is the growth in crime from the former Soviet Union, Russia in particular.'

Russia was back in the news as enemy number one again. Not quite the heady paranoia of the Cold War days, but there was pressure on Corrigan from his political masters to provide hard information and to be seen to crack down. The last thing the government wanted was to be made fools of domestically as well as internationally. Some form of crackdown on Russian criminals was called for, in their opinion. It would look as if they were doing something and it would be popular with the public. Above all, it would be relatively uncontroversial. It wouldn't upset, for example, the black and Asian or the Islamic community.

It wouldn't upset Brussels either.

Enver looked round the steam room, ghostly glimpses of naked men seen through the swirling hot mists. Sweat was pouring off him now. He'd used saunas in the past to make the weight when he'd been a boxer, shaving grams off before a weigh-in. He'd be a super heavyweight now. It was a depressing thought.

'Sir?'

Corrigan leaned forward. He spoke softly but Enver could hear the anger in his voice.

'I should be chairing a meeting right now involving the Borders Agency, HMRC, CEOP command and the NCA. Our star turn was to have been a man called Charles Taverner, a Foreign Office expert recently moved to the private sector and well informed on Russian crime syndicates, particularly prostitution, the one that concerns me.'

'Yes, sir,' said Enver.

Corrigan looked irritatingly composed, relaxed in the intolerable heat, like a huge lizard.

'Taverner was supposed to give us a presentation on something called a *skhodka*,' he said, 'a special meeting of criminals in which a *vor v zakone*, that's a kind of Russian crime boss, a sort of Godfather figure, would be elected or chosen to further Russian interests in the prostitution sector in London.'

'That's fairly clear, sir,' said Enver. It was obviously a case for Serious Crimes, not for him. 'Why would they want to come over here? Aren't they busy enough in Russia?'

Corrigan smiled mirthlessly. 'For much the same reason as the oligarchs; it's a relatively safe place to do business and to bank your money. Particularly with the rouble going tits up.' There was a brass tap on the wall and a small, metal basin. The AC filled it up and tipped it over his head, the cold water soothing him. He pushed his greying, dark hair back, obscuring his bald patch. 'If you're Russian and legit you're always worried that the government are going to confiscate your assets, the way that happened to Berezovsky or Khodorkovsky, and if you're a criminal they might crack down on you because a rival has paid the police off to eliminate you. It's a murky world, Demirel.'

'I daresay it is, sir.' And it's not my problem either, Enver thought smugly. I'm busy liaising with the London Turkish community. I'm building bridges, as they like to say.

As if reading his mind, Corrigan shifted his weight and leaned forward confidentially. 'It's always good to learn new things, isn't it, Detective Inspector?'

'Yes, sir,' agreed Enver reluctantly. The mention of his rank alarmed him. It was a none-too-subtle reminder that he owed it to Corrigan's influence. He felt this was an overture to something he did not want to hear. There was a jocular, wheedling tone now in Corrigan's voice. He'd heard it before; it was a softening-up tactic that the AC was fond of.

'Here's a new word for you, *smotriashchya*.' Corrigan said the word again, as if savouring its exotic syllables. '*Smo-tri-ash-ch-ya*. It means a watcher, a watcher who looks after the interest of the *vor*. Taverner was going to tell us the name of the watcher and the *vor*, but he wasn't at the meeting.'

'No, sir?' said Enver innocuously. Corrigan shook his head.

'A no-show, Detective Inspector. And he wasn't at Monday's meeting either. Now. . .' he tapped Enver on the knee for emphasis '. . . I know Charlie Taverner well. He's not that kind of man.' The assistant commissioner sighed. 'I enquired about him. Missing for two days. Men like that do not go missing. He's not some bloody teenager.' He shook his head.

'Something tells me I shan't be seeing him again in this life.' Corrigan leaned further forward so his battered face was nearly touching Enver's. 'There are always leaks, as you know, DI Demirel, in the police, but this information was restricted and I need to know who gave it out. We're not talking about someone giving info to the papers or blabbing when they're pissed in the pub. This is high-level leakage with very serious consequences. We're talking major corruption. The Russians talk about a *krysha*, a roof or protection. In this case an officer, a senior officer, probably in Serious Crimes, is acting as the *vor*'s *krysha*. Are you with me so far?'

'Yes, sir,' said Enver. It was fairly clear. That someone was presumably responsible for Taverner's death and would also be in a position to monitor all details of any police investigation. Corrigan wanted a parallel investigation, an unofficial one. PR was part of Corrigan's job and this would be a disaster if it got out.

He had realized immediately that Corrigan was terrified this would get into the press. There was almost an alphabetically long list of embarrassments and scandals surrounding the police right now. This would be horribly newsworthy – murder, Russians, corruption, bribery. No wonder Corrigan was concerned.

'I'm not going to put anything in writing,' the AC said.

Of course you're not, thought Enver somewhat bitterly.

'But, informally, I want you to look into something for me.'

'What might that be, sir?' asked Enver. He regarded the affable giant opposite suspiciously. The last time the AC had made a similar request he had come close to being killed, the circular scar in his foot from a .22 bullet a permanent reminder.

Equally, he knew he owed his last promotion to Corrigan's patronage and Enver had found his first real grip on the career ladder exhilarating. He was not the kind of man to admit it, maybe not even to himself, but Enver Demirel was an ambitious man. He knew he had the qualities it took to climb all the way to the top of the ladder and he knew Corrigan could make or break him. If you wanted to get to the top table, you had to take risks. Corrigan's smile broadened and Enver had the uncomfortable feeling that the man could read him like a well thumbed copy of *PACE*.

'There is a Russian in Oxford called Arkady Belanov,' began Corrigan. Enver's face remained impassive but he was thinking furiously. He knew Belanov courtesy of DCI Hanlon and he certainly knew Belanov's minder, Dimitri. He knew him because he had beaten Dimitri up in East London, late at night in a deserted side street in Bow. GBH, Section 18, added Enver's remorselessly tidy mind. 'I think he's the *smotriaschchya*, the watcher for the *vor*. That's Thames Valley CID's patch, not ours, so walk carefully. This Belanov lives off immoral earnings. That's who I would like you to look at for me.'

'Unofficially, sir?'

'Exactly. Say his name came up in some routine context, any questions you can refer them to me. But I'd rather you kept everything off the radar. Presumably you know one or two of the Oxford lot from courses, that kind of thing. Plus you were down there a few times for the Philosophy Killer, I believe.'

'Won't that raise suspicions, sir?'

Corrigan looked at him levelly. 'Always good to shake the tree, Detective Inspector, see what falls out. If Belanov is the watcher, we can maybe find the *vor*. If we find the *vor* we can find his police contact. I surely don't need to remind you, Demirel, that police corruption is very much in the public mind at the moment. I want to nip things in the bud. I'm fed up with officers on the take. Is that all clear?'

Enver nodded, not altogether happily. He knew a detective inspector in Oxford who could help. In fact, he had a shrewd idea that she might well know who the police informant was. But Enver was very reluctant to reveal this information that he had acquired, to his own discomfort, in an unorthodox way. Equally, he knew that if he scratched Corrigan's back, it would be reciprocated.

Off-the-record investigations were, in his opinion, PR disasters waiting to happen. He could think of two high-profile ones that were currently in the papers; he didn't want to add to them. 'I do know someone from Oxford CID reasonably well, sir.'

'So, there we are,' said Corrigan. 'I knew my faith in you would be justified, Detective Inspector.'

There was an unmistakeable note of dismissal in the final sentence. Enver said, 'Why not ask DCI Hanlon, sir?'

She knew Arkady Belanov better than anyone. She'd humiliated him and Dimitri. Then Enver immediately felt ashamed of himself. What he had really meant was, Let her take the risk. She's already as good as destroyed her career, what would another high-profile controversy matter? Keep me out of it.

It was a deeply cowardly suggestion on his part.

No sooner had he asked the question than he knew he'd made a mistake. But a mistake of a different kind. The expression of genial affability on Corrigan's face froze and was replaced by one of pure aggression. It was an astonishingly speedy transformation. Like many people, he'd fallen into the trap of assuming that Corrigan was some slow, lumbering old-time copper. An elderly has-been, slightly out of touch with the modern world, on the point of retirement. Doing things the old-fashioned way on a whim.

But Corrigan was a hard old bastard, ruthlessly efficient, still ambitious and frighteningly bright. A friend of his was probably dead, police complicity was suspected and Corrigan didn't just want answers. He wanted results. And he wasn't going to take any nonsense from inexperienced, junior officers.

Particularly from patronizing junior officers.

And certainly not at the expense of a woman who, although unbelievably troublesome, he deeply respected.

'Don't try and tell me how to do my job, sunny Jim,' said Corrigan. He leaned forward close to Enver's face so he could see the expression in his eyes. His voice rumbled ominously 'In fact, don't even think about trying to tell me how to do my job. Is that clear?'

'Totally, sir,' said Enver.

Corrigan didn't need to add an 'or else'. He never did. He never made threats; he didn't need to.

Corrigan sat back and stared at Enver with hostility.

'You can go now, Detective Inspector Demirel.' His voice was dismissive. 'You have my personal number. When you have something worth telling me I suggest you use it.' Corrigan nodded a curt farewell.

Enver stood up, one hand clutching the towel covering his groin. To have saluted would have been ridiculous in the circumstances.

'I'll be in touch, sir,' he said.

'You do that, Detective Inspector, you do that. And don't be long either. I want this put to bed asap.' He looked at Enver and said, cruelly, 'Give my regards to DI Huss, DI Demirel.' With satisfaction, he noted Enver's eyes start from his head and a kind of muscular ripple run up his body as if he'd been electrocuted. Serves you right for questioning my judgement, Enver, he thought.

'Yes, sir,' said Enver in a strangled tone. How could Corrigan have known?

'Off you go,' said Corrigan.

Corrigan watched Demirel's broad, muscular back disappearing through the clouds of steam. Strange that Enver Demirel had brought up Hanlon's name. Hanlon would be safe where he had put her. Twice she'd nearly got herself killed. Corrigan was going to make sure there wasn't a third time.

He thought with exasperated affection of Hanlon's corkscrew hair and angry eyes. If anyone had a genius for getting into trouble, he reflected, it was her.

She'd be safe in Thames Valley for now, chasing missing old ladies, looking for lost cats. Safe until this IPCC business had blown over and she could return to the Met. People have short memories.

I bet she's cursing me, he thought, but I most certainly don't want her involved with the Russian mafia. Let Enver do something strenuous for a change, other than building bridges.

CHAPTER THREE

Langley High Street was a five-minute walk away from the industrial estate. Hanlon and her new colleague Shona McIntyre were walking back to the office with some sandwiches from a local deli. Hanlon had spent half an hour in the quiet company of her new boss, DS Mawson, while he'd explained to her the role that they played in the Thames Valley Police. Mawson was particularly keen on the potential uses of social media such as Twitter and Facebook. He seemed disappointed by Hanlon's obvious lack of expertise at social networking.

She and McIntyre had spent the morning looking at the two prominent missing person cases. One was Peter Baranski, the Pole, aged twenty-seven, who had gone missing from a squat in Chalvey, a suburb of Slough. Slough was home to an enormous number of Polish immigrants and, as Hanlon was becoming increasingly aware, there was a whole secretive illegal immigrant community too, many living parallel lives crammed into slum-style outhouses built in the backyards of the town's backstreets – 'sheds with beds', as they were known locally.

One of the obvious side-effects of this hidden population was an unwillingness to talk to the police. Things did not bode well for the investigation.

'Why are we interested in him?' asked Hanlon. 'Maybe he just moved away; maybe he'd had enough of Slough.' God knows, I

27

have, she thought. It wasn't that there was anything particularly wrong with the place; it was just so very dull. It was famous for a huge Mars confectionary factory, a John Betjeman poem, 'Come friendly bombs and fall on Slough', and for the fact that the TV comedy *The Office* had been set there. Other Slough highlights included the first linked traffic-light system in the UK and a stuffed dog in a glass case on one of the platforms at the railway station. She was practically weeping with boredom.

McIntyre explained that the squat was well known as a junkie hang-out and there'd been a number of criminal incidents surrounding it.

'This Peter,' she said, 'Peter Baranski, is a heavy heroin and ketamine user. He hasn't got the energy or the inclination to go far.'

Hanlon nodded; that made sense. Strung out on smack and special K, he'd find doing his shoelaces up a struggle, let alone disappearing anywhere. 'Who reported him missing?'

'His girlfriend,' said Shona McIntyre. 'She thinks he's been murdered. She'll be coming to the station at eleven; we'll meet her down there with DI Hennessy.'

The trip to the police station was a waste of time. Paris Dowd, the girlfriend, was a no-show and her phone resolutely switched off. They stayed long enough for Hanlon to have her suspicions confirmed that she really didn't care about Peter Baranski with his list of previous convictions, mainly drug-related petty theft in his native Poland and two over here for affray and Grade A (heroin) drug possession.

At the station she was aware of the curious glances of her colleagues, keen to take a look at the controversial DCI Hanlon, foisted on them by the Met. At times like this, she felt like some sort of freak. But then she thought, In a sense I've created this image. I can hardly feel hard done by.

28

They turned off the High Street, past a pub into a lane that was a cut-through to the industrial estate. Parked illegally on the kerb was a battered pickup truck. An aluminium extension ladder was wedged against the rear nearside tyre where a decorator had been painting the soffit boards of the property, just under the eaves.

He was taking a cigarette break and he leered aggressively at the two women as they walked past. Attractive, confident, well dressed, they more or less represented everything he hated in female form. Hanlon looked him over with disdain. Her brief glance summed him up. He was short, stocky and bald and he had an unpleasant, slightly fat, aggressive face. He was like a sneer in human form.

He registered her contempt.

It was his eyes or, rather the look in them, that struck Hanlon as his least attractive feature. Their gaze was on the lookout for any kind of weakness that he could exploit. If they'd been disabled or students, or had learning difficulties, he would have tailored the abuse to meet the target. Cripple. Poof. Spaz. He was the kind of guy who got his rocks off trolling on Twitter. As they were women, he'd obviously decided upon sexual harassment.

Her sharp eyes noticed that the tyre by the passenger door was bald, well below the minimum legal tread. Momentarily she was tempted to nick him for that, three points on his licence.

The truck was a mess, an exposed jumble of old paint cans and detritus. The lackadaisical attitude extended to safety. He'd left a pot of paint balanced precariously on the penultimate rung of the ladder. What a cowboy, thought Hanlon contemptuously.

Their eyes met, hers coolly disparaging, his actively hostile. Two successful attractive women, a sight he hated. I just bet your sex life centres around Internet porn, she thought. No woman with an ounce of sense would touch you with a bargepole. Good job you've got a right hand.

'Give us a kiss, darling,' he said to Hanlon, with a suggestive pout. The jut of his body was full of displayed aggression. 'You know you want it,' he said, thrusting his crotch at her. What a target, she thought, entertaining a momentary vision of driving either her knee or her Chelsea-booted foot between his legs. No, don't think about it, she told herself. I haven't been here long; I mustn't cause trouble. Annoyed at her lack of reaction, the absence of fear, he turned his attention to McIntyre as they drew level with him.

'Oi, nigger bitch, show us your tits!' he called out to her.

McIntyre ignored him, keeping her eyes averted, stony-faced. Hanlon, feeling a sudden familiar rage surge through her body, gave in to it almost joyfully. Sod it, she thought. I should keep on walking, she thought. I should rise above these things. I should act professionally.

But, she thought. But. . .

Hanlon despised bullies. Those who picked on the weak she regarded as fair game. It was a personal urge to redress the balance. She also liked fighting. There was a berserker streak in her that craved release. Any old excuse would do. She had it here in spades. She let it out.

Here we go, she thought.

She kicked hard and sideways with her foot at the ladder as she walked past. It was a vicious kick. The ladder quivered, moving a few centimetres with a metallic scraping noise as its aluminium tips scratched at the exposed brickwork of the wall, and the three-litre pot of white gloss paint toppled forward, jolted off the rung by the motion, voiding its contents as it fell.

It went even better than she had dared hope.

There was no lid on it and a wave of thick white emulsion, followed by the now almost-empty tin, hit the man. It clattered loudly as it fell to the pavement. McIntyre stared at him in horror.

The stuff covered half of his head and one shoulder. More paint pooled over the lower half of his body, his boot and the pavement. For a second they all stood rooted to the spot by the spectacle. The man had the presence of mind to fumble in his pocket for a rag to clear the paint from his right eye so he could see.

Hanlon surveyed her handiwork with satisfaction. 'Oops,' she said loudly.

He advanced towards her, left arm outstretched to grab hold of her, the right arm drawn backwards, fist clenched. Sexual harassment, verbal abuse, the unexpressed threat of rape, had disappeared now. He wanted violence; he wanted to give Hanlon a good kicking.

Hanlon didn't shout, *Come on, then!* She grinned at him. It was so much more enraging.

'You fucking bitch!' he hissed, advancing on her.

Hanlon didn't retreat. She moved with her customary speed and grace, sure-footed and with an accuracy born of long years of practice. She seized his outstretched wrist and pushed it back on itself, transferring her iron grip to his splayed fingers, instantaneously bending them back. It stopped him in his tracks before he could throw the punch with his right.

His fingers were on the point of breaking. He automatically reached forward with his right hand to pull her hand and arm away.

Hanlon was so close to him now she could smell the paint, the cigarette smoke on his breath and the stale sweat of his unwashed body. But, above all, the paint. There was so much of it, its heavy fumes were eye-watering. Below his thin hair, plastered to his balding head with emulsion, two small bloodshot eyes, one rimmed with white, shone with malice and pain. She pushed the fingers back some more. He grabbed her arm and she swept out her right leg in a scything motion, forward and back. The rear of her calf hooked round his and he stumbled with the unexpected pressure and fell to the ground. Hanlon still had control of his wrist. He was now on his knees and Hanlon inhaled sharply as she prepared to break his carpal bones. She looked at his face and just as she leaned in for a final push that would shatter the bone, she felt McIntyre tugging at her jacket.

'Leave him be!' she said to Hanlon. Her voice was shocked and angry. 'Come on, let's go!'

Hanlon did as McIntyre asked. The two women hurried away down the side street, Hanlon's victim kneeling on the pavement, paint-spattered and clutching his injured forearm. He made no move to pursue them. He'd had enough.

McIntyre was slightly taller than Hanlon and longer-legged. She increased her stride to make Hanlon work to keep up with her. Hanlon, who had previously found McIntyre's relentless good nature irritating, was now discomforted by the woman's obvious ill humour. The other woman didn't need to speak. Her erect spine, shoulders thrown back, and the look on her face made speech unnecessary.

She followed McIntyre's angry back for two streets until she'd had enough. She suddenly increased her speed, overtook McIntyre, wheeled round and blocked her on the pavement.

'What's the matter? Have I upset you?' she demanded.

The other woman stopped dead in her tracks. McIntyre's brown eyes met Hanlon's grey ones.

'Yes, yes, you have. What was all that about?' she demanded. She was furious with Hanlon, outraged by her behaviour.

Hanlon glared at her irritably. 'You heard him,' she said,

pointing back in the direction they'd come from. 'He sexually harassed me and racially abused you, what more do you want? What do you suggest I do? Nick him?'

McIntyre shook her head angrily. 'Just because he acts like an asshole doesn't mean you should too. And, DCI Hanlon—' she stressed her rank sarcastically '—I would say it's very much up to me to decide if I've been racially abused and what I choose to do about it. It's not for you to decide for me.' She paused for a moment. 'In fact, what you did is arguably even more racist, in a subtle way, than what he did.'

She looked at Hanlon, visibly angry. She was actually shaking with emotion. Any minute now, thought Hanlon, she'll literally start jumping up and down on the spot. A passer-by looked at them curiously. A mother with two children crossed the road to avoid them, a worried look on her face.

'Who do you think you are, anyway, DCI Hanlon?'

Hanlon started to calm down. She'd better nip this one in the bud. She could do without an aggrieved McIntyre complaining to Mawson.

'OK,' said Hanlon to placate her, 'it won't happen again.'

McIntyre glared at her. Something more was needed. 'I promise it won't happen again,' said Hanlon.

She noticed that McIntyre had been looking at her hands. Incredulously, Hanlon guessed that it was to make sure she hadn't crossed her fingers when promising. God, we're back in the playground, she thought. Cross my heart and hope to die. Hanlon mentally shook her head. Her colleague was too nice to be doing this job, she thought. Maybe that's why I've ended up working with her, to make the scales balance.

Hanlon practically never apologized to anyone for anything and Shona McIntyre did not realize how unusually privileged she was.

'It had better not,' said McIntyre fiercely. 'You might come here from the Met with your big city ways of doing things, but. . .'

Hanlon forced herself to look contrite and not smile as McIntyre seemed intent on portraying Slough as some innocent, bucolic, country paradise. *Your big city ways.* McIntyre gestured wildly to indicate Langley.

This was what Hanlon saw.

There was a small park behind them, bordered by a mangy privet hedge.

On a bench three street drinkers sat clutching super-strength lager. A woman walked by with an English bull terrier and a Staffordshire straining at the leash. The Staffie added a curl of excrement to the others on the pavement. 'Good boy, Tyson,' said the owner.

More of the endless jets flying to Heathrow roared overhead through the grey skies. An old BMW with a new paint job and a wobbly exhaust, filled with Asian kids smoking weed, passed by. Aggressive rap thundered through a sound system more powerful than the car.

Oh, Jerusalem, thought Hanlon, England's green and pleasant land.

McIntyre continued, 'But out here in Berkshire we don't need patronizing, OK?'

'OK,' said Hanlon.

'And it's not up to you to go around like some loony vigilante.'

'No, I'm sorry,' said Hanlon contritely.

'And I'm a Christian,' said McIntyre.

Hanlon was puzzled. 'I'm afraid you've lost me there, Shona. I don't really get your point.'

McIntyre's elegantly braided hair swayed as she shook her head vigorously. 'It's just that, well, I take my religion very seriously,' the other woman said. 'And in the Bible it's very clear that we should forgive those that trespass against us, and not start handing out self-imposed punishments. Well, that of course is police policy anyway, I mean the punishment bit, not the forgiveness. Well, you know what I mean, but that's by the by. *Vengeance is mine, saith the Lord.* Wouldn't you agree?'

Hanlon nodded her head. During her short acquaintance with Shona McIntyre, she had decided that McIntyre was one of the nicest people she had ever met. Niceness shone out of her eyes.

The nice-people list was surprisingly short. Most of her colleagues wouldn't make it. Enver Demirel, her former sergeant, yes, but even Corrigan, her long-suffering boss who had often gone out on a limb for her, had faults that called niceness into question. He was politically ruthless and highly ambitious. He was happy to use her as his gofer. On occasion he had used her to discomfort colleagues, or simply get things done, knowing she'd ask no questions.

She knew she herself would never make the list. She didn't think of herself as nice. She knew she was violent. She liked intimidating people. She knew she was intolerant. She was over-competitive, hypercritical. Several high-ranking Metropolitan Police had given her a kind of nickname as Corrigan's attack bitch. It was almost justified. She had done questionable things for him and kept her mouth shut afterwards. Mark Whiteside, her former partner whom she adored, was also flawed. Like Hanlon he had a vicious streak. She hadn't equated McIntyre's silver cross around her neck with anything other than ornamentation. Hanlon's encounters with the faithful in the past had led her to unflattering conclusions about religion.

But McIntyre exuded goodness and Hanlon appreciated that.

'Fine,' said Hanlon.

McIntyre held out her hand formally. 'Please let's be friends,' she said. Hanlon shook her proffered hand. Like the rest of McIntyre, it was long, cool and elegant.

'Friends.' McIntyre, satisfied, gave her one of her brilliant high-wattage smiles and they set off together back to the office on the small industrial estate.

This is so unlike me, thought Hanlon as she walked beside her. McIntyre was explaining about how important bridge-building was with the community, particularly in multi-ethnic Slough. It was DS Mawson who had the vision, she explained. He was very well regarded in community-planning circles. Hanlon feigned interest.

'That station in Langley, it's only open part time. It just seems to work quite well, us being out here. We're also handy for Heathrow,' she said. 'We've got parking as well, which is a bonus. But, of course, it's more than that.' A messianic tone entered her voice. McIntyre was a woman with a mission.

'Old-style police stations are expensive and old fashioned,' she continued. 'We need to put policing back into the community. People have negative feelings about the police station. If you've got a missing loved one you'll be feeling worried enough without having to turn up at some local nick where we're dragging in lowlifes, all that effing and jeffing, speaking to whoever's on the front desk through reinforced glass. No, this way's better. Better for us, better for the community.' She pointed at a woman with a toddler in a buggy. 'Better for her, better for him. I think in the future you're going to see a lot more contact points for the police and neighbourhood bases rather than the traditional fortress-like cop shops. It's the way forward.'

'Oh,' said Hanlon. McIntyre felt quite passionate about policing. She carried on. A year with Mawson had expanded her horizons. He was passionate about his vision and so was she. Policing was, after all, a social contract; it could only work if the public let it work. They had to shed the 'them and us' image. The new-style police stations would help to do it.

McIntyre adored Mawson. He really cared about people, she explained to Hanlon. If only more coppers were like him.

'Our colleagues in the probation service usually operate these days out of buildings much more accessible to the public. We need to be more accessible to our clients.'

Hanlon looked at her colleague dubiously. She had a small scar on her ironing-board flat stomach where she had been stabbed, another one hidden on her head by her thick hair where she'd been knocked unconscious, and both arms had been broken at different times. Forgive me, she thought, looking at McIntyre's pleasant face, if I feel less than trusting of our 'clients'.

'Of course, the boss won't be around when we get back,' said McIntyre. 'He'll be down at Bisley.'

'Bisley?' said Hanlon in surprise. It was the home of British shooting.

'They shoot down there,' said McIntyre.

'I know that,' said Hanlon with a touch of impatience. 'Does Mawson shoot?'

McIntyre looked at her haughtily. 'Detective Superintendent was the small-bore champion at Bisley a few years ago, and he does still instruct firearms courses. So, yes, he does shoot.'

Hanlon nodded, impressed. They turned into the industrial estate.

Then McIntyre's quotation came back to her. *Vengeance is mine, saith the Lord.*

Hanlon thought of the injured painter and decorator nursing a hugely sprained wrist and sore head, from where the heavy can had struck him, as well as a bruised ego. He could wash the paint away and the bruises would fade, but at least, thought Hanlon, he'd learned that women aren't always an easy target. Another Bible quotation, this time from her school years, further ago than she cared to admit, came to her.

And I am the avenger, who carries out God's wrath on the wrongdoer.

She smiled grimly to herself. That's more like me, she thought. And, she thought, I wasn't crossing my fingers when I promised, but I was crossing my toes.

And that counts.

CHAPTER FOUR

Danny stared at the two bodies and the other thing, with horrified, sickened astonishment. He, and they, were at 50 Beath Street, Marylebone, London W1. It was a nice flat in a nice place in a nice street. Marylebone is a wealthy, exclusive London neighbourhood. It didn't have a racy reputation like, say, Chelsea. It was respectable. Number 50 was respectable too. It was a tall, narrow, discreet red-brick Georgian townhouse, subdivided into three apartments. Its neighbours in the terrace were service flats with a transient population, private doctors' surgeries and a clinic for rich people with minor psychiatric problems.

Number 50 wasn't a clinic. It was one of a number of flats owned by a man called Dave Anderson, a North London criminal, and used as a place for prostitution. It was both home and working premises to a girl called Tatiana, whose dead eyes were now looking blankly at the ceiling.

The brothel's customers were wealthy, powerful and discreet. They had that in common with the clients of the medical neighbours on either side, although number 50 was catering for sexual rather than residential or psychiatric needs. Beath Street didn't advertise its presence. It didn't need to. Money bought access to everything.

The brothel was not far from Harley Street, and the street it was in had more than its fair share of private medical businesses. If anyone had asked, not that they would, Tatiana would have said it was a private treatment centre, which in a sense it was.

People came and went, everyone minded their own business and number 50, as it was known, passed unnoticed and unremarked.

He looked around him again, shaking his head. Danny had seen some things that few people not involved in violent crime would ever see, but nothing like this.

He'd known before he'd arrived that something untoward had happened, but he certainly hadn't expected this.

Danny had seen execution killings; he'd helped Anderson do two. He'd seen prologue, deed and aftermath. What he was now staring at was in a totally different league.

There were two bodies, a man and a woman, sitting side by side on the sofa. And the thing on the table. Danny, gagging slightly, had forced himself to check the bodies. There was a smell of death in the air, a scent of corruption, and he'd opened the window, letting the sounds of the traffic enter together with the merciful fresh air. He recognized the woman, one of Anderson's East European girls, Tatiana. The man was middle-aged, balding, overweight with glasses. He had a shirt with double cuffs; the cufflinks were gold with an enamelled British bulldog embossed on each. His glasses had expensive-looking frames. His face, now expressionless in death, looked as if he'd been clever and humorous. His jacket was thrown over a chair, blue pinstripe like his trousers.

Both he and Tatiana had been shot in the chest. The blood from the entry wounds had long since oxidized to a dull rust colour. Danny guessed they had both been sitting down where they were now when it had happened. The same could not be said of the other victim.

The head that had been placed on the coffee table and now looked sightlessly at Tatiana and her last customer had a face Danny knew well. It was Jordan, Dave's impulsive elder brother, not that long out of Armley prison in Leeds.

Armley. He'd been there to see him a few times. Danny thought fleetingly of the prison's crenellations and Gothic fortress facade. It had been like visiting Windsor Castle. It had looked great lit up at night. Jordan's eyes, angry and restless in life, mournful in death, gazed sightlessly across the expanse of polished mahogany tabletop.

Danny went round behind the bar in the large living room of the flat and poured himself a stiff brandy. His hand was rock steady, but his heart was beating wildly and his mouth was dry. He took a healthy mouthful of the powerful spirit, an aged Courvoisier, and looked at the clock on the wall opposite. Eight thirty a.m.

He took a packet of Marlboro out of his coat pocket and drummed the fingers of one hand on them while he thought about what to do. Well, that wasn't quite true. He knew what he was going to do; it was just he hated being the bearer of bad news.

He would dearly have liked to light up a cigarette, but Anderson's father had just died of lung cancer and it seemed somehow disrespectful. Two dead in one week in the Anderson family. He picked up his phone and called Dave Anderson.

'Yes?' came the toneless voice at the other end of the phone. Dave Anderson was always emotionless, not like his brother Jordan. Jordan had been a nutter but at least he'd been human. Dave was something else. Danny took a deep breath.

'I'm at 50, Boss, I can't really describe it, but you need to see it with your own eyes.'

There was a momentary silence. Danny could imagine Anderson, his thin, sunken face, and those eyes that looked as if they belonged to some religious fanatic. Funny, thought Danny, his eyes burned, but his voice never did.

He could see Anderson in his imagination, in his memory, his face framed with his longish, lank hair, holding his mobile. Morris Jones, his lieutenant, would be with him. He always was. Like a faithful dog. Jones's eyes wouldn't be burning; they were dead and fish-like, glazed. Anderson didn't waste words. He trusted Danny and knew he would never exaggerate. If Danny said he needed to see it, he meant it.

'One hour,' was the reply. Danny thought of logistics, North London to here, a small crew to organize. It couldn't be done any faster.

He automatically straightened his back. 'As soon as possible, Boss, please.' He took a deep breath and looked around the bar. 'We need cleaners.'

There was a pause on the phone. 'Jordan?'

'Jordan's here,' said Danny. No need to elaborate; Dave Anderson would see what had happened to his brother only too soon.

'Within the hour,' said Anderson coldly. His voice wasn't ice; it was liquid nitrogen.

The cleaners arrived within thirty minutes. Impressive speed by any standards. By 'cleaners', Danny had meant people to deal with the crime scene. Anderson wasn't a messy criminal. He always made sure that things were tidy and the people who worked for him, whether full or part time, knew it. He hated sloppiness, hated untidiness. There were three of them, accompanied by Morris Jones, Anderson's right-hand man.

For Danny, with only the dead to keep him company, the half-hour had seemed a very long time indeed. He thought about going elsewhere in the flat, the bedroom or the kitchen, but the thought of leaving the corpses alone was even less appealing than being with them. He had experienced a kind of hallucinatory thought that the bodies might somehow, horror-film fashion, rise up from where they sat so patiently, to come and find him, to traipse through the doorway in single file, searching him out. At least in here, he thought, slightly hysterically, in here I can keep an eye on things.

The sense of relief when his mobile rang to tell him they had arrived was enormous. He opened the door to the four men and ushered them inside. They followed Danny into the living room and stood there silently, taking in the charnel-house scenario. Their faces revealed a mix of horror, revulsion and bewilderment, but not Jones: his face was its usual deadpan blank.

Jones was tall and formidable with an impressive pedigree of violence, but that wasn't why Anderson employed him. Muscle was ubiquitous. He was a superb organizer. The three cleaners, junior employees of Anderson, stood awaiting their instructions. They cast fascinated, horrified looks at the bodies round the table. Particularly the head. The severed head. Nobody had seen anything remotely like it. On the TV, yes, on the news, at the cinema, but not in real life.

Jordan's disembodied head dominated the room as he had never done in real life.

Morris Jones was always beautifully dressed. Today it was a charcoal suit and a camel overcoat. He was tieless; it wasn't a fashion choice. He didn't like wearing ties purely on utilitarian grounds. He was a man used to violence and in his youth, when he'd been in a great deal of fights, he'd had opponents use his tie to grab hold of him. So the hint of colour that he felt was needed in his ensemble was provided by a brilliant-red silk scarf hanging around his neck.

'Where is he?' asked Danny. He didn't need to elaborate as to who 'he' referred to. Jones checked his watch. A Patek Philippe.

'He'll be about ten minutes,' said Jones. 'It's the old man's funeral next week, and now this. What a fucking mess.' His tone of voice carried more a sense of weary irritation than anything. A harassed housewife faced with some more mess that thoughtless children had left behind.

'You two,' said Jones to the men with him, 'start in the other rooms, you don't need me to tell you what to do, and you, Mickey, down to the van, start bringing up those bags, OK. I need a quiet word with Danny here.'

The three men nodded and disappeared to their allotted tasks. Jones looked at Danny.

Danny nodded at the bodies and the table. 'I just don't understand all of this. I really don't.'

Morris Jones gave him a contemptuous look. I don't care what you make of this, the look said, your opinions are of no interest to me whatsoever.

Jones went over to the bar and poured himself a bitter lemon. He gazed at the green/blue drink and sipped it appreciatively. He ran his eyes over Danny speculatively.

'Seen Jackson around, have you?'

The question was anything but innocuous. After Jordan's release from Armley a couple of months previously, Anderson had assigned a reliable man called Barry Jackson to him as his minder. Dave Anderson had told his brother it was because he had received death threats and he wanted extra security, but the real reason was to make sure Jordan, loyal but hot-headed, didn't do anything stupid. Well, nothing too stupid anyway. To keep him out of trouble.

Jordan had had a tendency to lose his temper and cause trouble. The incident that had got him sent to Armley was a road-rage explosion, pure and simple, nothing to do with business. He'd forced a motorist who'd cut him up off the road and beaten him senseless. It had been stupid, thoughtless and violent. That was Jordan for you. Jones or Dave Anderson might kill or injure you, but only for professional reasons. Not Jordan.

And now Barry Jackson was missing.

Danny shook his head. 'No, Morris.' Jones nodded, then stretched his powerful arms as if relieving stress or tension in his muscles. He had a very long reach. Danny was a stocky, muscular six feet, the other man was taller, rangier. Jones opened his mouth wide and took the plate that held his top teeth out of his mouth. A baseball bat in the face causes havoc dentally, as does a steel-toed boot. Most of Jones's face had been broken or fractured over the years. Mouth included. He put the denture down on the bar. Its pink plastic, set with replica front teeth, grinned wetly at Danny. Morris Jones smiled humorlessly at the other man.

For a second Danny wondered what Jones was doing. Only for a second. Then he found out.

Danny had known some people who moved fast and Jones was up there with the best. Before he knew what was happening, Jones had grabbed his right wrist and spun him round so his back was against Jones's stomach, then the taller man twisted his right arm back and upwards in a form of hammerlock.

He forced Danny over the back of a heavy, leather Chesterfield sofa, the twin to the one that Tatiana and the unknown man sat companionably on, and applied pressure viciously. Danny could feel the ligaments in his shoulder start to give.

'Jesus, Morris, you're breaking my arm,' gasped Danny.

'Where's Barry Jackson, Danny?' asked Jones. His mouth was close to Danny's head and he spoke in an unnerving whisper. 'It's him I want, not you.'

'I don't know,' he said. He could smell the leather of the sofa and the smell of Jones, cigarette smoke and some kind of expensive aftershave.

Jones increased the pressure. Danny groaned again in agony. It hurt so much he could see stars floating in his vision. He tried to move but Jones's body weight was on top of him. Jones repeated the question and Danny could feel his hot breath on his ear.

'Jesus, I don't know,' he repeated. He knew Jones would have no compunction about breaking his arm, or anything else come to that. Anderson wouldn't care; he also knew that.

Danny's left arm was trapped under his own body by his chest. He tried to move it out but Jones leaned more of his own weight forward to prevent this and reached his free hand down between Danny's legs, seizing his testicles and squeezing hard and rotating at the same time. He'd known some pain in his life, but nothing remotely like this. He'd been kicked in the nuts before and that had been bad enough, bowel-churning, sickening pain, but this was worse and it went on, and on and on. He had always felt that things were never as bad as you might expect. Not any more. Now he knew that some things were exponentially worse than you could ever have imagined. The pain was excruciating. He thought he was going to vomit.

If Danny had known, he would have told him. Not only was the pain dreadful, so was Jones himself. There would be no point holding out against Morris Jones, no point at all. Not if you knew what was good for you.

'Where is he, Danny?' Jones's voice was merciless in his ear. 'Tell me what you know.' Tears ran involuntarily down Danny's face. Jones had a terrible reputation. Once Danny had unexpectedly walked in on him in the cellar of the Three Compasses. That was the name of the North London pub that the Andersons owned. He'd stammered an excuse and left, but not before he'd seen a huddled form on the rough concrete floor, covered by a blanket, and the bloodstained long-nosed electricians' pliers in Morris Jones's hand.

One naked foot, a man's foot, had been poking out from the blanket. It hadn't been moving. Jones had looked at Danny impassively. He'd been bare-chested, his shirt and suit jacket hanging neatly on the back of a chair. Danny had assumed he didn't want to get them dirty.

The pupils of Jones's eyes had been like pinpricks. Danny had heard the rumours about Morris Jones's heroin habit; he guessed it was true.

'I swear to God, I don't know.' More pressure on his arm and testes. He tried to resist, to push away, but Jones's strength was terrifying. He felt a roaring in his ears and thought he was going to black out. Fleetingly he thought, If Jones is a junkie, he's in bloody good condition.

Then he heard a voice saying, 'Leave it, Mo, he's had enough.'

Danny felt the remorseless grip slacken and stop. The weight disappeared from his body and he sank to his knees, coughing. The pain in his lower body was intolerable. For another long moment he thought he was going to vomit. He leaned forward on all fours, breathing deeply, willing the pain away.

'Boss,' said Morris Jones to Anderson. He moved back to the bar and replaced his teeth. He glanced at Danny incuriously. Danny hauled himself upright. His knees were trembling from the incredible ache in his pelvis. He retched drily and staggered to his feet.

Anderson stood looking at the silent figures on the sofa and Jordan's head on the table.

'Did you know, Danny, on average there are two to three murders per week in London? Statistics, eh, Jordan.' He picked up his brother's head gently and looked into the dead eyes as if seeking confirmation. Something about the face puzzled him and Danny and Jones watched as he gently tilted the head and, using his thumb and forefinger, opened Jordan's jaws to look into his now open mouth.

Danny, his pain subsiding, watched his boss with awed fascination. Anderson was taller than Jones, gaunt, his hair hanging in its almost shoulder-length rat's tails. His cheeks were sunken and the eyes glittered, as always, with a kind of unhealthy fire. With the severed head between his hands, he looked crazier than ever. He looked like an insane prophet.

He kissed his brother's cold forehead gently, placed the head back down on the table and turned to Jones.

'Check their mouths,' he said. Jones nodded and went to the sofa. He didn't need to ask what for. It had to be obvious or Anderson would have told him. He started his grim task with his face expressionless. Anderson came over to Danny.

'Feeling better?' he asked, with no real interest. Danny nodded. Anderson looked at him thoughtfully.

'Whoever did this was known to Tatiana,' he said. 'Someone who works for me. She let them in. Someone knew where this place was. Someone knew where to bring Jordan's head so I'd find it. I'm satisfied to see it wasn't you.' Anderson's eyes held Danny's momentarily. It was a frightening sensation. 'If I thought you might. . .' said Anderson, indicating the bodies behind him.

He didn't need to finish the sentence.

Anderson produced an iPad from the leather briefcase he had with him and tapped at it. Google Maps appeared and he pressed a couple more keys.

'There's a tracker installed in Jackson's car,' he said matter-of-factly, 'and right now Barry Jackson, or at least his car, is here.' He pointed with a long, strong finger at the screen.

Danny looked at the map. A display marker hovered over the countryside near Ongar in Essex, north of London. 'Jackson's from Essex,' said Anderson. 'Do you know Essex at all, Danny? '

'Not really, Boss.'

'Well, today's your lucky day.'

Morris Jones looked up from the table, his task finished. He put Tatiana's head back down gently as if replacing an ornament. 'Nothing there, Dave.'

Anderson nodded. 'I'll leave you here, Morris, to finish off tidying everything up. Get rid of the bodies, usual place.' Morris Jones nodded.

'Look at this, Morris, when you're done here. I want you to wait for us there.' His finger indicated a place on the screen. Jones came over, stood beside him, looked and nodded.

'Just there?' he asked.

'Just there,' confirmed Anderson.

'And Jordan?' Morris Jones asked.

'Put him in the lock-up in the freezer there. Until we decide what to do with him. He deserves better than the others.' Morris nodded.

'And the others?' asked Morris.

'The usual,' said Anderson.

Morris Jones nodded. 'Same old, same old?'

'Yes,' said Anderson. 'Oh, Morris, I take it they both had their tongues?' He indicated the heads.

'Yes, Dave,' said Jones. They might have been discussing the weather, thought Danny.

'Jordan didn't,' said Anderson. 'Come on, Danny.' He switched off the tablet, his face expressionless. 'Let's pay Barry a visit. In lovely, leafy Essex. He will be surprised.'

CHAPTER FIVE

Hanlon stood in the picket line outside Belanov's sizeable house on the Woodstock Road in Oxford with the other protestors, and waved her placard. Underneath the strap heading of the Socialist Worker Party, a slogan read:

Pay Parity.

Twenty-five women of varying sizes, shapes and ages stood in an orderly crescent shape and chanted harmoniously.

'What do we want?'

'*Pay equality.*'

'When do we want it?'

'*NOW!*'

Hanlon's features were concealed behind a V-for-Vendetta-style plastic mask. Normally these sent her blood pressure soaring with rage: she associated the smug Hidalgo- style features with middle-class anarchists attacking the police. So it was with a certain ironic satisfaction that she used it to hide her policewoman's face.

This wasn't a collection of sex workers outside Belanov's brothel; this was a demonstration by twenty-four short-term contract university administration staff (plus Hanlon) protesting about their pay conditions. When he had bought the house, Arkady Belanov hadn't realized that the property to the left of his contained one of the offices of the finance department of Oxford University. More specifically, it housed the office of the finance director.

Women employees at the university finance office, it seemed, who were on part-time contracts, were not being paid bonuses and overtime entitlements that full-time staff received. In effect, this was dragging their pay down. This was what the demo was about.

Hanlon had flashed a forged NUJ card she had and, claiming to be a freelance journalist, had joined in. One of the protestors, Beth, had lent her the mask. Beth had one too. Hanlon was hoping to catch a glimpse of her real quarry, Arkady Belanov.

This demonstration was beginning to cost the Russian a great deal of money. None of Belanov's customers wanted to use his brothel while the protestors were there. Belanov charged a couple of hundred pounds an hour for use of a girl, minimum. More for specialist services. His clients were well heeled, well connected. Many of them worked directly or indirectly for the university. Many were dons, lecturers in the colleges. They were frightened in case one of the protestors knew them or local media might appear with cameras. They certainly didn't want spouses, students or colleagues asking them what they were doing there. They were as camera-shy as wild animals.

It was setting him back several thousand pounds a day. He watched the demonstration now out of one of the upstairs windows, together with Dimitri, his minder, and a third man, local to Oxford and non-Russian.

The two Slavs made a distinctive couple. Arkady Belanov was porcine, extremely obese, virtually hairless, his eyelashes and eyebrows so pale they were practically invisible. He looked like a huge, malignant baby. His enormous stomach presented him with a perpetual clothing problem, familiar to all fat men: trouser belt under, so the rolls of fat overhung, or belt over the gut, like a parody of pregnancy wear.

The onesie had been a wonderful development, ideally designed for someone of Belanov's shape. He often padded around the brothel in one. Today, though, he was wearing a turquoise velour two-piece tracksuit. A mockery of athleticism. Heavy rings adorned his strong, sausage-like fingers.

His companion, Dimitri, a head taller than the other two, was also wearing a tracksuit. But with his overly developed muscular physique, a hard-core bodybuilder's ridged, ripped and defined muscles, it seemed appropriate. Non-ironic.

He had on a sleeveless, low-cut vest beneath the unzipped top, his pecs like hot-water bottles, and the third man, Detective Inspector Joad, surreptitiously examined Dimitri's intricate array of tattoos that were visible over the inverted arc of the material. He didn't like tattoos usually, or Dimitri, come to that, but even Joad was impressed with the artistry and theatricality of the body art. One evening Dimitri had been very drunk and had good-humouredly explained them to Joad.

The colourful multi-onion-domed cathedral on his chest (Joad had thought it was the Kremlin at first), one dome for each year served in prison.

The dagger round the neck showing he had murdered while in prison. The two drops of blood that dripped from its end the number of murders.

The spider on one shoulder in its intricate web denoted a high criminal rank.

There were plenty more. Skulls, slogans in the Cyrillic alphabet that Joad couldn't read. One of them, he remembered, meant *I live in sin, I die laughing.*

There were universal symbols that needed no explanation,

like a roaring tiger and a swastika that covered his arms. Unseen, but the policeman knew they were there, were thieves' crosses on his knees, indicating that Dimitri kneeled for no man, and fetters around his ankles that referred to the length of Dimitri's various prison sentences. All of Dimitri's criminal history, like a graphic autobiography, inked on to his skin. The illustrated man.

Although it was only ten o'clock in the morning, all three men were drinking Ruskova vodka, a cheap, potent brand that reminded Arkady of home in Moscow. Good old Nizhny Novgorod, he thought with affection, thinking of the city where the vodka came from and where he'd opened his first brothel. He'd worked for the owner, then made him a business offer, later burying him in a field outside the city. Happy days, his first steps as an entrepreneur.

'*Suki*, bitches,' said Arkady, glowering at the women. Women should know their place. He hated this aspect of Britain, career women. No wonder the country was in such a mess. What were women good for? Cooking and fucking.

Dimitri in turn glowered at the other man present, DI Joad. Joad might have been there as another type of physique to contrast with the fat, spherical Arkady and the raw-boned, muscular hulk of Dimitri. Joad was thin, wiry and narrow-shouldered, his hair, showing no signs of thinning despite his fifty years, greasy with a side parting. Broken veins on his cheekbones from years of heavy drinking added a splash of colour to his unhealthy pallor.

'You should do something about those *bliyad*.' Joad looked blank. 'Bitches. You are police. We pay you,' said Dimitri irritably.

Back in the industrial·slums of Moscow where the Russians came from, they owned the local police – at least they owned enough of them to get a minor protest like this broken up.

Dimitri sometimes found adjusting to life in Oxford hard. Joad should be out there directing a couple of police with batons, in Dimitri's view. Crack a couple of those lesbian bitches' heads open. Job done. He took another drink. He'd love to do it himself.

Joad shrugged and sipped his vodka. He raised his glass.

'*Nu boudem*,' he said. Cheers. A bit early in the day, even for him, but when in Rome. He was aware of Dimitri's provocatively unfriendly gaze, deliberately running his eyes contemptuously from Joad's scuffed shoes, up his cheap, dated shiny suit, to his dandruffed head. He knew that Dimitri was trying to humiliate him. Joad didn't care. He'd weathered worse than Dimitri. He was blissfully disdainful of others' opinions. Buddha-like, he had reached satori. He didn't give a rat's arse what the Russians thought of him, so long as they kept paying him.

'And you say you have no information on the *bliyad* Hanlon?' said Arkady, changing the subject. She was omnipresent in his thoughts. He saw her face last thing at night. He saw her mocking grey eyes first thing in the morning. Belanov didn't like women and didn't like the police. Hanlon was both and Hanlon had caused him to lose a great deal of face as well as physically hurting him. He very much wanted her dead.

Every day he prayed to God to deliver Hanlon to him.

Joad looked at him. This was why they were so antsy. Hanlon had humiliated Arkady and kicked the shit out of Dimitri. God knows how, the Russians never spoke about it, but he'd seen the aftermath. Dimitri bandaged around the head; Arkady walking in a strange, bow-legged way. No prizes for guessing where Hanlon had left her mark. They were desperate for revenge.

'I told you,' said Joad. 'After she was discharged from hospital she was on sick leave. Then suspended from active duty pending the IPCC report, and now God knows where. Maybe transferred out of London.'

Arkady looked at him in annoyance. 'I think maybe I'm wasting my money on you,' he said to Joad. 'Eh, Dima?' he added, using the diminutive of the bodybuilder's forename.

'I'm looking into it,' said Joad affably. He was in no hurry, no hurry at all. He was like a taxi and the clock was running. Arkady glared at him and added something in Russian and Dimitri laughed unpleasantly.

'Sure, Arkady Mikhailovich,' he said, using Belanov's patronymic.

Joad looked at them with equanimity. He didn't know what they were saying, although he had recognized the word *zhopa*, which he knew meant arsehole. He didn't care. Sticks and stones, boys, sticks and stones. The way he saw it, the world had spent fifty years trying to bring him down and he was still here, with a swelling bank account and a luxury villa in Spain. He liked Spain. Hot and cold running water, hot and cold running whores. Cheap booze, good food. He'd retire there soon. He didn't know what the future would bring these idiots, but he thought an early grave likely.

And when that happened, he'd make a point of visiting and then piss on them. Until that happy day. He finished his drink.

'Well, I'd better be off. Terminal Five, Heathrow.'

Arkady nodded. 'You have details flight, his mobile. He will be with companion, just one. You have sign?'

Joad nodded. *Konstantin Myasnikov* printed in Cyrillic on a laminated sheet of A4 paper. Dimitri pulled on his tracksuit top.

'Come, time to go.'

The two men left the lush, panelled room and Arkady

Belanov continued staring at the women below with unconcealed irritation.

Disruptive bitches.

Hanlon had grown bored with the demonstration. She had joined in so she had the chance to check out the front of the brothel to see if anything had changed. It looked the same as before. She noted a couple of CCTV cameras swivelling backwards and forwards atop ornamental, retro lamp posts in the front garden.

The sight of the house brought back memories of her last time there – the naked, fat bulk of Arkady Belanov, the giant form of Dimitri, the printed menus of the girls available, smiling strained smiles to the camera, for ageing, wealthy men to drool over their firm young flesh in such contrast to their own. Still in business, then, by the looks of things. Sex never dated.

She looked at the women on the picket line next to her, oblivious of the horrors that lay about fifty metres from where they were standing. It wasn't that Belanov was selling sex; it was that his hookers were essentially slaves. Some drug addicted, some forced to work for him for fear of family reprisals back home, some brought to Britain on false promises of nannying or bar work and intimidated into prostitution. Work or die, and Belanov liked hurting people very much. So very much.

The terror of the Russian criminal system is no longer hidden behind an iron curtain, thought Hanlon. It's not thousands of miles away. It's behind those expensive-looking net curtains just over that attractive garden wall. And the criminals aren't behind bars. They're behind that expensive, ornate ironwork scrolled around the gates, and your husbands, ladies, or their colleagues are subsidizing it.

What had Oksana called Belanov? One of the *smotriashchyi*,

one of the watchers who looked after the interests of the *vor*, the criminal boss.

She'd wondered at the time how he'd got the money to pay for this large house in the centre of Oxford; it must have been worth a couple of million. Now, courtesy of Charlie Taverner's notes and Oksana's explanations, she had a better idea. It was money from the *obschak*, the trough or the criminal fund based in Moscow. It was an international investment.

She'd parked her car in the street to the rear of the house. Now she walked back there. This road was quiet with residents-only bays. Belanov's house had the back garden tarmacked over so his clients wouldn't have to search for parking. High-security gates blocked access and there was an intercom built into a post so the driver could speak and be buzzed in.

Hanlon slid behind the wheel of her Audi and scratched her head thoughtfully. They were near the centre of Oxford and an intrusive development like Belanov's car park, extremely visible gates and security system would have required hard-to-get planning permission. Whoever had signed off on that from the council would be well worth investigating, thought Hanlon. Money, big money, must have changed hands. She had a feeling too that if you converted your garden into a hard surface area you were responsible for making arrangements to deal with the water run-off from rains and storms.

Hanlon was a big fan of harassing criminals with unexpected visits and inspections. She would have no compunction about threatening whoever was responsible for these things into action. The thought of council JCBs tearing up Arkady's forecourt and ruining his business filled her with glee.

Joad and Dimitri climbed into one of Belanov's cars from the car park that had attracted Hanlon's attention. It was a Mercedes S-Class saloon. Joad was behind the steering wheel, the first time he had ever driven a car that cost in the six-figure mark. House price rises in Oxford had swelled the value of Joad's modest one-bedroom flat, but he was acutely aware that Belanov's car was not far short of his property's value.

As they buckled their seat belts, Dimitri said to him, his voice dripping with scorn, 'Arkady Mikhailovitch might want to employ you, but I think you are fucking waste of space. You make one more mistake and I'll kill you. And you'd better fucking find Hanlon.'

Joad said nothing. He raised an unimpressed eyebrow. Dimitri might be as strong as an ox, thought DI Joad, but he was as bright as one. He was unfazed by Dimitri's threats. He noted dispassionately that Dimitri had mastered 'fuck' as an adverb but was still at sea with 'a' and 'an'.

'I'm glad to see your English is improving,' he said to his passenger enthusiastically. 'It's getting quite idiomatic – "waste of space" and all that, very impressive, me old cocker!'

Dimitri was dimly aware Joad was mocking him. He hadn't got a clue what Joad had just said, but guessed it was insulting. 'Idiomatic' sounded like idiot; what was a cocker? Something to do with cock?

Joad was the kind of man who would sell his grandmother, who had only a hazy idea of concepts of morality, who even among his colleagues was a byword for laziness and rumoured corruption, but he was no coward. In the pocket of his long, unfashionable suit jacket Joad had a set of high-quality brass knuckles and Joad also had a fast, vicious, practised punch. He looked forward to the time when they'd come into contact with the Russian's face.

Not just Hanlon who'll have left their mark on you, he thought, unaware that Dimitri's recently broken nose had come from DI Enver Demirel.

Joad pulled into the Woodstock Road, heading for the ring road that circled Oxford and would lead them to the motorway. He looked at Dimitri. He couldn't resist another jibe.

'Hope you do better against Hanlon than you did last time, eh, Dimitri,' said Joad. 'I hear these small women can be quite tricky sometimes.'

He smiled inwardly as he felt Dimitri bristle with rage. Joad knew that only Dimitri's implacable loyalty to Belanov prevented him from attacking Joad, and the policeman saw no reason to try and placate him. Bring it on, thought Joad. Bring it on.

The powerful car surged towards Heathrow. Joad was an excellent driver. He was falling in love with the Mercedes. He had good traffic and hazard anticipation and superb all-round awareness of the road, the conditions and his fellow motorists. COAST, he thought to himself, the key to good driving: Concentration, Observation, Anticipation, Space and Time. True of other things too. He hummed a song as he drove, a man at peace with the world.

'You just find her,' growled Dimitri.

'I'll do my best, Dimitri,' promised Joad.

That shouldn't be too hard, thought Joad, glancing in his mirror. In fact, nothing could be simpler. C for concentrate; I'll concentrate on that.

COAST. O is for Observation.

I should really tell you, Dimitri, that I observe DCI Hanlon is currently two cars behind us in the outside lane of the eastbound M40, but I don't think I will.

COAST. A is for Anticipation. Not just yet. Not until I've found out a bit more what she wants with you.

Joad switched to the middle lane and a nice sedate seventy

miles an hour.

COAST. Space and Time.

Let's go slowly, give Hanlon plenty of time to follow us. I don't know what she wants but I know what I want; your head on a platter.

He'd hate for Hanlon to lose them.

CHAPTER SIX

Barry Jackson regained consciousness where he would have least wanted to, in the company of the people he least wanted to see. The place: the back bar of the Three Compasses in Edmonton. The people: David 'Jesus' Anderson and Morris Jones.

The pub belonged to the Andersons. To call it a public house was technically, but not literally, true. Admission was by invitation only. If you had walked into the scruffy, down-at-heel dead-end street where it was located – the terraced houses with peeling paint, saggy gutters and the occasional EDL flyer in the window, white and proud but not house-proud, their small front gardens choked with weeds – and tried to enter the small backstreet pub, you wouldn't have got in. Anderson's praetorian guard, two shaven-headed, Crombie-wearing men, always stood intimidating watch outside the door to the street.

'Sorry, mate. Closed for a private function,' they would have said. But you wouldn't have tried anyway. It was that kind of pub.

Only the chosen got in. Whether or not you wanted to be chosen was a different question. It was that kind of pub.

Jackson came to pleasantly enough. Jones had injected him with a high dose of diazepam after they'd bundled him into the back of Anderson's Range Rover. Morris Jones was a big fan of diazepam. The drug had kept him under for the relatively speedy journey back to North-East London and its relaxing side-effects eased the trauma of the unwelcome return to the real world.

Now he was back in the room, mentally as well as physically, and wishing he wasn't. Confused memories of a dash through the woods at the rear of his cottage, Anderson and Danny in pursuit, driven like a pheasant by beaters into the arms of a waiting Morris Jones, and now this.

'Hello, Barry,' said Anderson quietly. Jackson had never heard him raise his voice. He never needed to. Today was no exception. When Anderson spoke, you listened.

Anderson moved close to where Barry Jackson was sitting, gaffer-taped to an old wooden Windsor chair. Barry Jackson started praying, mentally, to a God whose existence he doubted, promising him anything if He'd allow him to live.

'I don't particularly want to hurt you, Barry, but you know I will,' said Anderson reasonably, 'if I have to. I want to know what happened and why, and your part in it.'

Please God, let me live and I'll go to church on a weekly basis and renounce crime.

Morris Jones lit a candle that burned steadily in the gloomy light of the small back bar with its stained pool table, the baize shiny with years of use, and the crooked, old-fashioned chintz light fittings with their dim bulbs. They provided the illumination; the candle was certainly not there to enhance the mood. Danny stood by the door, hands folded in front of his body, Anderson's attack dog. Jackson had seen him in action; he was a useful man in a fight, vicious and fast and strong.

'I'm waiting, Barry,' said Anderson.

I'll atone for my sins. I'll do good works.

Jackson and Anderson watched as Morris Jones tipped the contents of a small folded packet, a greyish-brown powder, into an old tablespoon and took two syringes from his jacket pocket. He put one down on the bar. It made a dull clatter. It was made of glass. He filled the other with water, depressed the plunger and carefully voided the liquid into the bowl of the spoon. He stirred it around with the end of a match, warming it over the candle.

Jackson watched as he cooked the heroin mix, Morris Jones's face impassive. He watched the mixture dissolve, bubble and thicken. Barry Jackson knew what it was; he could smell its slightly bitter, aromatic scent from where he was sitting.

Please God, don't let them kill me.

Jones squinted down at the spoon, his narrowed eyes glittering, the pupils pinpricks, and, satisfied, broke the filter off a cigarette and removed the paper. He fitted a needle to the hypodermic, inserted it into the cotton-wool filter and put it into the spoon. He pulled the plunger back gently and they all watched as the body of the syringe filled with the drug.

Jackson knew approximately how much heroin would be in the syringe. Enough for a fatal overdose. Enough to kill him. Jones would know exactly how much; he was very knowledgeable about opiates.

Morris Jones put the syringe down. He walked round the bar, through the open hatch, and reached for something below the wooden counter. He put the bottle on the bar. Not heroin this time, or any opiate. Drain unblocker. Designed to dissolve hair, grease, soap, organic matter in general. The bottle was predominately coloured red, acidic-based, thought Jackson.

Jones looked at him steadily as Anderson leaned forward, put his mouth close to Jackson's ear and said gently, 'You're a grass, Jacko, and now Jordan's dead. Like I said before, just in case you'd forgotten, you're going to tell me why, when, how and above all, who. One of those syringes is for you, Jacko. You get to choose which one.'

Jackson felt Anderson's breath on his ear as he spoke; he was that close.

Please, my Lord. Please. This is my Gethsemane.

Jones dipped the needle of the glass syringe into the bottle and filled it. He put it down next to the heroin-filled one.

Jackson looked at the two syringes: one if he cooperated; one if he didn't cooperate.

Jones put a piece of crumpled tissue paper on the bar counter, gently tipped the bottle and carefully poured a few drops on to it. The paper shrivelled and blackened.

'The destination's the same, Jacko, but how you get there is in your hands,' said Anderson.

'Decisions, decisions, Baz,' said Jones. Heroin or Drain-O.

'Can I have a drink?' Jackson asked. His mouth was very dry. 'Scotch.' He had indeed reached a decision.

Have mercy upon me, oh Jehovah, for I am in distress.

Jones looked at Anderson who nodded. Jones took a bottle of Bells from the back of the bar where it stood with the other bottles and poured three fingers into a tumbler.

'Water?' asked Jones pleasantly, as if they were having a convivial drink together. Danny, watching from his place by the door, noticed that the bottle of Cointreau standing with the other liquor bottles was half-full. Who drank that? he wondered. In this place?

Blessed be thee, Jehovah, for he hath showed me his loving kindness.

'No water for me,' said Jackson. Jones gave Anderson the glass and he held it to Jackson's lips while he drank greedily. The Scotch tasted wonderful. Anderson withdrew the glass.

Into thy hand I commend my spirit.

'Eight days ago my mobile rang,' began Jackson, and started to tell his story.

CHAPTER SEVEN

Joseph Huss looked sympathetically at Enver Demirel standing in his muddy farmyard, obviously ill at ease and out of place. He'd met his daughter's London colleague several times before and had quite liked him. In some respects the two of them were not dissimilar, big men, powerfully built, placid by nature with a tendency to worry about things. Joseph Huss had a farmer's natural pessimism nurtured by a fear of DEFRA, bad weather and government/EU regulations, while Enver's gloom was fed by police hierarchy, crime and government/ EU regulations.

They were both naturally shy too, a similarity that led to a lot of foot shuffling and verbal awkwardness when they met as they both devoutly wished they were elsewhere. Huss, happy with animals, cows in particular; Enver content with criminals.

Huss Senior was in a faded blue boilersuit and steel-toed, rubber workboots. A fine drizzle fell from the grey, Oxfordshire heavens that to Enver seemed huge and unfriendly after the more restricted London skyline. His cheap, dark polyester suit was sodden with moisture and his highly polished black shoes were caked with mud. He hadn't given much consideration to his clothes. Footwear just wasn't a city problem, other than style. He hardly ever left the capital and he'd given no thought to the practicalities of walking around the farm.

The silence prolonged itself. Enver stroked his thick, dark drooping moustache, Joseph Huss scratched his grey one. He knew that Melinda, his daughter, and Enver had been seeing each other and there'd been a break-up. Shame, he'd thought. He'd liked the quiet policeman. He had pushed the matter away. He had every faith in his daughter's abilities; boyfriends were not his field of expertise. Joseph Huss was not given to dwelling on his daughter's love life. That was nothing to do with him. Well, anyway, here Enver was again. Not dressed for the occasion either.

'She's in the workshop,' he said, pointing across the farmyard.

'What's she doing?' asked Enver. It didn't really matter, of course, but he felt he should say something. *Are the cows well?* would have sounded inane. He never knew what to say to Joseph Huss.

'Fixing the clutch on the Freelander,' said her father. Enver nodded. He knew nothing about cars. He knew a clutch changed gears when depressed, or something like that. He knew a Freelander was a kind of Land Rover. There were another two parked in the yard, a Defender and its precursor, a 1964 Series Two, looking like a prim old lady on its narrow wheels. They were both army olive-green drab. Joseph Huss said thoughtfully, 'They're pigs to work on, Freelanders.' Enver made a non-committal noise, nodded again and squelched his way across the mud covering the cobbles of the yard.

More mud. More mud on his shoes.

Joseph Huss watched him go, a wry smile on his face. His daughter had painted her nails that morning over breakfast. I thought you were fixing the clutch. I am, she'd said. He had shrugged, baffled; now all was explained.

Enver walked into the workshop through the open door and looked around him. He shivered. The Husses, like most country people, were outdoor types. Doors and windows tended to be left open; draughts predominated. He was always cold when he visited Huss at her home. The air in the workshop was chilly and heavy with the smell of engine oil. A black SUV was in front of him, like a dead animal, rearing up at a thirty degree angle, held in the air by two trolley jacks, one on each side. The bonnet was open; there was no sign of Huss.

He walked to the rear of the car. His shoulders brushed a board devoted to spanners, arranged in order of size. Silhouettes had been drawn round every one of them so they wouldn't be misplaced when they were returned after use. There were three metal toolboxes on the floor, one containing a huge array of sockets, and various other tools neatly attached to the wall. His gaze travelled over a workbench with a vice that you could fit a man's head in, a generator and then, rounding the rear of the car, he saw DI Melinda Huss, crouched so far inside the near-side rear arch she was practically invisible. Most of her seemed to be under the car apart from her backside encased in a boilersuit, although hers was a faded green as opposed to her father's blue one, that jutted out from beneath the curve of the car.

Enver coughed discreetly. He didn't want to startle her, not with all that metal hanging over her. He had somehow managed to crush their relationship; he didn't want to add her body under a ton or so of Land Rover to that unfortunate score.

'Oh, it's you,' she said from inside the car. Her voice sounded unfriendly. For the thousandth time, Enver wondered what he'd done to upset her. They'd seen each other socially maybe a dozen or so times, things had even progressed as far as passionate kissing, which was fast work by Enver's standards – he was a shy man by nature and had body-image problems. He would occasionally look back to photos of himself in his prime as a boxer – had he so wanted he could have found some of his fights on YouTube – and compared himself unfavourably to what he had become in just a few short years. He hated seeing himself naked these days, and when he showered he'd avert his gaze from his flabby body like a prim Victorian.

He was unaware that Melinda Huss found him physically very desirable indeed, despite heavy hints on her part. Huss had no idea of Enver's self-loathing. She assumed, correctly, he was either shy or, incorrectly, playing hard to get. Huss had reached the stage of actively planning to drag him bodily into her bedroom, if necessary, but then the fault lines had widened irrevocably.

He stood behind her now. He could see the blonde curls of her hair spilling over her frayed collar as she tightened something under the car. The wheel that was missing was propped against a workbench, Huss's body pressed against the axle end.

'Pass me the clutch, Enver,' she said. He looked around him. He'd never knowingly seen a clutch. On the bench was a metal object the size and shape of a small dinner plate that looked a bit like a landmine. On the floor by his feet was a much larger object like Darth Vader's helmet made of grey metal.

'Um, what does it look like?' he asked hesitantly.

'Oh, for heaven's sake, Enver,' said Huss. She manoeuvred herself out from under the car. Propped up at this weird angle on the jacks, its wheel off so you could see the silver steel of the axle, the large Freelander looked oddly vulnerable, pathetic, as if it was patiently undergoing surgery. Huss rose graciously from the floor, light on her feet despite her sturdy body shape.

She stood in front of him. The sleeves of the boilersuit were rolled up over her powerful forearms. She was stocky in build and wore a beanie pulled over her blonde hair to protect it from engine grease and oil. The top buttons of the boilersuit were undone and Enver could see she was wearing a white tee underneath, its fabric stretched taut by her upper body. Huss was a curvy woman. She was wearing latex gloves, which she snapped off. Her fingernails were red.

'That,' she pointed at the landmine-like thing, 'is a clutch.'

'And what's that then?' said Enver, indicating the grey cowling on the floor.

'That's a gearbox.' Her tone was slightly sarcastic, her broad attractive face slightly hostile. 'And what brings you all the way out here? Other than automotive curiosity?'

Enver thought, She obviously wants me to apologize but I don't know what for. His gloom deepened. He'd been in this position once or twice before in his life. It was a conversation that went, *Tell me what I've done to offend you*, the answer to which was, *If you have to ask there's no point in me replying.* An argument as circular as a clutch seemingly was. I'm no good with women, he thought. Or cars.

He scratched his moustache, trying to think of something to say.

'Can I buy you lunch, then I'll tell you,' he said. Huss's face brightened at the thought of lunch with Enver. She had meant to be severely unpleasant to him, but the sight of his slightly battered, mournful face and his powerfully muscled body outlined by the wet fabric of his rain-soaked shirt and jacket softened her heart. She liked Enver very much. She'd forgotten how much she actually wanted him until this moment.

'Maybe,' she said. She pointed at the gearbox. 'Could you put that on the bench for me?' she asked. Enver nodded, bent down and lifted the Freelander's gearbox effortlessly from the floor and put it down on the workbench. That must weigh about fifty or sixty kilos, thought Huss. She breathed deeply, running her eyes over Enver's shoulders, back and backside as he experimentally inspected where he'd placed it to make sure it was secure. Desire, she thought. That's what I'm feeling now.

She glanced down at where she'd been working. 'Well, I suppose the dual-mass flywheel can wait,' she said. 'Where did you have in mind?'

Enver's face brightened. Melinda Huss was almost smiling at him.

'Wherever you want.'

Upstairs, my room, now, she thought. She wondered what he'd do if she said that. Faint probably.

'There's a new Lebanese in Woodstock.'

'Fine,' said Enver. Now she was smiling. It was all going better than expected.

'I'll get changed.' As Huss crossed the yard to the back door of the farmhouse she thought savagely, If he so much as mentions that other bloody woman. . . DCI sodding Hanlon. . .

CHAPTER EIGHT

Joad parked in the short-term car park at Heathrow's Terminal Five. As the automated gate barrier rose to let him through, he could see Hanlon's red Audi three cars behind. Driving along slowly, looking for a space to park, he thought about Hanlon's following them. It was a fairly risky manoeuvre, a one-car tail. It was so transparently obvious. Dimitri probably wouldn't notice but, then, Dimitri was thick. You could tail him in an ice-cream van playing 'Greensleeves' and he'd be oblivious. Belanov would have spotted her. It was also such an indiscreet car, so vividly coloured. Hard to miss really.

Hanlon was no fool, as Joad knew. If she was doing it this way it was either because she didn't care if she was seen or because she had to. Joad would take a guess on the second option. He had noticed her doing her best to keep a discreet distance. She had a track record of unilateral action. Haven't we all, he thought, although in fairness mine are all pretty much illegal. He was willing to bet a great deal of money that Hanlon had no official backing for this. If she had, it would have been more professionally done. He shrugged. At the moment it was no concern of his. His own story, should he be called to account, was that he too was befriending the Russians as part of his investigation into a brothel ring in Cowley.

In the interim, he wasn't going to tell the Russians about Hanlon. He would squirrel that piece of information away for later. For when it was needed. Joad was built for survival. Someone had once called him a rat by way of an insult. He hadn't been offended. Rats were smart, they had unbelievably tough teeth and could chew through steel and concrete, they could swim half a mile and they could take on opponents many times their size. They could survive radiation that would kill a human and live longer without water than a camel.

And, like the mythical rat on a sinking ship, Joad had a finely balanced nose for danger. All in all, he was happy to be a rat. He had a feeling that his association with the Russians was coming to an end and he certainly wasn't going to lift a finger to help them. If Hanlon wanted to bring them down single-handedly, all the best to her.

In fact, he thought, I might even help. It all depends.

He started wondering about the plausibility of borrowing a large amount of money from Arkady. And the car. He was falling in love with the car. With a bit of luck, with Hanlon on one side of the equation and the Russians on the other, they'd manage to cancel each other out. Then it would be a loan that need never be repaid. And if Hanlon succeeded in putting Arkady away or forcing him out of the country, he wouldn't be needing the Merc. Either way, he was going to come out of it in credit.

It was the way things had always been, Ian Joad versus the world.

So far, he was ahead on points.

He drove up and through the short-term multi-storey car park at Terminal Five with practised ease, manoeuvring the large car with enviable skill and confidence through the confined, claustrophobic space. He could have let his passenger out before parking but didn't. Joad was an excellent driver and he'd spotted the empty space in the bay and parked almost before Dimitri had time to think, reversing neatly in one smooth, swift move. The space he had found for the Mercedes was between a Range Rover and a transit van. The bay was small, the car wide. Joad, toothpaste-tube thin, easily slid out from behind the door. He stood by the bonnet of the elegant vehicle, smiling to himself, as he watched Dimitri struggle out of the narrow gap between the Mercedes and the Range Rover like a man playing Twister.

He waited patiently, the infuriating smirk still on his face, then he and his giant companion headed off to the arrivals hall.

Hanlon concealed herself as best she could in a far corner of the huge international arrivals area. She leaned against a wall, hands in the pockets of her jacket, trying to look innocuous. She could feel the silk fabric of a headscarf she'd forgotten she had in the right-hand one. She was pleased to find it again; it had cost a great deal of money. She had assumed she'd lost it. Her fingers caressed its smooth, light creases.

She too had parked quickly and had run down ahead of the two men, her hair bouncing as she moved, vaulting over concrete and steel barriers and taking the stairs in a series of elegant leaps. She could see Dimitri now, walking through the car park entrance doors with his customary hard-man swagger, accompanied by another tall, slim man that she guessed was Joad.

Her eyes narrowed at the sight of Dimitri. She had a visceral loathing of him and his fat boss Belanov. Belanov's favourite way to keep his girls subservient was to use a plumber's blowtorch on them, nearly two thousand degrees centigrade of concentrated blue flame on a woman's skin. Belanov found that arousing.

And Dimitri found it funny. She'd hurt them both once, but not, in her considered opinion, nearly enough.

She'd known about Joad from a previous case she'd worked on. Her colleague, Enver Demirel, had warned her about this criminal informant in the Oxford CID, but they had no hard evidence and she had no wish to start an official investigation in which her own behavior at the time would be seen as highly questionable. She'd never seen Joad in person, but Enver's one-word description, 'sleazy', even at this distance seemed appropriate. She had known somehow he'd be an amalgam of polyester, dandruff, faux leather and cheap aftershave. Even from here she could see her intuition was correct.

She mentally cursed herself for not having brought along some form of camera. She wanted a record of who Dimitri was meeting. She had a feeling that Heathrow required a permit for photography but as police she'd get away with it, should anyone ask. But all she had was her phone and there was no way she could get close enough to use it. Dimitri would probably attack her on sight if he saw her. She doubted his ability to control himself. He certainly wouldn't forget what she looked like, unless he'd suffered memory loss after she had felled him with the butt of a shotgun. I probably haunt your dreams at night, she thought with a grim smile.

Hanlon had no idea how much he and Belanov burned for revenge.

International Arrivals, Heathrow, Terminal Five. The space was vast, the ceiling immensely high, glass and steel predominated, the primary colours silver and black and yellow and white. It was teeming with people. She was pleased by the numbers. She felt comfortably inconspicuous.

In the distance she could see Joad and Dimitri. They were almost certainly there to pick up some crony of Arkady Belanov's from the motherland. Maybe even the *vor* himself. But Charlie hadn't known his name and Charlie hadn't known what he looked like.

The more she thought about it, the more Hanlon had a growing feeling that today she would find out. Why else would Belanov have sent this welcome committee? Today she would get to see the face of the *vor* and begin to take revenge for Oksana.

Whoever he might be. Charlie Taverner's files hadn't been as informative as Oksana had believed.

The information contained on the memory stick was the outline of a PowerPoint presentation to be given to Corrigan at the meeting that Taverner had failed to attend. It was an overview of the sex industry in London. Plenty of money to be made by energetic Russian criminals. There were several graph-based pages of statistics and figures, showing the rise of East European prostitutes in the capital, and the message was quite clear. That whether or not the rise in former Soviet Union sex workers was the result of increased activity by the *Bratva*, the *russakaya* mafia or, in plain English, the Russian mafia, or if the criminal gangs followed the girls, it would mean an increase in crime.

Taverner thought 'increase' was an understatement. There'd be an explosion in crime and one that the Met would be ill equipped to deal with.

Hanlon could easily imagine Corrigan wishing to defuse any potential threat to his position from the Home Secretary.

But this was all theoretical. Here the situation was not a briefing; it was real. She moved political considerations about the Russian crime threat to the back of her mind and concentrated on the here and now.

Hanlon tilted her head back and her keen, grey eyes scanned the arrivals board. A BA flight from Sheremetyevo Airport in

Moscow had just landed. She guessed that was what Dimitri and Joad were waiting for.

Moscow. Charlie Taverner was obsessed with an unnamed man known as the Butcher of Moscow. He controlled a significant amount of the city's prostitution. Prostitution at the high-end level.

Moscow, for Charlie, had meant crime.

There were two main criminal gangs in Moscow, the *Solntsevskaya Bratva* and their rivals, the *Tambovskaya Bratva*. The latter – who had been prosecuted in Bulgaria for laundering $1.4 billion of profits, Taverner noted, to give some idea of their financial worth – had the lion's share, and both were committed to the removal of the Butcher as a business competitor.

The Butcher, *Miasnik* in Russian, was small scale compared to his gangland rivals. All of the gangs were violent. Most of their soldiers were or had been just that, soldiers. Trained to kill in Chechnya and Ossetia; some of the older ones trained in Afghanistan.

But the Butcher specialized in flamboyant killing, shock and awe murder. That was his calling card. Beheading, seemingly, was a speciality.

And now, thought Hanlon, now he was coming over here. Coming to a brothel near you. Coming with his soldiers, former paratroopers and former Spetsnaz and the finest graduates of Russia's dread prisons.

The noticeboard changed to *Baggage in hall* for the Moscow flight. Two passing police, Heckler and Koch automatics slung around their necks, regarded Hanlon suspiciously, slowing their measured walk as they did so. It wasn't her slightly tough good looks or even the black eye that caused them to give her a professional once-over. It was the calm air of certainty that surrounded Hanlon, an aura of hard-edged competence. She met their gaze with rock-steady confidence. They walked past her and carried on by.

Hanlon knew that one of her major faults lay in not seeing the bigger picture; she tended to concentrate on the now, rather than worry about the consequences. Trying to do, say, Corrigan's job – marshal large numbers of officers and support staff to fight not just crime but terrorism, whilst steering a deft course through government policy, the police federation, civil liberties and human rights, a fickle public constantly veering from opinions that 'all coppers are bastards' to 'string 'em up or lock 'em up and throw away the key', budgetary constraints, the media and maybe ten to fifteen million Londoners – she'd have been disastrous. And then all the tedious meetings with Data Processing, monitoring the traffic on mobiles and computers, the technicalities and legalities of what they were and were not permitted to access, which she was hopeless at. Her mind just switched off in such situations. And as for tact and trying to keep the public on side, well, even a Hanlon enthusiast would duck that question. Hanlon and PR, a key part of Corrigan's job, were irreconcilable.

Corrigan had once said to her that the criminals were the easy part of their job. She was beginning to realize the truth of what he had said. But if she lacked strategic vision, she made up for it in the tactical.

She noted the increased tension in the officers' posture. Hanlon was failing the attitude test. Most people avoid the attention of heavily armed policemen. Hanlon's slightly arrogant poise and athletic build together with her black eye, an injury from sparring at the boxing gym she used, had aroused their suspicions. One of them had even checked her footwear as they'd passed. Hanlon was wearing knee-length boots with a short skirt. Good for running in. The officer had added it to his checklist.

In a minute they'd be back. While they engaged her in polite, meaningless chat, wanting to confirm ID, etc., Joad, Dimitri and whoever they were meeting could have come and gone. She looked around her for inspiration.

She saw them immediately. The answer to a prayer.

Salvation.

It wasn't a Guido Fawkes V-for-Vendetta mask – it was a piece of very expensive silk cloth, courtesy of Hermès, but it was equally effective. The arrangement of the barriers at International Arrivals was asymmetric and, as the metal curved round, Hanlon joined a group of about twenty Arab Muslim women waiting to greet arrivals from, she guessed, a Middle Eastern flight. The women all had their heads covered and half of them were wearing the shapeless, figure-concealing clothes favoured by the religious, the other half wearing Western clothes, jackets and jeans predominating.

Hanlon, her hair covered by her dark Hermès scarf, tagged along at the end of the group. The crowd that assembles at Arrivals is always excitable, always vibrant, never static. The attention of the greeters is universally concentrated on the focal point of the door through which the travellers appear. The women in the crowd, too, all seemed armed with mobile phones, either using them to talk to whoever they'd come to pick up or photographing their loved ones as they arrived.

Hanlon followed suit. She would be able to use her phone with impunity. Everyone else was. The images she had through the screen of the camera weren't perfect, but they were good enough. Dimitri and Joad were just a few metres away but their attention was fixed on the doors to Arrivals. They'd glanced at the Muslim women but it had been a glance of dismissal. No threat there to them and, also, nothing to ogle. All they'd seen was a mass of headscarves; that was enough for them. Hanlon got busy with her phone.

Click. Dimitri glowering at the floor, Joad looking bored.

Click. Joad yawning, holding his sign. Hanlon couldn't read the Cyrillic letters; she'd have them deciphered later.

It suddenly occurred to Hanlon that Dimitri obviously didn't know what the Butcher looked like, otherwise why bother with the sign. Clearly he was a man who valued his anonymity.

Click. Dimitri and Joad in profile now, both looking alert, like pointers who have scented the prey.

Hanlon changed the phone's camera to video as the first-class Moscow passengers started to arrive, filtering through from airside to terminal.

She would have missed Myasnikov if he hadn't gone to greet Dimitri and Joad. Middle-aged, average height, conservatively dressed with a neatly trimmed greying beard, he looked as unlike her mental image of a blood-soaked gang leader as it was possible to get.

She had enough images of the Butcher now. She turned away and disappeared into the crowd.

Twenty minutes later, Hanlon stood on the top floor of the car park overlooking the huge airport and the enormously long runways. The planes came and went. The wind tugged at her thick hair as jet engines screamed overhead from take-offs and landings, while more planes circled round, waiting for their allotted slots.

To her east lay London, her city that she loved with a passion; to her west, Langley and Slough, hateful place of exile. Below her, the Russians, maybe her ticket back to where she wanted to be.

She leaned across the red bonnet of her car while she scrolled through the photos. They were all there, all good enough to use.

She'd study them later. Particularly Myasnikov, Charlie's killer. She scratched her head, toying with the idea of a police-to-police request for a photo of the *vor* from the Russian authorities. Probably not the best idea, not if the Russian cops were as corrupt as Oksana said. She thought again of Oksana. I doubt if I'll be able to find your husband, she thought, but at least I have an image of his killer. And you'll be able to translate his name. That'll be a start; we can take it from there.

She got in her car and drove thoughtfully down the labyrinthine ramps of the car park, and once through the barrier turned towards the M4 and Slough.

Dimitri and Arkady, you'll be seeing me again, I promise, she thought.

CHAPTER NINE

Sam Curtis didn't have a therapist bound by the rules of his trade to confidentiality. He didn't have a priest bound by the rules of the confessional, but he did have Chantal. Right now he was quite drunk in her studio flat, one room plus bathroom, in Cowley on the outskirts of Oxford.

She listened patiently as, sprawled on her bed, he told her about Jordan Anderson and Taverner and the girl and what had happened on Monday night. She took another sip of the Baileys that she was drinking to keep him company and lit a cigarette. She didn't want to hear any of this but her boyfriend was not to be stopped. He was out of his mind on the booze and the drugs. Totally mullered, she thought. Curtis opened another can of Stella. That was twelve so far. It was only the coke that was keeping him from collapse.

'First we had to go to Chelsea Harbour and we met this geezer called Barry. In Barry's car there was this other bloke, sparko. Out for the count. We put him in the Merc and I drove them up to that industrial estate in Slough where I got them that warehouse. We carried out matey, inside, that's where, well, let's just say that's where it happened.'

Curtis was lying next to her in his underwear, singlet and pants tight against his muscular body. The skin was taut against his powerful frame but it was goosefleshed and coated in a sheen of cold sweat.

Chantal nodded. She was wearing the lingerie set that Curtis liked, the one she'd got from Ann Summers. She might as well have been wearing a bin bag. Curtis didn't have sex on his mind; he wanted expiation, not orgasm. He wanted forgetfulness. He wanted oblivion.

He imitated the Russian's voice. *'You pass me knife, you never do this to pig before, no, "dou'shit", what is English? Yes, must suffocate him first or blood goes everywhere, we want in bucket.'*

Curtis was a skilful mimic and accurate. He could have been good at languages – he had a good ear, a good memory – but it was a road he had never taken. Education had never been his forte. He had chosen crime. Up until now it hadn't seemed a bad choice. He had earned respect, a lot of money and an enjoyably hedonistic lifestyle. All it had cost had been a spell in a juvenile facility and a couple of months inside a low-security prison. A price well worth paying.

He did Dimitri again. *'Go get bag for head, this is "mest", what you say, payback time.'* But now, now he was beginning to regret working for the Russians. He was in the deep end, he couldn't swim that well and his toes didn't reach the bottom. Panic was setting in.

In his newfound awareness of detail – the huge empty, dark space of the warehouse, the damp concrete smell of the floor overlaid with the butcher's smell of Jordan's blood, the whine of the electric saw and the silencing effect of Anderson's tissue as the teeth of the saw made swift work through his spine and neck – he noticed how Dimitri, when he spoke English, didn't use pronouns, no *the* or *a/an*. Presumably they didn't exist in Russian. It was a piece of information whose accuracy he guessed he would never find out.

'Then we drove back to London,' said Curtis. 'Down the

Euston Road, down to Marylebone. With the head wrapped up in cling film, in a couple of bags.' Jordan's head had been surprisingly heavy.

He was rolling a joint now, the coke, two grams of it, all gone. Traces of it frosted his nostrils, his eyes were huge and she could smell the rank coke sweat on his body, floating like a top note on the metallic alcohol sheen that beaded his skin. The room stank of weed and sweat and booze. He was in a terrible state, she thought. She wished he'd shut up about the events he'd seen. She didn't want to know and she was certain that she wasn't meant to know. If Belanov ever found out, well, he would. . . She shut down the thought. He would burn her. Burn her. That's what he liked to do, and Dimitri liked to watch.

'Sh,' she said. 'You need to relax, Sam.' Chantal moved provocatively on the bed and shrugged off one shoulder of her dressing gown. Curtis stared blankly at her cleavage. He drank some more lager and lit the joint. He carried on his narrative.

'The girl knew Jackson. She let us in. There was some bloke on the sofa. The Chinaman had said he'd be there. The girl was in on it, but the Butcher doesn't like loose ends, so she died and he died. Bang, bang, simple as. Easy, I suppose, after what we'd just done. Dimitri gave the head a wash in the kitchen sink. It needed a clean.'

Back in the present, Curtis shuddered. 'And then Dimitri and I dropped Jackson back in Chelsea. Back to Slough, got rid of the body. In that warehouse I told you about, you know, the one I rented for them.'

'Poor baby,' said Chantal, and put her arms round Curtis. The money that he'd been earning from Belanov had been great. She remembered how she and Sam had laughed for pleasure at the huge amount he'd earned in his first fortnight for the Russian. It was all cash, of course, straight from the brothel's takings. Four grand in tens and twenties. They'd strewn it all over the bed. It had been like winning something on the TV, not like 'earning' it. But he had earned it; that was the problem. It had terms and conditions.

Chantal was concerned that they could easily end up very dead, and dead in some absolutely awful way.

She thought, That could be us in that warehouse. In that barrel where Anderson's body had ended up, covered in cement. That could easily be us. And there was no way out. It wasn't the kind of job Curtis had that you could resign from. You couldn't give a month's notice. Arkady Belanov had his own idea of a confidentiality clause, his own way of imposing a gagging order. It didn't involve lawyers. And you couldn't even grass him up, he'd got two police contacts, that sleaze-bag, that bell-end Joad who'd already been round trying to cop a feel, and once when she'd been bent over for some reason, casually pushing his groin against her chuff. *Go on, Chantal,* he'd said, *just a quick one, I won't take long.* And now this other one, this Chinaman whoever he was, if indeed he was a copper and not just some other high-powered civilian that was on side for the Russians. Like that bloke on the council. Not the chief constable, though. She was a woman.

She caught sight of the two of them reflected in the mirror above the bed, the view that her clients loved. Curtis's slim, muscular body and the back of his head as he buried his face into her chest and her long blonde hair, the roots beginning to show their natural mousy colour.

It had been better when he was just dealing, with a bit of debt collecting on the side, she fucking the occasional punter, five hundred to a grand a week and relatively risk free. Not this.

Chantal had a nose for trouble; her whole life had been nothing but. She could see that Curtis had responsibility but no power and the more he knew, the more likely it was that Belanov would decide one day to get rid of him. Thank God he didn't know who the policeman was. Thank God he didn't know who the Chinaman was. Ignorance was bliss. He'd delete Curtis with as little compunction as a text message and she'd probably be processed too. Or shipped off to somewhere in Russia where a British whore might have curiosity value.

She'd opened the window earlier to get rid of some of the heavy smoke from the skunk Curtis was smoking. Now a cold breeze shook the curtains and she shivered, but not from the evening air.

She pushed her nose into Curtis's sweat-drenched hair and tightened her grip round his back to feel the comforting heat and hardness of his body. She heard him mutter something, his low voice inaudible, his mouth pressed against her breast.

He lifted his head so that he could see her and their eyes met.

'What, babes?' she whispered.

'I'm shit scared, Chantal,' he said.

She nodded. 'Me too.'

CHAPTER TEN

Corrigan left the meeting room at the Home Office in a foul mood. He walked down the front steps of the startlingly ugly modern building, its facade reminding him of slatted blinds. It had won an architectural award. Of course it bloody well had, he thought angrily. Bloody idiots. He turned on his heel and glared venomously at 2 Marsham Street, a ten-minute walk from his office at New Scotland Yard.

He noticed a camera crew on the steps, filming a well-known TV political correspondent. They always liked this shot. It was emblematic of the Home Office, like Westminster Green for politicians or New Scotland Yard for police stories.

There had been two main issues on that meeting's agenda. The first, dictated partly by the surge in popularity of anti-European sentiment in the country, had concerned East European prostitution in the capital. The government was worried by the growth in support for anti-immigration policies and had decided it was time to get tough, or rather to be seen getting tough, on sex crime, tax evasion and non-EU issues. Hence Operation Tomboy, a crackdown on brothels and street prostitution.

The second was budget cuts.

As he'd sat in the meeting, watching a PowerPoint presentation on the 'Nordic approach' to prostitution – criminalizing the customer – Corrigan idly wondered where the spokespersons were from the English Collective of Prostitutes. Surely, he thought, if anyone knew about the sex industry it would be somebody who worked at the coalface, so to speak. Did an academic from the University of Sussex really know as much as someone who actually worked the streets, or shouldn't they at least be allowed their say? Evidently not. As far as policy was concerned the prostitutes could be studied like, say, macaque monkeys, but not allowed any voice or input. That had to be done by a specialist in prostitution. Not, God forbid, by a working girl.

He had tried raising the point and had been asked, patronizingly, if he was in favour of inviting, for example, murderers or armed robbers to comment on Home Office policy on police tactics.

Polite laughter.

Corrigan's sympathies were with the whores. They got shafted every which way, literally and figuratively.

Corrigan thought of all the outreach and consultancy work that went into community and gang-related crime and relations. Not into prostitution. It reminded him of mental health care, the right ignored it because of cost implications and fear of 'nanny state' accusations; the left because of complex libertarian issues. As per usual it would be the police responsible for the mess. The civil servants at the table and the representatives from the London Assembly didn't care what he thought. He was old and out of touch, and nobody liked the ECP because they didn't toe anybody's line but their own and, like him, they didn't have academic qualifications, which evidently meant their opinions didn't have any validity.

Poncey university bastards.

He didn't have a degree. Perhaps that was why he felt they secretly despised him. Them and their degrees. Their cherished bits of paper.

He increased his pace as he walked along Horseferry Road towards the pub in Pimlico where he'd arranged to meet Mawson. People moved out of his way as he bore down on them. At six feet five, with his battered, raw-looking face currently wreathed in a scowl, the assistant commissioner was an alarming sight. He looked like a doorman untethered from a nightclub entrance rather than a senior policeman. A bad-tempered doorman at that.

He passed a bar that purported to be an Irish pub. It advertised the joy of the 'craic' as well as Guinness. It was the kind of pub that would have kitsch Irish decorations like an oversized wooden spade labelled Finn McCool's spoon, and a Blarney Stone. Leprechauns! London Irish himself, he hated phoney Irish bars with a passion.

They could kiss his fucking Blarney Stone. His frown deepened.

He felt his blood pressure rise another notch with every step of his large Dr Martened feet. They beat out a rhythm of resentment. Civil servants, bastards. Stamp. Fake Irishry. Stamp. Unfair hounding of the police. Stamp. Being forced to use unorthodox methods for fear of his emails/mobile being hacked. Stamp.

He felt the blood thundering through his heart, felt a vein pulse in his temple. Calm down, for God's sake, he told himself.

Make an omelette, but don't, for God's sake, break any eggs.

He tried to remember if he'd taken his morning beta blocker. Thank God it's Mawson I'm meeting, he thought. He'll calm me down. Despite his degree. And fill me in on Hanlon. I hope to God she's behaving herself.

He passed a newsagent's, where the paper on display caught his eye, its headlines shouting.

Police Corruption, Scandal Deepens.
His blood pressure rose another couple of mmHg.

And I'll have the pasta melanzane, please,' said Mawson, handing back the large, stiff pseudo-parchment menu to the waitress. He looked around the airy, modern Italian restaurant with pleasure, a man at ease with his life, his surroundings and his character, and beamed at his dining companion, Assistant Commissioner Corrigan.

'Still not eating meat?' asked Corrigan. The two men looked at each other affectionately. He'd calmed down now. Mawson had that effect on him. They'd known each other since Hendon, more than thirty years now. Corrigan's career had taken him more or less to the very top of the career tree but Mawson's, although not unsuccessful, was considerably more low key.

Mawson pulled a face at the thought. 'I don't like killing things,' he said.

Corrigan replied, 'Yeah, but it's only natural, nature's way.'

'What, like murder, then?' Mawson replied.

Corrigan smiled bleakly. 'It's always been there, Harry. I suppose it keeps us in a job.'

'Oh well,' said Mawson, 'I guess it does.' He leaned forward. 'I've been reading a book, the *Tao Te Ching*. That in a way makes the same point.' He closed his eyes and quoted from memory.

'Heaven and earth are impartial, to them all things are
*   straw dogs.*
The Sage is impartial, to him the people are straw dogs.'

He smiled at Corrigan. 'In other words, Eamonn, we're all utterly unimportant in the grand scheme of things. None of it matters.'

'Well, there we are, Harry, very comforting.' Corrigan shrugged. 'I can't say they're sentiments I'd disagree with, but in the meantime there are still villains to nick.'

'Or,' countered Mawson, 'we could be concentrating on reducing crime, thus freeing ourselves from the need to nick so many people.'

'You're such an old hippy, Harry,' said Corrigan. He waved his fork. 'All this airy-fairy mysticism.'

'Peace and love aren't really that silly, Eamonn. Not really. And I'm doing my bit, aren't I, promoting user-friendly police interfaces and, yin and yang, I'm teaching the firearms unit to shoot straight. That's an uphill task, believe me.'

It was a classic case of opposites attracting, the differences between the two men widening as the years rolled by. Corrigan, enormous, raw-faced, a bull of a man, and the small, sleek figure of Mawson, who looked more like a teacher or a librarian than a policeman. Mawson was the bookish one. He even had a degree, a BA from SOAS in London. He was also a highly experienced firearms officer and, of course, former Bisley champion, although he no longer worked in that sector of the police. Corrigan, by contrast, had left school at fifteen and the only exams he ever passed were internal police ones. But the two men had always got on well despite, maybe because of, in Corrigan's eyes, an eccentric streak of mysticism in Mawson. Mawson's Taoist quote was typical. Harry Mawson would have said it was his yin to Corrigan's yang.

'I'll have the beef carpaccio followed by the saltimbocca,' said Corrigan to the waitress, 'and another large Barolo.'

Mawson said, '*Di me acqua minerale frizzante per favore,*' and added something in Italian that made the waitress laugh. Corrigan rolled his eyes.

'Show-off,' he said. For all his modesty, Mawson liked parading his achievements, his abilities.

Mawson smiled. 'You know I don't eat meat, Eamonn. I just don't like killing things.'

Corrigan looked at him quizzically. It was odd that a man who could hit a playing card dead centre at five hundred yards with a bullet should be so implacably opposed to killing animals. Particularly as Mawson had shot and killed two criminals in the course of his career as a police marksman. Maybe that had put him off.

Mawson smiled at Corrigan again. It was almost as if he was psychic. 'That was years ago, Eamonn, and, besides, the last thing I shot was a runaway bullock that had escaped from a field. And that was with a dart. I'm not even an authorized firearms officer now. Although they let me train still, in an "advisory capacity". But really I'm just Missing Persons and Community policing, you know that. And, of course, your chaperone.'

Corrigan shrugged. 'How's Hanlon?'

'Oh, fine,' said Mawson. 'A bit sulky.'

'She usually is,' said Corrigan.

'A bit panda-eyed at the moment,' said Mawson, removing his glasses and circling his eye socket with his forefinger for emphasis.

Corrigan felt a sense of foreboding. 'What's she been up to?'

Mawson polished his glasses on his napkin. 'A sporting injury, she said.' He squinted at his glasses and held them up to the light. 'I didn't say anything to her, sleeping dogs and all that, but I'd rather not have my officers look like they've been scrapping unless it was in the line of duty. Maybe you could have a word.'

'I wasn't planning on seeing her for a while,' said Corrigan. 'She's a bloody good police officer, Harry, go easy on her.

Anyway,' he said, 'yin and yang, I'm sure Hanlon's black eye restored equilibrium in the cosmos somewhere.'

Mawson laughed. 'Touché,' he said. 'I'm notoriously easy-going, anyway, Eamonn. Face it, that's partly why you asked me to create a vacancy for her. Which of course I did. '

Yeah, thought Corrigan, and I'm paying for her. She's on my budget, not on Thames Valley's.

'I'm even taking her shooting,' said Mawson. 'When I can find the time.'

'She'll like that,' said Corrigan. He had a sudden picture in his mind of Hanlon, prone on the ground, one grey eye squinting down a telescopic sight, her long, strong index finger gently squeezing the trigger, her coarse dark hair pulled back off her forehead.

'I bet she'll be bloody good.'

'We'll see,' said Mawson. 'There's a lot more to shooting than just pulling a trigger. Believe me, a lot more.'

'*Ecco, li,*' said the waitress. Their starters had arrived. '*Carpaccio per lei* and *carciofi alla Romana per lei, signori. Enjoy.*'

Corrigan looked down enthusiastically at his translucent slices of very red, wafer-thin, sliced raw beef, drizzled with olive oil. Nicer-looking than Mawson's artichokes. Baffling bloody vegetables.

'So, Hanlon's behaving herself?'

'Impeccably,' said Mawson. 'Now, you were going to tell me about some Russians.'

CHAPTER ELEVEN

Hanlon sat at a table in a pub opposite number 50 Beath Street, Marylebone. Oksana had given her the address; it was where Charlie had gone to meet his contact in the Russian sex trade. Oksana thought that Tatiana would have some idea of what might have happened to Charlie Taverner. Hanlon thought, Even if she did, she would keep her mouth shut. But she wanted to have a look, maybe meet the girl.

She should have been hard at work at the office in Langley, Slough, not engaged in this unofficial exploration of the whereabouts of Charlie Taverner.

But Mawson had a day off, Shona McIntyre wasn't the kind who would hassle her and she wanted to see where Taverner had met up with his London source of information. Whoever Tatiana was, thought Hanlon, she wouldn't have come cheap. A flat in the building opposite would be worth well over a million.

Once Hanlon had the bit between her teeth, she was unstoppable. Arkady Belanov represented everything she hated in one unattractive parcel. It would be fair to say that she had become obsessed with him. Obsession – a habit of hers that was both her strength and her Achilles heel. It led her to stupidly thoughtless actions. She didn't care. Hanlon, like many highly successful people, had an unshakeable belief in her own abilities, in her own righteousness.

Right now she was thinking of Oksana. She was thinking of her grief for her dead husband and her fatalistic belief that she would never see justice done.

Hanlon's bleak grey eyes narrowed as she remembered Arkady Belanov. His rolls of fat, his piggy, sadistic gaze. She remembered how the girl who had worked for Iris Campion had shown her Belanov's legacy to her, the angry, red scar tissue from where he had burned her with a butane torch. The Russian liked hurting women. Hanlon had hurt him. Not enough.

She ran her eyes over the expensive, desirable mansion block opposite. She nodded to herself. Now she knew that she was right to have come. This was where Belanov was seeking to expand his business.

Hanlon thought again about Belanov's legacy, a litany of hurt, the dead husband of Oksana, God knows how many others. And they were dead and mutilated while Belanov and his hired help, Dimitri, lived in a state of some luxury, insulated from justice by the power of their money, the power of their influence and the power of the fear that they spread.

She, however, couldn't be bought, she couldn't be intimidated and she couldn't be scared off. I'm your worst nightmare, Belanov, she thought grimly.

CHAPTER TWELVE

Overlooking Hanlon, staring out of a third-floor window at the street below but not seeing her, not seeing anything in the present, in the here and now, was Danny. Mentally, he was back in the Three Compasses.

'He got me to arrange a meet with Jordan, your brother,' Jackson had said.

'Who's "he"?' Anderson's voice was patient. He might have been discussing the weather.

Returning to the Beath Street flat had brought all the memories flooding back.

'This Myasnikov geezer. He couldn't come himself, he sent some other Russian. They call them "shestiorka", it means a gofer. This shestiorka told Jordan they wanted to buy Beath Street. With all fixtures and fittings. Jordan laughed. "How much?" "Five hundred," said the Russki. Jordan said, "You're having a laugh, aren't you, the flat alone is worth one point seven five." "Let me finish," said the Russki, "five hundred and we let you live."'

At the table outside the pub, Hanlon drank some of her tonic water and looked at the photos on her phone taken at the airport.

In Danny's head, Jackson's voice resumed its monologue from beyond the grave.

95

'"OK," Jordan said, "give the big man a bell. I want to speak to the organ grinder, not the fucking monkey." "I don't understand," said the shestiorka. Hardly surprising really. "What, don't you speak fucking English?" said Jordan. I could see he was getting angry. He was quite pissed and he'd been taking jellies. He was out of it, really. Really fucked, and nasty with it. You know how he loved downers. Phone your boss, I said. That's what he means. The Russki was mystified by Jordan, hadn't got a clue what he was on about. Phone your boss, I said.'

So there was Dimitri, mused Hanlon, man mountain, six and a half feet of pointlessly sculpted muscle; there was Joad, his head and mouth reminding her of an eel, and there was the *vor*, the crime boss, the man responsible for the death of Oksana's husband, looking like an unimportant, unassuming businessman.

Danny dragged himself away from the window and got on with his job of checking the flat to make sure that all traces of the killing had been removed. All of Tatiana's clothing and personal effects were now gone as well. He forced himself to look at all the rooms, inspecting everything for traces of blood or forgotten personal effects. It didn't have to withstand a police forensic team, it just had to look presentable until Anderson moved another girl in. That would be easier said than done. Rumours were spreading. The Anderson name was becoming synonymous with being killed.

He sat down on the sofa and the interior recording of Barry Jackson's voice resumed.

'The Russian stank of sweat and cheap aftershave. He spoke into the phone in his own language, he waited, then he said to Jordan, "Is 'vor'. Big boss. You want to speak to him." Jordan had

one hand in front of him, the other behind his back. He took the phone from the Russian, spoke into it. "Can you hear me?" he said.'

Danny took his wallet out and chopped himself a line of coke on the glass coffee table. The new glass coffee table, not the old one, which was irreparably stained where Jordan's disembodied head had rested. A nice new glass one from an expensive interior design shop round the corner. He snorted the coke down and sat back on the sofa. The new sofa, not the one where Tatiana and the client who looked like a Conservative MP had died.

'The Russian sneered at Jordan and started to speak. He said, "Is offer you can't—" The next word he said should have been "refuse" but Jordan's other hand appeared from behind his back. He was holding a gun and he shot the Russian in the kneecap. The Russian screamed and clutched at his shattered leg. Blood was everywhere, blood through his fingers as he tried to stop the flow, blood soaking his trouser leg. Jordan's eyes were big with killing lust. He held the phone near the guy's head so the vor could hear the screams. "Hear that?" Jordan shouted. "Hear that, you Russian cunt?" Then he brought the gun up and shot the Russki between the eyes. "Hear that? That's my answer."

'Arkady arranged everything,' Jackson said. 'He found me. He said you were history, Boss, his words not mine. He said they wanted number 50 and he was going to take it. You'd been offered a fair price and said no.'

Anderson had looked bored. 'Arkady,' he'd said. Jackson nodded. 'Arkady Belanov, based in Oxford.' Anderson had smiled thinly. 'Well, well, well.' He'd looked at Morris Jones and said, 'I've heard enough.' Jones had picked up the heroin-filled syringe and Jackson had swallowed and closed his eyes.

Again he saw Anderson, a look of bored disinterest on his face, as Morris Jones had gently inserted the silver sliver of the hypodermic needle into the thick vein in the crook of Barry Jackson's forearm, Jackson looking away, sweat pouring off his forehead, biting his lip to try to control himself. The swirl of red blood as Jones gently drew back the plunger to check the correct positioning of the needle, and then the slight pressure forcing the lethal dose of smack into Jackson's arm. Jackson had grunted with pleasure as the morphine rush hit him like a freight train before it carried him away into a final oblivion.

He'd sighed and stiffened, then his body had slumped as unconsciousness had claimed him and the black waters had closed over his head.

They'd watched him die dispassionately.

'Not a bad way to go,' said Morris Jones thoughtfully.

Danny stood up, put his wallet back in his pocket and left the flat. He locked the door behind him and thought, I wonder who'll be next.

From her table across the road, Hanlon saw him leave. She'd met him before once, a long time ago it seemed now. She didn't know his name, but she knew his face and she knew who he worked for. She wouldn't need to see Tatiana now. The jigsaw puzzle was becoming clearer. The *vor* and now Taverner's contact.

What part did Anderson have in this? she wondered.

Well, she knew one way to find out. She stood up and flagged down a black cab; she leaned into the open window,

'Dean Street,' she said to the driver as she crouched down and stepped inside. 'Soho.'

CHAPTER THIRTEEN

Lunch at the Lebanese restaurant was not going well. The two of them sat unhappily opposite each other at a table by the window overlooking the High Street like an illustration from an article about unhappy relationships. *Broken Dreams* might have been the title. Melinda Huss was low-key elegant. Back home she had changed into a low-necked blouse that discreetly but emphatically emphasized her chest, and trousers that slimmed down her muscular thighs.

Rubens would have liked painting Huss, there was quite a lot of her and it all looked good.

She'd picked the restaurant to flatter her partner. To allow Enver, who was highly knowledgeable about the cuisine, to sparkle with information, to maybe entertain her with some funny anecdotes about working in the family restaurants or the eccentricities of his Anglo-Turkish family. She'd have been more than willing to listen, applaud his insights, laugh at his jokes.

What could go wrong?

Enver, unused to driving in Oxford, unused to driving full stop, nearly collided twice with cyclists (angry exchanges), stalled the car in traffic on Broad Street (multi-horn honkings) and made a meal of parking in a multi-storey, reversing in and driving out of a bay about four times. Huss was a highly competent driver who not only was police-trained but had grown up manoeuvring tractors and horse boxes in confined spaces. If it had been anyone else, she'd have ordered them out of the driver's seat and done it herself. She'd noticed Enver's powerful fingers tightening on the wheel, the muscles in his arms beneath the fabric of his cheap suit swelling with impotent rage at the unusual stress of handling a car. He never drove in London.

They left the car, angled at a slight – but to Huss irritating – diagonal in the bay. Outside, the drizzle turned to rain. She had an umbrella; he didn't.

'Do you want to share my umbrella?' she asked.

'No, I'll be fine.' His voice was tight and stiff with irritation. Typical, thought Huss as Enver strode beside her, relishing his discomfort, silently blaming her for his driving incompetence and the Oxford weather. Huss's blue eyes narrowed. She was getting cross.

The restaurant was deserted apart from an irritable-looking bald man at a nearby table, expensively dressed and reading a copy of the *Economist*. Enver noticed, with a pang, that the fellow customer was quite slim. As he breathed he could feel his stomach pressing against the fabric of his shirt, tight against his belt. How had it got so big? How come he wasn't doing anything about it?

Conversation was stilted, awkward silences cropped up with increasing regularity and grew wider and wider, cracks widening into chasms. The lack of any kind of buzz in the restaurant, the absence of distractions, only deepened their mutual discomfort. Their conversation became brittle, disjointed and stalled. Enver wished he wasn't there.

Huss sat opposite him, stony-faced. She felt her artfully chosen clothes, flattering with more than a hint of sexy, were lost on Enver. She might as well have kept the boilersuit on. Silence enveloped the table. The waiter took their order, trying to jolly things up with smiles and remarks about the weather. He guessed they were an old-established couple. He'd have put them down as married but they had no rings. It was usually the married people who chose to come to an expensive restaurant to argue about things. You'd have thought you could do that at home. For free. Where was the sense in paying good money for a bust-up? Soon they'd probably start hissing at each other, the way the middle class always argued, quietly, venomously. In a *let's not make a scene* kind of way.

'It's all your fault.'

'God, how I despise you.'

'No wonder the children hate you.'

He doubted he'd get much of a tip.

Enver wanted to tell Huss how nice she looked, how he'd missed her and would she like to go to the cinema with him. There was an old art deco picture palace near where he lived in Tottenham and it had been lovingly restored by a friend of one of Enver's brothers. An up-and-coming local chef, he'd worked at Le Gavroche and the Square, and was running a pop-up restaurant there. Enver had bought two tickets for a 'romantic evening' that included a three-course set dinner and a film viewing of the old classic, *A Room With a View*. They were in his pocket. Huss was free that night; he had checked with one of her colleagues that he knew.

Huss would love it.

Physically, Enver was a brave man. It took real guts to climb through the ropes of a boxing ring and face someone, a fit, trained athlete who has devoted his life to basically beating people to a pulp. In the police force he'd encountered varying levels of intimidation and violence and a certain amount of attempted bullying. He had even experienced being threatened with a gun. He had been shot. But he was nervous with women and he was not only attracted to Huss physically; he felt disturbed by thoughts bordering on obsession for her.

If I ask her out, and she says no, what then? he thought. He even worried that she might laugh at the idea, that he was out of her league. He feared rejection; he feared ridicule. A fat, has-been ex-boxer who might – if he was lucky – do OK in the Met. A man who came from a background of kebab shops and who lived in a studio flat in south Tottenham.

Enver, although born and brought up in London, had been instilled with his father's essentially peasant values. While some of them had stood him in good stead – thrift, hard work, a mulish refusal to be intimidated – he felt ill at ease in social situations like this. Huss, he felt, was a cut above him, a landowner.

He was nervous and out of his depth. He felt tongue-tied, clumsy, awkward. He kept putting his hand inside his jacket to check the tickets were still in the pocket, as if touching them would give him the courage to ask her out.

'So what brings you down to Oxford?' asked Huss. She wished he'd stop fiddling about in his jacket pocket. It was beginning to annoy her.

'Corrigan wants me to look into Arkady Belanov's business dealings,' said Enver. He'd maybe wait for a better time to ask her out. He knew he had bottled it. He was going to stick grimly to business.

Huss raised a quizzical eyebrow. The gesture mesmerized Enver. Her eyebrows were very shapely. They were light brown. His heart lurched.

'Oh. Does he?' said Huss flatly. Enver didn't recognize the danger signs. He carried on, marching to his doom.

'Yes,' said Enver, 'in an off-the-record kind of way.' He smiled winningly. Huss found it infuriating.

'So that's why you wanted to see me, is it?' asked Huss. She didn't like being made to feel a fool and she felt like one now. So much for her romantic expectations. 'To help you and Corrigan in some secretive Met enquiry?'

'Well, no, yes.' Enver could see the whole thing was going terribly wrong. He wasn't quite sure where, but he recognized the signs. Surely talking about work was like the weather, a neutral subject, something they both had to endure. He had thought they'd be on common ground, which evidently wasn't the case. He floundered on, flailing. 'Sort of.'

Huss stood up. 'Sort of!'

She was very angry indeed. She could easily imagine the conversation: *Sweet-talk Huss into helping you, she's a size 12, she'll do anything for a date.* And to think that she was harbouring feelings for this idiot. She glared down at Enver. 'You can get the bill, Enver. You can direct any further police-related questions to me at the nick via the proper channels.' A sudden horrible thought struck her. 'Is DCI Hanlon involved in any of this?'

'No,' said Enver, looking confused. 'Why should she be?'

Huss glowered at him. Because I can't stand that bloody woman, she thought, that's why. I'm not being logical. Sod logic. She gestured at the waiter, who came with alacrity. 'My coat, please.' She slipped it on while Enver sat motionless, looking at her helplessly.

'I'll make my own way home.'

She swept out of the restaurant. There was a taxi stand across the street. Enver watched through the glass of the restaurant window as she climbed into the back of an old, grey Mercedes and he watched its tail lights as it drove off. The rain beat down remorselessly.

The waiter looked at him sympathetically. 'Bill, please,' said Enver.

Enver walked slowly back to his car, his clothes completely sodden now. His right foot, the foot where he'd been shot a year or so ago, ached. It did that occasionally, particularly when it was cold, and Enver's feet were soaking.

He felt angry, depressed, sorry for himself.

He walked up the concrete stairs that led to the third floor of the multi-storey where he'd so ineptly parked. They smelled faintly of urine, damp cement and weed. He got into the car and turned the ignition on. The inside of the windscreen fogged up from his damp body heat and he turned the fan on to clear it. As he waited for it to demist he thought, Fuck.

He flapped down the sun visor and looked at his face in the mirror. The fat face of a loser. His hard, brown eyes were reflected back at him. His thick, black hair, his quite prominent nose, like an eagle's beak. The scar on the side of his left eyebrow. He remembered that fight. Comprehensively behind on points, a Southern Counties championship final. His opponent, a black kid, he'd forgotten his name, had opened up a cut there and it had been bleeding badly. He'd known the fight was more or less over.

Demir, in Turkish, means iron; *el* means hand. Enver's surname was Demirel, Iron Hand, a good name for a boxer, and true in his case. He was a poor mover – in boxing terms, awkward – but he had a big punch, and in the third round, on the point of defeat – the referee would stop it soon because of the cut – he'd caught the kid with a massive right hand. He'd gone down like he'd been shot, his legs crumpling under him. KO. Sparko. There was surely a lesson there.

He touched the scar again. He put the car in gear. He'd come from behind once; he could do it again.

Back on the farm, Melinda Huss had angrily ripped her clothes off. She stared at her buxom body in her white lingerie. A sight Enver Demirel certainly wouldn't be seeing, she thought. Her carefully chosen clothes lay accusingly on the floor of her bedroom where she'd flung them, and she pulled the stiff fabric of the boilersuit, with its smell of engine oil, over her body. The Freelander awaited.

There was a knock on her bedroom door and she opened it, expecting it to be either her mother or father.

Her eyes widened in surprise, as did Enver's. Huss hadn't got round to doing up the buttons of the boilersuit. It framed her generously curved body, her underwear a geometric arrange-ment of triangular, vertical and horizontal white stripes. Her body was all he could have dreamed, and then some. She made no move; she held the door open with one hand.

'I wanted to ask you out,' said Enver, speaking quickly so he wouldn't forget the lines he'd rehearsed in the car and so she couldn't interrupt. 'But I didn't. I hoped you might want to go out with me to see this.' He handed her the ticket. 'If you do, call me.'

She watched as he turned and clattered down the stairs. It was an old farmhouse and the ceiling where the staircase turned was low. There was an audible thud as his forehead struck the beam above the stairs. Huss winced. Enver kept going. He had a head like a rock.

She closed the door and sat down on the bed. *A Room with A View*, and dinner. She raised her eyebrows, but in a good way.

Enver was sitting stationary in traffic when his phone beeped. He glanced down at the screen. Huss. She would like to come. There was a name, Sam Curtis, and an address in Cowley. Try him, she suggested. He works for Belanov. A file was attached.

He remembered the night in Basingstoke, the sweaty, noisy venue. The referee holding both their wrists: 'A-a-a-a-nd tonight's winner, and the NEW . . . ABA. . . Southern. . . region Middleweight champion is. . . Enver. . . Ironhand. . . Demirel!'

Contentedly, he turned the car round at the next roundabout and followed the signs for Cowley back into Oxford. He felt euphoric. Everything would work out just fine.

Enver Demirel walked past the door to Chantal's flat twice before he found it, the entrance squeezed between a betting shop and a fast-food outlet. He'd read the documents in a car park off Cowley High Street. Huss had sent him a PDF file that contained what little relevant information she had on the Russian duo of Arkady Belanov and Dimitri. It had more information on Curtis, including the fact that Chantal was his girlfriend. It was a lot better than walking around pubs with dodgy reputations to ask about Curtis, whose name he knew from his previous run-in with the Russians. This information wasn't official police intelligence; it was part of Huss's vendetta against Joad.

The Russians were only of tangential interest to Huss. It was Joad that she was focused on. Huss hated Joad. It wasn't solely because Joad was bent. There were several police she worked with who fell into that category, from the trivial, falsifying expenses, fiddling overtime, to the more serious, turning blind eyes in exchange for favours, particularly sexual, and leaking information to media and suspects' lawyers for cash. But there was only one Joad. She wouldn't have cared if the man turned over a new leaf and became pope; nothing would change her visceral loathing of the man.

Joad was Belanov's man in Oxford CID and Huss was busy preparing enough hard information to present a rock-solid case against him. It was difficult because of Joad's innately furtive nature and his inexplicably numerous mates in the force, all fifty-year-old men. They would close ranks; there was no doubt about that. They were the kind who would hear nothing bad against Joad, saying he was old school (dinosaur, thought Huss), or 'a bit of a character' (rude, unhelpful) or 'not PC' (porn-obsessed, lecherous, racist, homophobic) and 'one of the lads' (drink problem, aggressive). The strength of his involvement with the Russian pimp was still a matter of conjecture.

Belanov was out of bounds to Enver. He'd only met Dimitri once: it was unlikely Dimitri would have forgotten. An enraged Enver had hit him in the face, shattering his already fractured cheekbone, then dragged him out of the van he'd sat in and given him a good kicking.

But Sam Curtis didn't know Enver and Huss had information he was at his girlfriend's address. Chantal Jenkins, twenty-three, two counts of shoplifting and one of soliciting, later dropped. Curtis had a lengthier, more professional criminal record.

Enver stood irresolutely by the shabby, narrow entrance and looked at the row of buzzers, the name Jenkins in a curly feminine script written on a peeling white sticker. 'Off the record,' Corrigan had said. To this end he'd taken a week's leave, told his colleagues he was going to France. He'd give it a week; he owed Corrigan that much. He had decided he wasn't going to bust a gut; he had a date with Huss at the cinema on Wednesday.

'Shake the tree, see what falls out.' Those had been Corrigan's words. Well, Enver wasn't one for confrontation; the Dimitri incident had been atypical. But he'd do enough to credibly claim a tree had been shaken. He'd see Chantal. She'd tell him where to go, or Curtis would. He'd leave. They'd tell Belanov some copper had been making enquiries and presumably Joad would go into overdrive trying to find out what was happening, who had authorized it, what was known. Then Huss would monitor whatever he was up to. It was a nice, simple plan.

Best of all, he wouldn't be involved. All he had to do was alarm Curtis.

It was a bit like the kids' game of ringing the doorbell and running away, and that simple. He wasn't interested in results, just doing enough to satisfy Corrigan.

He took out his warrant card and studied the photo under the Metropolitan Police banner. He only had one chin in that picture. Now that was no longer the case. He should exercise more. Maybe jogging? God, the very thought. He hadn't run since he'd given up boxing. He was beginning to lack confidence in the ability of his legs to carry him at speed. Any speed. Sometimes Hanlon's training involved running up and down a hill for an hour to increase her power and endurance. Enver shuddered. Even the idea of running was becoming strange, alien. Like being asked to tango or to belly dance.

Top-floor flat. He rang the bell and a girl's voice answered.

'Police,' he said. The door buzzed, he pushed and it opened. He stepped inside and sniffed the air. It was dark inside and the light grey walls were scuffed and discoloured. The stairwell smelled faintly of skunk and damp carpet. The grey, stained stairway stretched upward, gloomy and uninviting. Laboriously, the stairs creaking under his weight, he started the ascent.

At the top of the stairs, quadriceps aching, he knocked on the shabby white door, warrant card in hand. It opened and the girl who stood facing him asked, 'What do you want?'

It was probably the question that Enver heard the most in his life as a policeman. If the party concerned was innocent it usually came out as, *Can I help you, Officer?* but it was essentially the same question, and it came with a variety of intonations – curiosity, worry, fear, sarcasm. Rarely was it welcoming. The tone this time was unmistakeably one of fear.

'Chantal Jenkins?'

'Yes.'

'I'm DI Demirel. Can I come in?'

She turned and indicated the flat. Enver walked into a small bed-sitting room. The window was ajar and there was a strong smell of stale smoke and grass, overlaid with incense.

He looked at Chantal Jenkins. Like Huss, she was blonde, pretty and female, but there the resemblance ended. Chantal had a narrow face, pallid, and her complexion was poor. Huss looked like the farmer's daughter she was, broader-faced, broader-beamed. Huss too was sturdy; she had a solid, powerful frame. Melinda Huss also always looked ridiculously healthy – tanned in the summer, glowing in the winter. The result of a lifetime spent outdoors.

The girl before him looked as if she had never seen sunshine or natural light. Chantal Jenkins was slim to the point of thin, her eyes restless and haunted. Enver felt enormous standing in front of her. She looked so fragile – a sudden movement, a harsh word and she'd break. Enver felt a sudden twinge of sympathy for the girl with her worried and careworn face. He knew she was about twenty-three, but she could have been a decade older.

'What do you want?' she asked. She looked round the untidy, grubby room with an air of hopelessness. Discarded dirty clothing lay here and there. Her voice was nervous, as if she thought he might be bringing bad news.

He looked around him. 'Can I sit down?' he said. Chantal looked at him blankly and he gestured to the only seat, a stained armchair, cigarette or joint burns in the arms. He felt he would be less intimidating sitting down than looming over her.

'Please do,' Chantal said. She indicated the kitchen area of the bedsit. 'Do you want a coffee or something?'

Her gesture took in a sink piled with dirty dishes, a hotplate and plug-in convection oven to the left, a microwave and toaster on a shelf above. Three of these were connected to a single multi-adaptor. The shelf with the microwave and toaster, a dip in the middle from where the melamine bowed under the weight, was more or less directly over the sink. It looked potentially lethal.

Enver's childhood and adolescence had been largely spent in family-run restaurant kitchens and he found himself looking at Chantal's rudimentary cooking arrangements with almost an environmental health officer's eyes.

That set-up, electrical appliances over water, a death trap waiting to happen. He could only too easily imagine either the rickety shelf giving way or the microwave toppling into the scummy liquid that filled the washing-up bowl in the sink, while a zonked-out Chantal was going through the motions of washing up. Water and mains electricity. Enver shuddered.

The oven and microwave both had a patina of burnt food engrained onto the inside of their glass fronts.

The overloaded socket was yet another hazard, this time with an added element of fire risk. He could see a filthy-looking fridge by an overflowing bin. Campylobacter heaven. He very much did not want a coffee. He didn't want his lips touching anything in here.

'No, thank you,' he said.

Chantal sat down on the bed, the only other place to do so. She was wearing jeans and a tight T-shirt that outlined the top half of her body. She had a good figure. If she hadn't looked so defeated, if she cleaned herself up, she could have been really attractive. But, then, thought Enver sadly, why would she be bothered to do that – for clients? For Curtis? He thought, She's too sad and unhappy to want to do it for herself.

He wished he wasn't here. She crossed her arms in what he guessed was a classic defensive gesture.

Time to shake the tree, he thought. Just like Corrigan instructed me to. He felt a stab of self-disgust. Chantal looked as if she might cry any second. I'll shake it gently, thought Enver.

'I'm investigating the activities of a Mr Arkady Belanov and a Mr Dimitri Kuzubov. I believe that you know them, or know of them, and I was wondering if you had any information you would like to share with me.'

He spoke slowly and clearly; he didn't want to intimidate her. Chantal looked absolutely terrified now.

'No.' She shook her head. 'No, I don't know anything about them, nothing,' she said over-emphatically.

'No?' said Enver. It was such a transparent lie.

'No,' said Chantal. 'I've never heard of them. They sound. . .' she paused, searching for an appropriate word '. . . foreign.' She stared fearfully at the door as if she expected it to come crashing down and the huge figure of Dimitri appear in front of them. The big, bad wolf.

'Please, please go,' she said. 'Someone's been winding you up. I can't help you, I'm sorry.'

Enver thought to himself that maybe he should take the Hanlon route. She would have kept on at Chantal until she broke down and gave him something useful. But Enver wasn't Hanlon. He was kind-hearted. Besides, he thought, erroneously, Chantal wouldn't know anything important. Curtis wouldn't be stupid enough to unburden himself to someone so fragile.

'OK,' said Enver. He took his wallet out of his jacket pocket and took out a business card.

'Here's my card. It's got my mobile number on and my email. If you do have any information on the Russians, or if your boyfriend does, just get in touch.'

He gave the card to Chantal, who stared at it as if it were a court summons.

'I'll let myself out,' said Enver. Chantal nodded silently and Enver heaved himself out of the armchair and left the flat.

Across the street from Chantal's flat was a Starbucks. Sitting in the window was Dimitri, having a double espresso before he paid a visit to Chantal. Dimitri had been in the flat before and had drawn similar conclusions to Enver as to the advisability of consuming anything while there. He liked to have a coffee in more salubrious surroundings while he thought about Chantal. He liked the way she was terrified of him. He liked it a lot. He knew that Curtis would be away for a few hours, running errands, and Chantal would be in there alone. Dimitri enjoyed Chantal's vulnerability. He savoured her weakness and her terror. He loved frightening women; it turned him on.

He watched Enver leave the front door and step into the street. At first he thought he was one of Chantal's clients, then he turned and Dimitri saw his face. The Russian's eyes widened in surprise and anger. His fingers automatically touched his cheek. This was the man who had punched him through the open window of a van in East London, breaking the bone. This was the man who had dragged him out of the van, semi-conscious, and kicked him several times in the head and crotch. A professional, hard and vicious attack. He doubted he could have done much better himself.

He hadn't been beaten up; he'd been processed.

What was he doing here? He stared intently through the glass of the coffee-shop window to make sure it was him. The bull neck, the thick dark hair, the drooping moustache, he recognized those. Then, with a professional eye, he noted the swell of the arms through the cheap thin fabric of Enver's suit, the powerful-looking legs. Even Enver's paunch looked hard and dangerous. He'd have a low centre of gravity and if he launched himself at you, you'd better brace yourself.

Enver turned and walked away up the street. Dimitri watched him go. He noted Enver's confident, heavy tread, a man used to people getting out of his way.

He shook his head in wonder at Myasnikov's foresight. The Butcher was so right to have identified Curtis as a possible weak link in a chain that could incriminate them. And this man, well, soon he would know exactly who he was and what he was after.

God was great. He had delivered his enemy to him. He had prayed for this moment every night since his encounter with the man, and now he would have his revenge.

Slava Bogu! Thank you, God, he said to himself.

They'd meet again; this time he'd be ready. He drank his coffee and put the small cup down, like a thimble between his large fingers.

He stood up. Time to go and see Chantal. The girl had some explaining to do.

CHAPTER FOURTEEN

Hanlon paid off the taxi driver at the bottom end of Dean Street, near Piccadilly. The pavements of Shaftesbury Avenue were thronged with tourists, but as soon as you walked a couple of metres away from the main road the crowds magically vanished. Soho was almost peaceful.

She walked past the church at the bottom of the street, surrounded by its outwardly curved hard-mesh fence that kept rough sleepers out of its graveyard at night. She eyed it speculatively. She could climb it easily, she thought. The overhang would pose no problem. Hanlon was the kind of woman who could do a one-armed pull-up without batting an eyelid.

The pavements of the narrow street were busy with purposeful-looking young people in casual, expensive clothes. Post- and pre-production film and TV offices were the main employers here, the main visible employers. Sex and drugs had been Soho's main trade for years and, although hit hard by rising rents, they were here to stay. They'd been here since the outset, the eternal verities. Blake had been born in Soho, thought Hanlon. It was here he'd seen angels, seen the New Jerusalem shining amongst the filth and the squalor. Nothing changed here in the magic kingdom. Soho was still the same mixture of heaven and hell. It would see off any new technological advance with ease. The eternal verities, the unchanging faces of Los and Orc.

She saw her destination, a tiny alleyway between a Thai restaurant and a property that was being redeveloped, draped in dark green plastic mesh and shrouded in heavy, waterproof canvas sheeting to keep noise and dust levels down. Two hard-hatted builders, their hi-vis jerkins smeared in grey dust and cement, crouched outside, having a cigarette break. One of them gave his opinion loudly as she squeezed by to get into the alley.

'Nice arse.'

Hanlon stopped, turned and looked him up and down. Her gaze swept speculatively down, from his yellow safety helmet to his ripped jeans, scuffed black knee-protectors and workboots, the leather worn away at the front to reveal the metal toecaps. He was wearing a sleeveless vest showing his powerful forearms and muscular biceps, the main vein prominent under his tanned, dusty skin. He had the kind of vascularity in the muscles that bodybuilders would die for.

'Nice arms,' she said to him as she passed, staring straight into his eyes. 'Shame about the face.'

As she knocked hard on the big red door in front of her she heard the other say, 'Look, Dave, you're blushing.'

The door opened and Hanlon stepped across its threshold into the dark portal of the Krafft Club. Iris Campion's house. A place of pain and correction.

Tea, dear?' asked Iris Campion solicitously.

Hanlon nodded. 'Yes please.' She watched as Iris Campion, her bulk shrouded in a floral kaftan, poured from a Clarice Cliff floral-decorated teapot into a matching art deco porcelain cup. Hanlon looked round Campion's windowless sitting room. It was as chintzy as she remembered, every square centimetre of available surface covered in knick-knacks with no unifying theme. There were china shepherdesses, toby jugs, glass swans,

Wedgwood vases, art deco figurines, art nouveau flowery ceramics. On the walls were sentimental, kitsch paintings.

Hanlon's cold eyes studied Campion. The twin scars, like tribal markings incised deeply into the flesh of each cheek, were deliberately uncovered by the thick foundation that Campion used. They had been done by a pimp as a punishment decades ago when she'd been a teenage whore. The pimp was long dead; his handiwork lived on in her cicatriced face.

She could have had corrective plastic surgery but she elected to leave her face as it was. Her two fingers up at the world. Soho Iris, she was called around here, her world bounded by a kilometre square. Oxford Street, Regent Street, Shaftesbury Avenue, Charing Cross Road, the four borders of her kingdom. She never left the place.

'Who's the *polone?*' the man in the guest armchair asked, in an unfriendly voice. He was, Hanlon guessed, in his seventies, red trousers, pink, tiger-print brothel-creeper shoes and a lilac shirt. Despite his age and his camp mannerisms, his eyes were hard and contemptuous. Mind you, thought Hanlon, she was in the reception room of London's leading S&M brothel, not a drop-in centre for the over-sixties. You weren't going to meet upstanding members of the community here. Well, you might, but only as paying customers.

His white hair had a faint pink hue to it. Like candyfloss. One hand held an ebony walking stick with an ornate silver head. It caught her attention.

'Looking at my knob are you, dearie?' he said, angling the polished metal head in Hanlon's direction. She ignored the suggestive double-entendre. Hanlon had been wondering if it was actually a swordstick, a Victorian relic still deadly after all these years. Maybe a little like this pensioner. He looked the kind of man who would be perfectly willing to use such a thing.

'Milk?' asked Campion.

'No, thank you,' said Hanlon. Campion shrugged and sat down on the high sofa, which sagged noticeably under her weight. Hanlon noticed her ankles were badly swollen. She put her tea down on a small table and topped it up with an aged single-malt Macallan. I wonder what on earth that tastes like, thought Hanlon with a repressed shudder.

Campion looked at her two guests with amusement. 'Albert Slater,' she indicated the older man with a slight hand movement '. . . meet DCI Hanlon.'

The old man looked at her with unalloyed displeasure. 'I thought you was Lilly Law, when I *vardad* you.' He looked at Campion. He had the old queen's dated habit of using he for she and vice versa. 'Didn't think he was one of your *polones.* He's a bit *naff*, inne?'

He looked witheringly at Hanlon.

'Cat got your tongue, dearie?' he asked.

'I hope you mean *naff* in the original sense?' said Hanlon coolly. 'If you mean "not available for fucking", then yes.'

The old man smiled despite himself. 'Ooh, sharp, aren't we. Mind you don't cut yourself. So you know Polari?'

'Yes,' said Hanlon. She could have added, I learned it from my colleague and friend, Mark Whiteside. But, of course, she didn't.

She thought of him lying in his bed in hospital. Asleep in hospital. She never thought of him as in a coma or on life support, or in a persistent vegetative state. Just asleep, and one day he would wake up. She would make sure of that.

Mark was an *omi-palone*, as the old man would have called him, gay as it was now known. She smiled inwardly, her face externally as hard as ever. He had loved the old camp language of Polari. She remembered when she used to stay sometimes at his flat, Mark naked except for a pair of Calvin Kleins, the corrugated ridges of his abdominal muscles. 'How about that for a basket, ma'am?' he'd asked, indicating his well-packed underwear. 'Fantabulosa, Mark,' she'd replied.

Alone now in his hospital bed, the only physical contact when the team of gentle, patient nurses turned him periodically, like a piece of meat, to prevent pressure sores from developing.

She'd killed the man who'd put him where he was now. Fat lot of good it had done.

'So, Detective Chief Inspector,' said Iris Campion, bored by this lengthy pause, 'other than a linguistic trip down memory lane, how can I help? Or is this a social call?'

Hanlon looked enquiringly at Albert Slater.

'Bert's practically family,' said Iris Campion. 'You can say anything you want in front of him.'

Hanlon shrugged. 'Who owns 50 Beath Street?'

Campion had a comprehensive knowledge of the who's who of the London brothel world. She took a hefty sip of her whisky-enhanced tea. 'Dave Anderson. He's a mate of yours, isn't he? I'd have thought you'd have known that.'

So I was right, thought Hanlon.

'Tell her what's been going on.' It was Albert Slater who spoke. Hanlon noted the change of pronoun. Now he'd given her back her feminine identity, a form of politeness, she guessed.

Iris Campion frowned; she didn't like anyone telling her what to do. Then she relented.

'Someone's been killing Anderson's toms,' she said. 'And the clientele.' With that, she filled Hanlon in, more or less accurately, on what had happened at Beath Street.

'So far it doesn't seem like the Old Bill know,' said Campion. 'Anderson's boys don't shoot their mouths off, but I know because one of them talked to someone one of my girls knows and working girls share stuff like that, and these days news gets about faster than a dose of the clap.'

Hanlon sat in her chair, expressionless. It was a gangland killing designed to intimidate, designed to send a message.

Anderson would try to keep it private, and he might just succeed. The dead prostitute, well, working girls tended sadly to be friendless. That left Charlie Taverner and no one was busting a gut over him.

Only Oksana and her.

She knew now that Taverner was dead; she knew it for sure. She was police. There was no doubt as to what she should do, but she felt strangely reluctant to act. It was as if Oksana Taverner's scorn of officialdom had been contagious. The Metropolitan Police had let her down, packed her off to Slough, had made no secret of the fact that they considered her a liability rather than an asset, and she felt disinclined to share her knowledge.

Knowledge was power and what Hanlon needed above all was the power to get Sergeant Mark Whiteside transferred to somewhere private where he could be operated on. Whiteside was too high risk and the cost of the op too exorbitant for it to happen on the NHS. So she stored this nugget of golden information away while she thought of how she might use it.

Hanlon knew that Whiteside's days were numbered. His next of kin wanted the machines that kept him alive withdrawn or, the equivalent nutrition denied him, so he would pass on.

Over my dead body, thought Hanlon. I've lost faith in the system, she thought.

'Who did it?' she asked Campion.

'The Russians, I believe, dearie. Anyway, you remember Yuri.'

Hanlon nodded. He'd been Campion's manager. 'He fucked off once he heard, scarpered he did, couldn't see his heels for dust. Something about the Butcher of Moscow.' As Oksana thought, noted Hanlon.

'Well,' she said. 'Hard to get good staff, I guess.' Yuri will be no loss, she thought. 'What was it all about?'

'I dunno,' said Campion. 'Turf war maybe, revenge. Who knows. To be honest, I don't give a flying fuck.' She yawned ostentatiously. 'Dave Anderson's your boyfriend, not mine. He's a nutcase.'

'He's not that,' said Hanlon. 'I've seen his psychiatric notes. Dr Stein assessed him, the last time he was banged up. He's a prominent forensic psychiatrist. He knows them all, Iris. All our prominent killers. Dave Anderson is officially evil, not a nutcase at all. He's saner than you or me.'

'Speak for yourself,' said Iris Campion. She looked at her shrewdly. 'You don't seem overly excited by any of this, do you, DCI Hanlon.' She added some more expensive malt to her tea. 'You going to old man Anderson's funeral?'

'I wasn't invited.' The last time she had seen Dave Anderson's father, Malcolm Anderson, he had been dying of lung cancer. Hanlon had liked him, he'd retained a mordant sense of humour as the shadows had lengthened around him and the pain ratcheted ever upwards. Not only had he been stoic in the face of death; he'd managed to joke about it. Hanlon had found that very impressive. And now the old man was gone, leaving Dave Anderson to run things.

The king is dead, long live the king, she thought. She felt strangely hurt that she hadn't been told.

'You are invited,' said Campion. 'I saw Malcolm the day before he died. He said to ask you. It's next week, Wednesday, ten thirty a.m., Edmonton Cemetery.'

'I'll make it if I can,' said Hanlon. 'How were you going to find me anyway, to tell me?'

'Slough's not far away, dear. Auntie Iris knows where to find anyone, doesn't she.'

It seems like everyone knows my business, thought Hanlon. First Oksana, now Iris Campion, and there's me not even on Facebook.

CHAPTER FIFTEEN

Curtis repeated his journey of a week ago with Dimitri. There were, however, major differences this time around.

The most obvious was that it was daylight. The huge industrial area was busy now. It was the largest privately owned trading estate in the country, maybe in the whole EU, and by day it showed. It was spacious and the roads wide, so it didn't feel unpleasantly over-crowded or polluted, just quietly humming with activity, in contrast to the blank, shuttered, necropolis look it had at night. Another crucial difference was that Curtis wasn't carrying anything incriminating in the back of his van, just three empty oil drums, similar to the one that occupied the leased warehouse. There were also six bags of ballast and three of cement.

Curtis was feeling resentful, again at Dimitri's treatment of him. He glanced at the empty place in the van where his huge companion, sitting next to him, had radiated sour dislike. OK, buying used barrels and cement from a local builders' merchant might not be the hardest job in the world, but he'd done it efficiently and, best of all, anonymously. Dimitri couldn't have managed that. Not with his build, accent, looks and tattoos. And he'd done it perfectly. And it was he who had found this warehouse.

Did anyone say thank you? No, they bloody well didn't.

Curtis had never worked with anyone who really detested him before and he found Dimitri's hostility hurtful. If he'd written a CV about his criminal past he'd have had about four employers and, on the whole, he'd got on well with both them and the people he had worked with. And you get close to people if you break the law together. Not so with the Russians. He still, however, clung to the illusion that Arkady Belanov liked him, that he was really an OK guy, that it was Dimitri who was the problem.

He couldn't stand much more. Like most workers, he needed the validation of feeling valued. He needed banter, he needed appreciation for the hard work he put in and he didn't need Dimitri's constant intimidation. He had come to hate him as well as to fear him. He felt he could have put up with either one, but not the two together.

The problem was, now he had his job with the Russians he couldn't leave.

Curtis was beginning to formulate a plan of escape that involved getting nicked for some as-yet-to-be-decided offence. Something that would get him sent down for maybe a year so he'd be out in six months. GBH maybe, or possession with intent to deal. Long enough to get him away from the Russians, not serious enough to annoy them, something that could happen to anyone. Then he'd be behind bars and out of their reach, and for long enough to show them he wouldn't grass them up. And he'd be replaced, and still alive.

He pulled into the small car park with its reserved section for the Russians' warehouse. Warehouse was a slight misnomer. It was essentially two large workshops with a reception area in the middle, two very large rooms and a smaller space inbetween. The design was basically box-like, the only windows set under the roof about six metres off the ground. You couldn't look in from the outside, not without a cherry picker or a very long ladder.

The entrance to the warehouse was a double door, secured by three locks. Two of them were Yale and mortice, which Belanov had ordered upgraded from the originals. They were intricate and expensive, designed to ward off any stray burglar. A steel strip ran down the join of the doors to make crowbarring them open impossible. They also had hinge bolts set into the door and a steel kicking strap reinforcing the inside. It would have been easier to smash your way in through the walls than break those doors down.

The third lock was a magnetic one operated by a swipecard. It was an impressive display. Nobody was coming through these doors that shouldn't be. It was impregnable.

Curtis backed the van up so the doors were level with the lip of the loading bay near the entrance, unlocked the doors, swung them open and unloaded his cargo.

He started bringing it inside. The huge room with the one oil drum in it, containing the headless body of Jordan Anderson, was cold and shrouded in gloom. North-facing windows did little to dispel the permanent, crepuscular twilight. Curtis eyed the oil drum, squat and menacing, with almost fear. The place was like some strange art installation, unsettling. He placed the first of the three new drums by the old one, and shuttled backwards and forwards until the job was done.

Three oil drums. Three new repositories, metal reliquaries awaiting their contents.

He wondered who they were for.

He looked up, startled from his thoughts by the noise of an engine outside. Then footsteps, the noise of a door being slammed and Dimitri appeared. Curtis's heart sank. But big as Dimitri was, the warehouse dominated everything. The huge, cavernous room was shadowy and dark, with a smell of damp and cement. The oil drum that contained the body – Curtis had forgotten his first name, he just knew it was one of the Andersons – exerted a kind of magnetic attraction on his attention. He had been unable to get it out of his head for the past week.

Now he was standing in front of it, waiting for instruction, as Dimitri sauntered towards him.

The unlikeliest of things reminded him of Anderson's fate. He'd been in a supermarket and seen a jar of stem ginger in syrup. The sight of the ginger lying there in the thick, viscous solution reminded him of the body folded into its foetal position in the drum, covered in concrete.

Anything in a can brought his mind back to this place.

To the right of the filled drum stood the three others, patiently awaiting whoever the Russians would choose to fill them with.

Not whatever, thought Curtis, whoever.

Curtis breathed deeply. He was morbidly fascinated to see if he would be able to smell anything of the dead man, but all he was aware of scentwise was the lingering hint of oil from the four drums, the neutral damp smell of the empty warehouse and the cement from the half-dozen bags that stood awaiting use by the empty oil drums. There was also a spade resting on some tough polythene bags of ballast and a heavy, stained piece of tarpaulin that would be used for mixing the concrete on when the time came. It was these items that Dimitri was checking.

'Everything OK, Dimitri?' asked Curtis, his tone light and jocular, as if he hoped it would rub off on the Russian.

Dimitri scowled at him. He was wearing jeans and a T-shirt, his biceps massive.

'*Zasranets*,' he growled at Curtis. Curtis rightly assumed this meant something uncomplimentary.

He looked again at the oil drums and the bags of cement. The objects themselves were insignificantly small in the huge, echoing room, but they were imbued with a compelling sinister presence. Their aura filled the vast, crepuscular space.

Dimitri ignored him and fiddled with his phone, as if killing time. Curtis stood there and patiently waited to be told what to do.

For some reason he thought of Chantal. The previous night she'd been very withdrawn and drinking really heavily to no discernible effect. It wasn't like Chantal, he reflected, to go on the lash. She liked a drink but she rarely overdid it. He wondered if something had upset her.

He'd had sex with her while she'd stared over his shoulder at the ceiling, her body politely going through the motions, the palms of her hands mechanically running up and down his back, her mind obviously elsewhere. Occasionally she'd winced and bitten her lip as if she'd been in pain, even though he was a surprisingly gentle lover and fairly speedy.

As he rolled off her he could see a row of bruises on the skin of both shoulders. The marks were red. Curtis knew quite a bit about bruises. He had experienced more than a few in his life. These were fresh; soon they would turn blue. Bruises, like traffic lights, have a colour sequence. He guessed it was one of Chantal's customers. He didn't like her being on the game but they still needed the money, although now he was earning big time from the Russians she could maybe stop doing it soon. Already she'd cut down dramatically on the number of her clients.

'Who did that?' he said, rubbing a finger along the bruises. They looked like a massage gone wrong. Chantal sat upright and turned away from him, ostensibly to light a cigarette but so he wouldn't see the fear that she felt must surely be visible on her face.

As she turned away, she saw again in her memory the brutal face of Dimitri and revisited the rank smell of his body masked with cheap aftershave. She could still hear his amused laugh as her body had flinched in pain beneath his fingers. He had enjoyed hurting her. She had been too frightened to scream; she had whimpered like a hurt animal.

'*Bliyad*,' he had said contemptuously when he had finished with her, thrusting her away and poking her with the tip of his foot. She guessed, correctly, it meant bitch.

'It's not important, babes, doesn't matter,' she had whispered to Curtis.

Now, back in the warehouse, Curtis looked at Dimitri. More specifically at his hands. Like everything else about the Russian, they were very big. Curtis's memory compared the finger spread of the man in front of him to the size and spacing of the marks on Chantal's shoulders.

He'd been at Arkady's the day before; Dimitri hadn't been there. He'd been relieved. His long-term plan was to make himself indispensable to Arkady so Dimitri would be supplanted. Maybe sent back to Russia. Hopefully retired. Retired in a permanent way, the way Arkady seemed to like to do things.

'Where's Dimitri?' he'd asked. Arkady had been wearing enormous black slacks with an elasticated waist and matching satin shirt, the nipples atop his man boobs pushing through the fabric like bullets. The satin shirt was shiny and its fabric had crackled slightly when he'd moved. His sparse sandy hair had been carefully combed over his pink scalp.

He had smiled and said, 'Visiting nice lady. Her lucky day, yah! She will say thank you.'

Curtis had smiled politely back.

'All ladies like Dimitri.' And Arkady had laughed. Curtis had laughed too, dutifully.

Now he looked hard at Dimitri. Curtis wasn't smiling now. If Dimitri had hurt Chantal, he was going to hurt Dimitri. Easier said than done. He had often thought about it; now the time had come. Defeat wasn't an option. Backing down wasn't an option.

Dimitri had crossed the line by his actions. Curtis was frightened of Dimitri but that wasn't going to hold him back. It was like a fight in prison that would decide where you stood. Either you drew a line in the sand and went down fighting or you revealed yourself as a pushover to be forever exploited and abused.

Curtis breathed in deeply. He calculated the odds, not for the first time. Dimitri, six feet three to his five feet six. Eighteen stone to his eleven. If he'd planned ahead he'd have armed himself, a knife probably. Curtis was a hard little bastard and most of his fights had been against bigger opponents than himself. He usually used a baseball bat or a softball bat; he was unsure of the difference, if any. He had a nasty feeling that if he hit Dimitri with a baseball bat it might have little effect, like hitting a tree trunk. A knife, though, that'd be better.

He had nothing, but there was the spade by the cement bags, on top of the ballast just a couple of steps away, and Curtis could move very quickly indeed. Swung so the blade hit the Russian sideways, it would do a lot of damage. Aim for his face, thought Curtis. Jealous rage flared up inside him. It felt good; he felt strong for the first time in months. Now Dimitri would suffer, not just for Chantal, but for all the put-downs, all the insults, all the glares he'd given Curtis. No one hurts my woman, he thought. No one except me. Then he thought suspiciously, What else did he do with her? He took a step nearer the spade. It would feel good in his hand.

'*Zhopa*,' said Dimitri conversationally, staring at him contemptuously. Asshole. Curtis didn't know the word in Russian but he did know Dimitri and correctly guessed that it wasn't a term of endearment.

His eyes met Dimitri's,

'Where were you yesterday?' he demanded.

'Your girl very nice,' said Dimitri with a sneer. 'Maybe too thin, though, but nice *siski*, nice tits.'

The last word was like the starting gun in a race that both competitors were awaiting, keyed up for action, feet ready in the starting blocks. As an enraged Curtis moved to grab the handle of the spade, Dimitri came forward far faster than Curtis could ever have dreamed possible.

Dimitri's huge hands grabbed Curtis's shoulders, left and right and simultaneously his foot scythed out and kicked away Curtis's legs. He fell to his knees in front of the enormous Russian as if he was praying.

Dimitri spent on average two hours a day working out in the gym and one of his own personal favourite exercises was to use a grip trainer. In bodybuilding terms a 'grip king' can exert a three-hundred-pound grip, Dimitri could manage two fifty. To put that into context, an averagely strong man might do between seventy and eighty. Three times the norm, and now, with the adrenaline thundering through his body like a river in spate, fuelled with his own abnormal aggression, maybe four times normal strength – four times normal ability.

He had also learned, while doing two years in Solikamsk High Security Prison in Perm province in the Urals, how to really hurt people scientifically. He'd shared a cell with Yuri, an old-style crook classed by the authorities as an *osobo opasnyi retsidivist*, a particularly dangerous recidivist. Yuri had shown him where some nerve points were readily accessible to fingertip pressure. Yuri had learned the hard way; the KGB had shown him personally. He'd grinned gummily, wetly, at Dimitri while he showed him. The KGB had amused themselves with Yuri's teeth as well, only the back molars were left. They had been harder to get to.

Now Dimitri's iron fingers dug expertly deep with bone-crushing pressure into the nerve endings in Curtis's shoulder and upper back, as Yuri had taught him, just as he had with Chantal but with ten times the force. The nociceptors, the pain-transmitting neurons in Curtis's shoulders, exploded into sheets of agony and he screamed out loud, head thrown back, mouth wide open in his pain.

'You like it, like your *bliyad* bitch did?' hissed Dimitri. Curtis was howling with agony now as he kneeled like a supplicant in front of the grinning Russian. He couldn't stop himself. If only Arkady could be here, thought Dimitri regretfully, he would love this. Arkady appreciated the artistry as much as the floor show of sadism and Dimitri enjoyed a discerning, approving audience.

More pressure. Dimitri switched to a question that was bugging him. Did Curtis know about the policeman; had he sold them out?

'Who was policeman, who is this Enver Demirel? Who is Demirel, *otvechai*! Answer me.'

Through his tears, through the pain, through the swearing and the pleas and the begging, Curtis made it clear he didn't know who or what Enver was.

'Answer me, *zasranets*, arsehole,' hissed Dimitri. 'Answer me! *Davai vikladivai*.'

It was obvious from Curtis's contorted face that he had nothing more of use to contribute. If he had known anything of use he'd have said, to make the pain stop. Dimitri let him go and Curtis collapsed on his side on the cold, screeded, concrete floor of the warehouse.

Dimitri looked down at him pitilessly. Curtis lay on his side. He was crying now. His chest was heaving like a wounded animal's. Dimitri took one step to the left, to the first of the three empty oil drums Curtis had brought here earlier that day.

He dug his nails under the lid and lifted. It came off easily. Curtis had wondered earlier who the drums were for. Well, now he knew the answer to at least one of the questions.

Dimitri looked down again at Curtis. Myasnikov's words came back to him.

'Terminate Curtis's contract. . . close any loose ends.'

He bent over Curtis, who looked fearfully up at him. There was nothing he could do. He knew what was going to happen but he had no more fight left in him; he hoped it would be quick. Closing his eyes, compliant and submissive, he made no attempt to resist as Dimitri's hands circled his neck and then tightened.

It didn't take long.

Half an hour later, Dimitri patiently washed the grey cement residue off the metal head of the spade in the trough-like sink on one of the walls of the warehouse. He looked across the expanse of floor, the concrete shaded here and there by darker geometric patches where machinery belonging to the former occupants had been removed.

The art installation had been rearranged.

Before, there had been one barrel to the left, three to the right. Now there were two and two. Two full, two empty. Temporarily.

CHAPTER SIXTEEN

'Phone him and tell him you have information on me,' said Dimitri to Chantal. He was wearing one of his inevitable tracksuits and several heavy gold chains. She could see the onion domes of the cathedral he had tattooed on his chest clearly, looming over the scalloped top of his low-cut vest.

It was Wednesday morning and Chantal hadn't seen Curtis since the morning of the day before. He hadn't responded to any of her texts or voicemail.

It wasn't unusual for Curtis to disappear for a couple of days, but Chantal had his drugs stashed in one of her kitchen cupboards in an airtight container so no moisture would get to the thirty grams of coke he had given her to look after. He had also left a couple of grand in twenties and tens in a ziploc bag, hidden in a packet of frozen veg in the tiny freezer compartment of her fridge. It was unthinkable that he would go so long without either the Charlie or the cash.

She was very worried, but couldn't think of anything to do. There was nothing she could do.

Family. Her mother was a foul-mouthed drunk living in Woodstock; Chantal wasn't going there unless she had to. She was worse than useless. Chantal had been taken into care when she was young and even she felt that had probably been the right decision.

Friends. She didn't really have any, just Curtis and the phone numbers of a couple of ex-boyfriends, both violent, both untrustworthy. All she could do was text him and add increasingly desperate emojis. Now she was down to just sending emojis. The bright primary colours cheered her up a little.

Maybe he was with another woman. *He'd have phoned with some pathetic excuse*, a cold voice inside her head said.

Maybe he'd just got off his face with some friends, a stag do he hadn't told her about. *He doesn't have any, he's Billy No Mates,* the voice said.

Now here was Dimitri. He stroked her hair proprietorially and she flinched. He took his tracksuit top off and she could see even more of the sinister tattoos that covered his body. *I'll tell Curtis,* she imagined telling him. The inner voice laughed, coldly unimpressed. *What's he going to do against Dimitri? Him and whose army?*

Perhaps, she wondered, if the policeman came round he would be able to deal with Dimitri; he'd certainly looked size-able. But then her gaze took in the huge, muscled bulk of Dimitri, his horribly animal presence. The big policeman had looked kind and, although he had been bear-like in build, it was a cuddly kind of impression. She had found herself considering Enver Demirel in her professional capacity. Men like him were her favourite clients; he'd have been polite, gentle, no trouble at all. She had even quite fancied him. That comforting, muscular weight on top of her. Not like Dimitri.

His hand was still in her hair; now his fingers tightened and clenched and he pulled at it viciously. She gasped in pain.

'Call him now, *bliyad*, get him over here.'

She nodded and took the business card with his number out of the cutlery drawer where she'd put it for safe keeping.

133

She typed the number into her mobile, heard Enver's voice on the other end, a questioning tone when he answered as he didn't recognize her number.

He sounded pleased to hear from her. Yes, he'd be round in about an hour and a half's time. She hung up and looked at Dimitri.

'He'll be round in about an hour,' she said.

He started taking off his shoes. 'I heard hour and half. We have plenty of time.'

The other shoe followed. He was wearing white ankle socks. The right one had a hole in and she could see the nail of his big toe. It was quite long and grubby. Like the rest of him it looked strong, like a broad claw. It made her feel sick.

'Curtis might be back soon,' she said desperately.

Dimitri tugged off his sock and looked at her. 'He won't.'

The amused look in his eyes said it all. There was no hint of, *I don't care if he comes*; no hint of, *So what,* or, *Call him and tell him you're busy*. It was just callous good humour. She doubted if he would even care that she had noticed. It was then that she knew Curtis was dead.

Enver had lied about the time it would take to get to Chantal's flat. He was in Oxford when his phone rang, sitting in a café eating doughnuts. They weren't American-style donuts. They were jam, the real deal as far as Enver was concerned. Thick, sugar-encrusted, plumply seductive. He had meant to have just one but he told himself that, technically, he was on holiday and, as such, deserved a treat. He would walk them off later.

He had no idea how many calories were in a doughnut or indeed how long it would take on foot to negate their effects. The truth was, he didn't care. He was in a nice café, drinking good espresso and eating these hard-to-find excellent doughnuts.

Besides, he thought righteously, the café was independent, not part of a chain, so he was also benefitting the local economy. In fact, the more he spent, the better.

The proprietress eyed him in a friendly way from behind the counter. She liked a man who enjoyed his food. Enver was on his fourth doughnut, his eyes gleaming, his strong white teeth occasionally visible beneath his heavy black moustache, now dusted with caster sugar as he chewed. She noticed that his powerful fingers were free of a wedding band. The look in his eyes, unalloyed greed and good nature, reminded her of her Labrador when she fed it. Enver looked like the kind of man who would be as nice as her dog, and, she felt, he could do with a woman to advise him on clothes; that T-shirt did not go with that jacket.

He was surprised that Chantal had called him. She had looked so scared when he'd been in her tiny flat.

He stared at his phone and drummed his fingers gently on the table in front of him. He had a vague sense of disquiet but he shrugged it off. What could she possibly do to him? Equally Sam Curtis posed little or no threat. Enver's increased body mass, allied to his powerfully muscled physique, while of no use in a boxing ring, was ideally suited to successful brawling. He would have flattened Curtis like a steamroller.

He toyed with the idea of phoning Huss but decided against it. He thought of his approaching evening with Melinda Huss with excitement. He was going to invite her to stay the night, provided all went well, and he could see no reason why it shouldn't.

He'd checked that the film, *A Room with a View*, was on and that it was what it purported to be, not some porno version or a remake. He'd had another look at the menu, even eaten a solitary, exploratory lunch and made friends with two waitresses and the manager. His family name, or rather the restaurants associated with the Demirels, was reasonably well known in this part of London, plus of course he knew quite a few names that he dropped to good effect – catering is a tight-knit community.

Enver was a formidably good planner. Entertainment was sorted; dinner was sorted; his flat was nearly there. He was halfway through Operation Springclean in his flat. It was always clean and tidy; now it gleamed. All he had left were the insides of the windows to clean and the skirting boards, in case Huss got down on hands and knees to run an exploratory finger along them.

He pushed the chair back and smiled politely at the woman behind the counter as he left. What a nice man, she thought as she cleared away after him and pocketed her tip.

Enver walked to a nearby taxi rank and gave Chantal's address in Cowley to the driver. He'd had enough of negotiating the one-way streets of the town and the endless, problematic bicycle chaos the last time he had driven here with Huss.

As if he had conjured her up by thinking of her he felt his phone vibrate and there was a text message from her, asking about the coming evening. The mannered Oxford streets passed by outside the windows of the cab as he laboriously typed in the time of the train he'd expect her on at Paddington and where exactly at the station they should meet.

Enver was leaving nothing to chance. He thought of Huss's attractive curved body; he thought of her blonde hair. He thought of her clever, competent hands and the look of studious concentration on her face as she adjusted some tricky component on the exposed gears of a car. He thought of the scent of her body, wholesome and attractive, like rising bread. He thought of her lovely breasts and underwear as revealed by the half-undone boilersuit. He thought of her even white teeth. Melinda Huss, he thought wonderingly, I think I'm in love with you.

The taxi pulled up outside Chantal's flat. He got out and paid off the driver. The car pulled away and Enver's thoughts of Huss vanished as he looked at the doorway sandwiched between a betting shop and a fast-food outlet that sold fried chicken.

His good humour evaporated. Chantal's surroundings were as depressing as her life. *Win, win, win* screamed the betting shop, its frontage bright with vibrant primary colours, green and red and yellow, its lettering bold, emphatic, confident.

Its optimistic slogan was negated by its neighbour. The fast-food shop's photos of the takeaways it sold had been bleached and yellowed by the sun and time. The chicken in the pictures was gnarly with dun-brown corrugated batter, like growths waiting to be removed. The shop smelled sharply of rancid fat.

Enver could imagine only too well what the kitchen would look like, the cracked rubber seals of the fridge grimed with dirt like a tramp's fingernails, the off-putting reek of out-of-date chicken in stained plastic tubs and boxes of congealing coleslaw. He knew the horrors that lurked in crappy kitchens only too well – not in the Demirels' kitchens, but in rival places he'd worked when he'd been a student.

He walked up to Chantal's front door. Someone had pissed in the recessed doorway during the night and there was still a residual puddle of thickened, semi-evaporated urine in front of the scuffed white door, the smell mingling with that of the chicken joint next door.

He pressed the buzzer and heard Chantal's voice, sounding slightly out of breath, metallic and tinny on the scuffed, steel honeycomb of the intercom.

'Hello?'

'DI Demirel,' he said. The door buzzed and he pushed it open, stepping carefully over the puddle as he went.

He glanced at his watch as he stood at the bottom of the narrow, steep carpeted stairs, the beige fabric unpleasantly stained here and there. A smell of stale skunk clung to the walls.

He thought of Huss longingly. Only a few more hours, he thought.

He started up the stairs and knocked gently on the door. Chantal opened it and he went into the cramped flat. Enver looked at her with concern. She had obviously been crying. Her eye make-up had run, and her fingers plucked nervously at the hem of her dressing gown. It was a cheap, oriental-effect garment made of red synthetic fabric with a gold dragon, the kind of thing you bought on a stall in a not-very-good market for a tenner. It looked highly flammable. He had the feeling that she was naked underneath the tawdry gown, which added to his discomfort.

He hoped that her unhappy state had nothing to do with him. He had a sudden surge of resentment at Corrigan. All well and good for Corrigan from his bastion of gentlemen's clubs and the upper floors of New Scotland Yard to issue instructions on 'shaking the tree', but it was Enver who had to do the dirty work and it looked as if it was Chantal who had borne the brunt of things. There was a swelling by the side of her eye that she had attempted to conceal with foundation. It hadn't concealed it. It was now a foundation-coloured swelling. Enver knew a thing or two about bruising and contusions – what boxer didn't? – but there was a time and a place, and in his mind the place was never on a woman's face. Curtis, he thought. He had a sudden desire to give Curtis a good going over. See how he likes it, thought Enver.

'Are you OK, Chantal?'

She nodded, avoiding his eyes. 'I'm fine,' she said. Then she raised her gaze to his and opened up the dressing gown, flasher style.

It was the last thing Enver expected and it certainly caught his attention. He stared at Chantal's slim body, the strip of dark pubic hair, her surprisingly full breasts. What the hell is going on? he thought, unaware of the bathroom door opening quietly behind him.

His body suddenly exploded with pain and his legs gave way as if they'd been severed. He fell face forward, his head thudding heavily to the floor, dazing him even further as the pain increased and his body twitched while his mouth made inarticulate sounds.

Chantal watched in horrified fascination as Dimitri stood over the body of Enver, the yellow taser in his hands like a child's toy pistol, its primary yellow colour lending it an almost clown-like quality as it clicked away insect-like in a busy, threatening staccato manner.

'Give it thirty seconds,' Joad had said. It was a standard police-issue taser, property of Thames Valley Constabulary. Joad had stolen it a few months ago during a raid on a crack-house in High Wycombe. Whichever of the three views held by his colleagues on Joad – likeable rough diamond; sleazy, yes, bent, maybe, but a good copper; corrupt, lazy, a disgrace, should be locked up – everyone, even Huss, agreed he was very useful in a ruck. He was in great demand whenever physical trouble loomed. When things had kicked off during the raid and everyone's attention had been fully occupied, Joad had coolly expropriated the taser and sold it later to Belanov for three times its list price.

Joad had said the best place to use it was on the back, which was why Dimitri had got Chantal to engage Enver's attention.

Dimitri was also very wary of the bull-like policeman. Enver had hit him in the face once and that had nearly knocked him unconscious; Dimitri was taking no chances.

He dropped the taser and kicked Enver hard between the legs, so hard it moved Enver's body up off the floor. It was a precaution, but more than that it was payback. The first instalment. It was revenge, a cold revenge, one he had longingly rehearsed in his mind like a sexual fantasy.

We all have certain memories that we worry at like a loose tooth or picking a scab – unforgotten resentments that continue to fester and haunt us. Dimitri could still vividly picture being in the street in Bow in East London behind the wheel of the stolen white van. It had been dark, late at night, and he had only been half alert. He'd been waiting for Hanlon, waiting to settle his score with her, when he had become aware of a presence at the open window of the driver's door. He'd turned his head irritably and seen a face, Enver's face, before Enver's fist had slammed into his head, breaking his already damaged cheekbone.

The force of Enver's punch had nearly knocked him out. The next thing he'd known, he was being dragged on to the London pavement where he'd lost consciousness momentarily before coming round, his body a sea of pain.

Now God, or the Devil, had brought Enver back within reach.

He handcuffed Enver's hands behind his back and rolled him over. Enver was still moaning slightly from the excruciating pain in his testes and the residual effects of the electrocution. Dimitri had a roll of black gaffer tape and wrapped a length three times round Enver's mouth then flipped him back over, face down, and, sitting on his back so Enver couldn't move, taped his legs together at the ankles.

Enver was secure; now Dimitri could relax. Chantal watched silently. There was no fight in her, no resistance.

She sat helplessly on the bed, waiting to be told what to do. She had never really in her whole short life made a decision herself. Her mother had put her in and out of care, depending on how sober or remorseful she'd been feeling. Handed back and forth like a parcel, she'd never had any feeling of being anything but a burden to everyone. School, a disaster. Work, a disaster. No one had ever wanted Chantal. If she'd been a puppy she'd probably have ended up being put down. The runt that nobody wanted, that would never be rehomed.

Only sex had made her feel in demand and appreciated, even if it was pretty grim most of the time. But if you were out of it mentally enough it was bearable. Valium, temazepam, vodka and coke and weed, they all helped. And now her mind was practically blank with misery. She didn't want to allow herself the ability to think. Any rational thought would just bring further pain. Curtis was dead; no help there. The policeman helpless, as good as dead; no help there. She couldn't run away. As always, others would decide her fate.

'You're nothing,' her mother had said. 'You'll never amount to anything, Jenkins,' her form teacher had said in Year Ten.

And now her destiny lay entirely in the hands of Dimitri.

Well, that wasn't encouraging, was it? she thought. She felt a ridiculous desire to burst out laughing, hysterically.

Dimitri took a hypodermic from his jacket pocket and a small glass bottle full of a clear liquid. He put the needle through the cap of the bottle and filled the body of the syringe, then pulled Enver's trousers down slightly to reveal the swell of his buttocks.

Chantal watched silently.

She had once found a small bird – she didn't know what sort, it had been brown, terrified – on the doorstep of the home she'd been living in at the time. It had obviously been young, it wouldn't or couldn't fly; maybe its wing had been broken. They had looked at one another, its eyes terrified, and she had closed the door on it, hoping something good would happen to it. Later she'd found its small, dead body by the scruffy hedge in the front garden. She had dug a shallow grave for it in the weed-choked flowerbed.

She stood, as motionless as the bird had been, as Dimitri inserted the needle into the policeman's backside and pushed the plunger. Enver sighed and she watched as his body relaxed.

Yesterday had been her twenty-third birthday. There'd been no cards. Not even a text.

CHAPTER SEVENTEEN

It was eight o'clock on Wednesday morning, the day of Malcolm Anderson's funeral in Edmonton. Earlier that morning Hanlon had driven up through the City towards North London.

The differentials in character between the districts she passed through were as sharply defined as rings on a severed tree trunk. The City with its ancient names – Leadenhall, Ludgate, St Mary Woolnoth – but now all high-tech, steel and concrete, even the food angular and spiky, sushi bars and terse, monosyllabic takeaways, *Eat, Graze, Pret*. The names themselves sounded like commands. Then Hoxton, hipper and more boho, followed by Stoke Newington, the trailblazer in the gentrification stakes as the native middle class was forced out of the centre of London by the colonizers from abroad.

For Hanlon, the drive was becoming an exercise in nostalgia. She'd lived here once, a junior officer in the Met, with a growing reputation both for efficiency and as a troublemaker.

The early morning traffic was heavy and her progress was slow. The further north she went, the more Turkish the influence became. Ubiquitous kebab shops, names like the Istanbul Grill, Karadeniz Meats, branches of the Turkish Bank, halal butchers, a couple of Turkish mosques. It was round about here that her last partner – then DS, currently DI, Enver Demirel – had grown up, before the family had decamped to Enfield.

In fact, she thought, he still lives around here, somewhere in south Tottenham.

She thought of Demirel with nostalgia. His mournful face and his endless, doomed attempts to fight the flab. She'd seen him box once, back before he'd joined the Met. Then there had been no fat on his body. Then he'd been an up-and-coming young fighter. An eye injury had put paid to that. Now, although only about thirty, he seemed to be embracing middle age with enthusiasm. He had grown a thick, black, drooping moustache; he was growing a double chin. He still had his impressive musculature but it was well concealed under his collection of cheap suits and growing flesh.

But his hangdog demeanour was misleading. In some respects Enver was like a bear. You saw him and thought he was quite sweet, cuddly-looking, but if provoked (and here the analogy broke down, he needed a lot of provoking) he could take your head off. Hanlon had seen Enver flatten a man with one punch, and his gloomy pessimism hid a fierce intelligence and an equally fierce ambition.

Enver's father had arrived in London as a penniless teenager from Rize province in Turkey and died a relatively wealthy and successful restauranteur. The same qualities of hard work and ability ran deep in Enver. Enver had, at one time, been ranked in the top ten UK professional fighters of his weight. He was never going to be a world champion, never, come to that, be a British champion, but to have got as far as he did was one hell of an achievement.

He was doing equally well in the police. He held a fistful of aces in his hand. Young, intelligent, efficient, untainted by scandal, and the fact he was non-Caucasian would stand him in good stead. And he wasn't ethnic enough to frighten anyone. He'd be a potent symbol of racial diversity, something the Metropolitan Police could well do with.

Hanlon herself, despite an exemplary work record, had faced charges of tokenism – *yeah, well, it's because she's a woman* – although rarely to her face. She was too frightening a figure for that and she had some equally hard-hitting supporters. The Hanlon fan club was small, but fanatical.

And Enver had a powerful sponsor. Corrigan, one of the Metropolitan Police's assistant commissioners, had taken him under his wing. Enver, thought Hanlon, was going places, and he knew it. Whereas I, she thought to herself, I've reached the end of my time with the police.

The thought took her almost by surprise. It was a quiet epiphany. Startled, she repeated it to herself. *I've reached the end of my time with the police.*

She suddenly realized that she had known for a long time that enough was enough, but had never consciously admitted it. It was like being in a marriage that you knew wasn't working, then one morning decided was over. I don't love you any more. We're through.

It was an amazing revelation. A Damascene conversion. For nearly twenty years she had defined herself by her job. And the police force had, by and large, tolerated her. It was a useful, symbiotic relationship. Hanlon was undoubtedly a nuisance, but she was a good detective, she wasn't corrupt and she was useful to wheel out occasionally as proof that there were career opportunities for women in the force. She also could be relied upon to keep her mouth shut. The Met had, on the whole, backed her up. She had got results and any resulting mess had been swept under carpets. But this latest transfer was a signal that the party was over.

They'd both had enough of each other.

Hanlon had known for a while that she was as far up the

career pole as she could hope to get. With a record like hers, particularly in the past year, no promotion board would dream of moving her upwards. She didn't mind. She knew she was poor at administration, rash, hasty, not good at communicating and inclined to hoard information. In fact, she was everything you wouldn't want in a position of executive power that involved planning and attention to detail – stupidly impulsive, rash, intolerant. She needed a minder, a short leash. Where she was, she was perfectly suited.

But now, she thought, enough is enough. We define our lives as a narrative, a story, she reasoned, and mine's been to fight the enemy by whatever means I have at my disposal. I was DI Hanlon, the woman who did it her own way, but it's time to move on.

I'll find Taverner's killers, she thought. I'll do that for you, Oksana, then I'll resign. I'll even get some shyster lawyer to screw the Met over for me. If I have a leaving party only Enver and Corrigan will come. We can hold it in a stationery cupboard. Her eyes softened as she thought of Enver again. I wonder what he's up to now.

Hanlon missed Enver. She hoped he was well in his safe environment of protocol and meeting rooms, liaising with people.

She guessed too that she was lonely, not that she liked to admit it. Perhaps I'll make new friends, she thought, join a dating agency. Hanlon laughed sardonically to herself at the idea.

The traffic had only moved a couple of metres in the last five minutes. In the distance she saw a traffic light change to red. She flipped down the sun visor on her Audi TT and looked at her reflection in the mirror. Her sea-grey eyes looked back at her. Her eyebrows were dark and curved and her black corkscrew hair framed her face. There were dark patches under her eyes and she could still see the faint bruising around her cheekbone. It was a strong face rather than a pretty one.

On the passenger seat was a small black leather handbag. In it was her purse with warrant card. I won't be needing that soon, she thought. She put the car in gear and drove northwards to Edmonton.

She left her car in a car park near the Broadway and headed into the backstreets of the Andersons' manor. The streets were quiet. She found her destination quickly enough.

There were two things that surprised Hanlon about the cemetery in Edmonton. Firstly that it was surrounded by a three-metre-high wall topped with razor wire. It seemed out of keeping with the function of the place. You didn't associate security with a graveyard. Hanlon frowned to herself as she walked along the path by the towering wall that was more suitable for a low-risk prison than a graveyard. The wall to her left seemed endless; it was a brisk ten-minute walk from one end to the other. The opposite side of the walkway on her right-hand side was an estate of small, low-rise houses with landscaped public areas of grass. It seemed peaceful enough and the area by the path was litter-free. It was quite a pleasant spot.

She walked alongside the wall, searching in vain for a gate, until she came to its end in a cluster of more social housing, this time small flats. She looked around her. Most of the buildings here were low-rise, the only visible exceptions a sizeable tower block near the High Street and station back the way she had come and, in the opposite direction, the high, slim tower of the Edmonton Waste Incinerator, pointing skywards like an admonitory finger, the tallest chimney in London that she could remember. It dominated the area.

She looked at it again. She remembered one of her conversations with Anderson, his casual comment about how it was often the final destination for his business rivals. It was Anderson's own personal crematorium.

She paused and checked the map on her phone. The cemetery was the shape of an elongated triangle; she had walked down one side of it and was now at the base. This fronted on to the main road and it was here that Hanlon found both the entrance and her second surprise.

The cemetery was Jewish. She checked the sign on the gate just to make sure. No, no mistake there. Was Anderson Jewish? Based on what she knew of him it seemed unlikely, but then again, why shouldn't he be? The surname was Scandinavian, if anything, but it could well have been changed for assimilation purposes, anything for a quieter life.

Things now started to make sense. She guessed that the wall and the wire were to keep out anti-Semitic attacks. They were on the increase. All over Europe, as ever, Jews were being targeted. A virulent strain of anti-Semitism was now very much back in vogue. Russia, always anti-Jewish; in Hungary, there was Jobbik. In Greece, the Golden Dawn's symbol looked alarmingly swastika-like. There was a particularly virulent strain of ugly racism in France, adding to a new diaspora of Jews to the UK, USA and Israel. She'd read in an internal Met document that anti-Semitic attacks were up recently by as much as fifty per cent, and a graveyard like this would be a ripe target for desecration.

Hanlon guessed too that the recent Dieudonné Quenelle controversy would almost certainly lead to further attacks on all things Jewish. She'd seen photos recently, selfies that people had taken at Auschwitz, grinning, thumbs up in approval. Another photo, in Oxford Street, a Middle Eastern or Pakistani kid with a straggly bum-fluffy beard and a placard, *Kill All Juice*. As illiterate as it was hate-filled. If there was one high-profile hate crime, it often led to others. But here there was no sign of heightened security for now.

The gates to the cemetery were open and Hanlon walked in. It was well ordered and tranquil with neat rows of headstones arranged in grid patterns. Some of the headstones were surmounted with angels or decorative motifs. Aside from the odd Star of David here and there and the presence of Hebrew characters on a fair few of the stones, you could have been in any graveyard anywhere in the country. In the middle of the cemetery towards one of the walls she could see a small JCB digger at work. She walked towards it. There were three men there, two workmen and another man in a suit with a clipboard. Hanlon spoke to him and found out that this was indeed the site of the Anderson burial.

'Are you family?' asked the man respectfully. Hanlon was wearing a dark tailored jacket and matching skirt. She had pulled her unruly hair into a tight bun. Foundation masked the faint bruising around her eye socket. She looked the epitome of a respectable businesswoman. She owned very little jewellery but she did have an expensive diamond ring; this she'd put on especially. Money reassured people. You didn't expect the rich to be troublemakers.

'A business associate,' said Hanlon, which was true in a sense. Anderson Senior had been a well-known criminal so she guessed they were linked, even if they were on opposite sides. She had a sudden thought that some of her colleagues would almost certainly be turning up to pay their respects. Some would be pensioned-off former Flying Squad, looking forward to getting hammered at the doubtless lavish do afterwards; some would be older police mourning the passing of a generation, the 'they don't make them like that any more' school of thought – they'd get pissed with their age group from the criminal fraternity, old, fat bald men with red noses, bonding about how London was going to the dogs with all the niggers and Pakis and now the fucking Russians moving into Knightsbridge and don't let me get started on the Arabs. And one or two serving officers would be there, quietly on Dave Anderson's payroll.

Earlier, she had walked past Edmonton Police Station. The borough seemed a nice enough place, but whoever had designed the local nick had been taking no chances. The modern building looked squat and massive. Bunker-like, its featureless walls looked as if they could withstand attack by a tank. It was like a fortress built in hostile territory. She thought of her new office in Langley, and the rationale of more open, less intimidating, access to the public suddenly made a great deal of sense. Chalk one up to Mawson and his Public Relations ethos, she thought.

She was aware that the man was still looking at her expectantly.

'It's eleven o'clock tomorrow, isn't it?' she said. She had no idea of the time that the funeral was scheduled for. The man shook his head.

'Ten thirty,' he corrected her. 'Today.'

Hanlon clicked her tongue irritably. 'I was misinformed, thank you,' she said.

The cemetery manager nodded and said, 'We're expecting quite a crowd. I'd get here early if I were you.'

'I fully intend to,' said Hanlon curtly. 'Thank you for your help.' She turned and walked away. The manager watched her back as she disappeared from view down the path. He guessed that she was probably one of the doubtless expensive defence lawyers that the Anderson family were forced to engage periodically. Everyone in Edmonton knew of the Andersons. Today, he thought, if you dropped a bomb on this place you'd take out half of London's top criminals, all coming to share their last respects.

If the first part of his surmise was incorrect, the second was spot-on accurate. The Andersons were A-list criminals.

Hanlon watched the first of Anderson's security to arrive. She had parked her car on the other side of the busy main road in a small side street, diagonally across from the entrance to the cemetery. She was sitting behind the wheel, with half her mind on the situation outside, the other reflecting on her future.

Above all, she considered the intractable question of Mark Whiteside, in his drug-induced coma, in a hospital less than five miles from where she was sitting. She had looked into the cost of private surgery and the availability of surgical expertise.

It had been made clear to her that the NHS were not simply opposed to the procedure on cost grounds (the National Handbag as Albert Slater might have referred to government funding); it was the likelihood of success that was a major factor too. The chances were slim. And it wasn't just that. One British surgeon she'd spoken to had pointed out that she had to be aware that the success of the operation could be as devastating as failure. That the damage the bullet had left could be repaired – but it wasn't yet known at what cost to Whiteside's quality of life afterwards.

'Are you prepared,' he had asked her quietly, 'for the fact that you could well spend the rest of your life caring for a grown man who has become, to all intents and purposes, a helpless infant? That would be a worst-case scenario, worse in my view than death on the table, but it is a very real possibility.'

Well, thought Hanlon grimly. We'll deal with that if and when it happens. But if I don't do something soon there's a deadline looming and Whiteside will be allowed to die. Meanwhile there was today's funeral to think about, to take her mind off things. In many ways Hanlon was craving action, as she always did. Action was her way of coping, her solution to everything. Like a drug, it could successfully relieve the intensity of her morbid thoughts about her injured colleague and her part in it.

At nine thirty a black Range Rover with tinted windows arrived and four shaven- headed men in tight-fitting dark suits got out. The family praetorian guard. They were led by the man she had seen at the Beath Street brothel, Danny. The car drove off.

The other three listened respectfully while Danny issued instructions. Two of them nodded and took up positions flanking the gates. The other one, with Danny, entered the cemetery. She guessed that they were here to ensure the safety of Anderson. After the murder of Jordan they would all be feeling somewhat twitchy.

An hour to go, thought Hanlon. She wasn't a hundred per cent sure why she was here herself. Partly, she guessed, to pay her respects to Malcolm Anderson, whose bravery in the face of his impending death had genuinely moved her, and partly out of curiosity to see which London villains would turn up at the funeral.

She was also interested to see if she'd recognize any police colleagues. A bent policeman had nearly had her killed in the past. Hanlon didn't feel outraged by the fact. Corruption was always going to be there; it was a question of scale and manageability. And she had known at least one policeman who was an exceptional copper but at the same time dirty. Yin and yang, she thought, as Mawson would have put it, and when you looked at the Taoist image, there was a speck of black in the white and white in the black. Nothing is absolute.

She drummed her fingers on the steering wheel and looked around her, an ingrained habit of mindfulness automatically taking over. The ability to concentrate fully was one of Hanlon's greatest strengths. Whiteside, her faltering career, everything was carefully set aside so she could give all of her attention to the task in hand.

She registered almost without thinking that to her left was a street of terraced houses and to her right, on the other side of the road, a three-storey-high office building with a flat roof that overlooked the road and the cemetery gates at the front, and the industrial estate and tall chimney of the incinerator plant to the rear.

Suddenly the inactivity of sitting placidly in the car enraged her. Hanlon was incapable of doing nothing for long; she lacked the gift of patience. She stepped out of the car and crossed the road. Ignoring the gates of the cemetery, instead she threaded her way through the small estate of houses to its left until she came to the broad path that bordered the Jewish graveyard.

The wall was as high as she remembered it from earlier, some three metres, and she eyed it thoughtfully. It was designed to keep people out, a statement reinforced by the razor wire. But every twenty metres or so there was a tree growing on the side of the wall by the path, a sequence of well-established trees some of whose branches overhung the cemetery.

Hanlon, in her dark, respectable two-piece suit, tailored jacket and skirt, wasn't dressed for climbing, but the skirt was short so she could run in it if necessary and her boots were flat for the same reason.

She walked alongside the wall in the direction of Edmonton Broadway until she found a suitable tree and glanced around her. Nobody was in sight. In the distance she could see the backs of a couple of women pushing babies in buggies. She took a short run forward and leaped upwards; her strong fingers made contact with the lowest branch of the tree.

It bent alarmingly, but Hanlon wasn't heavy and she pulled herself up. For her it was simplicity itself; she did a lot of chin-ups and pull-ups in the gym. She liked the sensation of just using the natural weight of her body to exercise. Sometimes she would strap on a couple of weights round her waist for added difficulty, to make her biceps really sing out. Occasionally, if there was an ostentatious, look-at-me kind of guy in the gym – the kind of idiot with a cutaway vest who swaggered with the sort of over-developed look she detested – she'd do a couple of one-armed pull-ups, her face studiously expressionless. The muscle-bound macho man would watch with baffled awe as Hanlon gracefully achieved what he never could. Her body was light, her sinews like thin cables of steel. The ratio of body weight to muscle was formidably on her side. She would seek to meet his eye with a contemptuous glance. Suck on that, Mr Universe, she would think. Let's see you try.

Once in the tree, she climbed up to the branch that overhung the graveyard and, nimble as a squirrel, careful not to lose a boot, she moved along its length until she was over the wall.

She looked out over the enormous graveyard, an elongated rectangle full of the geometric rows of grey gravestones. Near to the entrance by the wall she noticed what looked like a storeroom, a building almost like a lodge house, with a low-pitched roof slanting backwards towards the road. From there, she would have an excellent view of the mourners by the grave without having to join the throng. Some of those attending she would probably have nicked at some stage or other. She'd certainly had dealings with Cunningham, the Andersons' coke-addicted lawyer, and he'd be there, that was for sure, glassy-eyed and sniffing loudly. Despite her invite, she'd rather watch informally.

She could see Danny and his helper quickly patrolling the rows of gravestones. It confirmed her earlier theory. If what Iris Campion and Albert Slater said was true, and Hanlon never took information for granted, that Dave Anderson's brother Jordan had been murdered in some turf war, there was every possibility that those responsible might take the opportunity to have a pop at another Anderson.

The two minders were working their way from the cemetery gates to the back of the graveyard, row by row. It was a simple job, the marker stones virtually all uniform, the monotony varied only occasionally by an angelic statue. It wasn't like a higgledy-piggledy necropolis full of vaults, mini graveyard housing and other stone follies and monuments – the kind of place that was full of cover. In Highgate Cemetery, a veritable jungle of trees and overgrown bushes and shrubs and jumbled masonry, for example, you could hide a regiment if you were so minded. Here there were just the endless, neat markers written in Hebrew and English. The paths between each row were ruler straight. One quick glance down each row would suffice.

Hanlon swung down from her branch and dropped down gracefully to the stone chippings of the path. She made her way towards the front of the cemetery to the small building she had seen earlier. It was slightly offset from the entrance path and in the corner formed by its side wall and the brickwork of the graveyard perimeter was a large, green wheelie bin. She climbed on top of this, stood on its lid, put her hands on the edge of the parapet, hauled herself up and lay on the roof of the lodge. From this vantage point, as she had worked out earlier, she could see over the top of the gravestones to the place delineated by ropes and discreet bunting where the internment would take place.

She checked her watch, nine fifty-five.

At a quarter past ten the guests started to arrive. First came the pall-bearers, carrying the simple plain pine coffin, followed by the immediate family. Hanlon had a small pair of old Zeiss binoculars in her bag, and she took them out now and adjusted the focus.

There was a stout, balding man with glasses and an officious air, presumably a rabbi; Hanlon knew nothing about Jewish burial protocol. She didn't even know if this burial was religious at all or secular. The Andersons' word in Edmonton was law. Whatever religion Malcolm Anderson had been, if Dave Anderson wanted his dad buried here whoever ran the cemetery could either accede to the request or end up here himself. Whatever he was, he seemed to be in charge. There was Anderson himself, tall, thin, his lank hair trailing the thin high shoulders under his dark suit. There was a shorter, fuller-faced version of him that she guessed was Terry, the other brother, and a woman in her sixties with a blonde beehive hairdo that Hanlon thought must be Andrea, Dave's mother and Malcolm's ex.

More and more people filed into the cemetery, virtually all of them hard-faced men – various versions of the same type. Her vision, seen through the tunnel-like prism of the binoculars, swept here and there.

The grim faces of the Anderson family; the coked-out, stoner look of Cunningham, the lawyer – how did no one notice? marvelled Hanlon. Even at this distance he looked out of it. The sun was glancing off the bald and shaven heads of London's most prominent villains, all there to pay their respects.

She idly swept the glasses upwards to look beyond the family by the side of the grave. It was taking her a while to get over the strange sensation of the world as viewed through the constrictive narrowness of the Zeiss lenses of the binoculars. She had lost most of her sense of peripheral vision.

There was an impressionistic sensation of a montage of funeral black, a large amorphous grouping of bodies, with occasional detail. The very stoned face of the lawyer, Cunningham, the hard-as-nails facelifted features of Anderson's mother, more vicious-looking by far than her dead bank-robber ex-husband had been. The fatter features of Anderson's younger brother. The plump, bulky rabbi.

She'd noticed a sudden movement and raised the binoculars slightly, looking over the heads of the crowd. There, perched on a gravestone, was a small robin. Its fluttered wings were what had caught her attention on the extremely limited periphery of her vision. If it hadn't been for the bird she wouldn't have seen what happened next.

There was a sudden puff of masonry dust and several cracks appeared on the gleaming black surface of the grave marker with its sombre gold Hebrew lettering. The robin flew off, alarmed. For a fraction of time Hanlon looked on, uncomprehending, before she realized that what she had seen was the result of a bullet hitting the grave marker.

She swung her binoculars down to the mourners. They remained where they were, oblivious of the danger. The impact of the shot had gone either unheard or unnoticed in the general noise surrounding the burial.

The target was obvious. Hanlon leaped to her feet and looked round to where the bullet must have come from. It had to have come from above. She knew the direction from which it had travelled. Only one place really fitted the bill. The office block over the road.

To think was to act. Hanlon acted.

She leaped to her feet on top of the roof. From there, she jumped onto the parapet of the engirdling cemetery wall, mercifully free of barbed wire on the section that fronted the main road, hung briefly by her fingertips, then dropped on to the pavement.

Danny, standing at the cemetery gates with the other two,

Polite Paul and Robby, spun round at the sound of her feet hitting the ground as she sprang down to the pavement a few feet away from them.

It was as if she'd fallen out of the sky. The three of them stared at her in amazement. She had risen up from where her legs had folded under her to take the impact of landing on the hard pavement, pointed to the building over the road and shouted, 'Gun!'

Danny understood the implication of the word immediately. He turned, shouting, 'You go with her,' to Robby and sprinted into the graveyard, pulling his own firearm out of a belt holster where it had been hidden by the cloth of his jacket.

Now, head down, arms pumping, Hanlon ran across the road. Cars braked furiously, horns sounding, as she sprinted towards the office block opposite the cemetery gates. Hanlon hit the far pavement running and accelerated down the pavement opposite her car towards the flat-roofed office block. She was followed by the lean, shaven-headed figure of Robby. From a distance, in their dark, formal clothes, it looked as if they were in some odd white-collar race.

Up on the flat roof of the third-floor office building the *uzkoglazik*, the Chinaman, clicked his tongue irritably. He glared at Nikita.

The roof had a metre-high parapet. On this, the *uzkoglazik* had folded his jacket to rest the .243 rifle he was using. A slug from this rifle could drop a red deer stag at five hundred metres. He had Anderson a moment ago perfectly in the cross-hairs of the sight when he held his breath and gently squeezed the trigger back.

The rifle kicked against his shoulder, the suppressor on its barrel reducing the sound of the shot to that of a .22 air rifle.

It would be inaudible at street level. Mounted on a tripod was a pair of binoculars he had used to check the target area; the field of vision in a sight was so narrow it was often hard to locate a given object in a wider field.

A lesser shooter would not have bothered with checking where the bullet had gone. They'd have fired and almost immediately, and unconsciously, raised their heads. The Chinaman didn't. He wanted to know exactly where his shot had gone.

He could still see Anderson standing. The Chinaman had unaccountably missed. He put the rifle down hurriedly and squinted through the binoculars. He swore, ejected the casing, pocketed it and put another round into the breech of the rifle. The day before he had painstakingly centred the sights at five hundred metres, adjusting them so they were perfect, putting several bullets one after another through the bullseye at the centre of the target to make it as sure as sure could be that the sights were accurate. They had been; now they weren't. Someone had almost certainly knocked the telescopic scope out of alignment.

That someone had to be Nikita, the balding idiot that Belanov had foisted upon him. Well, there wasn't time for recriminations. God knows how long he had now. It should all be over. Anderson should be lying on the ground, a small hole in the front of his black jacket, a much larger one in the rear, while the mourners milled around wondering what, where and who.

Should, should, should. Now he'd have to readjust the sights or he might as well go home.

'You. Here. Look through these.' He pointed at the binoculars. 'See that black angel?' To save time he kept his sentences short; he also mistrusted the Russian's ability to understand English. Nikita did as he was told, then nodded. The *Kitayets,* the Chinaman as they called him, could see his scalp where the few sparse long hairs had been trained over the top of his head where they grew on the side, glued down to keep them in place.

'Tell me where the shot hits.'

The body wasn't yet buried. He had maybe five minutes before they moved away from the graveside. The mourners were oblivious to the drama behind them and the danger from the rooftop overlooking the cemetery.

Five minutes to recalibrate the sights and finish the job. Three hundred seconds. He didn't really care about Anderson one way or another; it was a question of pride. He did not want to be known as a man who missed targets. He slid the bolt back, put a shell in, closed the breech, aimed, the black marble angel filling the sights as he centred on the angel's navel, where it would have a navel were it human, and fired.

Two hundred and forty seconds to go.

'Top left,' said Nikita. He moved the barrel slightly, scoping that direction. He could clearly see the mark the bullet had left where he said. His practised fingers twirled the screws to adjust the sight. He reloaded, fired again. This time the angel's gown was marked dead centre. He could see the fractured, chipped impression that the bullet had left.

The muzzle of the rifle depressed slightly as he adjusted his aim. Anderson's face filled his telescopic sight: the cruel, chiselled structure of his face framed by the lank, shoulder-length hair. He toyed with the idea of a head shot; it would be elegant. But heads could move quickly; there was an increased chance of a miss and one miss was bad enough. He dropped the muzzle down to focus on the gangster's body, the slight breeze playing with his black tie.

But this Anderson wasn't the target. It was the brother.

He moved the scope so he was focused on the body of the remaining sibling.

His breathing, as always, was deep and even. His mind floated free and serene. A line from the Taoist texts came to him.

Only through purity and tranquility can the world be ruled.

He was aware of the breeze on his face, of the sun in the sky, the throng of people at the graveside.

In the midst of life we are in death.

The speed of a bullet is round about two thousand miles an hour. Even if Anderson were able to hear the rifle, the bullet would arrive before the sound.

By non-action everything can be done.

The Chinaman's finger started to tighten on the trigger.

The sound of the three shots had an electrifying effect on the crowd of mourners. Virtually every one there was either directly or indirectly involved in crime. The crowd was made up of former criminal associates of Malcolm Anderson, other crime families temporarily setting aside their business differences. Everyone in violent crime liked a good funeral; you never knew when yours might be. There was also the added plus that it wasn't you who was in the box. One day it would be, but not today.

The heightened bonus of being alive.

As well as the criminal guests, there were people the dead man had done time with and, of course, his own crime organization, now run by Dave. Even the handful of non-criminals, friends and family, all went shooting and knew what a gunshot sounded like.

Danny saw the crowd of mourners almost immediately he entered the graveyard. There were so many people they had backed up on themselves as far as the main central pathway through the graveyard. He slid the safety off his firearm, pointed the gun skyward and pulled the trigger three times in succession.

The throng by the grave threw themselves down on the ground. The Anderson brothers, their reactions faster than anyone's, got there first. The Chinaman's bullet passed over Terry's body as he fell. Antony Brooker, a former cellmate of Malcolm Anderson's, fifty-eight, twenty stone, reactions slowed by the surplus fat, beta blockers and the three pints he'd sunk prior to the service, took the shot in his chest. He died instantly.

Now the crowd was moving, taking cover behind gravestones and funeral ornaments, people pulling concealed weapons from wherever they'd hidden them about their bodies.

Up on the roof the Chinaman looked at the scene far below, a disturbed anthill, with resigned acceptance. Nikita, peering over the parapet, had seen Hanlon and Robby start across the road. He turned to the Chinaman to warn him.

It was his last action on earth. The *Kitayets* had reloaded and as Nikita pointed and started to speak, he shot him in the heart at point-blank range, killing him instantly.

As Hanlon, followed by Robby, started up the outside stairs of the building, the Chinaman abandoned the binoculars and the body of Nikita, gathered up his rifle and jacket, and thrust the spent shell casings into his pocket before running for the doors that led into the building. Pushing them closed, he entered the internal stairwell that ran down to the ground. Its doors on to the roof were fire doors and didn't open inwards.

Nikita lay on his back on the tarmacked roof, blood pooling outwards from the exit wound by his spine. His sightless eyes stared at the blue heavens of a perfect London day and the wind patiently unravelled his comb-over, strand by strand.

CHAPTER EIGHTEEN

Assistant Commissioner Corrigan looked at the agenda for the meeting which was neatly set out on the A4 piece of paper with its standard crown and portcullis logo. It was helpfully headed *Agenda*, in bold type. Then he looked at his watch, trying to calculate how long the meeting would last, then at his fellow attendees around the long, rectangular table. Corrigan was not a meetings man.

Back to the agenda. The date: today; the location: the Home Office, Marsham Street, fifth floor. The meeting room, a meeting room like just about every meeting room he had ever sat in, although the table here was real wood, which made a change from laminate.

His eyes dropped down to the list of attendees: Eamonn Corrigan, Metropolitan Police; Francine Edwards, Home Office; Serg Surikov, Thanatos Institute; Paul Fredericks, MOPAC; Sarah Lansdale-Brown, Home Office Immigration Compliance and Enforcement.

Apologies: Edward Li, Thanatos Institute.

Lansdale-Brown opened the meeting. She was very tall and slim, made even taller by improbably high-heeled shoes. Balanced on these, she was nearly Corrigan's height. Even sitting down she appeared taller than anyone else there. Her back was fearsomely erect. She was intelligent, efficient and no-nonsense. Corrigan liked her a lot.

She quickly ran through the agenda of Project Volga, an offshoot of Tomboy, which was the monitoring of prostitution and people-trafficking from Russia and the various republics of the former Soviet Union. Amongst the older generation of government employees there was a feeling that things had been a lot simpler pre-fall of the Berlin Wall. Better, much better, from our point of view. The Cold War might have been unpleasant, but it had been kind of a Garden of Eden time with clearly defined enemies and clear boundaries. You'd known where you'd stood. It had been a more innocent, pre-Lapsarian epoch of good and bad, black and white. Now everything was a dispiriting shade of grey.

There were seven items on the agenda, actions from previous meetings, updates on requirements and legal compliance, current status and tasks in progress, project plans, actions required, financial overviews and AOB.

Corrigan found his attention wandering. Project Volga had seemed to him a typical example of departmental time-wasting, but someone had considered it of sufficient importance to have Charlie Taverner killed. He had been killed to stop him attending a meeting rather like this, as dull as this. Just to protect the name of the *vor*, the Russian god-father. Taverner had been planning to produce it like a rabbit out of a hat. He wondered when Demirel would get back to him. He wondered if Demirel had found out anything worth reporting on.

He guessed he might have been naïve in blaming a police informant for Charlie's death. The leak could easily have come from anyone around this table. Was that what had happened? The criminals had so much money to spend and there had been no pay increase for anyone in the room for several years. Had that affected someone's morality?

His gaze rested speculatively upon Charlie Taverner's replacement, Serg Surikov. And what about the Thanatos think tank that both of them had worked for? Thanatos monitored criminal as opposed to ideological threats from around the world. It analysed trends and Charlie Taverner, ex-Foreign Office and ex-Moscow Embassy staff, had been their key Russian adviser. Someone from Thanatos could have tipped the Russians off. Possibly even this man sitting opposite him, Serg Surikov.

Tall, thin, a feline kind of face with eyes that were slightly almond-shaped; maybe he had some Tartar blood in him, thought Corrigan. Maybe Chinese. He had a wispy beard and moustache that belonged on a schoolboy rather than a businessman. Corrigan was old enough to remember Bjorn Borg, the Swedish tennis player that women had swooned over. He too had had similar skimpy facial hair. In Corrigan's view you shouldn't have a beard unless it was a proper one.

He rubbed his own sizeable chin. It rasped satisfyingly.

Their eyes met momentarily. Surikov seemed to guess what Corrigan was thinking and stroked his straggly beard with an air of self-mockery. His eyes were bright and amused. He obviously didn't care remotely what anyone thought.

'Can we start now, ladies and gentlemen,' said Lansdale-Brown. There was a general shuffling of papers and clearing of throats. Francine Edwards, from the Home Office, short, dark-haired and buxom, had laid her things out in a neatly aligned pattern. Bright and alert, she looked as if she was ready to sit an important exam. An exam she was confident of passing. The man from the mayor's office for Policing and Crime, Paul Fredericks, pointed at Surikov.

'Does he have clearance?' he asked aggressively, and, 'Where's Edward Li?'

165

Li was the Hong Kong-born head of the Thanatos think tank. A shining example of upward mobility, from the dockyard slums of Kowloon to the boardrooms of London, New York and Berlin in four decades. Rumour had it he had once been an enforcer for the Triads. It was a rumour Li never denied.

'I said, where's Li?' repeated Paul Fredericks.

Corrigan knew Fredericks well. He heartily disliked him. He always had to be difficult, always wanting to make some point.

'I have been exhaustively and painstakingly vetted by DVA and FCO Vetting Unit,' said Surikov, his voice silky. It sounded very musical after Fredericks's estuary English accent. 'I believe I have, to the *nth* degree, bounded over hurdles put in my way.'

He chose his elaborate phrasing slowly, as though he was picking his way through an interesting maze of vocabulary, thickets of lexis.

'As to your other point, allow me to elucidate. Mr Li is very unavoidably busy and cannot extricate himself from coils of pressing business.'

'Well, I think that covers that point, Paul,' said Lansdale-Brown firmly. Fredericks scowled. Lansdale-Brown scratched her head with the end of the biro she was holding. She had wiry, scrunchy hair that she'd piled up and secured on top of her head, adding to her considerable height.

Surikov smiled sarcastically at the man from the mayor's office and the meeting proceeded. It covered the areas that Corrigan had outlined to Enver Demirel in the previous week and two things rapidly became very clear to Corrigan.

The first was the extraordinary lack of information held by the Home Office and the Border Agency on the extent of Russian involvement in UK crime, indeed, in UK business in general. Even numbers of Russians in the country appeared to be a matter of conjecture. We're basing policy on guesswork, thought Corrigan gloomily. I don't know why I should be surprised.

The second thing was how impressive Surikov was. Most of us have some, possibly exaggerated, knowledge of what we consider to be a weak spot, and for Corrigan it was lack of a formal education. He had left school at sixteen and that was that.

The older he became, the more it rankled. He was slightly in awe of Hanlon for her relentless autodidacticism, the way she would devour history, geography, anything non-fiction. He envied Mawson for his degree, even though he outranked Mawson astronomically, and he was always intimidated by Lansdale-Brown and Francine Edwards with their respective degrees in PPE (Oxon) and Economics (Cantab). He knew it was stupid of him, but it was there, as irrational but as powerful as his dislike of sports jackets, golf and TV presenters.

Edward Li, whose absence Fredericks had bemoaned, was cut from the same cloth as Corrigan, working class made good, but Li, chamaeleon-like, had insinuated himself into the educated, ruling elite. Suave, distinguished-looking, in his well-cut bespoke suits and handmade shoes, you would never have guessed he had quite literally at the beginning fought his way up and into society. Li had managed to acquire a degree and solid academic credentials, but for Corrigan it was too late.

Corrigan, battered face and raw, pitted features, looked like a labourer dressed up for an unexpected day at the office. He had risen high, but he never felt he belonged and he never felt part of the establishment he represented. He was there as an equal of everyone around the table at the meeting but, deep down, he didn't feel equal and he suspected that privately they were looking down their noses at him. He guessed it was why he got on so well with Hanlon. They were both, in their own ways, outsiders. Both mistrustful.

Surikov, who was an outsider, dominated the small meeting. He effortlessly laid out facts and figures from what was obviously a prodigious memory. He was insightful, informative, even managing to make the thickets of Russian acronyms, MVD (Ministry of Internal Affairs), OBEP (Department for Combating Economic Crime), RUOP (Regional Department for Combating Organized Crime) intelligible and interesting. His ornate English, Corrigan decided, was a significant factor in the weaponry Surikov deployed, of charm, intelligence, lucidity.

All qualities that Fredericks, in Corrigan's opinion, lacked.

Fredericks's scowl deepened as Surikov held the interest of the women in the room, the Home Office ladies practically flirting with him. Corrigan was quite pleased. He had been hoping to avoid a series of potentially tricky questions about the Metropolitan Police's contribution to combating the rise in sex-trafficking in London, but all eyes seemed to be on the Russian end. The Home Office because they were swooning over Surikov, the mayor's office because Fredericks was busy trying, ineffectually, to score points over the Russian.

The meeting finally broke up, Lansdale-Brown and Francine Edwards handing business cards to Surikov.

Corrigan watched them, amused. He wasn't the kind of man that women made a beeline for, but he didn't care. Popularity meant little to him, although he was exceptionally good at personal PR. He had hit upon a winning strategy years ago, to be himself. And as he was fundamentally a decent man, it worked.

Fredericks came up to him.

'Cocky little bastard, isn't he?' he said, jerking his head at Surikov. Corrigan shrugged, disliking Fredericks even more than usual. Fredericks had the kind of mouth that held a perpetual sneer, as if there were some kind of specialist curling tongs that he used on his lips on a nightly basis. It was rumoured he had political ambitions. He would become the kind of politician the people love to hate, thought Corrigan.

'When you're that good-looking and that bright you can afford to be, Paul,' said Corrigan, his tone implying Fredericks was neither. 'Brains and beauty, Paul, God rarely gives both.'

It had been warm in the office and Surikov had removed his jacket. As he left the room, Corrigan noticed Lansdale-Brown and Edwards frankly appraising his backside. 'I think they like his ass as well, Paul, particularly Francine,' said Corrigan helpfully. He knew Fredericks fancied Edwards. 'She's almost drooling. Oh, to be that good-looking, eh, Paul?' he added. Fredericks frowned in annoyance, glared at Corrigan and left the room.

Surikov was still waiting for the lift when Corrigan joined him. Surikov smiled politely. 'Allow me to say what an honour it is to have met you, Assistant Commissioner Corrigan,' he said.

Corrigan looked down at the Russian from his great height. It was hard to know if Surikov was being serious or sarcastic. He noticed for the first time that his eyes were a strange greenish-blue colour, like a cat's.

'Thank you,' he said.

'Serg,' said Surikov, proffering his hand. Corrigan enfolded it in his own enormous paw and shook it. He made no attempt to give his own forename. The lift arrived and they got in; Surikov pressed the ground-floor button. He toyed with the visitor's pass hanging around his neck.

'Edward Li intimated to me that I should jog your memory regarding a DCI Hanlon,' said Surikov as the lift doors closed. Corrigan looked at him coldly. Not this again, he thought.

169

'I was very close to Charlie Taverner,' said Surikov. 'I know that the police will be exploring every avenue but I have inferred from several hints dropped by my employer that DCI Hanlon, whilst maybe impetuous, precipitous, even, has in the past produced extremely effective results.'

'Ground floor,' announced the lift, in modulated tones. Corrigan thought, Thanatos seems to view Hanlon as some kind of magic solution if a situation seems intractable. God, I'm getting as bad as Fredericks, he thought, intractable.

He was growing heartily sick of Li telling him what to do. He'd already had a couple of private emails from the man, asking that Hanlon be assigned to Taverner's disappearance. Corrigan was damned if he was going to endanger her life in the pursuit of Russian gangsters. And, he thought, how come Li knew so much about Hanlon?

He felt an almost irresistible urge to lean forward, to morph into an old-school London copper, say something along the lines of, *Word in your shell-like, sunshine, fuck off!* Let Serg ,with his deep knowledge of idiomatic English, try and work out the meaning of the first half of that sentence.

'I have every faith in the ability of all my officers, Serg,' said Corrigan. The doors opened and Surikov politely waved him ahead.

Corrigan strode towards reception security without looking back. Thanatos seemed strangely obsessed with Hanlon, he thought.

Serg Surikov stood in the lobby and watched him go. His face was inscrutable. He took his mobile phone from his pocket and saw there was a message from Francine Edwards, the young, sleek brunette from the meeting.

Thanks for the chirps, call me!

Surikov frowned and looked up chirps on the dictionary app. *To make a short high-pitched sound like a bird or an insect.*

Obviously another slang expression. It must have a second meaning. A polyseme, a word with multiple meanings. Francine Edwards's voice was quite low and husky. It certainly wasn't high-pitched. Most definitely not insect-like. His face brightened and he entered *chirp* into his list of words to learn. He made a note, *idiomatic usage.*

He loved vocabulary.

Maybe Francine Edwards would like to explain it herself. He started to tap her number into his phone.

CHAPTER NINETEEN

Arkady Belanov's mobile rang. It was Dimitri.

'Mitya has the policeman under control now,' said Arkady to Myasnikov. 'What do you want doing with him?' He knew, but he wanted confirmation.

Myasnikov raised surprised eyebrows. 'I thought we'd agreed we'd take him to that warehouse in Slough. I certainly don't want him here and the farm isn't ready yet. We're still waiting for the Yusopovs. I want this place to look as innocent as possible just in case his colleagues come looking for him.'

He shook his head at the stupidity of his subordinates.

'And remind all the girls here of what will happen to them if they speak to the police. You did film cutting off that scum's head.' Arkady nodded. Myasnikov said, 'Show them that. When we kill the policeman, record that too. Let them know no one is above my law.'

Arkady picked up his landline phone and issued the relevant instructions to the Yusopov twins. They'd pick up Dimitri and the girl and drive them and Enver to the trading estate.

'And the girl, Arkasha?' asked Dimitri, still on the mobile. Arkady looked at Myasnikov. Myasnikov considered the question; it was a pleasing one. He felt like the emperor in a Roman amphitheatre. He had the power of life or death.

Thumbs up or thumbs down. It was a great feeling, known only to a select few.

'Is she trouble?' he asked. Arkady relayed the question. Dimitri, a few miles away on the other side of Oxford, looked at the hunched figure of Chantal, sitting on the bed staring bleakly into space, meekly awaiting whatever fate had in store for her.

'No.'

Thumbs up then, thought Myasnikov. The emperor had exercised his power. In the Circus Maximus the crowds cheered, applauding his magnanimity. Soon, however, they would see his other side. They needed to question Enver before they got rid of him; they'd let her watch. After that there would be no doubt that she would do what she was told, and he could take her to Moscow and sell her. She was near the airport; they might as well make use of it. He'd fly her to Poland and drive her in that way, save messing around with visas. He knew people at a border crossing there; it would be easy.

She would have novelty value, a genuine British whore. Nobody liked the British, so the chance to defile at least one of them would make her very marketable. After she'd seen what they would do to the policeman she would beg to serve them.

A shame for the *politseyskiy* that when the quietus came he wouldn't be allowed the luxury of what the defeated and condemned-to-die gladiator used to do, to wrap his face in his cloak to hide his death agony.

Although when the time came, the *politseyskiy* would be begging for death, that was for sure. He would oversee it personally. He didn't like getting his hands dirty, but he liked to watch.

Another barrel for the policeman, then make arrangements for their disposal. So much to do in such a limited time. He gathered that Anderson's lawyer, Cunningham, who Arkady had contacted, was busy arranging the documents for sale of the Marylebone flat. The police, according to both Joad and the Chinaman, knew nothing of the killing of Jordan, Taverner and the girl Tatiana, but rumours had leaked out into the criminal community and Anderson's prestige had taken an almighty knock.

He sipped his tea gently and looked at Arkady sitting opposite him, holding a large vodka.

Myasnikov knew what Anderson would be going through. He had experienced lows himself in his criminal career. Right now whores would be looking for other employers, creditors would be asking for repayment of loans or money up front and there would be a general rise in absenteeism from Anderson's hired thugs. It was very much like a run on a bank, and fear would feed fear. Anderson's stock had been irrevocably devalued and he would be feeling it.

Only Myasnikov's death could restore Anderson to his former glory, and who would dare attempt that? No one. You wouldn't be able to find a single person in London with the balls to try and kill him. Not one.

A couple of weeks ago Dave 'Jesus' Anderson had been one of the most feared men in London. An invincible criminal who had once crucified a man who had crossed him, hence the nickname.

Now the Moscow Butcher was the man to fear. A man who killed people at funerals. A man who beheaded his rivals. Myasnikov was furious at the Islamic terrorists in the Middle East. They were stealing his thunder. He felt that he was being devalued by their actions. How dared they chop heads off. People might think he was a copycat, that he lacked originality. He took another sip of tea.

It's strange, thought Arkady, how normal Myasnikov looks in his conservative blue suit and tie, his thin, ascetic features, bald head and mild-mannered expression. Like a teacher marking homework. Then again, look at Lenin, who he faintly resembled. He had no qualms when it came to signing death warrants.

'Tell Dimitri Nikolyavich to bring the girl along when he comes. I want as few loose ends as possible. We'll speak to the cop tomorrow. Make sure that the cop has an uncomfortable night. Do we know anything about him?'

Arkady took a mouthful of vodka.

'Joad says there is nothing unusual, nothing strange locally. No one is interested in us. This cop is Metropolitan *politseyskiy*, London, not Oxford. The Chinaman says nothing unusual too in London. They don't seem to know about Anderson's brothel. He's covered that up.' Arkady was wearing voluminous cream linen trousers and a bright blue Hawaiian shirt with a motif of yachts. It was loose-fitting but his huge gut strained at the fabric. The top of his slacks were darker than the rest where sweat had soaked through. He swirled the ice around in his drink. 'Anderson must have got rid of the bodies effectively.'

Myasnikov frowned. 'The Chinaman didn't do very well with terminating Anderson's brother at the cemetery. It was a fuck-up, Arkasha.'

Arkady nodded. 'Yes, Konstantin Alexandrovich, but not the Chinaman's fuck-up. Nikita dropped his rifle, messed up the sights.'

'Mmm-hmm, and the Chinaman certainly messed Nikita up, I gather.' Good, he thought. He didn't like loose ends. It saved them a job.

'So, all in all, Kostya, not too bad. And the Chinaman gave me the lead on Anderson's lawyer, Cunningham. They're ready to negotiate.'

'Good,' said Myasnikov. He thought for a minute and then looked out of the window. The gardens of the brothel were immaculate. He'd checked everything with his usual rigour, including the accounts.

The brothel was registered to his UK company, Godunov Holdings. The brothel was technically a 'wellness' centre. The dozen or so girls who worked out of it were qualified masseuses and reiki practitioners, nutritional experts and NLP counsellors. He'd bought a job lot of qualifications for them over the Internet. They were framed and sat on the walls of the girls' bedrooms. They were all perfectly genuine qualifications. In Myasnikov's opinion it was scandalous that you could buy such things legally. How could you know who to trust?

His filed accounts kept him just slightly over the wire, tax-wise, enough not to excite the attentions of HMRC, not enough to hurt. The warehouse in Slough was part of the portfolio. Myasnikov always did enough to stay on the right side of the authorities when he could.

The farm outside Oxford was registered in another name. Security within security. He had made millions through his hard work and he wasn't going to have his wealth jeopardized by the government taking it away, if, God forbid, he were ever caught and sentenced. It's partly why he was in England, a safe haven for his money. You couldn't trust the Russian government and he most certainly didn't trust the rouble.

If England was good enough for the oligarchs, it was good enough for him. Maybe he would take out citizenship.

He checked the slim, expensive watch on his wrist.

'Tell Dimitri to make sure that the girl watches while he works the policeman. I want her to be in no doubt as to what will happen to her if she doesn't cooperate fully. Oh, and, Arkady, tell Dimitri not to be too enthusiastic. I want him alive and able to talk tomorrow morning. They're fixing the farm to hold him for a couple of days. Just to recapitulate. Move him and the girl to Slough now, store them there till tonight, then we'll move him back to the farm later when it's ready. You and me will call in tonight, Arkasha. I want to see the girl. I want to see my investment. I want to make sure she's worth keeping alive. Face it, Dima will fuck anything. I also want to make sure this Demirel is more or less in one piece. Tell Dimitri if he kills him, well, I'll be unhappy.'

'Yes, Konstantin Alexandrovich, it will be done.'

It was a day of meetings. While Myasnikov and Belanov were meeting at the brothel in Woodstock Road in Oxford, Anderson, Morris Jones, Danny and Robby were in the back bar of the Three Compasses, Edmonton.

It was a lot less salubrious than the brothel in Oxford.

'Did you get a photo, Morris?' asked Anderson. Today, Morris Jones was wearing a paisley shirt and faded blue jeans; his training shoes with blue stitching had been handmade in Jermyn Street. Anderson was also casually dressed, in an old tracksuit that had been cheap when he'd bought it at Edmonton market. He was unshaven and Danny thought he looked crazier than usual.

Danny wasn't feeling too clever himself. He'd spent the weekend on the piss, drinking himself unconscious. He couldn't seem to clear the images of death out of his mind. He was alarmed to find himself trembling every now and again. It wasn't dramatic but it worried him. He found that his heart would start racing at the same time and he would feel cold sweat on his brow. His nerves were pretty much shot. He was terrified that someone would notice. He didn't want to end up like Barry Jackson and he didn't want to end up like Jordan Anderson. He was between a rock and a hard place.

What with the Russians on one side and his employers on the other, Danny was beginning to feel very much out of his depth.

Morris Jones rested a speculative eye on him. Danny glared at him aggressively. Why are you looking at me like that? he thought. He felt his palms starting to sweat. Please God, not a panic attack, he prayed.

Morris Jones nodded and handed over a glossy head and shoulders print of a woman. Robby looked at it briefly. He'd had the best look at the woman. She had been caught looking into the camera. The expression was confident, maybe slightly arrogant, the dark hair thick and kinked, almost corkscrew-like. Her eyebrows were black and gracefully arched. Her jaw was determined, the eyes grey, but there were dark shadows underneath them as if she didn't sleep well. It was a handsome face but hard. She had an attractive mouth yet it was somehow difficult to imagine it smiling.

'That's her,' Robby said. 'She can't half run. Who is she anyway?'

Anderson smiled. He'd known it would be her. How many other women would jump from a twelve-foot wall at a gangster's funeral, issue instructions to his security team, instructions that they'd all obeyed without thinking, and then outpace Robby up all those stairs to confront an armed man?

Danny had thought it might be her, but he'd only met her once, briefly, a while ago. He was unsure of her, but then he had been behaving a bit oddly of late. Anderson made a mental note. Maybe it was time to get rid of Danny.

'That, Robby, is DCI Hanlon of the Met.'

Robby looked puzzled. 'She didn't stick around, not when we found matey up there. What was all that about then?'

'That,' said Anderson, 'is what we're going to find out.' He turned to Morris Jones. 'Arrange it, Morris. Cunningham will know where to find her.'

Anderson looked at the photo of Hanlon he held between his strong fingers. I knew we'd meet again, he thought pleasurably.

CHAPTER TWENTY

Enver Demirel woke up feeling terrible. He felt sick, sore and disorientated. There were no effects from the taser but the ketamine that he had been injected with had left him tired and lethargic. Its pain-killing effects had worn off and he was aware of an aching pain in his groin from where Dimitri had kicked him.

He shook his head to clear it and looked around. His thoughts were still slow and confused. He was mentally zoning in and out of the here and now like a randomly focused lens.

He was in a very large empty room with a high corrugated roof. Light filtered in from small windows set up in the walls near the ceiling. The overall impression was one of dark, damp, grey gloom. The only objects in the vast space seemed to be several oil drums, nothing else. He shifted his attention to his own body.

His hands were behind his back and he was secured by his wrists to an old-fashioned radiator. Handcuffed with what looked suspiciously like his own police-issue rigid cuffs. The cold radiator was made of heavy iron and securely bracketed; he wouldn't be going anywhere in a hurry. His ankles were gaffer-taped together.

He sank back into unconsciousness.

He awoke again with no knowledge of how much time had elapsed since he had last come to. He was still feeling disassociated from his surroundings by the drug. He closed his eyes and maybe he drifted off; he wasn't quite sure. He opened his eyes again and this time noticed that he wasn't alone.

Chantal Jenkins was also attached to the other end of the radiator. She looked at him unhappily. 'Are you awake now?' she said. 'How are you feeling?'

Back at her flat, when she'd opened the door to let Enver in and seen this big, powerful man with the kind face, the floor creaking under his heavy tread, momentarily hope had flared in her heart. For a flickering instant she had thought of pointing at the bathroom door where Dimitri was and mouthing something. A warning; a plea.

But equally quickly had come the knowledge that even if Enver overpowered and arrested him, Dimitri would be released by the end of the evening. Or, even if he wasn't, Belanov would come for her and, if not him, someone else. And where could she hide, where could she go? Nowhere. They would come for her. Nobody had ever helped her in her life and they weren't going to start now.

The best it ever got had been Curtis. That was far from brilliant but he had cared for her in a way. Now he was gone.

So she'd done what Dimitri had told her, distracted Enver with the sight of her body, allowing Dimitri to emerge and taser him in the back.

'Hello, Chantal,' said Enver. He remembered everything clearly up until he had been tasered. Dimitri, he guessed. He bore her no ill will. He rubbed his thick hair against the radiator, tested the metal of the rigid handcuffs. Oh, for a malfunction. They were working perfectly; he was going nowhere.

'Do you know where we are?' he asked.

Chantal shook her head. 'We were in the back of a van,' she said. 'You were in a box,' she added unhappily. 'I looked at my watch, we're about an hour from Oxford. Most of it was on the motorway.' She paused. 'Does it matter?'

'Not really, I suppose,' Enver said. He tested the mounting of the old-fashioned radiator with his strong hands. It didn't move a millimetre.

Enver briefly considered his fate. All in all, he decided, it didn't look promising. Dimitri could hardly release him – well, not unless he planned a return to Russia. The odds on a successful extradition attempt would be low. That was his only chance really. That, and being rescued by some fluke. Still, at least he was still alive. That was something.

But his work colleagues thought he was in France. The only person who would miss him would be Melinda Huss.

'Have you still got your watch?' he asked Chantal.

She shook her head. 'They took it.'

What would Huss do? thought Enver. He pictured her getting off the train at Paddington, failing to find him. The unanswered calls to his mobile, her rising anger, her returning on the train to Oxford. He clamped down on the thought as best he could.

Enver was one of those people who would fret about trivial things – *what will happen if . . . ?* – and construct elaborate, doom-laden scenarios based on nothing but pessimism. Faced with real and terrifying danger, such as the inevitability of much physical pain when boxing and the possibility of severe injury, even worse, he was cheerily fatalistic.

He had confronted the certainty (at the time) of death and he had been pleased by the stoicism he had shown. He had survived that. It was a good precedent. Perhaps he would survive this. Well, he wasn't going to worry about it any more than he had to.

'Well, Chantal,' he said, 'since we're here and there's nothing else to do, why don't you tell me everything you know about Dimitri and Arkady Belanov?'

Chantal thought about it. She had little to lose. She looked at Enver, shackled to the other end of the radiator. He had lost his shoes somewhere along the way; she assumed Dimitri had removed them for some reason. After he'd been injected with the ketamine, two men – they had to be twins, they were so alike – had turned up at her flat carrying the empty box with its reinforced base, like a pallet, so a forklift could slide its prongs underneath. She guessed it had been used once to carry something like a washing machine. The unconscious Enver had been jackknifed into it, the box sealed and slid down the stairs, then put into the van waiting outside on the pavement. Then she'd climbed in after him.

It was all very well planned. Of course it would be, she thought unhappily. Her thoughts were drawn to the oil drums, their squat, sinister shapes unpleasantly suggestive of menace. It was the way they had been placed in the centre of the big, empty echoing space of the warehouse that drew the eye to them.

Dimitri had left her a bottle of water and she took a mouthful. Only one of her wrists was attached to the radiator; her other arm was free. Enver watched enviously as she drank. He was desperately thirsty.

'I've been with Sam, Sam Curtis, for eight months,' she began. She was determined to begin at the beginning. No one had ever expressed any interest in her life story before and she had a horrible feeling that Enver would soon be in no position to repeat anything.

The sky as revealed by the row of small windows changed to a deeper and deeper blue and the light gradually faded in the warehouse. There were obviously streetlights because a dim orange glow from outside cast enough of a diffuse illumination to make out close-at-hand objects.

They could see each other and the suggestive oil drums revealed themselves only as deeper cylinders of darkness in the gloom of the warehouse.

Chantal had finished speaking and the two of them were silent, Chantal too miserable to think, Enver only too glad to consider a subject other than his own fate.

There was a lot to think about. The murders of at least four people and the Russians' criminal connections. The Russians had someone on Oxford Council, they had minimally one tame policeman, they had maybe another high-ranking police official or civil servant or NGO on board. They had the brothel on the Woodstock Road. They had this place. They had a great deal of money and probably half a dozen men working for them plus subcontracted local criminals such as Sam Curtis. And they had a keen brain running them in the form of this *vor,* Myasnikov.

Well, I've done what Corrigan wanted, thought Enver bitterly. I've shaken the tree. I've found that Belanov is the watcher and I know the name of the *vor.* All I have to do now is unshackle myself from this radiator and get out of this building and I can go and present my report in person. He will be delighted. I now know more about this than I ever would have thought possible.

His reflections were broken by the noise of an engine outside the warehouse. It was a vehicle pulling up and parking.

'Chantal,' said Enver quietly, 'if we're lucky that could be a security patrol. The estate probably has one. I'm going to count to three and I want you to shout *Help* with me, OK?'

Chantal nodded.

'One, two, three,' said Enver, 'and *HELP!*'

The dead air and acoustics of the warehouse made a mockery of their calls for assistance, but they tried again. Then Enver's straining ears heard something, the sound of a key turning in a lock, and briefly there was a flash of light as the outside door to the loading bay opened. Then it disappeared as the external door closed, and then the electric light in the entrance lobby came on. There was an opaque glass panel in the double doors that led to the lobby and the light, diffuse as it was, seemed very bright after their virtual darkness.

The doors opened and the giant form of Dimitri stood there, looking at them. In his left hand he held a sports bag. He walked towards them. Enver heard Chantal gasp in fear. He could certainly sympathize.

The huge Russian walked up to them with a slow measured tread. He stopped a couple of metres away from Enver and stared at him. Their eyes locked. It was like when two boxers met before the fight, that first moment that could sometimes decide the outcome.

His brutal face, which seemed composed of flat planes, with little that was rounded in it, looked down at Enver in sadistic satisfaction. Enver's eyes conveyed angry, defiant contempt.

Dimitri said nothing but slowly unzipped the sports bag and took out a variety of objects. A plumber's blowtorch. A chisel. A hammer. Pliers. Duct tape. A screwdriver. A lighter. A Stanley knife.

He carefully lined these up in a row.

'All for you,' he said to Enver. Enver was silent; what use were words? He wouldn't give Dimitri the satisfaction of pleading. Chantal was silent too, but she was crying. Tears ran down her cheeks, glistening in the light from the door.

'Who sent you to her and why?' asked Dimitri, addressing Enver.

'Fuck you,' said Enver, almost conversationally.

Dimitri smiled. 'You don't know how happy I am to hear you say that,' he said.

185

He picked up the duct tape and neatly severed a length, which he attached over Enver's mouth.

'Where to begin?' he asked no one in particular. He looked at his array of tools and picked up the claw hammer. He walked over to Enver.

'We start with this.'

Chantal closed her eyes as Dimitri bent over Enver. Enver couldn't make any noise but she heard the hammer and she heard Dimitri.

That was maybe even worse.

CHAPTER TWENTY-ONE

Anderson was waiting patiently for Hanlon near the office building where she worked. He had used his lawyer, Cunningham, with his extensive list of police contacts, to track down her whereabouts.

The first time they'd met, he'd been in prison on remand for cocaine possession. A lot of cocaine. Hanlon had freed him in return for his help to find a child kidnapper. He had provided the information, and she had tampered with evidence so that it would be declared inadmissible. It was with grim amusement that he learned from Cunningham the blame for this had fallen on several other Metropolitan Police who had also coincidentally been tampering with evidence in exchange for money. Their vehement denials of their involvement in *Crown* v. *Anderson* had fallen on sceptical ears. He'd heard that one of them had, in fact, confessed to it as part of a kind of plea bargain.

The last time he'd had dealings with her had been to give the nod to Iris Campion to let Hanlon know the address of the Russian brothel in Oxford. Now the Russians were back to haunt him. Anderson didn't care that much. He had a messianic belief in his own destiny. He felt, he knew, that he had been put on earth for a special purpose. Like Aguirre, he felt he was the Wrath of God. To him events were preordained, predetermined by some divinity or fate, and occasionally the veil parted and God, or fate, allowed him if not a glimpse into the future then a sense of the way the wind was blowing.

He'd known he was going to see Hanlon again soon before any of this kicked off. He had, by chance, seen her overweight, boxer sidekick in Tottenham a fortnight before, a mere glimpse out of a car window but a sure sign to his mind. She was associated with certain numbers too in his personal numerology. Fifty-one meant Hanlon. It had been part of the number plate on her last car, and he'd seen it outside a restaurant he'd eaten in and on a bus that had passed by in Woolwich, where he'd gone to pick up half a kilo of coke. Finally, there had been the kestrel he'd seen when he'd been hunting down Jackson. The bird, motionless, graceful, deadly, hanging effortlessly in the Essex sky; obviously it was her.

The boxer. The numbers. The bird. Signs and wonders. Some things were meant to be.

When Hanlon had appeared at the funeral he hadn't been remotely surprised. It had been foretold.

Hanlon slowed her car down as she approached the side road that would turn in to the car park for the office block where the MPU was situated and there, leaning against the sign advertising the names of the businesses in the industrial park, was the unmistakeable figure of Anderson.

His tall, wiry figure, wearing a dark blue Adidas tracksuit and trainers, conveyed sinister malice. Like Death getting in shape for a track-and-field event. She stopped and opened the driver's window. Anderson put his hands on the top of the car door and bent his head down to look in.

She saw his unshaven face, the high cheekbones and hot, restless eyes. His unkempt stringy hair framed his bony features. She was conscious of his magnetic presence filling the small car.

She was very aware of his large, powerful hands, the fingers splayed above the groove where the glass of the window had disappeared.

His gaze took in her face, her hair, her upper body. It was incurious, almost robotic. As always with Anderson, there was a sense that he wasn't entirely present, as though he were listening to some other voice, like a TV presenter with an earpiece. Now he cocked his head slightly as he looked at her.

'Nice car,' he said. London accent, proper London, she thought, almost snobbishly; echt-London, not Slough wannabe London.

She nodded. She had no wish to discuss the finer points of an Audi TT. She waited, then raised an interrogative eyebrow. Anderson smiled, genuinely amused. Most people who knew his reputation needed a change of underpants when he spoke to them. Oh, Hanlon, he thought, you're so cool.

'Like Slough, do you?' he enquired.

She looked him in the eyes. 'Love it,' she said with crisp certainty. Anderson wondered what she was doing here. Cunningham's mate in the CPS had guessed she was being punished, but you never knew with the woman he was looking at.

'I'd like a word,' he said.

Hanlon nodded again. Not the Three Compasses. She'd had enough of Edmonton for a while. She thought back to the incident with the painter and decorator; there'd been a pub on the corner. 'There's a pub down the road, the Three Barrels. I'll meet you there, four thirty.'

'Is it nice?' asked Anderson. He was immediately struck by the recurrence of the numeral, three. Three Barrels, Three Compasses. God is in the detail.

It was foretold. How could it be otherwise?

'I very much doubt it,' said Hanlon. She smiled icily at Anderson and put the car in gear.

He stood and watched as the car drove off.

Hanlon spent the rest of the afternoon occupied on her official business. She checked through the details of those reported missing over the previous twenty-four hours, prioritizing and making sure that protocol had been followed for the several teenagers who had disappeared in the past seventy-two hours.

DS Mawson was busy working on budget updates for an internal audit. He won't have me to worry about. I'm not costing him any money, thought Hanlon. I'm still on the payroll of the Met, as far as I know. At least that's what her last payslip had said.

Missing persons was not occupying much of her mind at the moment. Foremost in her thoughts was the link between the dead Taverner and Arkady Belanov via Dimitri.

She called up Companies House on her screen and did a quick check of Woodstock Wellness Clinic, the name she'd made a mental note of when she'd been demonstrating. A call to Oxford Council had established that was the name under which, unbeknown to them, Arkady Belanov's brothel operated.

Hanlon's dark eyebrows lifted in increasing interest as she read under Overseas Company Information that it was now a subsidiary of Godunov Holdings. Its penultimate filing history was the appointment of a Mr Arkady Belanov as managing director.

Godunov Holdings wasn't listed as a UK company, but further digging and a one-pound fee elicited the information that it also had a mortgage on a property in Slough. A warehouse. She noted down the address.

So how did this tie in, if it did, to the disappearance of Charlie Taverner? According to Oksana, Taverner, researching Russian growth in the prostitution market, had come across Belanov – a man known to Hanlon as being involved in the trade. Belanov worked for a senior crime figure, the *vor*. Probably the man that she had seen at the airport. The Butcher of Moscow.

Then there was the other piece of the puzzle. Anderson. If Iris Campion were to be believed, there was some sort of ongoing feud between Anderson and the Russians, again centred around prostitution, in this case Anderson's Beath Street brothel. A turf war?

She tapped her even white teeth with the end of a pen.

Then the attempt on Anderson's life. The dead man on the roof, a Slav.

Finally, what was she going to do? In her mind the agenda was simple: find Taverner, or at least his body, for Oksana's sake. The chances were that Anderson would know where it was. It was he who had disposed of the corpses from Beath Street. If it was unofficial, he might even tell her where Taverner could be found.

The unusual thing was that so far she hadn't done anything too outrageous. The deaths at Beath Street were, after all, technically only rumour. Others could open or not open that can of worms. So she could, with a fairly clean conscience, do what she was supposed to do.

I don't know, she thought. There doesn't seem to be any real rush. The dead are dead anyway and there appears to be no threat to anybody living. I've usually acted too quickly in the past, was her conclusion. I'll see what Anderson wants and then sleep on it. Tomorrow is another day.

Hanlon put her head down and ploughed on with her officially sanctioned work. Mawson walked past her desk a couple of times on his way back and forth to the coffee machine in the corner of the office. He was quietly pleased to see Hanlon settling down. Proof to him that good police work stemmed from the top. In the past Hanlon had either had demonstrably disastrous managers – here he thought of Peter Bench, currently doing fifteen years – or Corrigan himself, too lax with Hanlon. Obviously, what she needed was some useful, undramatic work in a carefully supervised environment.

He watched with a sense of pride as she left the building and crossed to her car down below in the car park. She'd politely said goodbye and that she'd be in bright and early the following day. There's progress for you, he thought proudly. Bright and early.

Hanlon started her car and drove out of the car park. Anderson, here I come, she thought, bright and early.

The pub lived up to her unenthusiastic billing. The Three Barrels wasn't a bad place but it lacked charisma. She walked in and immediately checked the layout, an automatic habit. It was L-shaped with the bar at the top of the letter, entrance at the bottom and a room just off on the right that she guessed in the old days would have been a separate bar, now knocked into one.

It was a working-man's pub with no concessions to family or women. Four thirty p.m. was builders' drinking time, most construction workers following an eight-until-four day. She'd guessed this would be the clientele from the pickup trucks which were parked outside. There were also a couple of small Nissan flatbeds with scaffolding and the scaffolders' names emblazoned on the sides, which were crammed into the small car park behind the pub. She had glanced down at the pavement and seen there were still splashes of paint on the grey stone from her altercation with the painter and decorator.

Hanlon had turned the corner and entered the doorway of the pub. As she walked in she could see the backs of half a dozen plaid shirts lined up at the bar, and an old TV tuned to a sports channel.

Curious heads turned to examine her. The pub obviously didn't attract a female clientele. One of the faces was familiar, all too familiar despite not being covered with white paint. Decorator Man.

Hanlon didn't pause or flinch. Retreat was not an option in her mind. The sensible thing to do would have been to just turn and leave, but she wasn't made that way. Sensible wasn't part of her character. When she went to bed that night she couldn't have faced closing her eyes, knowing that she'd backed down. She'd have despised herself.

She walked up to the bar and ordered a Coke. There was a strange, almost eerie silence as the builders stared at her, not impolitely but obviously all wondering what she was doing in here, an attractive woman in a skirt and jacket. She guessed it was the office clothes more than anything that puzzled them. A man in a suit would have been baffling, although a woman in here of any description would have been a rare enough sight.

Decorator Man said nothing, but stared at her menacingly while he rolled a cigarette. The barman said something to him, he was obviously a regular, and he nodded without listening. All his attention was fixed on Hanlon. He was as unattractive as she remembered, his face sneering and piggy-eyed. She suddenly thought, I bet he hasn't told any of his drinking buddies what happened, why he was coated in paint the other day. He wouldn't dare say he'd been beaten up by a woman. He wouldn't be man enough to bear the teasing. He wasn't the kind of guy to go in for humorous self-deprecation.

In fact, she thought, he probably hasn't admitted it happened even to himself.

She paid for her drink and nodded civilly to the sweat-stained scaffolders, then went to sit down in the bottom part of the pub, out of sight of the bar round the corner. She sat with her back to the wall, awaiting the inevitable.

Her keen senses heard the conversation by the bar start up again and then the squat figure of the decorator appeared from round the corner. He was carrying a pint of Guinness, which he put on the table that she was sitting behind. He sat down opposite and stared at her. The unlit cigarette that he had rolled hung from his lip.

'Aren't you going to say hello?' he said. His voice was surprisingly high-pitched, as unappealing as the rest of him. She had obviously been preying on his mind, beaten by a woman, and here she was, an answer to a prayer.

He leaned forward menacingly across the table, bringing something out of the pocket of his paint-stained dungarees. He held his right hand around something fist-sized, there was a click and a slim blade appeared.

'Cat got your tongue, bitch?' he said, in his hoarse, squeaky voice. He was looking intently into her face, obviously hoping to see fear, something he could taste. Something he could feel. He wanted to see her suffer. Hanlon sat immobile, her cold grey eyes staring him out, relying on her peripheral vision so that if he did slice at her face with the knife she would have a chance to react.

She felt a rising rage at her own stupidity. She should have known that for Decorator Man his humiliation would have been festering like a boil, and now here was the chance to lance it. She had thought that what he wanted to do was frighten her. It was only now that she realized she had seriously underestimated him. The knife was wholly unexpected. He had gone nuclear.

He hadn't produced a knife just to scare her. Now she suspected it was to mark her forever, so that whenever she saw herself in a mirror from now to the end of her time she'd think of him.

He would go for her face any second now. That was for sure. That was a given. She rehearsed what she could do. She couldn't jerk her head back, away from the knife, there was a wall there. She'd have to go sideways. His arms were short; he'd have to stand to make sure of reaching her face. So, as he rose, she'd flip the table towards him, using the momentum to propel herself away and then throw herself forward at him. He wouldn't be expecting that. He wouldn't be expecting her to attack; he would be expecting tearful pleading.

'Bitch,' he repeated, provoked by her lack of reaction. Ever since he'd been humiliated by her he'd been fantasizing about what he'd do to her and now the moment had come. Now she was going to pay.

Hanlon smiled contemptuously and rested the palms of her hands on the underside of the table. When she reached three she would act, explode into action. She started counting in her head.

One, two—

The door of the pub opened and Anderson walked in, flanked by Morris Jones and Danny.

Decorator Man wouldn't have noticed if a brass band had walked in. All his attention was on Hanlon. Absolutely nothing was going to distract him. Even if he had been aware of the door opening he wouldn't have cared. From a casual entrant's perspective there was nothing strange or potentially violent going on. What would anyone coming in see? The back of a man's head as he sat opposite a woman. Nothing unusual. Nothing to worry Decorator Man about anyone walking in. He was just annoyed by the absence of fear on the bitch's face.

Hanlon watched impassively, her eyes not moving from Decorator Man's face. The stocky figure of Danny in jeans and an expensive-looking bomber jacket moving out of sight to the bar, Morris Jones in chinos and a red-and-white striped shirt, what looked like diamonds in his cufflinks sparkling, advancing purposefully towards Decorator Man's left and Anderson to the right. Dave Anderson's face was hard, menacing. His eyes glittered in their deep sockets.

Decorator Man became aware of Anderson only as Anderson leaned over him, his rat's tails of long hair brushing his bald patch. Decorator Man twitched, but was so intent on Hanlon he didn't look round.

'Boo!' said Anderson, softly in Decorator Man's ear.

That got his attention all right. Decorator Man jumped and twisted his neck, looking up in surprise at Anderson. It was maybe that action, presenting his nose as a target, that determined what happened next. Anderson drove his forehead with practised skill hard into the man's nose, just at the bridge where it met his forehead. There was a crunching noise, as if someone had stepped on a pair of glasses. Simultaneously, his large, powerful hand descended onto the man's wrist as fast as if he was swatting a fly, to trap the blade, and Morris Jones's knuckles thudded in, hard and vicious, to the back of Decorator Man's skull.

Head, hand, fist. Bang. Bang. Bang. The whole process was unbelievably quick and efficient. It must have taken less than two seconds.

Decorator Man's head had been driven into the table from the force of Jones's short punch. The table was heavy and sturdy. It barely moved as his forehead made contact with its surface. He was still conscious but in no shape to do a great deal. The three short, sharp blows to his head – nose, back of head, forehead – had taken their toll. Blood started to trickle from his nose as Jones hauled him upright, the legs of his chair screeching on the cheap lino of the floor, and bundled him out of the pub door.

He went in an unprotesting sort of way. Probably he was barely conscious or, if he was conscious, not wanting to provoke his attackers any more.

Anderson took the vacated chair. He picked up the flick knife from the table and inspected it. He raised his eyebrows, retracted the blade and put it in the pocket of his tracksuit jacket. He said to Hanlon, 'Friend of yours?'

'We'd met before,' said Hanlon.

Anderson smiled at her. 'I guessed so,' he said quietly.

They looked at each other, both conscious that Anderson had evened things up after the cemetery incident.

'Not Russian, is he?' asked Anderson.

Hanlon shook her head. 'A domestic incident,' she said.

Jones reappeared and Danny joined them with a tray of drinks. Anderson nodded at Decorator Man's half-drunk Guinness. He looked at it with disfavour. The froth from the head had congealed, like a slug trail, up the side of the straight glass.

'Take that back to the bar, Danny. Buy his friends a drink. Make sure the natives aren't restless.' He turned to Jones. 'What did you do with chummy, Morris?'

'I left him with Robby. Robby's taken him round the back.'

Anderson nodded, satisfied. Jones turned and positioned himself near the entrance to the alcove-like part of the bar where they were, to prevent any newcomer, if there were any, from sitting near his boss.

Anderson had a bottle of Pils in front of him and a glass. He poured the contents of the bottle into it and watched the bubbles. Hanlon waited for him to speak. His eyes flicked from the glass to Hanlon.

'You heard about my problem.'

It was a statement, not a question. Hanlon nodded.

'Turf war, eh, Hanlon.' Anderson rubbed his chin. 'I haven't had any problems since I nailed that cunt to a door.'

Hanlon's eyes narrowed. 'I'd rather you didn't use that expression,' she said.

Anderson gave a short bark of laughter. She hadn't expressed any reservations about the incident to which they both knew he referred, when he'd used a nail-gun to attach a rival named Phil Woodward to a door, crucifix fashion. But here she was, objecting to his language.

Jones looked round in surprise. He didn't hear his employer make that sort of noise usually.

'OK,' said Anderson, raising his palms in a placatory manner. 'I won't.' He dipped a finger in his lager and removed it, inspected it and tasted it with his tongue. 'Now, I know it's Russians. I know they want me out of the running. I could do with some names confirming. And addresses. Could you help?'

He studied the woman opposite, slim and elegant. She'd taken her jacket off. It lay folded neatly beside her on the faux leather of the banquette bench seat that ran across the wall of this end of the bar. It was a navy jacket and he could see its lining, cream with blue spots. The jacket looked very small and fragile, strangely feminine. He examined his sizeable right hand. He could probably lean forward, pick it up and enfold it within the grasp of his powerful fingers. He looked at the face of its owner as she considered his question.

Hanlon looked up. The nails on her hand, which she'd been studying, were cut short. Earlier that day she had done twenty-five slow, perfect form push-ups, supporting her weight on the ends of her fingertips.

She raised her eyes to Anderson, to the burning eyes under the rat's tail of stringy hair. Her gaze took in the elegant, expensively dressed figure of Morris Jones. His red and white, double-cuffed shirt with its gleaming cufflinks was not designed to hang outside trousers as it did at the moment. The shirt tail was too long; it was meant to be tucked in. Jones was not the kind of man who would make a sartorial mistake like that. There would be a gun under there. She knew that for a certainty.

Anderson was obviously a concerned man.

Decorator Man, although he'd have been processed by now at the hands of Robby, could count himself lucky he was still alive.

Anderson looked at her quizzically. She was annoyed with herself that she actually quite liked him.

She reached a decision. 'Arkady Belanov, Woodstock Road, Oxford, and his minder, Dimitri something or other, are the two who will have organized the hit on you and the one on your property in Marylebone. They are working for a man known as the *vor*.'

'You know about Marylebone?' said Anderson, not smiling any more.

Hanlon stood up. 'I know lots of things. I'm a knowledgeable woman. I know that the *vor* is called Myasnikov. I know his nickname is the Butcher of Moscow. I don't, however, know where I can find the body of a man called Charlie Taverner, and that I would like to know.'

She slipped her jacket on. She had no bag; it was in her car. She took a card from her jacket pocket.

'My number.'

Anderson nodded. She walked past Morris Jones.

'Mr Jones.' She nodded goodbye and left the pub.

He looked at Anderson in surprise. 'How come she knows my name?'

'She knows lots of things,' said Anderson. He stood up too. 'Come on, Morris, let's go.'

From behind the counter, the barman watched the three of them leave the pub. He breathed a heartfelt sigh of relief.

He turned to the three scaffolders. 'Drinks are on the house. I'm having a fucking large one.'

CHAPTER TWENTY-TWO

DI Huss waited with mounting impatience for Enver Demirel at Paddington Station. She checked the watch on her wrist yet again, even though she was hardly unaware of the time. The electronic information board for Arrivals and Departures, the constant announcements of train movements, the phone in her other hand and the frantic busyness of the place at six in the evening, filled with commuters desperate to get home – she would have had to be deaf, dumb and blind not to have realized that it was around six o'clock and that Enver was late, and she had heard nothing from him since the day before.

Enver and late were not a collocation, words that went together naturally. If ever there was a man who was pathologically early, who would normally provide updates on his progress on a practically minute-by-minute basis, it was Enver.

Huss wasn't by nature a frantic clock addict. On the farm, where she'd grown up, time was dictated at a more leisurely pace. If you had to start work at five to milk cows it didn't matter if it was four fifty or five oh five that you started, you just had to be up round about then. Similarly, in lambing season, when you were putting in twenty-hour days, it was fairly elastic. Things took the time they should take. You couldn't make barley grow faster by screaming and shouting at it. Fence repair, drainage issues, feed time, all the enormous number of jobs around a farm – they all had times to be done, but clock-watching was no help.

Enver, by contrast, had come from a catering background, which was ruled by clocks. Opening times, closing times, food-preparation times, service times, cooking times, order times: everything was done at the bayonet point of time. Seconds counted.

And then boxing, at first a sport, then semi-pro, then – all too briefly, six months – fully professional. Time was king again. When he trained, a stopwatch was always in someone's hand. And in the ring, the length and number of rounds, defeat, survival or victory – the tyranny of the clock.

For him to be late was a non-issue. Huss, although by nature placid, easy-going, was starting to get more than a little worried.

Two texts later to Enver's work colleagues and she was even more concerned. She knew that Enver was not in France on a well-deserved break but probably busy with this ill-conceived, face-saving exercise for Corrigan.

She bought herself a coffee and sat down on a bench. Her overnight bag by her feet mocked her. She tried Enver Demirel again; no reply. Huss was not one to shy away from troublesome thoughts. If Enver wasn't here, it was because someone had made sure he wasn't here. Work could be ruled out. Arkady Belanov couldn't.

What have you done, Enver? she thought with increasing alarm. Where are you? At last, she could stand it no longer.

Huss clicked on to the contacts list of her phone. She looked at the name she'd thought she would never need to use, someone she heartily disliked.

'Sod it.'

She pushed her finger against the screen. The answer came almost immediately.

'Yes?' Just the one word, the usual arrogant tone.

She gritted her teeth. 'It's Melinda Huss.'

'I know that.'

'It's about Enver. I'm worried.'

'Where are you?'

Huss told her.

'Half an hour,' said Hanlon.

Hanlon had said half an hour and she was as good as her word. Huss saw her striding across the station concourse, grim-faced, the commuter crowd unconsciously parting to let her past as she cut through them like a torpedo slicing water. Huss explained what had happened in the back of a black taxi as it ferried them through London.

Huss didn't know London that well, but she recognized St Paul's as they drove past, and the style of the buildings surrounding it – modern, massive, simplistic, temples and shrines to money – as the City. Then the taxi stopped, they got out and she followed Hanlon's slim, muscular back down a couple of narrow, mysterious streets, not much wider than alleys.

It was now nearly seven and the City – London's financial centre – was virtually empty, which, Huss guessed, was how Hanlon liked things. The large, imposing buildings rose up around them, eerily quiet. It was like a deserted film set. The two women slipped through a narrow gate at the back of a tall, darkened, office building, the entry to a shadowy, tiny yard, and squeezed past some wheelie bins overflowing with shredded paper. Hanlon unlocked a nondescript door and motioned ahead of her, locking the door behind them. A secret tradesman's entrance. Huss, still carrying her overnight bag, trotted up a narrow, dingy staircase. She guessed it was the fire exit for the floors that lay the other side of barred emergency doors. It was a part of the building the workers would rarely get to see. The secret world of service corridors, access shafts and service elevators. Not for the general public. Three floors later the staircase ended in two plain green doors, one labelled *Roof access,* the other *Staff only.* She stood to one side while Hanlon unlocked the latter and they ascended a last flight of steps to Hanlon's rooftop eyrie.

Huss gasped in surprise at the stunning view, gazing south over the Thames. It was blocked in part by another couple of office buildings, but you could see the great fast-flowing tidal river, the lights of the Embankment, the buildings like Tate Modern and the Globe on the other side. They were brilliantly illuminated far below.

'What is this place?' she asked.

'Home,' said Hanlon irritably.

It was, in fact, a planning mistake on the architect's part. The space she inhabited had originally been designed as a penthouse for the directors of a company that leased one of the floors below. A change in building regulations regarding fire and purpose of usage had made it impracticable. Unusable.

It belonged to the offshore owners of the building itself and Hanlon, who knew one of the partners, had been here ten years. The room was a footnote in an inventory of the portfolio of a British Virgin Islands company, as noteworthy to the auditors as the concrete shed in the yard they'd walked past, where flammable cleaning products were stored, or the underground storage facility for bicycles for people who worked in the building. The office workers didn't really know of its existence and the maintenance staff remained incurious.

Hanlon never brought people here. Only Mark Whiteside, her friend and colleague, and even then she'd preferred visiting him at his own flat in Holloway. She was furious that Huss was here, furious that fate had conspired to make this inevitable. She was fiercely solitary. She hated having people in her space.

They took up too much room. They polluted it.

'Have a seat,' said Hanlon shortly. The seat. There was only the one, a hard wooden chair by a small table with a laptop and an anglepoise lamp. Its metallic, slim, engineered functional lines reminded Huss of Hanlon.

Huss sat on the chair. She looked around Hanlon's one-roomed apartment. She thought, She obviously doesn't do much entertaining. Then she immediately rolled her eyes mentally at the stupidity of the notion that Hanlon might entertain. Not Hanlon.

These two items, chair and table, were the only visible pieces of furniture. Hanlon's flat was amazingly bleak, not minimalist chic, just bleak. The front of the flat, a rectangular box, was mostly glass. One side was given over to fitted cupboards. The other side was more glass, opaque building blocks of the stuff, and a door leading out to the flat roof of the office building with its maze of ducting and extractor-fan cooling hoods. The other wall had a door, through which they'd come, louvred doors that would open out to reveal a sink and two hotplates with a glass plug-in convection oven and fridge, Hanlon's kitchen, and another door concealed shower and toilet.

The only other things the room contained were a steel frame like a U-shape that supported a bar Hanlon could use as a squat rack, or position above her head for pull-ups, and a pile of weights from twenty kilos downwards to add to the barbell.

The sole decoration was a large framed photograph, black and white, of a seated man in his late forties, in jeans, workboots, shirt and a fisherman's vest. He was wearing a kind of Homburg hat and looked faintly anguished. His eyes were soulful, his build powerful. It looked like it had been taken in the sixties. It had been signed but Huss couldn't read the signature.

The table had a copy of a triathlon magazine and a history of Iran.

The room was frighteningly spartan.

Huss sat down on the chair as instructed and watched as Hanlon opened a cupboard, pulled out a pair of jeans, a hooded top and, from a shoe rack, a pair of calf-high army boots. Ignoring Huss, she stripped off the clothes she was wearing, hung up the jacket and skirt, and put her blouse and tights in a basket in the cupboard. Huss looked enviously at Hanlon's gymnast's body revealed in her black, minimalist underwear. The effort and the discipline it would take to make it look that way was awe-inspiring.

'Where are you going?' Huss asked. Hanlon zipped up her jeans, her flesh above her hips taut over the waistband. Huss could see the outlines of Hanlon's stomach muscles under the skin above her navel. She stood holding the hoodie.

'I think I may have some idea where Enver is being held,' she said. 'So I'm going to take a look.'

Huss stood up. 'I'm coming with you.'

'No, you're not,' said Hanlon, putting on her hoodie. She pushed the legs of her jeans up, showing shapely muscular calves, and pulled on socks.

'Write this address down,' she ordered Huss. Melinda Huss felt irritated at Hanlon's high-handedness, but it was a huge improvement on feeling sick with worry for Enver.

She dictated the Slough address to Huss, who keyed it into her phone while Hanlon laced up the army boots. They were US Army issue, light, perfectly fitting and sturdy. She could run well in them, climb in them, kick in them, and they were amazingly comfortable.

'That's where I'm going. I'm collecting someone to help me get in. I'll be back about midnight.'

She stood up, collected her phone and car keys and another couple of items Huss couldn't see, and shoved them in a small black rucksack.

Hanlon's face was grim but confident.

'And if you're not back by midnight?'

'Call Corrigan.'

'We could do that now,' said Huss. 'Make it official.'

Hanlon stood up. 'I want a run at this by myself. If we call Corrigan now he'll have no choice but to do everything by the book, you know that. And from what you tell me, then Belanov will know everyone's coming. Joad will tell him, this other guy he's got will tell him, and he'll put Enver where he won't be found. And if they bring Belanov and Dimitri in for questioning they'll lawyer up. In fact, they'll probably demand an interpreter,' she said irritably, 'buy themselves even more time.'

Huss knew she was right, but discipline ran deep. 'But we've got resources if we do it properly.'

'We'll get nothing if we do it officially,' said Hanlon. 'Just give me four hours, then we'll know one way or another. Besides,' she added, 'Enver might not even be there. It's just an educated guess on my part.'

'OK,' said Huss warningly. 'Get in touch before midnight or I'll call Corrigan.'

'You do that,' said Hanlon contemptuously. 'You just go ahead and do that.' Huss silently watched her leave. The door clicked to behind her. Enraging and rude, but if anyone was going to find Enver, she'd bet on Hanlon.

Alone, feeling annoyingly useless, Melinda Huss looked

around Hanlon's one-roomed apartment. She sighed and stood up, went over to the cupboard that contained what passed for Hanlon's kitchen and put the kettle on. She opened a cupboard and found some tea bags. There was little else in the cupboard – tins of tuna, dried pasta, rice.

Huss found a cup and opened the fridge. Some cheese, eggs, no milk. She found salt but no sugar. Her stomach rumbled; she was starving. She should have been in the pop-up restaurant with Enver.

Where was he?

Enver, she thought, what have you done?

There was a full-length mirror on the wall facing the bars, where she imagined Hanlon would do intense workouts, checking her form in the mirror. It wouldn't be there for vanity, although it had to be admitted, she thought, that Hanlon was a highly attractive woman. Huss had seen her virtually naked and the effect on a man would be electric.

It was strange but she no longer resented Enver's obsession with Hanlon. The woman was weirdly compelling, as if she exerted an irresistible gravitational pull. Huss was beginning to understand the respect that Hanlon seemed to command, not just in her colleagues from Corrigan down but the world in general. But at what cost? Hanlon's apartment said it all really. A life devoid of comfort, fun, friends.

Oh, well, thought Huss, she's chosen this path, good luck to her. I wouldn't want to be her, although I wouldn't mind those abs. She looked at herself critically in the mirror. She prodded her own stomach experimentally. Bit more give there than on Hanlon's. A lot more, if she was honest. Well, she was attractive too, in a large, generously proportioned way. She smiled at her reflection. Her best dress and jacket were wildly inappropriate for her new, monastic surroundings. She thought, I'll probably have to spend the night here. Huss, in happy preparation for her night with Enver, had packed an Agent Provocateur kimono and a ridiculously skimpy nightdress. She groaned at the thought of wearing them in front of Hanlon; she could imagine her sardonic amusement.

Huss was thinking of anything to avoid thinking of Enver Demirel. Please God, let him be all right, she prayed.

She kicked her heels off and looked around again. No TV, Hanlon's laptop was almost certainly password protected, her own iPad was at home. She hadn't been expecting this. What could she do to kill time? To take her mind off Enver?

She picked up Hanlon's book. She didn't want to be reading this, or anything, for that matter. She wanted to be watching Helena Bonham Carter in a dark cinema, holding Enver's large hand and feeling the sap rising. She shook her head in disbelief. God, I hope he's all right. She started reading about pre-Achaeminid Iran circa three thousand BC. She read that the Elamites destroyed Ur round about two thousand BC. And they're still at it, Huss thought. She turned another page.

It was going to be a long night.

CHAPTER TWENTY-THREE

After meeting Albert Slater at Iris Campion's, in an idle moment at work, Hanlon had looked up his criminal record, which had begun when he was sixteen and had gone on, in various forms, until he was sixty. It took in everything from sex, when being gay had been a crime, to real crime. There had been importuning in a public toilet and gross indecency, Slater's gay martyrdom, that would only end in 1967 when homosexuality was legalized. However, this sexual persecution was leavened with his first conviction for burglary at eighteen and a string of other offences, mainly other counts of burglary of commercial premises. Sex crimes (i.e., convictions for homosexual behaviour) ended in 1967, and real crime, burglary and robbery, took over until the late eighties. His record was sprinkled with occasional affray and a couple of GBH convictions. Slater was quite a violent man.

Something about the aged villain had stimulated Hanlon's curiosity and she had gone for a quiet drink with a copper, now retired from the force, who she had worked with years previously. McClennan had worked with Tremayne, her guv'nor from way back, when she had been a probationer. He knew Albert – *Vicious little bastard, he used to get pissed and cause fights. He'd really camp it up to provoke a reaction and then go for it.* McClennan had taken another sip from his pint. They'd been in a pub in Wardour Street, very close to the Krafft Club, an establishment he would have known well by name, not as a punter.

Francis McClennan had leaned over the small, heavy, circular wooden table and put his face close to hers. The pub had been packed, the noise deafening.

'I tell you something, Hanlon, he was very good at breaking and entering – neat, tidy, knowledgeable. I think he got used on some big jobs, couple down in Hatton Garden, very high security, but Albert was good with electronics. He moved with the times.'

She looked affectionately at McClennan, paunchier, jowlier, redder of face and nose than he had been fifteen years earlier, but still good-looking in a kind of dad-off-the-leash way. He'd got carried away once, drunkenly frisky, and had tried to grab her at a police do when he was very pissed. She'd kneed him hard in the groin. Neither bore the other any resentment. Now McClennan had a business running background checks on people for companies seeking in-depth profiles of potential employees – high-risk, high-responsibility jobs where the employer wanted to know every scrap of carefully buried dirt that may have stuck to the candidate in question. McClennan had the expertise and the contacts and the mindset that made his services highly sought after. He'd been delighted to hear from Hanlon and assist her.

'Albert, hey. I think he sells Chinese stuff now; goes to Hong Kong a lot.'

'Drugs?' asked Hanlon hopefully. McClennan shook his head.

'No, all legit. Furniture, rugs, that kind of stuff. *Chinoiserie*, that's what it's called, isn't it?' He shook his head ruefully at the way of the world. Hanlon could smell his industrially powerful aftershave; his hair was swept back and lacquered into place.

He had a consoling mouthful of beer. She looked at him with genuine regard. '*Chinoiserie*. I don't know, Hanlon. A grown man selling knick-knacks.'

'Do you know his address, Frank?' she asked innocently.

McClennan smiled at her. 'Same old Hanlon, eh?' he said. She had a reputation for leaning on people, for extorting favours. He wondered what she would want from Slater. He considered her request. Hanlon was tainted goods, but she had been his mate's protégée and she had an odd effect of charming people when she wanted to. McClennan looked at her and pushed a hand through his hair, still thick and abundant at sixty-four. He looked at her hard, attractive face, the gleam of her eyes. I wish I was thirty years younger, he thought.

'I'll find out and email it to you.'

And he had. Before he had left Hanlon, he had turned to her. 'You've got my mobile number. You need info on anyone, any time, Hanlon, I'll drop what I'm doing and help. You know that, don't you?'

'Thanks, Frank,' she'd said, touched by the affection in the old copper's voice.

After leaving Huss, Hanlon went straight to Albert's place. It was at the end of a street in Kentish Town on the way up to Tufnell Park, near the Forum. It had been a crappy street in a crappy part of town but now, with the tide of gentrification spreading inexorably from the epicentre of Camden, it had become desirable.

His house was at the end of a terrace. She guessed that there had been another house at one time next to it but it had been demolished, making space for a kind of yard that abutted on to Albert Slater's property. Yellowing bricks that made up the high wall were topped by sagging barbed wire to deter intruders.

Hanlon thought to herself that if anyone knew how to prevent a break-in it would be Albert Slater. She looked more closely at the rusty, sagging barbed wire, saw a double row of gleaming razor wire concealed by the old stuff. A suitable metaphor for Albert himself.

Access to the yard was via a gate wide enough to allow a single vehicle through. The red, rusty metal gates looked old and rickety, but when you got close you noticed that the hinges holding them up were massive and recessed into the brickwork. You also noticed the state-of-the-art computerized keypad, again recessed neatly into the bricks, and a couple of small skeletal cameras monitoring the gates.

She moved on to the house and rang the doorbell. All the windows that faced on to the street were protected by ornamental wrought-iron metal grilles. She noticed again that there was a small camera above the door that inquisitively moved around on its gimbelled mounting as it surveyed her.

The intercom by the door asked, 'And who might you be?' It was Slater's voice, tinny and robotic through the small speaker.

She pushed back the hood of the top she was wearing and stared up at the camera. Their unblinking gazes, her grey eyes, the lens of the camera, met and held.

'DCI Hanlon,' she said. 'Lily Law.'

Hanlon and Albert Slater looked at one another. The elderly criminal was wearing an ornate Chinese mandarin-style dressing gown, the style of which Chantal's Rayon copy had tried childishly to emulate. He was wearing a white silk shirt underneath it, black trousers and black kung fu-style slippers.

The clothes suited him. He looked like a sinister tai pan from Hong Kong. He was dressed more for Kowloon or Canton than Kentish Town.

He had led her from the doorway, a state-of-the-art console just inside the door providing views of the doorway and the street. Her professional eyes had noted the three bolts that would slide into the wall of the house from the door when he closed it. They were activated by a palm-sensitive motion detector that she could hear engaging other locks with synchronized precision. It would have cost thousands. The frame was steel-reinforced. The hinges belonged on a safe. Good luck trying to break that door down, she thought, if the police tried to raid him.

'This way, Hanlon,' he said.

She followed him down the narrow hall passage, piled high with cardboard boxes done up for delivery or receipt, then into Slater's front room.

It was very warm in there and smelled of smoke, stale air and incense. It was dimly lit and crammed with artefacts and handicrafts, some cheap and gimcrack, some obviously extremely expensive. A couple of battery-operated, plastic cats, the kind that you saw in cheap and cheerful Chinese restaurants, their white faces with fixed, painted smiles, endlessly waved their paws in a hypnotically metronomic way. There were expensive-looking oriental rugs, rolled up and stacked like logs of wood, a Chinese suit of armour on a frame – 'Tang Dynasty,' said Slater – ceremonial swords on racks, and other lethal-looking antique weaponry, familiar to her from Hong Kong kung fu films. There were vases and a phalanx of replica terracotta warriors. As well as the chinoiserie, there were reminders of another more techno-savvy Slater. Steel shelving held carefully labelled electronic equipment and circuitry, a bank of monitors flickered randomly, showing images of the front and back of Albert Slater's property, the yard adjoining the house with an old classic Mercedes sports car from the late sixties – '1968 280SL,' said Albert Slater – and next to it a nondescript white Ford

Transit van. Other TV screens stacked on top were broadcasting Sky News, a Chinese channel and several showing a variety of hard-core gay porn like a homoerotic TV showroom. Sucking and fucking, fisting and golden showers, waves of cum sprayed and dripped over faces, buttocks, groins and eager tongues and mouths. The good-luck battery-powered cats sat waving their paws tirelessly at them. The screens displayed the silent, heaving bodies, money shots and the black-and-white exterior of street and yard.

The walls of heavy red-flock wallpaper were decorated with Tom of Finland prints, some signed, Robert Mapplethorpe male nudes and classic Chinese landscapes. There were Japanese *shunga* prints, serious-looking oriental women being penetrated by eye-wateringly large Japanese penises, their owners also serious-looking, inscrutable. The room was dominated by a huge, black-lacquered desk.

Hanlon was inspecting a print showing a gay orgy, more fucking and sucking – there are only so many variations after all – enormous engorged penises, ferociously intent anal sex. Brows were furrowed. More of the same was going on silently on the TV screen.

'Did your *omi-palone sharpy* friend like Tom of Finland?' asked Slater from behind his desk. His voice was sarcastic, the usage of the archaic Polari gay slang a deliberate anachronism to disconcert Hanlon. He had an oriental opium pipe in his hand, a long, thin stem and small bowl.

'He preferred action to looking at pictures,' said Hanlon. 'He was kind of old fashioned that way.' She sat down opposite Slater. The room was lit by a Tiffany lamp. The shadows were deep. The desk had an Apple Mac connected to some kind of external drive before the cable snaked away into the gloomy recesses of the room.

215

Slater touched the device gently. 'Firewall,' he said. 'Can't be too careful.'

Next to the Mac was an old-fashioned telephone with a circular dial. The front of it was given over to numbers 1–9, arranged like a clock. You didn't key the numbers in; you inserted a finger and turned. A receiver was balanced on top: one end for speaking; one end for listening. A curly cable connected it to the box.

'No, no, you can't,' said Hanlon. Slater lit his pipe and inhaled deeply. A plume of greasy black smoke rose upwards. Hanlon could smell the burning opium now, heavy, stifling, powerful. Slater closed his eyes luxuriantly; the room was extremely hot. There were stacks of currency on the desk, tens, twenties, fifties, euro notes and ones she didn't recognize with Chinese characters, presumably yuan. The lazy, oily, fragrant smoke curled into the dark, heavy shadows that surrounded the circle of warm light from the lamp.

'Very daring of you to come and visit an old fruit like me,' said Slater drowsily. 'Sticking your *esong* where it doesn't belong.'

'I need your help,' said Hanlon simply.

'Do you now.' His voice was bored; he sounded extremely stoned.

He didn't see her expression. His eyes were closed. Hanlon stood up very quietly and walked over to behind Albert Slater. She eyed the cord that connected the telephone receiver to its box. She toyed with the idea of wrapping its coiled wires round the old man's throat, and tugging.

'I'd be careful where you put your *luppers*, darling,' said Albert Slater. His right hand was tucked inside the silken folds of the dressing gown. Gun or knife? wondered Hanlon.

She put a gentle hand on his shoulder and leaned her face close to the side of his head, as if she was going to kiss him.

He could smell her perfume. Her hair brushed his cheek. 'A firewall's only good if it can keep things out, and some things are harder to keep out than others. Some things are already here, and some things you can't keep out, you know that, don't you, Albert,' she breathed into his ear. 'Now, you do what I ask you or I'm going to make a call to Dave Anderson.' She paused to let the idea and its implications sink in, before continuing.

'You know the Andersons, don't you, Albert, you know monsters exist.' Her voice was soft, cajoling, almost erotic. 'You know the kind of things they do, Albert, and you know how easily old bones, old bones like yours, can break, don't you, darling, and he'll come visiting with his friend Morris Jones.'

Albert Slater's chair swivelled and Hanlon spun it gently through ninety degrees so Slater was facing her. She placed her hands on the armrests of the chair and leaned forward so their faces nearly touched. He looked into her burning eyes. Her voice was so quiet it was almost a whisper.

'And they'll huff,' she murmured, her eyes holding his hypnotically, 'and they'll puff, and they'll blow your house down.'

She stood up and folded her arms, looking down at Slater. He put the pipe down on the desk and looked at her in an unfriendly way.

'You're a *meshigener* bitch, aren't you, Hanlon,' he said quietly.

'I know,' she said. She clapped her hands together, twice. The noise was almost explosive. 'Now chop-chop, get dressed, Cinderella, you shall go to the ball.'

CHAPTER TWENTY-FOUR

Hanlon parked the Ford Transit near where she'd left her car just a few hours ago. It was now nearly midnight. The roads were hallucinatorily quiet. The industrial park was deserted, the only sign of life an urban fox that had paused to look at them rather insolently at a T-junction. There was something furry in its mouth that had looked suspiciously like a small cat.

Next to her in the other front seat her reluctant passenger grumbled, 'Well, this is all very nice. *Fantabulosa* I very much don't think.'

'Stop moaning, Albert,' said Hanlon. 'We're here.' Albert Slater stared intently at the door in front of him. He was dressed more or less like Hanlon – boots, hoody, jeans. Although he was pushing seventy, and obviously a heavy drug user, he was in surprisingly good shape, she thought.

The warehouse rose up in front of them. In the heavy shadows of the loading bay by the front entrance, screened from the CCTV on the streetlights by a concrete pillared portico, in their dark clothes they were as good as invisible.

There were three locks on the door that Albert had to deal with. He stared at them with an expert eye. Initially, he'd been furious with Hanlon both for threatening him (he knew of the Andersons and they frightened him) and for forcing him into action when all he wanted to do was stay at home.

But now here he was, like the old days, and he was enjoying himself.

He looked hard at the locks. Two of them were straight-forward, a Yale and a Banham mortice lock, old friends, and he had picks in the dark sports bag by his feet to deal with them. Hanlon had told him not to worry about an alarm. The kind of people who had rented this space would most certainly not want to be hooked up to a security company or the police in case the alarm went off, for whatever reason.

The third lock was much more modern than the others technologically, a magnetic lock that he guessed was installed by the new tenants of the warehouse. It was this that had been causing the problem. It was easy to put up, and a bastard to open. He could see why they'd fitted it in addition to the others. Ridiculously simple to fit; practically impossible to break. Because it was just a metal plate and a powerful magnet, there was no need to drill into the doorframe. Albert could have installed it in minutes flat: simple and horribly effective.

It had a key-swipe mechanism attached to the wall to allow access. Unlike the other locks it was brand new.

The lock was pretty secure. Albert guessed it would need about twelve hundred pounds of pressure to force it. Well, that wasn't going to be happening. Or, if it was fail-safe, all you had to do was disrupt the electricity supply. You could dig a hole in the ground where the jacketed mains cable came in, then sever it. Well, that wasn't going to be happening either. Or disable the sub-station. You could always pray for a miraculous power cut.

He scratched his head in frustration. There was something he could try, but he had a feeling it wouldn't work. Not unless he was very lucky.

'Sod it,' he said. Hanlon looked at him questioningly. He shook his head in irritation, rummaged in his bag and held something like a silver, ridged cylinder in his hand. 'Magnet,' he said by way of explanation. If he was lucky and it was an old model, the powerful neodymium magnet should scramble the sensitive internal electrics and release the mechanism. He tried. It wasn't an old model and nothing happened.

Hanlon looked at him angrily.

'What's the matter?' she hissed. Slater indicated the key-swipe mechanism. 'It's magnetic and I can't open it.' He had a sudden thought. 'The fire alarm probably will, that should trip it. Should have that as a safety feature.'

Hanlon rolled her eyes. Any sensors would be inside the building. It'd be a catch-22 situation: to open the door, you'd have to get in first. To get in, first you'd have to open the door. Well, she'd have to find another way in. She'd thought it might come to this. She said to Slater, 'Have you got anything to break glass in there?' She pointed at his bag.

Slater nodded and pulled out a small break-glass hammer. 'Won't work,' he said. He thought she was going to try it on the keypad, to try smashing it.

'Yes, it will,' said Hanlon. She put it in her rucksack. 'Lighter?'

Slater reached again into his bag. He looked quizzically at Hanlon. She was looking upwards at the side of the building. Now Slater guessed what was in her mind. She asked him, 'So the fire alarm will open the door? '

He nodded. 'Yeah, it's a safety feature so people don't get trapped if a fire breaks out. So if you activate it by lighting a fire under a sensor, it should work. But there's probably a release button by the side of the door anyway, on the inside. It's designed to keep people out, not in.' He nodded at the other locks. 'I can open these for you if you want. So all you'll have to do is pop that beauty.'

Hanlon was now sitting on the ground, unlacing her boots. 'You do that,' she said. 'I'll deal with that one.'

She pulled her socks off and stuffed them in her bag; her boots she tied together and hung from round her neck. She stretched and flexed her toes. Then she stood up and motioned to Slater to follow.

The walls rose up about eight metres sheer until the windows appeared. There was a ledge below the windows, a ledge she could use. The concrete portico by the door would gain her a couple of metres of distance less to climb and there was a plastic drainpipe that ran from the guttering above. She wasn't going to put her weight on it; she doubted it would take the strain. But she could use it as a partial climb-hold while her toes took the main weight of her body. Balance and angle were everything.

Slater guessed what she wanted him to do. He laced his fingers in front of him and Hanlon stepped into the cup of his hands, and he boosted her up. Momentarily he felt the cool, taut muscle of the underside of her foot, and then she was up onto the flat surface of the portico.

She walked across the small flat roof to the wall of the building. The concrete felt cold beneath her feet. She touched the wall experimentally, examining it carefully. It was made of large breeze blocks, the only weight it supported being the lightweight roof. The mortar between the large blocks was worn and grooved; it needed repointing. She nodded her head, satisfied. The slight indentations would be enough to give her purchase.

Hanlon pushed her body close in to the wall and, using her right hand to grip round the pipe, reached up with her left until she got some hold on the narrow, shallow gap between the blocks and, body pressed hard to the wall, she started her climb.

She thanked her lucky stars that the weather had been dry and the composite man-made stone wasn't damp or slippery. Her fingers, from years of push-ups balanced on their tips, were like iron. Hanlon loved natural workouts, and her grip from exercises as simple as squeezing a tennis ball or pinch-grip holds on a chin-up bar had made her slim forearms intensely powerful.

Albert Slater watched her ascent from the shadows below with professional, evaluative admiration. He'd done his share of cat burglary when young, mainly hotels where there were umpteen hand and footholds from balconies and ornamental stonework like friezes and decorative ridging. Easy stuff compared to this. He appreciated the strength and grace of Hanlon's ascent.

She was now just below the window and he watched open-lipped, his teeth clenched in worry, as she reached out with her left hand. Now was the point of greatest danger. If she slipped or her grip failed, she'd fall to her death, no doubt about it.

She's got some nerve, he thought admiringly.

She was holding the ledge with the top joints of her fingers of the one hand, hanging her whole weight there as she pulled the emergency hammer Slater had given her from the top of her boot, which held it like an improvised scabbard, and swung it in a short explosive arc against the glass. God, she's strong, he thought. He heard the glass shatter, a sharp, brittle noise, and he watched as Hanlon, still hanging one-handed, gently swept her right hand over the ledge, checking for glass, moving what there was off the ledge so she didn't cut herself. He heard it land on the concrete below, near where he was standing. Most of it had fallen inwards and now she was able to pull herself up and lean her weight on the sill of the window, her legs outside, her torso invisible in the building.

He exhaled slowly. Only now did he realize he'd been holding his breath as he had watched.

He momentarily wondered how she would get down inside, then, as he watched, she smashed the adjacent window so the metal strut of the frame was exposed, and took something from her bag. She snapped a carabiner, such as climbers used, like a steel D-shaped ring, round it. She pulled a rope from her rucksack, tied a quick double clovehitch round it to secure it to the carabiner and disappeared into the blackness of the warehouse.

He checked his watch. Five minutes. Slick and quick.

Time for him to open the other two locks. He set to work.

Inside the warehouse, Hanlon climbed down the narrow rope hand after hand, holding on tight to the knotted thin line to avoid any friction on her palms.

The warehouse was dark and silent. And as her eyes adjusted to the gloom, the orange streetlights from outside providing some illumination, she saw the barrels in the centre of the room and on the far side a figure seated on the floor.

Hanlon let go of the rope and jumped the last few feet lightly to the concrete floor. She crossed over to the far side of the warehouse and as she got nearer saw that the seated figure was a young woman with blonde hair. She flinched as Hanlon came closer and she could see that the girl was attached to the radiator by a pair of loose-link handcuffs.

'It's OK,' said Hanlon soothingly. 'I'm not going to hurt you.'

The girl drew her knees up to her chest, her eyes wide with fright, and said, 'Who are you?'

Hanlon crouched down to be at her level and said, 'I'm going to fetch something to cut you free. What's your name?'

'Chantal. Chantal Jenkins.' She still looked terrified, her face a mass of matted, dyed-blonde hair and tear-streaked eyeliner. She smelled of sweat, cheap perfume and fear.

'Well, Chantal, I'm Hanlon, DCI Hanlon. I'm police. I'm looking for a colleague of mine, Enver Demirel.'

Chantal nodded. 'He was here.' She spoke clearly and earnestly like a child. 'But Dimitri took him away.'

Damn it, thought Hanlon. A horrible thought crossed her mind. 'Was he. . . ?'

Chantal guessed her meaning and shook her head. 'He was alive,' she said. Just, she didn't add. She had kept her eyes firmly closed during Dimitri's assault on Enver. It had been audible only as a series of grunts, thuds and oaths in Russian. Enver of course couldn't speak, couldn't cry out, couldn't scream, not with the tape over his mouth. Once she'd heard a muffled snap that had almost made her howl.

She had opened her eyes and seen blood, a lot of blood. Even now she could see dark spots of it on the floor, blacker shapes on the shadows of the concrete. They looked like oil stains. But they weren't. Periodically she would hear a tearing noise as the tape was ripped from Enver's mouth. She'd heard him speak, his words punctuated by gasps of pain, and once she had opened her eyes to see and hear the big policeman say, 'Corrigan. Corrigan sent me.'

Dimitri had squatted down. 'And what does he want to know?'

Enver was silent and Dimitri turned round and picked up a small chisel and a hammer. He showed them to Enver. 'And what does he want to know?' Enver shook his head. Dimitri tore another strip of tape off and bound Enver's mouth.

The Russian's phone had rung again. He answered it and Chantal had heard him get increasingly irritable. He had stopped his interrogation. Soon after that two men had arrived, both Russian, one hugely fat. She recognized him from Curtis's description. It had to be Arkady Belanov. The other was nondescript, thin with a swelling, nascent gut and a very expensive-looking suit. His black shoes gleamed in the faint light and she could smell the polish. Then footsteps and a third man joined them, Joad.

Hanlon interrupted Chantal's account.

'I'm going to fetch help. I'll be back in a minute.' She pulled socks and boots on, not bothering to lace them up, and stalked across the floor to the internal door. She entered the lobby and switched the light on. There, to the left of the door, was a panel, where Albert Slater had predicted it would be. It had a round control button that she depressed with the side of a clenched fist. There was an audible clunking noise as the magnetic lock disengaged.

Chantal saw the light go on. She re-ran the memories in her head. Hanlon would want to hear everything. Black shoes had filled her vision as someone had crouched down in front of her, taking her chin between thumb and forefinger, and tilted her head to the left and right. He'd said something in Russian to Arkady Belanov.

'He says open your mouth.'

She did so and he examined her teeth, as if she were an animal, a horse or a dog. He appeared satisfied and stood up. More Russian.

'Bring him with us,' said Belanov to Joad, pointing at Enver. They unlocked Enver from the radiator. He was unconscious. His head was beginning to swell and it was horribly misshapen. His flesh was like rising dough. They cuffed him again, wrists and ankles, then Dimitri took his armpits, Joad his feet, and they carried him out. Belanov and Black Shoes turned and followed. Arkady said, 'We'll be back for you in the morning.'

***

Now Hanlon was returning with another man carrying a holdall. He was wearing a beanie and Chantal saw that he was old, really old, although you wouldn't know it from the athletic way he moved. He sat down on his heels beside her and took a small pair of bolt cutters from the sports bag. Then she was free.

She stood up, rubbing her arms. She was desperate to leave. She kept thinking that any moment Dimitri might return. If Hanlon was police, why were there only two of them? Where were the uniforms? she wondered.

'Come with us,' said Hanlon.

'Where are we going?' Chantal asked nervously. As she watched, Hanlon looked down at where Enver had been secured. Blood, looking like rust in the dim light, streaked the faded cream paint of the radiator. She looked hard, rubbed it with a fingertip and sniffed it. She crouched down and did the same where more of Enver's blood had pooled. She looked at Chantal. She nodded at the policewoman.

'His.'

Hanlon nodded. Her face was mask-like, sinister. She said silently to herself, *And I am the avenger, who carries out God's wrath on the wrongdoer.*

She turned to Chantal, nodding at Albert Slater. 'We're going to his place.'

'What's wrong with your gaff?' grumbled Slater. 'Why my *lattie*?'

Hanlon glared at him. 'Because it's so *dolly* compared to mine.' She emphasized the adjective sarcastically. Albert Slater wasn't the only one who knew Polari. She turned and jerked her head. 'Come on, I've had enough of this place.'

The three of them turned and left the warehouse. Before she

turned off the light in the deserted bare reception area, Hanlon looked at the oil drums for a last time. It was a hard look.

She looked at her fingers. She had Enver's blood on her hands. Belanov, I'm coming for you, she thought.

CHAPTER TWENTY-FIVE

Joad parked the car on the outskirts of Oxford in the part of town near Blenheim Palace, a grateful nation's gift to Winston Churchill's ancestor. He and Dimitri got out and the Russian took his place at the wheel and drove off. He watched the tail light of the Mercedes disappear. His Mercedes, as he was coming to think of it. He'd already had the computerized details of the key copied by a friend of his who had a repair shop specializing in high-end German cars. Just in case. Soon it will be mine, he thought. I'll steal it if necessary.

Joad wasn't visiting Blenheim Palace. He was on his way to Leighton Crescent where a prostitute of long-standing acquaintance was waiting for him.

Elzbieta, Lizzy – blonde, buxom, forty, from Wroclaw – poured Joad a hefty vodka on ice and lit a cigarette. She looked at Joad amicably enough. She'd known him for ten years or so and although he expected her services for free in return for looking the other way, and once or twice handling troublesome clients and the odd pimp, he did pay her for information and, in fairness, if he stayed for a longer session he did recompense her for lost business. As Joad grew older, he found it was taking more and more time to engage his body in sensual activity. He didn't know if it was age or laziness, but sex was increasingly a bit of an effort.

Viagra, here we come, he thought. He wasn't troubled at all.

'So, what can I do for you, Ian?' Lizzy purred, stroking Joad's thigh and placing one of his hands on her large right breast. He absent-mindedly stroked it like the old friend it was and took a drink of his vodka. The cold, raw spirit burned his throat in a pleasing way and he took Lizzy's Marlboro from her other hand and inhaled a deep lungful of smoke. His GP had told him to stop smoking, but so far he'd stopped buying cigarettes and just smoked other people's. He was amazed at the money he was saving.

He took his phone out of his pocket. Back in Slough, he and Dimitri had loaded the unconscious, bound Enver into the boot of the Mercedes. Joad had spread a tarp across the fabric of the well of the space to stop any blood seeping into the pile of the fabric. He wasn't concerned with the possibility of forensic evidence, but he didn't want the carpeted interior getting dirty. He fretted about the car. He tore some holes in a plastic bag and fitted it over Enver's motionless, swollen head.

'He will *doushit*,' protested Dimitri. Plans had most definitely changed. He really didn't want Enver dead now.

Joad looked at him blankly. 'Do what?'

Dimitri said, '*Doushit*, I do not know word, die when is no air.'

'Oh, suffocate. No, he won't,' said Joad. Most of Enver's blood was coming from his head and hands. He wrapped some plastic sheeting over the raw wounds on Enver's fingers where Dimitri had obviously been busy. He didn't want trace blood in his car. No mess in his nice car.

'He's got plenty of air through those holes. He'll be fine.'

He tucked the policeman up in the tarp and closed the boot. He got behind the wheel; Dimitri and Belanov were in the back. Myasnikov had been picked up by someone on the corner, out of Joad's sight. He heard Dimitri make reference to the *Kitayets*. The Chinaman. They'd really got some respect for this Chinaman despite the botched assassination attempt on Anderson. He added this fact to his mental file on the Russians that he carried within his excellent, police-trained memory. A lifetime of orderly and methodical information storage stood him in good stead. Like most policemen he had very good recall.

While he'd been arranging Enver in the boot, he'd switched the recorder of his phone on. The Russians obligingly started talking the minute he switched the engine on.

Joad's inbuilt alarm system, even more sensitive than the Mercedes, had told him that crunch time was coming. He still knew very little about what had happened in the brothel in London or the incidents in Slough, not in detail anyway, but he was aware of the disappearance of Curtis and obviously the far from rosy fate of Chantal. The half-dead policeman in the boot of the car was a clear sign that things were ramping up in a highly ominous way.

Myasnikov and the other two could always hightail it back to Russia. It was all right for them. There were almost certainly people there who would swear blind they'd never left the motherland, while the British police gnashed their teeth impotently. Litvinenko all over again. They'd never be extradited. This luxury wouldn't be available to Joad. Joad wouldn't be able to flee; he'd be stuck between a hard place and a rock.

No sunny retirement in Spain. Carrying the can for a dead cop. Carrying the can for God knows what. I should cocoa, thought Joad. Fuck that.

He handed his phone to Lizzie, explaining what he wanted her to do. Lizzie, he knew, spoke good Russian; she used to work in St Petersburg. She went next door to her kitchen to transcribe Joad's recording and he put on one of her porn DVDs that she kept for her customers. He refreshed his drink and watched while two girls pleasured an athletic-looking black guy. He yawned and closed his eyes.

'Oh yes, baby, oh yes, that feels so good,' one of the girls was saying. 'Ooh, it's so big.'

Joad nodded off; it had been a long day.

Lizzie rubbed her eyes in the kitchen and put her pen down. Her Russian had been good but it was rusty now. She hadn't bothered to write down the conversation verbatim, but it was fairly straightforward. The Russians had a man – she gathered, although it wasn't made explicit, that he was a policeman – as a *zalozhnik*. She puzzled over the word, then it came to her: hostage. They were going to use that man as a hostage to lure some woman, a *bliyad*, a bitch, presumably another cop, to where he was being kept. How they would do this, they didn't seem to know themselves. But they did want the woman.

Lizzie found it hard to listen to what they planned to do to her. It was a question of revenge, that was for sure – *mest*, Russian for revenge – but they went into stomach-churning details, *golaya*, involving naked, graphic descriptions that she found nauseating. She wouldn't want to be in that woman's shoes, that was for sure.

She knew of Belanov and Dimitri by reputation. One of the girls from the Woodstock Road brothel had worked with her and some other girls at a party organized for some high-ranking VIPs, diplomats and senior legal advisers to the British government, who had been at a Commonwealth civil rights conference held at a large, exclusive hotel not far from Oxford. Anastasia (her working name) had told her of the dreadful lives they were leading. A few months later she had seen an e-fit of Anastasia's face – *Do you know this woman?* – in a local paper.

Dead of a drugs overdose, found in the River Evenlode near Oxford. Foul play wasn't suspected, but Lizzie knew that the girl from Donetsk had escaped from Belanov and his cruelty the only way she had felt certain would work.

She wondered what this Hanlon had done to them to make them both hate her so much. The two Russians were keen to keep all of this from another Russian, sometimes they called him Konstantin Alexandrovich, sometimes *Miasnik*, the Butcher. She gathered that this campaign against Hanlon was of their own devising, that she had humiliated them in some way that they didn't want to tell their boss about. *Miasnik* wasn't to know.

Then they started talking about *yborka doma*, house-cleaning, and Lizzie really started to pay attention.

Lizzie woke Joad up from his sleep in the armchair in a state of agitation. She switched the TV off.

'Calm down,' said Joad, yawning. 'What's the matter?'

She started talking. Myasnikov had decided on a compulsory redundancy scheme of his own devising of his UK staff. *Vse izmenniki umrout*. Death to all traitors. Curtis was dead and Joad was next on the list. Joad nodded, entirely unfazed by this development. And what about the man from the council, he asked, Steve Berlington? Him too, said Lizzy, and do you know someone who is Chinese?

'The Chinaman?' said Joad.

Lizzie nodded. 'He's the one who's going to do it.' Joad asked when and where and Lizzie said, 'In the next two weeks. This Myasnikov flies home soon. He wants to make sure everything is arranged and in place before then.'

'Anything else?' asked Joad.

Lizzie nodded. 'This man Enver. They want to keep him alive to use as bait to catch some woman called Hanlon. They don't know how, but that's their plan.'

'Any idea where they're keeping him?' asked Joad.

'Either a farm or a cottage, does that mean anything?' Annoyingly, it didn't. Lizzie carried on. 'Their boss doesn't know about any of this plan concerning the woman. It seems to be their own pet project.'

'Is there more?' asked Joad.

Lizzie nodded. 'Myasnikov wants them to up the pressure on someone called Anderson. Myasnikov wants Anderson to sell him a place in London in the next two weeks. He's very clear that he doesn't want Anderson dead until he's signed off on this place in Marylebone.'

Joad nodded, satisfied.

He did a swift mental recap of his own position: the Russians wanted him dead; the police (as epitomized by Huss) wanted him out or in prison; he had no friends; he had no allies.

Business as usual then. Ian Joad versus the world. So far, Joad was winning.

On the other side of things: he wanted the Russians incapacitated; the police off his back; Belanov's Mercedes and a suitable amount of money to enlarge the Joad pension pot. He'd also like sex with Huss, despite the potential erectile problems, but he figured you had to be realistic.

He'd settle for shafting the Russians.

Lizzie looked at Joad with concern. She didn't exactly like him, but she felt some concern for anyone she knew who was going to cross swords with Belanov. There was an odd look on Joad's face.

Even Huss wouldn't have been able to fault Joad's ability to rise to a challenge. It had also rekindled his appetite for sex in a way that the hard-core porn had failed to do. Action made Joad horny.

Lizzie placed her hand firmly between his legs. 'My, my,' she said automatically, with practised skill. God knows how often she'd said it. 'Is that all for me?'

As they stumbled up the stairs together towards her bedroom, locked in a firm embrace, Joad's lips against hers, she realized that the strange expression on Joad's face was one of happy anticipation.

He's madder than I realized, she thought.

CHAPTER TWENTY-SIX

Serg Surikov stretched his long, muscular body luxuriously in the goosedown comfort of Francine Edwards's large double bed and looked at her shapely nakedness as she checked her emails on her laptop.

She was sitting cross-legged with her back to him. He gently ran his index finger down the ridges of her vertebrae at the nape of her hairline downwards. She tilted her head left then right, freeing the tension in the muscles at the base of her neck. She grinned at him over her shoulder; she had a goofy, infectious grin that was incredibly attractive.

Her fingers clicked away at the keyboard.

Golaya, obnazhenniy. Those were the Russian adjectives. In English *naked*, thought Serg, *nude, in the nuddy. Unclothed, unclad.* Other synonyms floated through his mind – *bare, stripped.* And not just single words but collocations, *birthday suit,* and slang, *stark bollock naked.* What a rich language English was. He loved words. I'm a vocabulary junky, he thought. Of course, appropriateness of language was always tricky, *a thorny question,* he thought, pleased with himself. Could he say that Ms Edwards was stark bollock naked, given that she was female, or would that only refer to men like him? He didn't like to ask. He'd had ample experience of adverse reactions to questions relating to non-erotic matters while making love.

His attention would wander from his partner and he'd follow a train of thought unrelated to sex. It was unpopular, that much was undeniable.

'How long have you worked for Thanatos?' asked Edwards. She scratched her thick dark hair and the heavy silver bracelets that she wore jangled as they slid down her forearm.

'A year or so,' said Serg. It wasn't true; it was a lie, an evasion, a falsehood, a porky. That was so beautiful, he thought, *porky*, a *porky pie* equals *lie*. Rhyming slang, fantastic, although now, sadly, beginning to die out.

'And they brought you over as Charlie Taverner's replacement?'

Serg nodded. 'I did a lot of work for him, information gathering, in Moscow. And, of course, I know Edward Li quite well. He was a good friend of my father's.'

Edwards looked round. 'Was?'

Serg shrugged. 'He died. Well, he was killed, in the first Chechen war.'

'I'm sorry,' said Edwards.

Serg shrugged. 'It doesn't matter,' he said. Another porky, he thought. His hand moved further down her body, gently massaging the muscles that ran down by her spine, and he noted Edwards's breathing deepen. She logged off and clicked the laptop shut, then turned round.

Serg's eyes, she decided, were kind of feline; they even gleamed like a cat's. He had the sensitive face of a poet with a hint of Cossack warrior, she thought. Was that fanciful? She didn't care. He was beautiful and she wanted him. She ran her eyes over his long, lean body, his elegant muscular thighs. She traced his ribs with one blood-red fingernail. She pushed her hair away from her face with both hands. Serg's eyes widened appreciatively as she knew they would. She had great breasts. She leaned her body over his. 'Darling,' she breathed.

Betrayal, thought Serg, as her dark hair brushed his face and her tongue sought his. *Stabbing in the back, duplicity, treachery, deception.*

Later, afterwards, Edwards was in the shower.

He opened her laptop and typed in her password, which, glimpsed over her shoulder, he'd memorized earlier. A nice, strong password. He had a couple of decryption programs on a memory stick but now he wouldn't need to use it. Just as well, he thought, it'd take too long. Quickly, his fingers an efficient blur, he found an address book and Hanlon's work address and mobile number. He had what he'd come here for. Bingo!

He closed down where he'd been and entered the details into his phone.

Edwards reappeared in the bedroom and started opening drawers and pulling on underwear. Serg watched her, half lasciviously, half running through his underwear vocabulary database in his head. A German word for vocabulary, and Serg's German was good, was *wortschatz*, word treasure. And this was, in a way, how Serg felt about lexis – a treasure chest of shiny adverbial rubies and ingots of noun gold and filigreed strings of verbal pearls that he could dive his hands into, like a miser with a hoard of Krugerrands or Maria Theresa thalers.

Pants, panties, knickers, he thought. But she's not wearing a thong or bloomers; they're different. Opposite ends of the underwear spectrum.

Francine Edwards looked at him sternly. 'You're a foreign national,' she said with mock severity. 'You shouldn't be looking at Foreign Office briefs.'

Serg pointed at the triangle of black fabric she was wearing. 'They are briefs?'

'They are indeed,' said Edwards.

'It is a pun?' She nodded. Fantastic, thought Serg.

'So what is the other meaning of *brief*? Not, I would estimate, *short* as in *Brief History of Time*.'

Wearily, Francine Edwards started to explain.

CHAPTER TWENTY-SEVEN

The Huss family farm lay at the end of a private road. Thick hawthorn hedgerow bushes grew alongside the main road and bordered the fields that lay on either side of the lane.

Huss glanced in her mirror, indicated left and turned into the narrow track, wide enough for only one car at a time. The car jolted over the cattle grid near the road with a rumbling, crashing sound and then she stamped on the brake as a Volvo estate pulled out of a passing place and drove straight towards her. She braked savagely, suddenly furious at this interloper on Huss property.

Huss's Golf and the Volvo were practically bonnet to bonnet like two snarling dogs, each unwilling to back down. Huss unbuckled her belt and angrily got out of the car, as did the other driver.

'Hello, Melinda,' said Joad with an unpleasant smile. His hands were hidden behind his back.

'What the fuck do you want, Joad?' spat Melinda Huss. It was a sign of how preoccupied she was that she hadn't noticed who was driving the other car. Unconsciously her fists had balled as she took a step towards him.

'Just this,' said Joad, bringing his hand forward and showing her what he had in his grasp.

Huss recoiled in horrified disbelief.

'That's right,' said Joad. 'Take a good look at it.' He gave what he was holding to Huss. Joad nodded grimly. 'I think you'd better come with me, don't you?'

Huss nodded unhappily.

'Now,' said Joad, 'reverse back, let me out and follow my car, have you got that?'

Huss complied. She followed Joad's car in her own, her thoughts dulled both by misery and confusion.

She followed him up to the main highway, her mind full of unanswered questions. They drove down some minor B roads until they came to a car park in the middle of nowhere surrounded by Oxfordshire woodland. There were several vehicles there, all estates, all with either mesh screens in the back or cages to restrain dogs.

Joad got out of his car and into the passenger seat of Huss's Golf. She held Enver's bloodstained warrant card in one hand. She had been crying as she drove. Now her eyes were dry and hard. She wasn't going to weep in front of Joad.

'You want to explain this?' she demanded.

Joad said, 'You don't much like me, do you, Huss?' He could see the rage in her eyes. Even Huss's blonde hair seemed to bristle with anger and distaste. Her blouse was unbuttoned a couple of notches and Joad stared with frank admiration at the top of her breasts. She was a very attractive woman in her own large way. He pulled his wandering attention back to the business in hand.

'If you'd like to listen, Huss, I might be able to help you save Enver Demirel.'

'Go ahead, Joad,' she said, a threateningly angry undertone in her voice. 'You go ahead and do that. And, Joad, it had better be good or I'll rip your balls off.'

Joad smiled at her. 'It's the real deal, Huss. We both happen to want the same things. Now, if you'll allow me to begin?'

And he started to talk.

CHAPTER TWENTY-EIGHT

Enver Demirel came to lying next to a wall in a small, window-less room lit by a single bulb. His hands and his feet were manacled together.

Another day, another radiator, he thought, staring at the only thing in the room beside himself. He was vaguely surprised to find he was still alive. Memories flickered and coalesced in his mind as his brain started to function again. Memories of Dimitri; memories of Slough and Chantal.

He sat upright with a great deal of effort and explored his aching body. In fairness, he had sometimes, once or twice, felt worse after a twelve-round fight. That had meant thirty-six minutes of being punched repeatedly. How long had Dimitri worked on him? He couldn't say.

He remembered the hammer; he remembered the chisel; he remembered the blowtorch. His body remembered the pain.

He explored his mouth with his tongue. His teeth were mir-aculously intact, but his eyes didn't open properly. He guessed his face and head were pretty badly swollen as he gingerly felt them. His hands were nightmarish. Agonizingly sore, they looked like fleshy oven gloves. Two or three fingers on each hand were probably broken; he was missing fingernails. He turned his gaze away. Just looking at them was making him feel sick, and every time his heart beat the puffy, tight, hot flesh on each hand throbbed as the blood tried to force its way through the constricted vessels. He wondered what he was doing here and where he was. He guessed he would find out eventually.

Dimitri and Arkady Belanov were not happy men. Normally, neither of them had to think long term. Arkady was a problem-solver. As a teenage hood, he'd beaten people up to order. As a conscript soldier, first in the regular army then Spetsnatz, he'd fought or killed to order. In prison, he'd provided the muscle for the *vor* and, of course, now Myasnikov gave the orders and he followed them.

But Hanlon, like all women in his view, had confused things. She had got in the way of his relationship with the Butcher. He'd been too proud to tell Myasnikov of his and Dimitri's humiliation at her hands. He could barely admit it to himself. Now Joad had informed him that Hanlon was determined to save Demirel, that they could use him as bait. It was his plan, but taken over and refined by Joad.

'It's what you said you wanted, Hanlon. I can find her now.' Joad's voice on the phone was clear and confident.

'How?' Arkady had asked. Suspicion and hope both waged a battle in his heart.

'I work with Demirel's girlfriend. She knows Hanlon. I can tip her off; she'll tell Hanlon. Hanlon will come.'

Joad's voice on the phone was calm and relaxed. It was an unusual experience to be more or less telling the truth to disseminate a lie. It made life a lot easier. Arkady looked at Dimitri, who shrugged.

'How do we know the police won't turn up?' asked Arkady suspiciously.

Joad sighed. 'Because both Hanlon and Huss know you have someone who works for you in a high place in the force. You can't mobilize an armed response unit discreetly. I'd know and so would that other copper you've got working for you. You'd know immediately if either of them made it official.'

Arkady nodded. It made sense. From what he knew of Hanlon she would prefer acting alone. It had happened in the past; it would happen again.

'What will you tell Huss to make her believe you?'

Joad grinned broadly as he held the mobile phone to his mouth. He was glad Dimitri couldn't see his face. 'DI Huss thinks I'm a bent copper, so I'm going to tell her a little bird told me that you were thinking of retiring me. Permanently. You follow me so far?'

'Oh, yes,' said Arkady. It was his turn to grin broadly now; so did Dimitri. 'It makes sense.' Of course it does, he thought, since that is what we were planning to do to you anyway.

'So,' continued Joad, 'I get her to fetch Hanlon to take you out. Now, you've met Hanlon. She's not one for sitting around, twiddling her thumbs. One of her ex-sergeants is in a coma, thanks to her. She'll do anything to avoid losing another one. I think we can safely say she'll be down at your gaff like a rat up a drainpipe. Oh, and, Arkady, Huss will almost certainly want to hear Demirel's voice or she won't believe me. Don't do anything stupid like kill him. Not for the moment.'

Silence on the phone. For an agonizing second, Joad thought, Christ, I hope they haven't killed him. Then relief washed over him.

'I like this idea,' said Arkady with approval. 'And this woman, Huss, afterwards?'

'I don't know,' said Joad tetchily. 'You could shut her up, permanently, but Huss lives with her parents. I'm sure that you can explain to her what the consequences of her talking would be, not just to her, but to them. But she's not my problem, mate.'

'Yes, that would work,' said Arkady. 'You have their address and details?'

'Yes,' said Joad. 'Thing is, Arkady, I'm going to find it hard working with Huss after this. I'll have to go for early retirement, until the pension kicks in. I don't want to lose money, even for a friend like you.'

'How much?'

'Hundred and the Merc. I've got attached to it.'

'One hundred, no Merc. I am attached to it.'

'Jesus Christ, Arkady,' protested Joad. 'Even Judas got thirty pieces of silver.'

'That was for son of God,' said Arkady curtly. 'You're just giving me one woman and one fat Turk. Come to Woodstock Road, one hour, we work out details.'

'I'll be there,' said Joad.

He turned his phone off and looked at the woman beside him in the passenger seat.

'This had better work, Joad,' said DI Huss. Until now she had been primarily concerned with Enver's safety. With a horrible chill of certainty she realized that what Joad had said was true. Belanov would not hesitate to have her silenced, or her family. It's what men like him did. He tortured women for fun with a blowtorch. Belanov had machine-gunned families in the Caucasus: men, women and children. He had strapped suspects to artillery shells in Chechnya and blown them to pieces so no shred, no trace would remain. It was called 'pulverization'. He would do the same again in Oxfordshire. He wouldn't care. And if he was arrested, a proxy would do it for him. The terrifying thing about Belanov and Dimitri was that there were a lot of them around. They weren't just isolated monsters.

Joad was genuinely aggrieved that she sounded so aggressive. Hadn't he just saved her boyfriend?

'Don't say thank you, then, fatso,' he said angrily. 'Let's just hope Hanlon doesn't let you down.'

Huss stared at him grimly. 'She won't, Joad. She won't.'

CHAPTER TWENTY-NINE

'No, your posture's still all wrong,' said Mawson to Hanlon. The two of them were at a range that the DS used near Slough. Range was a possibly over-descriptive word. It was a field screened by scrubby trees. At one end of the field there was an embankment where spoil had been dumped years ago, forming a natural earthwork to act as a barrier to the bullets.

Hanlon had been driving around with her .22 rifle in its gun bag in the boot of her car ever since Mawson had promised her a shooting lesson. Being taught to improve by a Bisley champion, one of the best shots in the country, was not an opportunity to be missed. Hanlon was always keen to learn from an expert. She loved learning new things and building on existing knowledge.

Mawson had examined her rifle, an old Ruger that she'd bought second hand from Tremayne, her former boss, way back when. Hanlon was a good shot. She belonged to a range in West London, and occasionally spent time in the summer with a box of cartridges, unhurriedly shooting at targets. It was quiet – her gun had a suppressor, although a .22 didn't make much noise anyway – and relaxing. She enjoyed the camaraderie of her fellow marksmen, generally placid, friendly, middle-aged men from a variety of backgrounds. Target shooting was very democratic, very egalitarian, unlike thousand-pound-a-day game shoots where the emphasis was as much on who had the most expensive shotgun as it was on marksmanship.

Mawson examined the gun, snapped it shut, squinted down the sights, put a shell in it and fired a shot at a target halfway down the field. The business of checking the accuracy of her sights had begun.

When that was done, when he'd made minor adjustments to the positioning of her scope, zeroed the sights to a hundred metres accuracy, he said to her, 'You see that "shoot n-c" target to the left.' Obediently, she looked down the sight at the piece of paper with the concentric rings of the target, a drawing pinned to a post. 'Six shots on that, please, in your own time. There's no rush.'

Mawson watched as Hanlon lay prone on the ground, her rifle resting on his tightly folded jacket, the slight breeze playing with the curls of her dark hair, her face concentrated as she worked the bolt.

He put the field glasses to his eyes and looked at the rings of the target she was shooting at. It wasn't perfect, but for an amateur it was extremely impressive. He studied the groupings of the shots and made a mental note of areas that needed to be covered.

Zero sights at 100 metres; not happy with her trigger action; think, press, rather than pull. Never snatch, you should know that, Hanlon. Another trick you can do is to start the press motion with the little finger and work upwards, little finger, ring finger, middle finger now. . . bingo. Always be gentle.

'Have you got that, Hanlon?'

'Yes, sir.'

'After you shoot don't look up. Keep your focus through the scope. If you miss, then at least you'll see where your shot went. If you hit, you'll see where you hit.'

An hour went by with Mawson patiently improving her technique, then he set up a new target at a hundred and fifty metres. She could feel herself improving under his expert instruction. Her spirits rose. She was almost happy. 'We'll make this the final one,' he said. Hanlon nodded.

She lay down on Mawson's coat, which he had gallantly spread on the ground for her, and rested the barrel of her rifle on her own rolled-up jacket.

'Remember what I said about posture,' he told her. 'And one little tip, Hanlon. If you're not using a bipod, and you're in a field somewhere in the country, think fence post or wall. You can always use where the horizontal bar meets the vertical, if necessary, for a prone shot. Got that? Now, clear to fire.'

The field was sizeable and there were only the two of them in it. Despite the sense of space, the whole universe for Hanlon had contracted down to what she could see through the circle of the scope and its cross-hairs. She concentrated hard on the placing of her shots, aiming high to allow for the fall in the arc of trajectory of the bullet. She fired, worked the bolt, ejected the spent cartridges, and then they were done.

They walked up and checked the shoot n-c paper target. There was a bull, then a circle to denote a score of nine and another to show a score of eight, in the black three-inch centre of the target. The first two shots were high left. Adjusting as he had shown her for the height and direction by a couple of notches on the scope, she'd dropped the next two bang in the centre, in the bull.

'Compare this to your other one,' said Mawson. There was a dramatic difference between her first attempt and the final one.

'Thank you,' said Hanlon to Mawson.

'Don't mention it,' he said.

They walked back together to the gate at the edge of the field, then Mawson patted his rifle. In one smooth movement he loaded a cartridge, snapped it shut, released the safety, brought it to his shoulder, aimed and fired at a small metal target at the end of the field. It was two inches wide. Hanlon heard the dull clang as the bullet hit.

It was a massively impressive piece of shooting.

He ejected the spent round and smiled at her. He was perfectly relaxed, his eyes kind behind his glasses. 'But just remember, Hanlon, the bullet and the target are one and the same. Successful shooting should transcend the act of shooting. Have you read the *Tao Te Ching*?'

'No.'

'But you know of it?'

'Yes, I do,' she said.

He nodded, satisfied. 'Good, you should read it,' he said. 'It covers everything really.' Mawson smiled at her and quoted, '*The great Tao pervades everywhere. . . Because it never assumes greatness, therefore it can accomplish greatness.* Don't forget that, Hanlon. It'll make you a much better shot. More than that, it'll make you a much better person.'

'Thank you, sir,' she said. 'I'd better get back to work.'

He nodded and watched as Hanlon turned and left the field, walking slowly and thoughtfully back to her car. Mawson thought, I'm really very lucky with my team. McIntyre and Hanlon, they complement each other.

But then, as he watched her, he was conscious of a cloud drifting over the sun, and the sky darkened. Everything is interconnected, he thought.

Another line from Lao Tzu crossed his mind. '*The daring and violent do not die a natural death.*'

He strongly suspected that it might well have been written with Hanlon in mind. There were probably Hanlons around in the Zhou dynasty in five hundred BC, or the equivalent. Nothing was new under the sun.

Her car started and she drove off.

CHAPTER THIRTY

DC McIntyre stared at Serg. The woman on reception in the building where the MPU office was located had called her to say there was a visitor for Hanlon. McIntyre, only half listening, busy posting stills of a missing Bucks New University student from a CCTV camera on to Twitter (please retweet), had assumed it was someone from the Specialist Search Unit about the reservoir and had irritably gone downstairs to fetch him.

McIntyre was irritated because she was slightly put out by Mawson whisking Hanlon away for a couple of hours. She knew it was unfair on Mawson. He worked extremely long hours and when he did contribute to armed police training, he was scrupulous about doing it in his own time, hours he had accrued in lieu when he'd been working unpaid overtime. Thames Valley had to make about fifty million pounds worth of budget cuts. Cost savings were being imposed everywhere, but Mawson was adamant quality wouldn't suffer.

The cuts were vindicating Mawson's views on policing too, noted McIntyre with satisfaction. Several large old inefficient stations were closing and small new customer-friendly ones opening. Like this one, she thought proudly. We're the vanguard. The man is a prophet, she thought affectionately.

But McIntyre – it was unfair and childish, she knew – felt that Hanlon had been taken on a treat (even though McIntyre was totally uninterested in guns), while she hadn't, and she was left with the dull job of putting out photos and descriptions of missing people on social media. Then she had a couple of upgrades to do on those who were already on the system but were causing extreme concern because of the length of time that they had been missing. Two people on her list fell into that category. They hadn't been gone that long, but they had left none of the usual footfalls that marked our lives. No credit card activity, no bank activity, their passports still at home, their friends and relations baffled.

She knew it was important work and that many of those listed as missing had loved ones who were frantically worried about them. But it was dull, dull, dull.

Having just put the finishing touches to people who had turned up safe and sound on the website, Karen downstairs called her. She walked downstairs and there, sitting politely on a chair in reception, checking his phone, was Serg Surikov.

She could see Karen's thin face eying the Russian clandestinely over her desk. Serg stood up and looked at McIntyre. Oh my God, she thought.

Serg was one of the most attractive men McIntyre had ever seen. He had the quirky, distinctive but symmetrical looks and the build – tall, angular, graceful – that male models had. The kind of man who could wear a bin bag and still look good. His mother had been Tatar from West Siberia, from Omsk, and this oriental/Mongol lineage showed in his slightly slanted green eyes and high cheekbones. He carried with him the danger and exoticism of the steppes and the Taiga, the effect of which in a humdrum Slough office, on a dull Thursday morning, under grey skies, was magnified a thousandfold.

McIntyre, like Francine Edwards, was smitten. Her religious upbringing and years of church attendance from Sunday school to choir, and her daily Bible readings, helped put words to feelings. (That morning it had been Romans and Psalms. St Paul had warned McIntyre against the temptation of desire.) Staring at Serg, she was only too conscious of the lure of the sins of the flesh.

O that you would kiss me with the kisses of your mouth! For your love is better than wine.

But she didn't quote from the Song of Solomon. Instead she smiled politely and asked if she could help him.

Serg stood up, elegant with loose-limbed arrogance. 'I apologize for disturbing your day,' he said.

What an amazing accent, thought McIntyre. Disturb away, please. She made an *it really doesn't matter* gesture.

Serg smiled. He had a slightly wide mouth, perfect lips and a strong jaw. She guessed he was about thirty. There was a deep scar between his eyes and a smaller one by the side of his left eyebrow, which was dark and shapely. The slight imperfection, the hint of dangers past, only enhanced his attraction.

She took the card that he proffered. 'And how may we help you, Mr Surikov?'

I arose to open to my beloved, thought Shona McIntyre, *and my hands dripped with myrrh, My fingers with liquid myrrh, I opened to my beloved.*

'I'm looking for DCI Hanlon,' he said.

'Oh,' said McIntyre. She felt thoroughly deflated. Serg looked at her with those amazing eyes.

'She's out for the moment,' she said. 'Can I help you? Or would you like to wait?'

Please wait, she thought. Please keep me company.

Serg smiled. 'What time are you expecting her back?'

'Lunchtime,' said McIntyre.

'I'll return at one.' He turned to leave.

'What shall I say it's in connection with?' asked McIntyre.

Serg smiled again. 'Tell her it's about some Russians,' he said. He turned and left the building.

Karen, the receptionist, looked at McIntyre and pushed back the fringe of dark hair that framed her forehead. 'OMG, as my daughter would say.'

His speech is most sweet and he is altogether desirable, as the King James Bible would say, thought Shona McIntyre.

CHAPTER THIRTY-ONE

Hanlon pulled into the car park and neatly reversed into her space. It was surprising, she thought as she put the handbrake on the small, powerful car, how quickly you could get used to things. Not that long ago the Slough/Langley Police Station had seemed almost alien; now it was like a second home. She did the drive through London and out down the M4 without thinking. The small estate where the place was located felt familiar. It all seemed so tranquil here. Even the roar of jets every few seconds from above seemed not just bearable but practically unnoticeable.

She had also started to shed her resentment at her colleagues and her new role at the MPU. McIntyre was so nice to be with, she was even starting to thaw Hanlon's heart, and Mawson's idealism was beginning to, if not exactly rub off, win her over more to his way of thinking. She had worked all her life in an aggressive, cynical environment, where it was a 'them and us' mentality typical not just of the police but anyone really who had dealings with the public en masse, the enemy being not just the criminal fraternity but the general public whose lack of appreciation of the police bordered upon the repellent. Nobody ever said thank you for a difficult job well done; it was always moan, moan, moan.

Mawson was like a breath of fresh air. He genuinely enjoyed his job. He was a happy idealist, feeling that utopia was within our grasp. She appreciated the fact that he was genuinely free of cynicism. He could have gone far – she'd done some digging into his background – but he seemed perfectly happy with the backwater position he occupied. His hearts-and-minds policy was, she felt, possibly on the right track and, besides, any man who could shoot like that couldn't be all bad.

If it hadn't been for Enver, all would be more than tolerable. Enver's fate occupied her every thought that morning when she wasn't concentrating on the range. To have missed him by a couple of hours when he was being held so close was horribly frustrating. The only good thing was that she knew he was still alive.

It was an unsurmountable 'but'. She had lost one friend and colleague through her own arrogance – Mark Whiteside, still in the limbo of his coma, awaiting without awareness the rapidly dawning day when his parents, his next of kin, would have their way and the life-mantaining machines would be turned off.

She still felt bitterly guilty. Her larger-than-life colleague who had enjoyed his time on earth to the full, an almost Rabelaisian figure, brawling and shagging and drinking and laughing. She suspected she had lived vicariously through him and now he was gone – well, not fully gone but hanging on by his fingertips – she felt alone, embittered, increasingly violent in her moods, wanting to lash out so that others would be hurt as she had been. It was driving her to take even greater risks than she would usually so that she wouldn't be able to think in the maelstrom of danger she created for herself.

Enver's disappearance wasn't her responsibility, wasn't her fault. It was Corrigan's. But, to Hanlon, saving Enver had become her duty, as if she might be able to atone for Whiteside's condition by rescuing this other life.

She sat for a moment in the Audi and leaned her head on the steering wheel. Her existence was almost schizophrenic, torn in two by the Russian mafia and Myasnikov, in a struggle that should have been nothing to do with her at all. Oksana Taverner and Charlie Taverner, the latter missing, presumed dead at the hands of Belanov and Dimitri. Oksana waiting patiently in her luxurious home in Windsor, just a quarter of an hour's drive away. Enver Demirel, missing, presumed still alive, in the hands of Belanov and Dimitri. Myasnikov and Anderson locked in a battle over ownership of a brothel and revenge. Sex and money and death. Selling women's bodies it was not their right to sell, from buildings they had no right to own, taking lives they had no right to take. And both with high-placed sources in the institutions that existed to stop them flourishing.

She thought of the framed yin and yang symbol in Mawson's office, the diametrically opposed symbols of light and darkness that each contained a seed of the other.

It was a fairly accurate depiction of the mess they were in.

Hanlon felt a moment of despair at the scale of what she faced, then she flexed her fingers and the powerful muscles of her biceps. She tilted the sun visor down and looked at her face in the mirror. Her grey eyes looked back evenly at her.

I've beaten you before, Belanov, she thought. And I've faced worse than you, Myasnikov, and I'm still alive. I'm a hard woman to kill.

She got out of the car and heard a voice say, 'DCI Hanlon?'

It was Serg Surikov.

From the window above, Shona McIntyre watched. She saw the tall Russian in his well-cut dark suit incline his head to the much shorter Hanlon. She saw Hanlon push her hair away from her face with a familiar impatient gesture and then point her hand at the red Audi. Its lights flashed as it locked, then she followed the Russian across the car park and the two of them got into a VW Golf that she guessed was the Russian's hire car.

McIntyre watched as it drove out of the car park. She felt a surge of resentment against Hanlon. It simply wasn't fair. First Mawson had taken her out shooting. OK, it was his day off, she knew that, and he could do what he wanted in his free time, and she was sure that her boss would have spent the time profitably discussing work with the DCI, but she hadn't been invited. Not that she wanted to be, but still.

Then one of the most attractive men she had ever seen in the flesh, as opposed to on film, had driven Hanlon off in his car.

It definitely wasn't fair. Equally, it wasn't fair to blame Hanlon.

McIntyre decided to have a quick pray, then a hot chocolate and a biscuit. That would cheer her up. Jesus, cocoa solids and sugar, a winning combination. She'd text Hanlon later. The underwater search people were getting irritated that she wasn't returning their calls.

Hanlon and Serg were in the bar of the Ibis Hotel near Heathrow, where Serg was staying. Thanatos normally put their senior staff somewhere more central and considerably more luxurious. Edward Li was at the Savoy. Not only was it regarded as a perk of the job, but it reassured clients. If they were staying at places like that, they must be worth every penny they were being paid.

Serg, though, disliked ostentatious luxury. There was a streak of puritanism that ran deep in him as it did in his family. Poverty was a badge of honour. His grandfather, the Hero of the Soviet Union, had been a commissar in the Party, and had remained a shining beacon of probity unusual as the old idealism had withered and died under the tyranny of Stalin and his successors.

Then Brezhnev had ruined the Hero of the Soviet Union medal by being awarded it, the highest honour the state could bestow, almost like the Victoria Cross, to celebrate his birthday. And he had accepted it. That's what Serg couldn't understand. He had accepted it. His own grandfather had been shot several times and destroyed a German platoon single-handedly in the hellhole of Stalingrad. Serg loathed the former president for demeaning his grandfather's achievements. For mocking the bravery of others.

The Party had betrayed the workers, betrayed Russia, become a corrupt institution of nest featherers, but the Surikovs gritted their teeth and kept the faith. Their juniors took bribes and had lifestyles far more opulent than they did.

Serg Surikov's grandfather had died in genteel, alcoholic poverty, surrounded by medals and photos of his dead friends. Serg Surikov's father had been murdered by corrupt superiors to cover their tracks. Serg Surikov had a bleak future. He didn't care. Serg, like Hanlon, wasn't sensible. He was incorruptible.

His nickname in Moscow was 'the Angel'. Not because he was holy or religious; he had thrown someone implicated in his father's death off a roof. They said if Serg came for you, you'd better grow wings, quick.

'You said you had information for me regarding Charlie Taverner and this Myasnikov character,' said Hanlon. She studied Serg thoughtfully as he drank his coffee. Like her colleagues, she automatically registered his good looks. Unlike her colleagues, she noticed the way he constantly scanned the room, continual risk assessment, the way he moved, the easy muscular grace, and the small signs of damage to his face, the scar between his eyes, the one to the left of his eyebrow, the kink in his nose where it had obviously been broken at some time, and the general air of good-humoured competence. She noticed the powerful muscles in his elegant wrists. The other women in the bar were looking surreptitiously not just at him but at her, to see what it was that this woman had to interest a man like him.

'I do. I suggest we share, we pool, our respective knowledge.' Serg's accent was extremely pleasant to listen to, she thought, although she wished he wouldn't talk so much like a dictionary. 'After all, we indubitably share a similar agenda. We both want similar things, do we not, DCI Hanlon?'

Perhaps we do, thought Hanlon. Indubitably. His green eyes held hers. He knew she would not look away.

Hanlon did not have the kind of face or figure that made her a traffic hazard, but Serg was keenly aware of her chiselled body and her hard, attractive face with that commanding gaze that he was looking into now.

Serg liked climbing. He liked the challenge and the risk, and the woman opposite aroused similar feelings in him. She was wearing a white blouse under her jacket, and when she moved he could see the way her taut neck muscle stretched where it ran from below her ear to the trapezius muscle. Occasionally she would push her thick, coarse dark hair back with her long strong fingers.

Serg found her alarmingly attractive. 'I believe we want the same things. I have my laptop upstairs,' he said.

'Do you now?' said Hanlon, her dark, curved eyebrows raised in an ironic look. 'I'm going to buy a drink,' she said, standing up. 'Do you want one?'

'Another double espresso,' he said. 'They'll bring it.'

'I'd rather get it myself,' said Hanlon. 'That girl took ages last time. I'm not noted for my patience.'

Serg watched as she walked to the bar and spoke to the barmaid, who turned and busied herself with the coffee machine. Hanlon checked her messages on her phone as she waited. He took his phone out and ran through his messages too.

From the bar, Hanlon could see his head and face reflected in the mirror. He was ridiculously attractive. She had never found it hard to reach decisions and she reached one now. She studied her own reflection. Was she good-looking? She guessed she was. She knew that she had an intimidating reputation. Any man trying to make it with her would certainly need the courage of his convictions, and still they tried. She guessed she was worth it.

She paid for the drinks and brought them back to the table. She took a sip of her cappuccino and watched as Serg drank his bitter double espresso in a single swallow.

Serg said, 'I'll go and fetch the laptop. I'll bring it down here.'

Hanlon shook her head, her eyes compelling. 'There's no need. I'll come upstairs with you.'

There was a pause that to him seemed to fill eternity. He looked into her confident, grey eyes. 'If you're sure?' said Serg quietly.

Hanlon shrugged. 'Like I told you,' she said, 'I'm not noted for my patience.'

He could see the outline of her bra strap through the fabric of her blouse. Time seemed to stand still, holding its breath.

Hanlon's phone beeped as her phone rang. She glanced at the caller ID and turned it off.

'Just an old colleague I know,' she said to Serg. 'It won't be important.' She stood up.

'Coming?' she asked.

CHAPTER THIRTY-TWO

Even Joad, ever the optimist, had to admit that the arrangements he'd made with Arkady Belanov hadn't gone as well as they could have. He had expected Belanov and Dimitri to be both excited and delighted by this unlooked-for opportunity to capture Hanlon and finally be revenged, or get closure as people seemed to say these days. They had, after all, been moaning about little else for ages. They were men obsessed.

Then too there was the unexpectedly good news of his discovery from friends in the Met that DI Enver Demirel was technically on holiday. His presence wouldn't be missed. It rather looked as if his reappearance in their lives had been caused by some personal agenda rather than an official one.

Instead he found the Russians cagey, nervous. Whenever Belanov's mobile rang, both he and Dimitri squinted anxiously at the screen to see who the caller was.

It's Myasnikov, thought Joad, in a moment of clarity. They never told him any of this Hanlon business and they're shitting themselves in case he finds out they've gone behind his back. They're worried in case he goes apeshit on them, chops their heads off or something.

'I spoke to Huss,' said Joad reassuringly. 'She believes every word I said and she's pinning all her faith on Hanlon.'

He spoke not just with the conviction and fluency of the practised liar; he was telling the truth. Sincerity poured from him.

'Good,' said Arkady. Having met Hanlon, he could understand how the myth of her invulnerability would have grown. But the higher you climbed, the harder you fell. When Huss discovered that her idol was dead, she would be shattered psychologically. It had been the same with the Chechen resistance fighters in the TransCaucasus. Take out a leader, you take out the followers.

If people thought their families would suffer horribly, you could make them do almost everything. The only exceptions to the rule were the evil, who didn't care, the stupid, who were incapable of risk evaluation, and the militantly religious who were confident in God's ability to sort the whole thing out. Huss fell into none of these categories. She could be relied on. Arkady Belanov knew that Huss could be trusted to do nothing to harm them. She'd be far too frightened. Besides, thought Belanov, she was only a woman. She would be incapable of serious action. Hanlon, although she had the outward shape of a woman, was some sort of hideous banshee in human form. Not really female.

'Tell Huss we will call you in one hour and she can hear Enver Demirel, so she knows he is alive.'

'That sounds good,' said Joad approvingly. 'And where are you keeping Demirel, so I can direct Hanlon there? I guess she'll want to come tonight, to get her beloved colleague out of your clutches asap.'

The two Russians looked at each other and spoke in their own language. Joad only understood 'Heathrow' and *vor* and 'Friday night'. They seemed to be arguing about the times of Myasnikov's flight. It was odd, thought Joad, listening to them, how certain things were expressed in English, *lya, lya, lya* 'International Departures', *lya, lya, lya,* 'piece of piss', *lya,*

lya, lya, 'keep his mouth shut', *lya, lya, lya.* They stood out like rocks poking up from a stream of language he didn't understand. They'd obviously been in the country too long. They were starting to get linguistically assimilated.

'Not tonight,' said Belanov finally. 'Tomorrow night. Tell her tonight is extra security for *vor. Vor* wants to hear what policeman has to say, then Saturday morning he is scheduled for execution.'

'That sounds fine,' said Joad. 'On Friday night, then, Hanlon will be walking into your hands. I'll stress the point that your other contact in the force will know if Hanlon tells anyone, so she'll come alone.'

'You do that,' said Arkady.

'So where's he being held?' asked Joad encouragingly.

'Tell her, here,' said Belanov. 'Then if she does tell people, there will be nothing for anyone to find. I'll close the place for one night.'

Shit, thought Joad. If he had been Belanov, he thought, he'd have done the same. Why compromise security when you didn't have to. But he needed that farm address for tonight, or all bets were off.

He ran a series of objections to Belanov's plan rapidly through his brain. None seemed remotely plausible. Well, he thought, at least he had kept Enver Demirel alive for another twenty-four hours.

He stood up and stretched and grinned affably at Belanov. It was one of Joad's strengths that he knew when he was beaten.

'Well, that all sounds fine, then. Get Dimitri to call me from wherever you're keeping Enver in about an hour, let Huss know he's still with us.'

Arkady Belanov gave him a nasty smile. 'For now, Ian, for now.'

CHAPTER THIRTY-THREE

Serg Surikov woke up in the place he most wanted to be in the world, dressed as he most wanted to be dressed, with the woman he most wanted to be with in the world. The Ibis Hotel, Heathrow, stark naked, and DCI Hanlon. He felt sleepy and relaxed. He stretched luxuriously, or tried to, but something was hampering his movements.

He opened his eyes fully, consciousness returning, and took stock of the situation. There was a chair in his hotel bedroom, a solid piece of construction, and he was tied to it. His arms to its arms; his legs to its legs. He glanced down at the thin cord that secured him. The knots were simple and wholly effective. Any struggle on his part would only tighten them. He looked up at Hanlon, fully clothed, sitting cross-legged on his bed in a perfect lotus pose. Her face was unfriendly, unsmiling.

He could remember what had happened now. The walk from the hotel bar to his room, Hanlon leading the way, his eyes clamped on her perfect backside. Her hips had been swaying mesmerically. Maybe with anyone else he would have recognized the warning signs, a slight dimming of vision, a feeling of heaviness in his muscles, but he had been completely distracted. He'd had only one thought in his head. It had crossed his mind at the time that she had been setting a fast pace. Now he realized it had been to get him to his room before the drugs kicked in. She had pushed him down on the bed, removing his shoes with an enigmatic smile, and that's all he could remember.

'What did you use?' he asked, out of professional curiosity.

'Rohypnol,' said Hanlon. 'The rapist's friend. Oh, and diazepam.'

Serg nodded. That would explain the feeling he had at the back of his throat and the rear of his head, the hospital sensation of floating and relaxation that he associated with the times he had been professionally injured.

His clothes were neatly laid out on the bed next to Hanlon. He nodded at them,

'What were you doing? Seeing if I was wearing a wire, checking for concealed weapons? Or trying to make me feel more vulnerable?'

All three were true but Hanlon shook her head. 'No, just for the hell of it,' she said.

She uncoiled her legs, stood up and stretched. 'I know you don't work for Thanatos. I know you're FSB. I take it you're not going to deny that.'

Serg shook his head. God, she's good, he thought admiringly. 'No. How did you know?'

Hanlon smiled tightly. She thought of McClennan, the text he'd sent her with the photo of Serg attached. She had messaged him to check on Serge en route to the Ibis. By the time they'd arrived and bought drinks at the bar he'd got back to her. The mighty FSB, outflanked by an elderly, retired copper. Then again, he always had been a cunning old bastard, not unlike Tremayne. She thought again of Mawson, of his yin/yang image, the fact that white always contained some black and vice versa. That was McClennan, eighty-five per cent good, fifteen per cent corrupt, if her judgement was accurate. She wondered if

Mawson had any guilty secrets. She shrugged and looked at Serg, seemingly unfazed by his situation.

McClennan had even asked her out for a drink in a later text, the one she'd switched off when she'd propositioned Serg. It had taken him less time to track Serg down electronically than to find a series of lewd emoticons to show how much he was attracted by her.

Well, she thought to herself, I am undeniably popular these days. Particularly with Arkady and Dimitri – they're just dying to see me again.

'I know a lot of things,' she said.

Serg watched as she picked her phone up and her fingers moved over the screen. She put the phone down and went to the window of the hotel room overlooking the car park. Through the glass he could see the planes taking off and landing with astonishing frequency. There was no noise; the soundproofing must have been excellent.

There was a tap on the door and Hanlon opened it. A man entered the room, tall, slim, thin-faced, about fifty years old. There was a lot of grey in his side-parted hair. The lining of his suit jacket as he sat down on the bed was an exquisite robin's egg blue. Raw silk. The suit was beautifully cut and his black leather loafers gleamed. He wore a blue-and-white striped Turnbull and Asser shirt and a carefully knotted matching tie. He ran his eyes incuriously over Serg.

He was carrying a tan Dunhill manbag, like a satchel. He carefully undid the strap and took out a folded canvas package, the kind of thing a chef used to carry knives. Serg could guess what it contained. Jones put it next to him on the bed. Within easy reach, just in case it was needed.

Serg had never met him before, but he had worked with people in Russia who had the same hard, dead eyes.

'This is Mr Jones,' said Hanlon. 'He'll be joining us for our discussion. How much you want Mr Jones to contribute to our little chat is very much up to you, Serg.'

Morris Jones steepled his fingers and looked at Serg with interest. The kind of evaluating stare a cat gave to a cornered field mouse.

'I want to speak to you alone,' Serg said.

Jones stood up. 'I'll wait in the bathroom,' he said.

The door closed and Serg said, 'What do you want?'

Hanlon looked at him levelly. 'I am curious as to why an officer of State Security is over here pretending to work for a government-employed think tank, but what I really want to know is if you have any information as to where Myasnikov and Belanov have a colleague of mine that they have taken.'

'It's that simple?' asked Serg.

'It's that simple,' confirmed Hanlon. 'I just need an address.'

'And Mr Jones is here to make sure I comply.'

'He is indeed. I think Morris Jones would make your life unbearable if you didn't, and he has a colleague downstairs to help carry you out of the building after he's finished.'

Serg smiled and shook his head ruefully. 'I had heard a lot about you, DCI Hanlon, and I am delighted to tell you, you are even more intriguing than I had dared hope.'

Hanlon drummed her fingers on the fake wooden table in the bedroom. It was an ominous sound.

'I have two addresses for Belanov,' she said. 'A central Oxford brothel and a warehouse in Slough. I need a third address. I'm looking for a farm not far from Oxford.'

Serg looked at her face. Composed, perfectly prepared to do whatever it took to get him to talk to save her colleague. He knew that she would have no compunction in killing him, if that was what it would take. He also knew she would take no pleasure in it either, unlike several of his colleagues.

'I'm waiting,' she said ominously. Whoever Belanov had taken must be quite a guy if a woman like Hanlon was prepared to go to these lengths for him. He felt a momentary stab of jealousy towards the unknown policeman. He reached a decision.

'Well,' said Serg, 'I can help you there. Tragoe Farm, East Nethercote, near Chipping Norton.'

Hanlon blinked in surprise. It had been that simple. She looked narrowly at Serg. It seemed too easy. He returned her stare, his feline eyes quietly amused. She shrugged on her jacket and banged on the door of the bathroom. Morris Jones emerged. Serg looked closely at him. The hitman's eyes were narrow, his movements slightly somnolent. His head gave an involuntary nod. Heroin, Serg thought. Hanlon paid him no attention. She looked at her watch.

'I'll be back before six a.m tomorrow to untie you.'

'That'll be nice,' said Serg. 'We can breakfast together and I'll tell you what I'm doing over here.'

'Serg,' said Hanlon, sighing deeply, 'I don't care what you're doing over here. I don't give a rat's arse if you're here to kill the prime minister. But if you've fucked me over on this address. . .' she leaned forward, her eyes startlingly clear and diamond hard '. . . Morris and his merry men will make sure you never see Mother Russia again.'

Hanlon turned and left the room. The door closed on her back with a solid click. Morris Jones's head dropped again suddenly and he scratched himself absent-mindedly. His glazed pupils never left Serg. In the Russian's professional opinion, Jones was a highly dangerous man. He would kill you like squashing a bug.

'So, just you and me, then, Mr Jones,' said Serg pleasantly.

Morris Jones sighed and took some duct tape out of his bag. He shook his head sorrowfully. 'That's enough rabbit from you, sunny Jim.'

He had carefully folded a bit of the tape back on itself so he could find the edge easily. He took a scalpel from his bag. Its tip gleamed ominously in the light, but he only used it to neatly cut a piece of the tape off. Even a job as simple as that called for perfection in Jones's eyes.

Rabbit, thought Serg, more rhyming slang, *rabbit and pork*. Mr Jones must be a Londoner.

Morris Jones sealed Serg's mouth with the tape and put the scalpel away, then the canvas roll back in his manbag. Then he polished his shoes with a special impregnated paper cloth provided by the room. They gleamed a fraction more.

'My employer needs me to go and watch his back.' Jones patted Serg on his head. His pupils were pinpricks, but Serg knew that the strung-out Jones would be just as deadly as he was straight. Maybe more so.

'Don't do anything I wouldn't do,' said Morris Jones. He left the room, turning out the light behind him.

Serg was alone in the darkness.

CHAPTER THIRTY-FOUR

'So where exactly are we going?' Danny asked Hanlon. They were heading west, down the M40 towards Oxford.

'We're going to a farm owned by Arkady Belanov, the fat Russian,' said Hanlon. 'We're going to rescue a friend of mine who he's holding there. He's called Enver. Enver Demirel. But first we're stopping off to see a woman called Melinda Huss.'

'We?' said Danny.

'You and me, Danny, you and me,' said Hanlon. Her voice was clipped and irritable, her driving fast and aggressive.

Danny fell silent. It was plain that she wasn't in the mood for talking. That was fine by him; he wasn't in a communicative mood either. He had come, he realized, to a crossroads in his life and he'd had enough. He was tired of being ordered around by Anderson, he'd had more than enough of Morris Jones and he was also frightened. He realized that now. He usually defined himself by his fearlessness. He had welcomed danger because it gave him a chance to prove himself. He had always felt before that he was immortal, that death was an abstraction or something that only happened to others. Well, that had changed.

He had seen too much death recently. It wasn't glamorous and it was happening uncomfortably close. He was twenty-six and he didn't want to die. Until now he had never thought it could happen to him. Now he did.

He looked at the woman next to him, at her hard, confident face. The only person he had ever seen his boss actually like. He envied her ability to feel so confident, so sure of herself. He wondered what she'd had to say to Anderson earlier that afternoon.

Hanlon glanced at the blond, crop-haired man beside her. She was glad he'd shut up. Tonight she was crossing a line she had never thought she would. She was about to take money from organized crime. She was about to become what she'd always despised, a bent cop.

Yin and yang, she thought. And now that nice, pristine clean circle that represents my life is about to have an unequivocal dirty stain in it.

She overtook a car that was dawdling along in the middle lane. Hanlon loved driving. There were so few external variables, just the car, the driver's ability and whatever was happening on the road. It was a level playing field. It was simple and straightforward. Not like the rest of her life.

She had bent more than a few rules in her time and she had broken a few too. But they had always been in the pursuit of justice. She had never had any doubt before that a hypothetical jury, whilst maybe rejecting her actual deeds, would applaud her motives. Maybe she had been totally misguided – she didn't think so but she was prepared to accept the possibility – but now it was down to money. Pure and simple. Selling herself for cash. Not too different from Chantal, or even Joad, come to that.

Her conversation with Anderson had been short and to the point. 'I can get the Russian, Myasnikov, off your back, Anderson, if you make it worth my while.' They were standing in the Ibis Hotel's car park, the jets deafeningly loud overhead, forcing an unnatural rhythm to the conversation as they could only really speak in short bursts between the roar of the planes' engines.

'Off my back, Hanlon?' he'd asked.

'I mean dead,' she said. 'I will kill him for you.'

He had looked puzzled. 'What, and make it look like a botched police operation?'

Hanlon shook her head. She had smiled mirthlessly. 'No, it'll look like an efficient contract killing. It'll look like murder because that's what it will be.'

'Fine by me,' he said, shrugging. 'What about Belanov and Dimitri?'

Hanlon said, 'No promises, but if they get in the way, then, sure.'

'And what's the price, Hanlon, how much is this going to cost?' he had asked, reasonably enough.

'Two things,' she said. 'The dead people at Beath Street. I asked you before, I'm asking again. Charlie Taverner. I'd like what's left of him back.'

'Too late,' said Anderson, shaking his head. 'Second?'

'You remember my colleague, Mark Whiteside?'

'Coma Cop?' he asked, surprised.

'Yes, him,' biting her tongue to stop an outburst, *How dare you call him that.* 'The cost of his operation and subsequent treatment.'

'OK,' he said.

'It'll be at least five hundred K,' said Hanlon.

'That's very expensive,' said Anderson.

Hanlon shrugged. 'Of course, but who else would do it, who else could do it, and I can do it tonight.' Anderson looked at her hard, attractive face. The gritty breeze in the car park ruffled her dark corkscrew hair. He was running out of time and resources. He had nothing to lose. If she failed, on her head be it. The monetary cost was liveable with. Myasnikov wasn't.

Anderson had looked up at the skies, at the wheeling air traffic. 'I'll guarantee his treatment up to seven fifty K,' he said. 'Things always cost more than you expect. For that, I would like Belanov or Dimitri too, and that hitman of theirs, the Chinaman. I don't want to be walking around knowing Charlie Chan's going to blow my head off at any minute.' He looked at her; his eyes pierced her. 'But you know about cost, don't you, Hanlon? Anything else, that's your problem. I'll send Cunningham over; he'll sort out the legal bit. You'll need some kind of independent escrow account to pay the bills. Something not associated with me. Even the dickheads the Met employ might notice if I start writing cheques for them.'

Hanlon nodded. Anderson was wearing a long, black leather coat with jeans and a T-shirt. The wind whipped at his stringy hair. He looked as sinister as he was. It's funny, though, thought Hanlon, I know I can trust him implicitly. If he says he'll do something, he will.

Then Anderson said an odd thing. He looked at Hanlon. 'You should stop torturing yourself about Coma Cop,' he said mildly.

'His name is Mark Whiteside. He's a friend of mine,' she said angrily.

'Whatever.' He looked at her steadily. 'You didn't shoot him in the head. Stop feeling guilty.'

'How do you know what I'm feeling?'

Anderson had laughed. 'I never feel guilty, Hanlon. I'm not wired that way. But, Hanlon, when I see you asking me to help you out with money, money not for you but for your injured colleague, I can recognize guilt.'

Hanlon said nothing. There was nothing to say.

275

'You can use Danny if you want him,' said Anderson off-handedly. He opened the door of his Range Rover. 'Not Morris Jones, he's too useful to me. Good luck with the Russian hunt. I'll be lying low until the dust settles. Cunningham can always find me.'

The door of the Range Rover slammed shut and Anderson drove away.

She turned her attention back to the driving. She glanced at the man beside her. You can use Danny, not Morris Jones. Danny was disposable, then. That was Anderson's subtext.

They drove through the dramatic gap in the hills that marked the descent from Buckinghamshire into Oxfordshire. Not far now, thought Hanlon.

And now I've become Anderson's woman. She had a horrible feeling that the high price he was prepared to pay her would end up leading to more favours done. I've sold my soul, she thought bitterly.

Danny looked up from his reverie as Hanlon, following the instructions on her satnav, turned off the main road on to the track that led down to the Huss farm. Towards the top of the track was a small stone building that stood near to where Joad had blocked Huss's path the other day. Huss's car was parked outside and Hanlon pulled in next to it.

Huss heard the engine noise of Hanlon's Audi and opened the door of the outhouse. Hanlon parked and she and Danny got out and joined her. The storehouse was large inside, tools and bags of feed for pheasant and various other agricultural products were stacked round the walls. There was a table in the middle of the room under the single, bare light bulb and Huss had spread out an Ordnance Survey map of the area.

She pointed out the layout of the farm. Access was similar to her own property, down a tarmacked private drive. They looked at an image from Google Earth on Huss's laptop, also open on the table. The fields on either side were large, wide and flat.

At the end of the fields was the farm itself. It was small. The aerial view showed a barn, some outhouses and the farmhouse itself. Like most farms, everything centred around the farmyard. Farms looked inward, not outward. They were introspective places. Huss pointed at the farmhouse.

'The stockman who works for my dad, Derek, used to work for Old Man Miller who had Tragoes Farm till he died about twenty years ago. He said the house was in a real mess, nothing had been done to it since the Second World War. The electrics were lethal. But he did say that off the kitchen there was an old-style meat store, no windows, to keep flies and insects out, really thick stone walls, big old door. It's probably there they've put Enver. It'd be soundproof as well as escape proof.'

She thought briefly back a few hours. Dimitri had phoned Joad on some pretext, and at some point he had stopped and said, 'Say hi to the police, Enver.' Through her tears, tears that she'd held back so Joad wouldn't see, Huss had heard Enver swear at him, then a gasp of pain as Dimitri had kicked him. You'll pay for that, she said to herself.

Chantal, too, had told them that it was Dimitri who had tortured Enver. The Huss family don't forget things like that, she thought. Huss's family had been in their village for at least six hundred years, almost certainly much, much longer. Huss's ancestors had fought in the Civil War at Oxford, dying by the side of Colonel John Hampden the Parliamentarian, at Blenheim, and in both world wars. Their bones had littered battlefields before now and, if necessary, would again, thought

Melinda Huss savagely. The Huss clan knew how to fight; the Huss clan knew how to die.

Hanlon nodded. 'Access?' she asked.

Huss pointed at the track. 'Down here obviously, but, as you can see, there's this wood here.' She pointed at the image. 'And there's a path through the woods, quite well used, it's part of some sort of heritage trail. Anyway, it comes out down here, the other side of the farm. Then it skirts the farm itself and runs more or less parallel with the track, up to the main road.'

Huss and Danny looked expectantly at Hanlon, the de facto leader. Quickly, Hanlon explained what they would do. It didn't take long.

When she was finished, Huss said, 'I think we should call the police, get backup. I don't see the point in us doing this alone.'

Hanlon looked at her. The point was that she was hoping to kill Arkady Belanov, and Myasnikov were he around, and, if not, to find out where they were so she could get at them. She could hardly tell Huss that.

But it wasn't going to be straightforward. Simply finding the Butcher could be a problem. Myasnikov would have to be very careful where he slept at night. Anderson was a formidable enemy. He too had contacts in the police as well as his own extensive criminal connections. Then there was Serg Surikov. It wasn't just Anderson interested in his movements; the FSB were – that meant either the Russian state or Myasnikov's Russian rivals. And, of course, to a lesser extent, Corrigan.

It was all too simple to see Myasnikov as some sort of deadly, criminal mastermind, which in a sense he was. But as well as being the hunter, he was himself the hunted. Easy, too, to forget, in the wake of the deaths he had caused and the human misery, that Myasnikov was in Britain because Russia was too dangerous for him. Bigger and more dangerous predators swam in those cold, faraway seas.

So finding Myasnikov might be far from easy. But in Myasnikov's death lay Mark Whiteside's potential rebirth.

'The point is that the Russians' man in the force will tip them off, Melinda,' said Hanlon. 'And we'll end up with either them moving him so we'll never find him, and he'll be dead, or there will be some sort of shoot-out or a prolonged hostage situation. Then, when – if – they are all nicked, they'll be out on bail and I would imagine they'll come looking for you and your lovely family, who have conspired to deprive them of their liberty and put them inside where Anderson can probably get to them. Isn't that right, Danny?'

Surprised to hear his name, Danny almost jumped.

'Oh, yeah. If they end up on remand they might as well top themselves, save someone the bother of doing it. The Russians are dead men if they get banged up. Anderson will see to that.' He shrugged. 'But they've got a lot of money, a lot of pull probably. They'll be able to buy a judge to keep them out, I'd have thought, or good enough lawyers. They can claim their human rights would be infringed, that they won't be treated fairly inside. I bet someone like Cunningham could get them out. The human rights issue will probably do the trick. Lack of a fair trial, questionably obtained evidence, that kind of thing. Plus they'd have a good chance of getting at the jury.'

Hanlon looked at Huss levelly. 'So, who do you trust more to keep Enver alive? Us, or the British justice system?'

Huss rolled her eyes. 'I'm not happy about this,' she said. She stood up and walked over to where the tools were propped against fertilizer sacks, and came back to the table with a bundle wrapped in a plaid blanket in her arms. She put it down on the table and opened it up.

'None of us are happy, Huss,' said Hanlon.

Huss passed Hanlon the .22 rifle that had been wrapped in the blanket. 'It's Derek's. He uses it for foxes. That's a night scope on it; sights are set to two fifty metres.'

Hanlon nodded. She'd have preferred her own gun, still in the boot of her car, but she needed a night scope.

Next to the rifle was an up-and-under pump-action shotgun. 'Is that for me?' asked Danny.

'No, it's mine,' said Huss.

'Can you use it?' asked Danny.

Huss shook her head disbelievingly. 'I live on a farm, Danny, and I'm the third best shot with a twelve bore in South Oxford-shire. That's official. Have you won many cups for shooting?'

Danny was silent.

Huss leaned forward aggressively, her sleeves rolled up over her powerful forearms. 'I said, how many trophies have you won for shooting, Danny? I've got lots. Have you ever shot anything at all. . . ? I'm sorry, what did you say?'

'No. No, I haven't.'

'There you are, then,' said Huss angrily. 'I suggest you keep your mouth shut unless you've got something useful to say.'

The two of them squared up at each other across the table. Hanlon could see they were both so on edge, so keyed up, that they were practically hysterical. There was a prospect of very real violence.

'Perhaps I'd better tell you how to use a shotgun or rifle,' Huss carried on with heavy sarcasm. 'You put a cartridge in this end, bullets or shot come out of the end with a hole, this wiggly thing is called a tri—'

'Let's all calm down,' said Hanlon acidly. 'Now, can we please go and find Enver.'

Huss and Danny glared at each other.

'Danny, you're coming in my car,' said Hanlon firmly. Huss and Danny exchanged looks of implacable dislike.

CHAPTER THIRTY-FIVE

Joad was in Arkady Belanov's office. He was busy doing what no sane man would ever dream of doing. He was burgling the safe.

When Huss had told him that Hanlon had found the address to the farm and it was tonight it was all going down, he suddenly realized that it would be practically impossible to get any more money out of Belanov.

It hadn't slipped Joad's mind that it wasn't primarily money that had caused him to want to betray the Russians. It was the fact that they were going to kill him. It was ironic really, thought Joad. The seeds of Myasnikov's destruction lay in the fact that he was too ruthless, too obsessed with housekeeping. If he hadn't decided to remove him for security reasons, then Joad wouldn't be busy digging a trap to catch him. If Joad hadn't stepped up to the plate, who knows where they'd be. *If, if, if.* Joad didn't deal in ifs.

DI Ian Joad was not the kind of man who dealt with conditional hypotheses and he certainly wasn't one to buckle under pressure. He was used to the idea that the world was out to get him. He knew that Huss certainly was. Myasnikov's threat was just one more example of what he was up against. Business as usual.

Belanov's safe was operated by a standard keypad. It wasn't

particularly large; it wasn't particularly sophisticated. It contained the takings for the brothel for two or three days, which was a great deal of money. Two hundred pounds an hour, per girl, and there were ten girls working. Clients preferred to pay in cash. Card payments would be listed as the Bulgakov Treatment Clinic to make it sound more therapeutic. But cash was king. No customers wanted awkward questions.

It also had the bar takings and a large float for the till.

The safe also contained quantities of recreational drugs with which clients could enhance their pleasure, plus Viagra for the older generation. There were a couple of handguns in there, some expensive man jewellery that Belanov liked to wear, and a manila envelope stuffed with euros, dollars and roubles, Belanov's just-in-case fund.

Tonight, the brothel was in full swing. There were fourteen clients, more men than working girls, as some of the customers liked to watch while they shared a girl with a friend. Joad had recognized a couple of senior figures from the more prominent colleges in the town, eminent dons, enjoying pre-coital drinks at the bar.

Good to see the university represented, he thought. Unbeknown to the customers, security had been ramped up. Myasnikov was concerned that Anderson might stage some kind of revenge attack. There were an extra seven men on duty. Two men at the front and back doors, and three in the room with the CCTV monitors. Myasnikov had been in earlier to give them a little pep talk about what would happen if they failed to spot anything untoward. He'd shown them some footage from his phone that he'd taken in Moscow.

'If a man can't use his eyes properly when he's paid to, why should he be allowed to keep them?' he had asked, in his reasonable voice.

One of the guards had rushed out of the room to throw up.

The following night all the genuine clients would be replaced by *balbesiy*, foot soldiers, in Hanlon's honour. Belanov would be taking no chances. And Myasnikov would be on his plane.

Joad had seen Belanov use the safe once and had memorized the combination. It had taken the fat man a while to actually open it. The safe was at floor level, bolted to the wall and boards, and to use it Belanov had had to laboriously get down on his hands and knees, which with his weight and girth had taken some time. Getting up had been even more of a struggle. Joad had had to take one of his enormously fat arms and haul him up. It had been like pulling a dustbin up from the bottom of the sea.

Now Joad crouched down lightly, keyed in the number and heard the click as the safe door sprang open. He took the manila envelope after eyeing the handguns thoughtfully. Better not, he thought, God knows what killings those have been linked to ballistically. He put the envelope away in the inside pocket of his seersucker sports jacket (no laundering required!) and brushed some dandruff off the shoulder.

He closed the safe door and stood up. It was fortunate he had finished. Belanov's office door opened and Myasnikov stood there, with another man wearing motorcycle leathers. In Joad's eyes he looked too old to be a biker, but these days even eighty-year-olds seemed to be throwing their aged legs over motorbike saddles.

The cult of youth, thought Joad sadly. Fifty-year-olds dressed as toddlers in Day-Glo T-shirts and granddad rockers. What is the world coming to?

Joad didn't miss a beat. 'Good evening, Mr Myasnikov. Can I help you?'

Myasnikov didn't look remotely surprised to find Joad in Arkady Belanov's office. He had come firmly to believe in his own myth, that no one would be crazy enough to try to cross them. He assumed the policeman had a valid reason to be there.

'Actually, you can. You can drive me to farm,' said Myasnikov. He turned to the other man in the leathers. 'Coming with us?'

The other man shook his head. 'I have some things I need to do first,' he said. 'I'll take my bike, meet you there later.' He nodded to Joad and left the room. He didn't look overly happy to have met the policeman.

'I don't know where the farm is,' said Joad.

'Well, I suggest you use satnav,' said the Butcher. 'It'll be on there, won't it.'

Now why didn't I think of that? thought Joad as the two of them left the office. The money in Joad's pocket made a hugely incriminating bulge. As he closed the door behind him he glanced at the grandfather clock in the foyer of the brothel. Arkady thought it lent the place a classy touch.

Eleven thirty p.m.

I hope to God Hanlon's on time, thought Joad. I wish I'd taken one of those automatics now.

As they got into the Mercedes, his Mercedes, Joad noticed a scuff mark and a small dent by the headlight on the driver's side. He got in the car and adjusted the seat. It had been pushed far back. Dimitri must have been driving. He was a careless driver. Joad felt a surge of rage at what he'd done to the blameless car with his selfish ineptitude. Dimitri had never really got used to driving on the left.

My car, he thought.

As he started the engine he patted the steering wheel soothingly. He'll pay for that, he promised the car.

CHAPTER THIRTY-SIX

A huge full moon illuminated the flat fields over the Oxfordshire farmland. A hunter's moon, they called it in the country. Hanlon had dropped Danny off at the top of the track that led to the farm from the main road. She'd told him to remain out of sight with his gun drawn and phone on silent, to await further instructions.

Quite frankly, she had no great faith in Danny. He didn't seem like the kind of man who had initiative. She didn't doubt he'd be useful in a fight. He wouldn't be Anderson's minder otherwise. But, like an attack dog, you'd have to explain who to go for. She also seriously doubted his ability to hit anything with that automatic of his. But what he could do was keep an eye on the road.

Huss walked behind her as she led the way through the wood. As Derek had said, the path was easy to find and it was only about half a mile across one field, then through the trees, before they came to the field behind the farm.

The path was a ghostly silver in the bright moonlight from overhead, the trees that lined it like columns in a church. Hanlon recognized the trees they were walking through, spectral, graceful, very tall with few side branches, as beech. As the ground fell away from the path the trees changed to spruce that had been planted in orderly lines.

It was very tranquil in the wood. The only sound was the faint noise of their footsteps, practically silent on the beech mast covering the path, and the occasional hoot of an owl. Once they heard a high-pitched yelping bark that Huss recognized as a fox.

They reached the end of the wood. The trees stopped abruptly at the edge of the field behind the farm. Huss recognized the plants in the field as oilseed rape. It was in flower and its heavy smell hung in the air. By day it would be a brilliant blaze of yellow. In the monochrome of the moonlight it was an expanse of silvery grey.

They were standing on a slight ridge overlooking the farm and Huss took a quick glance, then passed Hanlon the pair of night-vision binoculars. She focused them on the buildings in front of her.

Parked down below in the cobbled rectangle of the yard was a large white van she assumed was the one that Chantal had mentioned, a BMW estate and a Harley-Davidson chopper she guessed had to be Dimitri's. It had ape hanger bars and she could easily imagine him in sawn-off denims and mirrored aviator sunglasses cruising around, trying to impress the girls. It was the kind of bike that would almost certainly have red flames painted on to the gas tank. A pimped-up bike for a pumped-up pimp.

There was nobody around. She looked again, more closely this time. She could see an enormous stack of silage, packed into standard-size green plastic bales and stacked up six high like a pile of giant-sized child's cylindrical building blocks. A newish-looking tractor was parked near the silage heap next to several bewildering, spiky, dangerous-looking tractor attachments. The Massey Ferguson still had the bale-moving attachment for lifting the silage bags connecteded to its front.

The bale mover looked like two enormous metal grips on hydraulic arms that would move together like the jaws of a vice until the bag was securely compressed between them so it could be lifted up and manoeuvred. The grab arms meant that the tightly wrapped bags wouldn't get punctured and the grass inside would ferment, not rot. Not like if you used a forklift on them, which often risked tearing the packaging. Huss had used something similar on her father's farm.

The Russians appeared to be doing a reasonable job of running a farm. Huss would doubtless know what the other pieces of machinery were, thought Hanlon. Melinda Huss had been driving her dad's tractor since she'd been old enough to reach the pedals.

There were no lights on in the house. Hanlon scratched her head irresolutely. Part of her wanted to go down there and set something on fire, see who came out of the house to investigate and then shoot them, the targets hopefully illuminated by the flames. But that would risk burning Enver to death or suffocating him. Would it be better to break in?

She texted Danny, nothing happening where he was. Hanlon reached a decision. In a low voice she breathed her plan into Huss's ear. Huss nodded silently.

The two women walked down through the oilseed rape field down to the farm. The crop came practically up to their shoulders. The plants were densely packed but a tractor had made a track down which they could walk easily.

Soon they had reached the farmyard and were crouched down in the lee of the silage bags. Each bag was like a large, green, plastic-wrapped cylinder, shoulder high. They looked over the top of one of the lower bags at the base of the stack. The stack rose up next to them like a step pyramid. Hanlon unslung her rifle and rested it on top of the bag. She chambered a round, and looked at Huss and nodded.

Huss too had loaded the shotgun. She slid the safety off, and walked round the back of the silage pile to the outhouses. Fuel for agricultural vehicles, red diesel, was tax exempt, and somewhere in the outhouses would be a store of it. There were only three outhouses; all were unlocked.

She struck lucky in the second outhouse. There were a dozen ten-litre cans of the stuff. Diesel was hard to set alight, unlike petrol, but given a wick, or enough vapour coming off it or a sufficient accelerant, it would go up. Huss shone her torch along the shelves. Meths, good, then paint thinners, even better. Then, bingo, a five-litre drum of petrol. Hanging on a nail above the diesel was a Massey Ferguson key on a fob, almost certainly a spare for the tractor. Huss unhooked it and put it in her pocket.

Hurriedly, careful not to spill anything on to herself, she made her preparations, including two petrol bombs, simple Molotov cocktails. She'd done this before, aged thirteen, with a boy from a neighbouring farm. It had worked then, the target had been an already burned-out car at the bottom of a field. Her father had gone berserk. It would work now. Good job he never found out about the strip poker too, she thought.

Huss glanced at her watch. Twelve fifteen a.m.

She texted an OK to Hanlon. She glanced down at the phone; no signal here in the dip where the farmhouse was. She waved her arm instead. Seconds later, she watched as Hanlon soundlessly, lightly ran across the yard to the farmhouse. She could see from here that the lights in one of the upstairs windows were on, though nothing showed in the downstairs rooms. Huss guessed that the door leading on to the yard would almost certainly be the one for the kitchen; it was in most farmhouses. The main door for the house would face out to the drive at the front. It would be reserved for visitors and kept for best, like the front room, the old-fashioned parlour.

The kitchen window was in darkness. She watched as Hanlon tried the door handle and slipped inside.

Huss's heart was thundering in her chest like crazy and her mouth was very dry. As if to compensate, her hands were slick with sweat and her head felt it was encased in an iron band. The band grew tighter and tighter. I'm terrified, she realized.

Then almost immediately came the thought that she was in the middle of nowhere, outside a house containing a group of men, number unknown, who wouldn't hesitate to kill her and were holding the man that she loved hostage. It wasn't a game. It wasn't a training exercise. In a couple of minutes either they would be dead or she would.

She felt a terrible, almost overpowering desire to turn tail and run. And run and run and run. *No one will ever know,* said a voice in her head, *they will never tell. They won't be able to. They'll be dead.*

You've every right to be terrified, thought her brain, but you're going to carry on anyway. Fuck, I'm scared, thought Huss.

Seconds later, Arkady Belanov's Mercedes swept into the yard, an expressionless Joad at the wheel. It pulled up outside the house and the passenger door opened. Myasnikov had arrived.

CHAPTER THIRTY-SEVEN

Hanlon had slipped inside the dark kitchen through the unlocked door. She had a small flashlight the size of a pen, but there was enough light from the moon to see. There was an open door into the hall of the house opposite the one that led into the yard. From the inside of the house she could see bare wooden stairs leading up to the top floor and a door off on either side.

She risked a quick glance. One door was in darkness. Through the bottom of the other one she could see a strip of flickering light and hear muffled shouts and explosions. She guessed that someone would be watching an action movie. Hanlon's sensitive nose caught the sickly smell of weed and the more acrid tang of cigarette smoke in the hall. The house itself smelled musty, of age and disuse, of damp and coal and a hint of blocked drain. She remembered what Huss had said about the house belonging to an old farmer; it certainly had that look and feel about it.

The kitchen was dominated by an ancient, soot-encrusted range that had stood there for probably eighty years. It was coal-fired and the flue obviously leaked. The scent of coal dust was overpowering.

She wished she had some idea of how many people there were in the house. Joad had texted Huss earlier to say that neither Dimitri nor Belanov were at the house on the Woodstock

Road. She shone the torch quickly round the table. There on a chopping board was a large ham, half of it hacked away, and the remains of a supermarket Black Forest gateau. Another gateau with a breadknife sticking out of it, like Excalibur in the stone, stood next to it.

Protein for the muscle-building Dimitri, and no prizes for guessing who had wolfed down a cake and a half with what looked like 500 ml of extra-thick double cream. Belanov's distinctive spoor.

So, at least two of them; almost certainly more.

Encouragingly, there were two empty bottles of vodka on the table too. The more drunk the Russians were, the better.

Hanlon moved to where the pantry should be, through a low opening to the side of the kitchen. She shone her torch at a door that barred her way.

This looked promising. Nothing high-tech like the door of the warehouse in Slough. Nothing formidable like Albert Slater's metal-plated, hinge-bolted portal that it would take a battering ram to knock down. Just two big bolts, brand new by the look of things, top and bottom, and the old-fashioned keyhole by the handle. Enough to keep a man locked in, but not enough to keep a woman like her out. No sign of a key, though. She quickly ran the torchlight over the walls just in case there was a key hanging on a hook. Nothing. She did notice, though, that the walls of the farmhouse were heavy stone. In here there was no sound whatsoever from the deafening TV.

Quickly she drew the bolts back, top and bottom. She tried the door. It was locked and there was no give on it. Sod it, she thought. She put the muzzle of the rifle against the keyhole, angling the gun so the bullet would strike where the metal of the lock connected with the frame. She slid the safety off. Before she pulled the trigger, she thought with grim amusement of the time she had spent with Mawson practising shooting at tiny targets half a kilometre away. No need to be gentle with the pressure on the trigger now. No need to check her stance or regulate her breathing. Missing was not a possibility. Being blinded by shards of wood or splinters was, though. She screwed her eyes shut and turned her head away as she pulled the trigger.

The bang was like a clap of thunder to her ears. Thank God for the shooting on the TV down the hall. She broke open the rifle and put another round in. This was going to be a serious problem. How quickly could she reload a rifle? Ten seconds? Five? But she wouldn't be facing a stationary target, and Dimitri, Belanov and anyone they had with them would be armed. She was guessing handguns, automatics. She was pinning her faith on their drunken marksmanship and her ability to hit what she was shooting at. Plus she had Huss, and while she didn't like her, she trusted Huss's ability with a gun. Huss was capable of bringing down fifty to a hundred odd clays fired at different speeds and heights, Huss had shot rabbits, pigeons and foxes. She'd certainly be capable of hitting two lumbering Russians at spitting distance. Danny she discounted. She had seen his heart wasn't in it and anyone who felt like that was not going to arrive early at the party.

She wished she'd taken his gun.

She pushed the door. The old keyhole had looked worryingly intact but the bullet had wrecked the lock, shattering the century-old mechanism. The door swung open easily enough and she shone the torch in.

'Hello, ma'am,' said Enver. He was sitting on the floor, propped against the far wall. Relief flooded through her. Not dead. She shone the torch on him. Christ, he looked terrible.

'Can you get up, Enver?'

He was sitting down, propped against the wall. She leaned over and took his arm. He gasped with pain. His hands were handcuffed together.

'Pull me up,' he said with gritted teeth. He hissed with the effort as he straightened up, and then he was on his feet. She looked down at the shackles binding his ankles.

'Can you move?' she whispered.

He nodded. 'Yeah.' He shuffled forward slowly. That would have to do for now. He was in no fit state to move faster anyway.

'Come on, we have to get out of here. For God's sake be quiet.'

She turned and moved to go into the kitchen. As she did so, the headlights of a car illuminated the outbuildings as the Mercedes turned into the farmyard.

Hanlon froze. The car stopped and its horn sounded. She and Enver crouched out of sight below the top of the massive kitchen table as hoarse shouts came from the front room, followed a couple of seconds later by three men running through the kitchen into the yard. None of them had looked left in her direction, though they'd passed a scant metre away from where she and Enver were hiding.

Hanlon rose from her crouch and stood up in the kitchen, just as a fourth man switched on the light.

'Well, well,' said Arkady Belanov, a huge grin spreading on his face. 'Look who it is.' He raised the CZ 85 automatic in his hand, her face clearly triangulated by the sights on the gun, and pulled the trigger.

CHAPTER THIRTY-EIGHT

Francine Edwards was not a woman you said no to. She had been invited that morning by Serg to meet him at his hotel at nine o'clock to have dinner that evening. It was nine thirty and there'd been no sign of him at the bar. He wasn't answering his mobile either. Now she wanted to check his room to make sure he was all right.

She was currently speaking to the manager, equally determined to prevent her.

'I know you've called his room, that's not the issue here. I want to check his room personally.' Edwards was used to getting her own way and she could feel her temper beginning to rise.

The manager, Irek Czerwinski, was sensing jealousy issues. He'd had problems like this before. Automatically his eyes dropped to her left hand. No wedding band, probably irate girlfriend then. Twice, when he'd been at the Blenheim Hotel in Oxford, he'd had to deal with this kind of thing, guests subsequently found in flagrante in rooms by partners. He had been left with the noisy, disruptive fallout.

'I'm sorry, madam, but—'

Francine Edwards produced her trump card. She took her Home Office ID out of her bag. She let Irek study it in detail, let the implications sink in of who he was talking to.

'You let me in there right now or tomorrow I'm going to make sure that an immigration audit team is in here checking every member of staff who works here, right down to cleaners and the guy who sweeps the car park, and if any non-EU employee here does not have a valid work permit I'm going to come down on you like a ton of bricks.' She looked closely at his badge. 'Fines, deportations, financial audits, employee audits, the works, and I'll also make sure, Mr Czerwinski, your boss and his boss know whose obstructive attitude sparked the whole sorry mess. Have I made myself clear?'

Irek knew when he was beaten. Five minutes later he was opening Serg's bedroom door. As Francine Edwards switched the light on and her eyes widened with shock, the manager thought to himself, Happy now?

Five minutes after that, a now fully dressed Serg was heading down the M25 London ring road towards the M40 motorway and Oxford.

CHAPTER THIRTY-NINE

Arkady Belanov had sprung to his feet with the others, or tried to. He wasn't built to spring. He, Dimitri and Georgiy and Grigory, the Yusopov twins, had been watching an old Rambo movie when they'd been startled from their evening's relaxation by the sound of the car horn blaring outside.

There was a coffee table in the living room. On it were three old copies of *Hustler*, the current edition of *Muscle and Fitness*, a virtually empty bottle of Grey Goose vodka, a bottle of Bailey's Irish Cream, a bag of grass, some coke, two Makarovs, a CZ 85 automatic and a Ruger shotgun.

Dimitri and the Yusopovs were up and out of the door in a couple of seconds. Belanov was much slower. With his weight he found getting to his feet a struggle. He was in a lounger chair, which helped, but he'd been lying in it, the chair in its recline mode, his feet in the air, when Myasnikov arrived. His powerful fat arms pushed on the side rests of the chair until it resumed an upright position, and only then could he get up.

His back had been hurting badly, a permanent problem, and Dimitri had lashed him into what he called his *zhenskiy korset*, his lady's corset. He had owned it for a few years now but he was bigger these days than he'd been when he'd originally acquired it, and folds of fat extruded from the sides where the straps were, in strange fist-size bulges. But it meant he couldn't slouch. He had to hold himself erect, which helped his overworked spine, and its lightweight panel gave him a feeling of pleasurable control over the heavy flab of his gut.

Underneath he was wearing a pair of tartan boxer shorts and knee-length support socks for his white, varicose-veined legs.

The last owner of the house, the farmer, hadn't redecorated the room since he'd inherited Tragoes Farm from his parents, and the wallpaper was ninety years old. It had come adrift from the walls but was still attached at the top. It hung like wafer-thin tapestry and moved slightly in the draught from the door.

He caught a glimpse of himself in the old, fly-blown mirror that hung on the wall. Even he thought he looked a bit weird dressed like that. The carapace of the corset and his pudgy hairless limbs made him look like a huge beetle standing upright on its back legs, and the shifting backdrop of the walls gave an even more hallucinatory tinge to the image.

Belanov suspected that it was Myasnikov performing one of the late-night snap inspections he liked to carry out. He pulled on a kimono, rather like Chantal's, red polyester with a gold dragon motif, and hid the drugs. Myasnikov was quite puritanical. There'd be hell to pay if he saw them. The booze he'd tolerate, grudgingly.

He picked up the Czech nine mm and stumbled slightly. He paused to steady himself against the sofa. He was drunker than he'd thought. He looked again at his reflection. His face was flushed and his eyes were bulging from the effects of the coke. Bloody Myasnikov. He was in no fit state to be talking to his boss.

He went through the open door and could see down the short hall, through the open door of the kitchen, the backs of the Yusopovs and the much larger one of Dimitri. They were now outside. The courtyard was illuminated by the powerful headlights of the Mercedes that Joad had left on full beam.

He strode into the kitchen, where his hand closed round the antiquated raised brown Bakelite knob of the light fitting and he switched it on. It was then that he saw Hanlon.

Her dark hair was tied back and she was wearing a navy-coloured T-shirt, her muscular arms bare. Her left hand was on the table, palm down; in her right a rifle that she was lifting upwards.

Arkady was slow and ponderous most of the time, but now he moved with graceful speed. His combat reactions were excellent. Most people had a natural tendency to freeze in situations of extreme stress or danger. Belanov had been tried and tested in bar-room brawls, vicious streetfights, the Chechen conflict and some of Russia's worst prisons. He didn't have Hanlon's fitness levels and lightning reactions, but he had a lot more experience of life-and-death fighting. He and Hanlon were well matched. He had the advantage, though, that he was used to killing and she was not. She had taken two lives, it was true, but only in self-defence. He had lost count long ago. For Belanov, killing someone required as much thought as swatting a fly.

He pulled the trigger on the nine mm, his arm braced for the recoil from the handgun. The trigger didn't move. The bottle of Bailey's, shots of vodka and several joints had affected his judgement. He'd left the safety on.

Belanov swore at his stupidity and reached for the safety slide with his free hand. Hanlon didn't hesitate. She raised the rifle and pulled the trigger. The rifle cracked in her hand and the .22 bullet caught Belanov in the chest, knocking him off balance. He fell backwards, his head slammed against the wall and his eyes closed.

Outside the three Russians spun round at the sound of the shot. Hanlon was briefly illuminated like a fish in a tank by the bright single bulb hanging from the ceiling. She desperately swung her rifle at it, the barrel smashing it, and flung herself down as the Yusopovs opened fire at the window and door. The glass in the window exploded, but Hanlon had hit the floor unharmed and hurriedly reloaded. She crouched under the window sill, rose up, put the barrel out and fired a shot with no particular target, just to make them keep their heads down.

'Stay down, Enver,' she hissed as she reloaded. She didn't need to tell him to do that. The injuries he had received were too much for his system to cope with and he had lost consciousness again. He was slumped against the wall, unmoving apart from his laboured breathing.

'Shit,' muttered Hanlon.

The Mercedes' engine roared as Joad put the car into reverse and slammed his foot hard down on the floor. The car shot backwards at speed. Myasnikov, unarmed, threw himself down on the ground, out of the line of fire.

From her hiding place in the outhouse, Huss could now see the three men and Myasnikov lying on the ground. Dimitri had taken up a position sheltering behind the bonnet of the white van. She couldn't see him directly but he was resting the barrel of the shotgun on it, pointing it at the kitchen. The rear doors of the van faced her. In front of the van was Dimitri's motorcycle. One of the Yusopovs was now crouched underneath the window of the farmhouse kitchen, just the other side of the wall to Hanlon, the other twin was about two metres away from Hanlon, sheltering behind the giant rear wheel of the Massey Ferguson tractor.

Hanlon's only advantage was that none of the men knew for sure how many they were facing. Dimitri suspected it was Hanlon in there, which was just as well for her. The glimpse he'd caught of an armed figure before she'd smashed the light hadn't been enough for him to be absolutely sure, but who else could it be? He had a high respect for her abilities, even more so now she'd taken out Arkady.

The Russians hadn't been expecting trouble and were low on ammumition. Makarovs only took eight bullets in their small magazines. The Yusopovs had six shots left each in their guns, Dimitri just the two. He didn't want to waste them and face Hanlon unarmed. One of the shells too was problematic. It was a solid round, rather than one loaded with shot. This was used by Spetsnatz, the Russian equivalent of the SAS or US Navy Seals, although the design was fairly universal and most countries used them, as did armed police. It was designed to punch through solid metal. It was still utterly lethal, but given the chance he'd rather have had the shot. He would have to hit Hanlon direct if he used that. If it made any contact with her, it would be game over, but he'd rather have something that required less accuracy.

Huss, concealed in her hiding place, had her shotgun, but she would have to break cover to use it and she suspected she would have no time to reload.

She hardly dared breathe in case the twin, whose back she could clearly see, heard her. Georgiy was wearing a white T-shirt and the night breeze ruffled his short sandy hair. Hanlon's finger on the trigger was slippery with sweat. The gun in his hand was black in the moonlight. The lights from the Mercedes lit up the yard as brightly as a stage. Joad had backed it up some twenty-five metres, turned the engine off, jumped out of the car and concealed himself in a ditch out of harm's way. He watched the proceedings with interest. Hopefully, they'd all kill each other, although he'd settle for the Russians dead. One thing was for sure: he wasn't going to take any part in the proceedings.

All was eerily quiet, then Joad heard Dimitri's voice shouting something in Russian. Joad watched as Grigory flattened himself against the wall of the kitchen and edged slowly along to the opening by the door. Joad could see what his problem was. He had no angle of fire to shoot inside, and he sure as hell wasn't going to be dumb enough to put his head and shoulders through the window. He gathered himself into a crouch and ran across the empty doorway to the other side, where he drew himself up to full height. He held his breath and the pistol in both hands. He started counting to himself.

One, two, three, four . . . On *five*, he started to move.

Inside the kitchen Hanlon had seen the blur of movement as Grigory dashed across the doorway. She guessed immediately what he was up to and what would come. She glanced back at Enver, who had weakly opened his eyes. He nodded that he was OK. He'll never get out of here without being carried, thought Hanlon.

Beyond the kitchen table, somewhere on the floor, lay Arkady Belanov's handgun. She would dearly love to get to it, but felt that she would be too much of a target through the open door. She was also impatient for Huss to act. Please God, let her not lose her nerve, she thought.

As Grigory reached *five*, he leaned round the door of the kitchen and fired two shots in Hanlon's direction. He couldn't really see where he was shooting; he was just praying for luck. The bullets didn't hit Hanlon or Enver. One embedded itself in the two-inch-thick old oak table, the other into the wall. Hanlon returned fire, her bullet striking the wall.

The three shots shook Huss into action. She watched, tensely, as Grigory ducked back to his position of safety. Hanlon's bullet had driven a spray of brick dust across his left cheek. Another two centimetres and she'd have blown his head off.

He still didn't realize he was dealing with a single-shot rifle, didn't realize that he could have walked in with impunity and put his remaining bullets into Hanlon.

He breathed deeply and looked at Dimitri. 'Four shots,' he shouted. He was pretty certain nobody spoke any Russian other than them.

Myasnikov had meanwhile taken this opportunity to pick himself up and join Dimitri behind the van.

'Any minute now, the Chinaman will be here,' he said. Dimitri nodded. He didn't care. He wanted Hanlon dead at his hand and his alone. She had humiliated him and Arkady in the past and now his friend, mentor and protector was dead at her hands. Her life was his to take.

'I think it's just her in there,' he said. 'Her and maybe the other one, and he's in no state to do much. Georgiy,' he shouted, victory in his grasp, 'run across to where Grigory was, to the window.'

While Georgiy got ready to run, Hanlon reloaded. Or tried to. She blinked in disbelief and horror, and her nimble fingers checked again. There was no mistake.

In the shed where she'd met Huss she'd taken a few shells and put them in her front pocket. She'd put the box of .22 ammo for the rifle she'd been holding, minus these shells, in the side compartment of the door of her car. Also in that compartment, in a similar-sized box, had been .243 shells that she'd had for Mawson's rifle. It was these she had in her trouser pocket. The bullets wouldn't fit. Her rifle was now useless.

All she could do was sit there and await the inevitable.

Hanlon rarely swore. 'Fuck,' she said.

CHAPTER FORTY

Danny ran down the road towards the farm. He'd watched helplessly as the large Mercedes had turned down towards the farm, two men in the front. He quickly ran through the best guesstimate on the odds facing Hanlon and Huss down the track below him.

Hanlon had guessed that there would be Arkady, Dimitri and at least one, probably two guards to look after Enver. Now they'd been joined by two more men. Six against two. Well, he couldn't say he didn't have a choice. Hanlon's keys were in his pocket and her car was parked in the entrance to a field a couple of hundred metres away. There would be nothing simpler than to hang around here, wait for the inevitable noise to settle down, and, barring a miracle that she would be saved, take her car and drive off.

It would all be so easy. Nobody would be left alive to blame him. He had done his best, he could see himself now saying that. He would be believed. He thought of the dead bodies he had seen back at Beath Street, what seemed like a lifetime ago. He thought of Hanlon and Huss, their bodies riddled with bullets, decapitated for a Russian crime lord's amusement. He shook his head, angry with himself. Angry at what he was about to do.

I'm too nice for my own good, he thought. He started running down the track, the Glock comfortingly heavy in his hand.

Time to see if he'd be able to hit anything with it. Huss's remarks still stung. *Bloody woman!* he thought. From the distance he could hear the pop of gunshots. He increased his pace.

Joad watched the action unfolding before his eyes from his vantage place in the ditch by the car. So far, the Mercedes was unscathed, thank God.

Down below the Russians were closing in for the kill. He guessed that Hanlon was in the kitchen because of the rifle fire. The two blond men were by the kitchen, one under the window sill that overlooked the yard, the other standing by the outside of the door. Where was Huss? Joad wondered. He turned his attention back to the Russians. He could almost feel their tension. Dimitri barked a command and the two men started to move.

Suddenly an object sailed through the air. It was alight. He could see it burn as it described an arc and hit the ground near the Russians, exploding in a ball of flame, followed by another one that landed near the front of the van. The twin explosions of the petrol bombs were followed by a third explosion of flame as the bucket of diesel that Huss had placed underneath Dimitri's Harley went up. Diesel was hard to ignite but a petrol bomb exploding on top of it would do the job.

Under the black canopy of night, the farmyard was lit by the headlights of the Mercedes like a stage set, and the searing light of the sheets of fire, yellow, orange, red, added to the surreal sight. The Harley remained upright momentarily on its stand, its shape silhouetted through a sea of flame, like some motorbike from hell surrounded by blazing curtains of fire, then it collapsed over on its side as the petrol in its tank went up, the force of the explosion knocking it off its stand. The front of the white van was covered with burning petrol and another mini-explosion of fire roared into life as a second bucket of red diesel that Huss had pushed under the nearside wheel arch caught.

There were hoarse shouts in Russian and the twins ran forward into the centre of the yard, guns held in two-handed grips, looking for a target. Both of them had blackened patches on their white T-shirts where burning fuel had splashed on to them, but they seemed unscathed. Even if they had been injured, it wasn't enough to slow them down.

Huss stood up, still in the sheltering darkness of the outhouse, and stepped into the yard, her shotgun firm against her right shoulder. She shot Grigory with the first barrel. He was killed immediately, collapsing backwards on the cobbles of the yard, propelled by the force of the blast, his chest a red mass of bloodied flesh. Huss then turned the other on Georgiy.

It was now that Dimitri appeared from the rear end of the van. He'd seen the first Molotov cocktail appear and explode, and when the second one had arced towards him he had guessed what was going to happen. He'd pushed Myasnikov over and flung himself on top of him. The shockwave and flame of the explosion from the petrol bomb and the ignited fuel had rolled over them. He shook his head dazedly to clear it. So Hanlon wasn't alone. He looked backwards in alarm. The van had sunk down at an angle where the tyre had deflated on the nearside and black clouds of noxious-smelling toxic smoke were drifting from the burning rubber. He guessed that soon the oily detritus around the engine would start burning and then the fire would spread back to the gas tank. His Harley too, now fully ablaze, added to the heat and smoke.

He pulled Myasnikov up and approached the end of the van. It was at that moment Huss strode out and blew Grigory away. Dimitri grinned to himself. Huss was slightly in front and couldn't see him. He took a step forward, his finger tightening on the trigger for the barrel that held the cartridge with the shot.

'Behind you, Huss!'

Melinda Huss, pumped so full of adrenaline it would have been off the scale, twisted round and pulled the trigger on the other barrel. But Danny's shout had alerted not just her but Dimitri. As she fired, he ducked back behind the van and its thick panelled doors and sides, reinforced and thickened for refrigeration, took the force of the blast. Pellets from the shot punched holes in the metal of the van, but Dimitri was unscathed.

Danny, on the edge of the farmyard, shot at Georgiy and missed him. The Glock in his hand felt good. All of Danny's previous existential gloom was washed away in the excitement of the here and now. All there was in the world was the gladiatorial conflict between him and the blond man, silhouetted against the now dying flames of the burning van. In the foreground between them lay the bleeding body of Georgiy's twin brother.

Georgiy kneeled down as if he were on a range and fired at Danny, two careful shots. He missed. As he fired the second time, Danny shot again and this time the nine mm bullet found its mark. The remaining twin fell over backwards, the red and yellow light of the fire reflected in his dying eyes.

Huss saw the Russian fall and scrambled to her feet. She took shelter behind the comforting bulk of the tractor, shotgun still in her hand. She glanced over at the silent, dark kitchen. Where the hell was Hanlon?

CHAPTER FORTY-ONE

Hanlon was scrabbling around on the dirty floor in the blackness of the kitchen, searching frantically for Arkady Belanov's gun. Outside, God alone knew what was happening. Whatever it was, Hanlon's respect for Huss, already fairly high, soared. She risked a glance out of the window after she heard the first shotgun blast and saw the dead Russian twin on the ground. Belanov lay on his back on the floor of the kitchen. Blood covered his face. It was dark in the kitchen despite the fires burning outside and Hanlon crouched by Belanov's body, feeling for the handgun with her fingers. It had to be around here somewhere.

She heard Danny's voice shout something and then she saw the end of the automatic. Belanov's fat thigh had fallen across it. She could just see the butt of the handle underneath the white, hairless pudgy flesh. She slid her hand underneath his leg to retrieve it and just then Belanov's eyes opened, and his immensely strong arms grabbed her and pulled her on top of him in a macabre parody of a lover's embrace.

His powerful hands held each of her arms just below her elbows. She tried to pull away, but the sheer bulk and dead weight of Belanov's body made a secure anchor. The kimono he wore had come undone and she could see the dark shape of the Kevlar vest that he wore as his corset. Now she realized that the bullet that should have entered his chest had done no such thing. She could even see where it had impacted the body armour. It was just the fall backwards against the jutting edge of the sideboard that had knocked him out. Aside from the head wound he was unscathed.

And he was fearsomely strong. But so was she.

'Hanlon.' He almost crooned her name. He snapped at her like a dog and gave another heave to pull her head towards his face. Strands of her hair brushed his face and she could see the saliva wetly coating his crooked yellow teeth, some of them replaced with gunmetal- coloured bridgework. She was so close she could see fragments of gateau between the teeth. She could smell the sickly sweetness of his breath from the bottle of coffee liqueur and the cake he'd eaten, overlaid with stale smoke from the joints he'd had. He opened his mouth wider, craning his fat neck upwards, planning obviously to sink his teeth into her face.

She heard another shotgun blast and redoubled her efforts to escape from Belanov's grip, to no avail. His fingers were like iron bands. Then she felt a sudden constrictive weight on her left calf muscle. Belanov had lifted his right leg and hooked it over hers. In a second, the other would follow and she'd be irrevocably attached to him like a grim simulacrum of sex. Then her exposed face and his tearing teeth.

Danny sprinted over to join Huss by the tractor. About twenty yards from there was the bulk of the white van. Most of the flames had died away now and the explosion that Dimitri had feared was no longer likely.

'Where's Hanlon?' he gasped. The kitchen was dark. The headlights of the Mercedes still illuminated the farmyard and the bodies of the Yusopov twins.

'In there,' she said, 'with Enver.' She pointed at the van. 'Dimitri's behind that van, with Myasnikov.'

Both Huss and Danny were panting, as if they had run a race and were exhausted. The emotional strain had been incredible and they both shared a sense almost of resentment that they were still, at best, only halfway through all of this. The end was in sight; neither of them wanted to make a mistake now. They didn't want to die. They looked at each other with almost loving passion, bonded as neither could have thought possible in the terrible events of the last three or four minutes. Blood thundered through their veins; their hearts were beating as they'd never beaten in their lives.

Huss loaded her shotgun and gave it to Danny. She took the keys to the tractor out of her pocket.

'I'm going to drive this straight at Dimitri,' she said, patting the side of the Massey Ferguson. 'Either I'll run him over or you'll shoot him. Whichever way, Danny boy, he's dead meat.'

Danny grinned at her savagely and Huss stepped lightly up into the tractor, her movements lithe and athletic despite her size.

Huss settled down in the cab, the controls familiar and comforting. It was a welcome feeling of control in the chaos of the past few minutes. God, she suddenly thought, that's all it had been in all probability, five or ten minutes, nothing more. She took a deep breath. Come on, Melinda, she thought, you can survive this.

She looked around her. There was the small computerized control panel for the bale grabber attached to the tractor's dashboard. The height of the cab gave her a feeling almost of omnipotence. Up here, she was in control. She started the engine and momentarily frowned in thought.

The silage bale was still attached to the front of the vehicle by the grabber and its controls on the panel, about the same size and shape as a small tablet or large satnav, were similar to ones she was used to, but with minor differences. Now wasn't the time for subtlety. Her forefinger stabbed down and the powerful hydraulics swung the bale upwards so it was at a sixty-degree angle high in the air. That would do for now. At least it was off the ground and the tractor could move forward. She now saw the icon to disengage the grip; well, that would have to wait. It would only be in the way when she moved forward. She glanced down at Danny, who gave her a thumbs-up.

She switched on the tractor's powerful lights, and the van and the section of the farmyard behind were brightly illuminated. The noise of the engine was pleasurably deafening. The skeletal remains of the Harley at the front of the van were smoking gently. She put the vehicle in gear and moved forward gently and slowly.

Inside the farmhouse, Hanlon heard the tractor start up. It had to be Huss, she thought. She pushed upward against Arkady Belanov's grip and then slammed her right leg up and forward as she drove her knee into Belanov's groin. Hanlon regularly squatted with sixty to eighty kilos on the bar across her shoulders. Her thighs, her quads, were like iron. She saw his face contort in agony and kneed him in the balls again with all the strength in her muscular legs. She felt his grip slacken and that was enough for her to break her right arm free. She punched Belanov hard in the face just below his nose and heard a wet crunch as teeth gave way under her knuckles. But Belanov was from a hard school and he gave an almighty roll of his body, hurling Hanlon sideways. Now it was her turn to see stars as her head crashed into the sideboard. Belanov scrambled to his feet. Unlike Hanlon, he had no knowledge of the whereabouts of the gun, even though it was practically at his feet.

Huss had barely covered a couple of metres when she stopped the tractor and put it into neutral. Something was wrong, and momentarily she wasn't sure quite what it was. She looked around her.

Danny was lying face down on the ground, the shotgun next to him. For a second Huss was confused. What was he doing down there? Had he fallen? Then, as if on cue, she noticed the red patch of blood spreading from his back.

Dimitri stepped out from behind the van in front of the tractor. The pump-action shotgun was cradled in his arms. He had ripped off his T-shirt and the tattoos on his awesomely developed muscles were highlighted in the glare of the Massey Ferguson's lights. There were the onion domes, the bloodstained dagger, the swastikas, the ornate, bold Cyrillic script, his whole upper body an iridescent, brilliantly inked hymn to crime, death, murder and rape.

'Come on, Huss, come on, you bitch, and die!' he shouted at her.

Huss put the tractor into gear and stamped down on the accelerator. The engine roared and she bore down on Dimitri. He lifted the Ruger and aimed, but not at Huss.

The solid bullet from the twelve bore, a bullet capable of travelling through the engine block of a car, struck the tractor's radiator grill, and the motor whined and stalled and fell silent. The tractor stopped dead in its tracks.

Huss sat stock still in the cab, her body a perfect target for Dimitri.

Hanlon grabbed the automatic from the floor under the table, where it had ended up, when she heard the shotgun blast from the farmyard. Arkady Belanov turned and ran from the kitchen. But not in the direction of the farmyard. He ran down the hall to the front door. Hanlon fumbled with the unfamiliar gun, looking for the safety, found it and fired a shot at Belanov as he threw open the front door. She was lying on the floor and the unfamiliar gun kicked in her hand. The fanlight above the front door exploded into thousands of shards of glass.

The door banged shut behind him. She could go after him. She could run fast; Belanov couldn't. She was wearing her army boots; he was in support socks. She was armed; he wasn't.

Or she could help Huss.

Dimitri stared upwards in triumph at Huss and started to lift the gun to his shoulder. Her upper half was clearly visible through the glass of the cab.

Huss looked down at Dimitri and, almost casually, with her left hand pressed the icon that controlled the grab release.

High above Dimitri's head, unheard and unseen by him, the arms of the grab opened a couple of millimetres and a bale of silage, weighing eight hundred kilos and the size of a telephone box, crashed down on top of him. The ground around it shook from the impact.

Joad saw it happen. The bale didn't fall in slow motion; it plummeted from the sky at ten metres per second. In the time it took to blink, it had obliterated Dimitri from the land of the living.

He also saw Myasnikov run from the shadows, obviously intending to pick up the Makarov that lay near the dead Yusopov's hand. The unarmed Huss was still sitting in the cab; she had turned the tractor off. She was motionless in her seat, staring down at the dead Danny.

Joad thought, She'll be in shock, I guess.

'Leave it,' said a curt voice. Myasnikov stopped in his tracks as Hanlon emerged from the farmhouse kitchen. Her blue T-shirt was covered in dirt and sweat, her slim, muscular arms were scratched and grazed, as was her face. From under her dark, matted hair, her eyes were cold and unblinking. The CZ 85 in her hands was small but menacing.

Myasnikov put his hands up.

'Face down on the ground,' ordered Hanlon. 'Hands on the top of your head, do it now.'

She cursed herself mentally. She should have just shot him, for Whiteside's sake, for humanity's sake. But Hanlon was not a born killer. She knew then that she did not have it in her to execute someone cold-bloodedly, no matter how terrible their actions. Damn, she thought. I didn't think I'd be this weak. But even as she thought that, she refuted it. I'm not weak, she thought, I'm moral. And there's nothing I can do about it.

Myasnikov obeyed. He lay on his stomach, staring at Hanlon's scuffed army boots and olive-green combat trousers. There was a smirk on his face. He would have had no compunction in pulling the trigger. Hanlon was feeble and he had won. He knew that lying down he'd be utterly safe. There was no way she would stand over him and put a bullet through the back of his head, which was exactly what he would have done.

You stupid, weak woman, he thought.

In his hiding place in the ditch, Joad put his hand inside his jacket and touched his envelope. The lovely money was still there. Arkady was dead. Dimitri was dead. They were the only two people who knew about the envelope, and they were dead. He smiled to himself. He looked at the Mercedes, miraculously unscathed. Nearly there, he thought to himself, nearly home and dry.

Hanlon looked up at Huss. 'Melinda.' Huss didn't move. Hanlon spoke louder, but gently. 'Melinda, Enver's inside. We have to get him out. He needs to get to a doctor.'

The mention of Enver's name seemed to wake Huss from her trance. She slowly climbed down from the cab of the tractor.

She kneeled down beside Danny. Hanlon joined her. The wind ruffled his short blond hair. Huss stroked it sadly. There was no need to check his pulse now. He lay in a huge puddle of blood. Huss stood up and bleakly surveyed the farmyard.

Hanlon, still kneeling by Danny's body, frowned to herself and looked sharply at the wound on his back, just below the left shoulder blade. Not an exit wound, a carefully placed entry wound, designed to put the bullet straight through the heart. But it was on the wrong side of Danny's body. Very gently she lifted him up slightly so she could see his chest. Just as she suspected, an unholy mess of gore and splintered bone. Delicately she let him lie down again.

'Put the gun down and step away from the body, that's right,' said a voice from the darkness. 'Don't do anything silly, you know I won't miss. You too, DI Huss. Both of you into the light where I can see you clearly.'

They did as they were told. Myasnikov stood up and dusted himself down. He picked up the handgun he had been going for earlier. He was a cautious man.

'Well, *Kitayets*, you took your time coming.'

Danny's killer stepped into the light. 'Hello again, DCI Hanlon,' he said.

CHAPTER FORTY-TWO

Well, *Kitayets*, you took your time,' said Myasnikov. The Chinaman shrugged.

'The situation was always under control. But now, well, now we're all happy, aren't we? Except for you two ladies, of course. Perhaps you should introduce me to your friend, DCI Hanlon.' His voice was low, mellow and reasonable, as always. Compassionate and caring.

Hanlon said to Melinda Huss, 'DI Huss, meet Detective Superintendent Harry Mawson. He's also known as the Chinaman for some reason.'

Mawson smiled. 'It's because I've got a degree in Chinese Studies from SOAS,' he said. 'The Russians like nicknames. I've got quite fond of it myself, even if I am from Kent.'

She felt physically sick. At least Myasnikov had the grace not to pretend to be anything he wasn't. He was the *miasnik*, the Butcher, he was the *vor* of *vors* and he lived up to his name. Mawson had hidden behind this facade of niceness.

Myasnikov laughed. 'You know what is so funny, *Kitayets*, I was thinking to myself earlier back in Oxford, no one would have the balls to stand up to me in this shithole country. And you know what, I was right. The men here, they have to use women to try and kill me, and, of course, they have no balls at all!'

He laughed again, delighted with his joke. 'Do you get it, *Kitayets*, no balls. Hanlon is woman, and—'

Mawson rolled his eyes, interrupting. 'Yes, very witty. Well, Konstantin,' he said acidly, 'I think we had better crack on with things. We've got, let's see, the Yusopovs, Dimitri, I suppose that Belanov's inside – you did kill him, I take it?' he asked Hanlon. She didn't reply, just stared at him with unwavering hatred. 'I'll take that as a yes, that's four. If you could go inside, Konstantin Alexandrovich, finish off Enver Demirel, that'll make five, and these two, seven; oh, silly me, and him, eight.' He pointed at Danny. 'Can you get whoever you've got left working for you out here, please. We'll need at least two men and a refrigerated van. I want this lot done and dusted by five a.m.'

'I give orders around here, Mawson,' said Myasnikov. But his voice had lost a little of its old certainty. The past hour had been a frightening time. He was used to delegating death, to arranging it, not being caught up in it. Momentarily he wondered if he was doing the right thing in trusting Mawson. But Belanov and Dimitri were dead. He had to trust Mawson. He was the *krysha*, the roof under whose protection Myasnikov sheltered, and now Mawson was close to getting his hands on the *obschak*, the trough or the fund.

Well, first things first. He cocked the Makarov so he wouldn't have to apply any pressure to the trigger when he blew Enver Demirel's brains out.

'Turn round, ladies, please,' said Mawson politely. 'This will be very quick, I promise.'

Hanlon and Huss looked at one another for the last time. Grey eyes on blue. 'I'm sorry,' said Hanlon. Her face was grave. Huss nodded. She didn't trust herself to speak. She put her hand out and briefly touched Hanlon's arm. It was a final gesture of goodbye.

The two women turned their backs on Mawson. Both of them closed their eyes. They waited. Seconds later, two shots sounded.

CHAPTER FORTY-THREE

Huss stood stock still, her eyes screwed shut. She felt her chest rise and fall. She felt no pain. She opened her eyes. Everything looked the same, the smouldering van, the Harley, the farm buildings. And then she looked at Hanlon, who seemed equally surprised.

They both turned round. Mawson and Myasnikov lay on the cobbles of the yard. Or Hanlon assumed it had to be them. Very little was recognizable of their faces, or indeed their heads. Huss saw, walking slowly towards them, silhouetted in the lights of the Mercedes, a tall man in a peaked forage cap and old military fatigues. He was carrying a heavy rifle with a bipod attached and a heavy-duty scope. As he got closer she thought, My God, he's gorgeous. To Huss, he looked like an actor, an actor from the romantic section of leading men, playing an action role for a change.

Walking behind Serg was a far less impressive figure, managing to look furtive and yet arrogant at the same time. Joad. With all that had happened, she had completely forgotten that it was Joad who had driven Myasnikov to the farm.

'Hello, Hanlon,' Serg said.

'Saved by an angel,' she replied. You can say that again, thought Huss. Hanlon smiled. Huss thought, that's the first time I've ever seen her do that. It transformed Hanlon's face. Huss thought she looked beautiful.

The Angel surveyed the farmyard, the Yusopovs, Danny, Mawson and Myasnikov.

'Where is Belanov and where is Kuzubov?'

'If you mean Dimitri,' said Huss, 'he's under that silage bale.' She pointed at the solitary bale. It seemed perfectly level with the ground. She thought, Dimitri must have been squashed virtually flat. Good.

'Did you do that?' Serg asked Huss. She nodded. Serg raised his shapely eyebrows.

'Congratulations,' said Serg.

'Arkady Belanov got away,' said Hanlon. Serg nodded thoughtfully.

'Oh, well.' He didn't seem particularly concerned.

'Now,' Hanlon said, 'Serg, can you help me with an injured man? He's in the farmhouse there.'

Huss, Hanlon and Serg carried the unconscious Enver outside. They laid him gently down on the cobbles of the farm-yard. The fires that had burned so brightly were nearly out. Huss crouched down beside him and stroked his hair. Enver's eyes were swollen as were his hands and face, and there were burn marks on his chest visible through his unbuttoned shirt. He was covered in bruises but he seemed intact.

In Chechnya and Dagestan, Serg had served in Group Alpha, the feared A Department, the FSB equivalent of the US Delta Force. He had seen a lot of violence, a lot of death. To Serg's experienced eyes – he had seen quite a few survivors of torture – he looked in not-too-bad shape. Serg felt his pulse. It seemed strong.

'If you can get him back to London, I know a doctor who is FSB recommended. He worked in Afghanistan for us, then in Chechnya. He's very good, and discreet.'

Hanlon looked at Huss. 'It's up to you,' she said. She paused. 'We can take him to the John Radcliffe if you want.'

It wasn't just an invitation for expert medical treatment at the best hospital in Oxfordshire; it was an open invitation to go public with the whole thing. At the moment, all of what had happened could be covered up.

Hanlon was leaving it up to Huss.

Huss appreciated the gesture. She looked around at the farmyard. She thought of the media circus that would ensue and quailed. 'I'm not sure Enver's job would survive this,' she said. Or my own, come to that, she thought. 'He's had one career ruined with that business with his eye. Now he's got one foot on the promotion ladder, I don't want to mess it up for him. So, we'll compromise. Let's take him up on his offer.'

'OK,' said Hanlon. She was undeniably relieved.

'Who's going to clear this lot up?' asked Huss. Her gaze travelled around the farmyard. It was like a battlefield.

Hanlon looked at her. 'Dave Anderson will,' she said. 'He's good at that kind of thing. He'll be delighted to see what's happened to Myasnikov and,' she said sadly, 'he'll give Danny some respect. The kid deserves that at least.'

Huss nodded. 'Come on, then,' said Hanlon. 'Let's put Enver in the back of the Merc. Joad'll drive you two to Slater's. I'll text you the address when we get a signal. I'll go back with Serg.'

Gently, watched by Joad who stood there smiling his insufferable smirk, they loaded Enver on to the back seat and secured him as best they could with the seat belts. Hanlon wondered what on earth Joad had in the inside breast pocket of his jacket. He kept touching something in there almost continually, like it was a good-luck charm or some religious artefact that needed continual propitiation.

'Can't we put some sheeting underneath him, in case he bleeds on the upholstery?' complained Joad. 'That's expensive leather.' He resisted the temptation to touch the envelope again.

It contained far more money than he had dreamed possible, more money than he'd ever seen, well in excess of six figures. Tax-free, thought Joad, misty-eyed with emotion.

Hanlon rolled her eyes. 'No,' she said.

They closed the rear doors gently. Huss opened her passenger door, and then seemed to remember something. She walked round to where Joad was standing by the open driver's door, lost in thought, smiling his annoying smile.

Huss nodded. 'Oh, before we go, Joad?' She spoke as if she had suddenly remembered something that she'd previously forgotten. Something important.

DI Ian Joad looked at her, slightly startled to hear her call his name. 'Yes?'

'Just one thing I'd like to make clear.' Huss balled her fist and slammed it into Ian Joad's stomach, driving the wind out of him. He doubled up in pain. It was an upper-cut and the force of it nearly lifted Joad off his feet. Good punch, thought Hanlon admiringly. He straightened up, using the bonnet of the car for support, taking shallow gasps of painful air.

'Don't call me fatso,' she said.

Huss walked back to her side of the car and got in. She slammed the door shut. Joad straightened up, wincing, barely able to breathe.

Hanlon smiled and watched as the Mercedes reversed away and headed off round the farmhouse to the track that led to the main road.

'Shall we go?' she said to Serg.

CHAPTER FORTY-FOUR

Traffic was light on the M40 heading back to London. Hanlon had pulled over at a car park as they had been leaving Oxford, and called Anderson to tell him about the Russians and to ask him to clean up the resultant mess. She also told him to return Serg's car to his hotel and Huss's car to the park-and-ride car park at Headington. And she'd texted Slater's address to Huss.

Then she sent one last text. The most important one she had ever sent in her life.

'So it was Myasnikov that brought you over here to Britain?' asked Hanlon. The engine sounded good to her ears; she was aware of the compelling shape of Serg next to her in the small cockpit of the powerful car. For once she was obeying the speed limit. At seventy in the Audi TT, it felt as if she was deliberately dawdling, which in a sense she was. She felt an almost medicated sense of relief. To be alive, that was amazing. Everything felt wonderful, every breath, the comforting feel of the hard steering wheel between her fingers, the lights of the dashboard, the car seat under her thighs. She was alive. She could be lying face down with Melinda Huss, like poor Danny, but she wasn't.

And Enver was OK, and Huss, and for once, none of this mess was her responsibility. She felt a blessed freedom from guilt. Beside her, Serg nodded.

'Technically, yes. As you know, I am FSB, the Federal Security Service, a full colonel, in fact.' She could see a bitter smile on his face when she glanced at him quickly as she overtook a slow-moving lorry.

'But, really, it was just an excuse. Myasnikov, he was one of the *novye vory v zakone*, the new-style *vors*, and he was, as you know, *a nasty piece of work* – I think that is the correct expression?'

'It'll do,' said Hanlon. 'Understated, but it will do. What about Mawson?'

'Belanov was Myasnikov's UK bagman,' said Serg. 'The money that he controlled would have fallen under Mawson's control. He'd have become what we call *derzhatel obshchaka*, the controller of the money fund.' He remained silent for a moment and continued, 'Everyone, Russians included, thought of *Miasnik* as a great criminal brain. But he wasn't. Mawson would have bided his time, then killed him, or a Russian gangster would.'

'Or the state,' said Hanlon.

'But of course,' he agreed. 'The state is just a bigger and more powerful mafia than the mafia,' said Serg dismissively.

Hanlon thought of the trail of dead back at Tragoes Farm. She also thought in particular of Danny. So young.

'And you serve it?' she said to Serg, disbelief in her voice. 'This mafia state?'

'*Nyet*, Hanlon. I serve Russia,' said Serg proudly. 'Governments come and go, political systems come and go, presidents come and go. My duty is to Russia. That is who I serve. That is where my loyalty lies.'

First and foremost, my country is my love, thought Serg. As it was my father's. There was silence for a while as the Audi law-abidingly ate up the miles down the motorway through the black night. Then Serg resumed their conversation.

'I told my boss that Myasnikov was part of some unspecified plan to assassinate the Mayor of Moscow, that there was a *skhodka*, a special thieves' meeting, with disaffected Chechens and rogue police here in London, and I would go as a guest of Edward Li and Thanatos and investigate.'

'They believed that?' said Hanlon.

Serg shrugged. 'Who knows, who cares? It could well be true. Belanov was connected with all sorts of criminals. My boss let me come, that's the main thing. For all I know he works for some rival of Myasnikov. The Surikov family are like FSB royalty. We're part of the *siloviki*, the power guys. We run Russia.' He gave a mirthless bark of laughter. 'It's true in, oh, so many ways.' Serg's great-grandfather had been with the CheKa, forerunners of the NKVD where his grandfather had served, who had later become the KGB, who became the FSB. It was a distinguished lineage.

'That was my excuse anyway,' continued Serg. 'And it was good enough to get me here, and soon I shall write a report that I have neutralized the threat of Myasnikov and the Chechen-supporting policeman, and my superiors will be happy and Myasnikov's *vor* rivals who bribe them will be happy. Everybody will be happy.'

Hanlon could hear the bitterness in his voice.

'And what will make you happy, Serg?' Hanlon asked gently.

He turned his head and looked at her proud face in profile, fitfully illuminated by the lights of oncoming traffic. You could make me happy, DCI Hanlon, he thought. But here is what would satisfy me.

'My father was killed by Arkady Belanov. He had been sent to investigate something even bigger than the usual corruption in the 58th Army at their staff headquarters. That's in a place called Vladikavkaz near the Chechnya–Ingoushetia border.

The middle of nowhere. He was murdered. The army said Chechens, but I found out it was a Group Vympel elimination group. That's four men.' Another bark of laughter. 'They're FSB. My own kind. One talked to me, before I threw him off that roof.'

'That's why they call you the Angel?' asked Hanlon.

Serg nodded. 'They say when you see me coming for you, you will fly with the angels. Belanov was in the elimination group. He will lead me to the man who organized it. Belanov is nothing by himself, just a weapon, just a tool.'

They were now entering the outskirts of London.

'So I'm glad you didn't kill him. I need him to talk to me, then he will die.'

They drove in silence through the deserted streets of central London – orderly, quiet, well lit, beautiful in Hanlon's eyes – each lost in thought. Then up through Camden, past Little Venice where so many of Serg's countrymen were buying properties.

Hanlon pulled up outside Albert Slater's end-of-terrace house in time to see Joad about to get into the Mercedes. He leaned on the open door as she stopped alongside.

'They're in there, together with the doctor that he sent.' He pointed at Serg. 'The other copper seems OK, according to him. Anyway, I'm off. I'm feeling a bit under the weather.' He smiled his infuriating smile. He patted the roof of the car in an almost proprietorial way. 'I think I need a bit of time off work.' He looked seriously at Hanlon. 'Maybe a lot of time. I'd say it was stress. Adios, Hanlon.'

He slid into the driver's seat and pulled away.

Hanlon watched him go. She put the handbrake on in the Audi but left the engine running and got out, as did Serg. She opened the boot and took out his gun bag and gave it to him.

'Aren't you coming in?' he asked. The tension between the two of them was almost palpable, electric. They stood silently, looking at each other. Hanlon pushed her hair back from her forehead.

'Please,' said Serg gently. Hanlon got the feeling it wasn't a word he had to use a great deal.

She shook her head. 'I've still got things to do.'

She thought of Oksana; she thought of the man she had to speak to. Debts to be discharged.

He nodded. 'Can I see you again?' He was feeling almost light-headed with desperation. He hadn't felt like this since he'd been a teenager. I'm thirty-four, he thought, almost wonderingly. Not seventeen.

'I don't know,' she said. She got in the car. She didn't turn her head to say goodbye.

He watched as her tail lights moved away.

CHAPTER FORTY-FIVE

The bar at Corrigan's club officially closed at one a.m, but Corrigan had bribed the night porter to allow him to use it for his meeting with Hanlon.

She looked exhausted. James, the night porter, was ex-army. He had raised an eyebrow slightly at Hanlon, even though he'd been forewarned by Corrigan. The woman he admitted through the forbidding club entrance was unusual to say the least.

She smelled of smoke and sweat and blood. James knew the signs of combat when he saw them. She was wearing an old, faded, man's denim shirt over a navy T-shirt, and he suspected he knew what the dark stains were on her chest. Her combat trousers were filthy and her dark hair matted and powdered with dust. She was wearing high-sided army boots – not British, he knew what they looked like only too well – American, he guessed. There were several deep gashes and scrapes across her knuckles.

'I'm Hanlon,' she said, her gaze imperious. James straightened his back automatically and fought a desire to salute.

'If you'd like to follow me, ma'am,' he said.

They walked across the marble foyer, lit only by a single lamp, James leading the way, and then up the broad marble stairs with the red carpet and the golden brass runners at the base of each step. After the hellhole of the farm, the club seemed supernaturally opulent and so quiet she could almost feel the silence throbbing. The stairs ended at the broad gallery that overlooked the foyer and the members' bar was one of the rooms just off it. Like the foyer, it was lit by a single lamp.

'He's in there, ma'am,' said James.

Corrigan was sitting in a pool of soft light that did little to mitigate the harshness of his craggy, slab-like face. He had been to a black-tie dinner and was still wearing his jacket and bow tie that on him gave the impression of a high-class bouncer in a low-class club. He had undone his bow tie and it hung like a short scarf around his thick neck. His dress shirt was rumpled. He was holding a cut-glass tumbler of single malt; she could smell it from where she stood.

'Good evening, Hanlon,' he said. 'Have a seat.'

She sat down opposite him. He ran his eyes over her. She looked terrible, but she was alive. Enver's silence over the last couple of days had become to Corrigan a deafening roar. Now, thank God, he would get some answers.

His eyes were hard as ever, but inside he felt a terrible anguish as he looked at Hanlon. He had tried to keep her safe and had failed spectacularly.

'How's Enver Demirel?' he asked.

How are you feeling, Enver?' asked Huss. Enver Demirel was lying in Albert Slater's guest bedroom, which was mercifully free of oriental or whimsical touches. It had clean, hard, modern Scandinavian lines and its colour scheme consisted of greys and shades of white, with the occasional strip of black and clever lighting. Mirrors made the room bigger and lighter than it was naturally.

The lights had dimmer controls and the bedroom was bathed in a very soft light. He was feeling tranquil and relaxed. He looked at the tall, bald Russian doctor with sleepy eyes and yawned.

Enver lay propped up in bed. Huss, her touch sure and gentle from handling sick animals, had helped the doctor to clean Enver up, treated his wounds, mainly bad burns and occasional deep cuts, bandaged his head and strapped him up where necessary.

'Fine,' he said and closed his eyes.

'It seems pretty much superficial,' said the doctor, satisfied. 'I've given him morphine-based painkillers. Give him two of these.' He pressed several bottles and blister-packed packages of tablets on Huss. Antibiotics, anti-inflammatories: it was a comprehensive pharmacopoeia. More instructions followed. Three days' worth. In a day or so she'd get him checked over properly. Enver appeared to be sleeping.

She accompanied the doctor downstairs. In the front room Slater was at his desk, Chantal pouring him tea.

'Let Dr Zhivago out, Chantal, there's a good *feele*,' he said to her. Chantal nodded. Huss thought she seemed to have adopted the role of PA to Slater. Chantal said politely to the doctor, 'If you'd like to come this way, Dr Zhivago.' She led the baffled-looking doctor to the front door. Chantal was dressed demurely in a white blouse and dark skirt. She looked relaxed and content, so much better than the wreck from a couple of nights before.

'I think I'll let the little *palone feele* stay,' said Albert Slater. 'Poor tart. I know what it's like to work the meat rack. I was a *dilly boy* once and very much in demand, may I tell you, not that you'd guess it these days. But,' he said, 'you've got to be tough to survive and she ain't that.' He shook his head. 'She's street, but she's not tough.' He sipped his tea. 'How's the *charpering omi*?'

'I don't know,' said Huss. 'I don't know what you're talking about.'

'He means your policeman friend,' explained Chantal sweetly, as she came back into the room. 'Mr Slater's been teaching me Polari. *Palone* means a woman and *feele* means a child.'

Slater looked at her approvingly. 'It's all very Pygmalion,' he said. 'In a way.'

'He's fine,' Huss said, and yawned. 'I'm sorry.'

'You left your bag here the other day,' said Chantal. 'I put it in the same room as the policeman.'

Huss excused herself and went upstairs.

Enver seemed asleep. She found her bag that she'd packed for a night of cinema, food and sex. It felt like an awfully long time ago. She took out the exotic nightwear she'd been planning to wear just in case Enver still hadn't got the message.

She padded into the bathroom, undressed and stood under the shower for what felt like a very long time, washing and scrubbing her hair and body with intense concentration, cleansing every bit of the day from her. She could feel the tension and the excess adrenaline flowing away down the drain with the dirty water. Tomorrow I'll get a sauna somewhere, she thought, exfoliate even more. She had brought a bin bag upstairs with her and she had stuffed it with the clothes she'd been wearing. Everything connected with Tragoes Farm would go.

Eventually she got out of the shower and towelled herself dry. She felt renewed. She put on her ridiculously sexy nightdress and lacy kimono, feeling slightly absurd, and looked at herself in the bathroom mirror. My, my, she thought. She slipped quietly through the door into the bedroom.

'Is that for me?' asked Enver. His eyes drank in the sight of her, exceeding his wildest dreams. He had never seen such an attractive-looking woman wearing so little. The bandage round his head looked like a turban in the half-light, his powerfully muscled arms dark and naked against the white sheet that covered him.

'In your condition?' asked Huss. She was backlit by the light from the bathroom door, her nakedness and the curves of her body emphasized by the nightwear.

'Particularly in my condition,' said Enver. Huss smiled and slipped under the sheet next to Enver. They reached for each other hungrily.

I would imagine Enver Demirel's fine,' said Hanlon. She didn't add, *No thanks to you.* It would have been a cheap shot.

'Drink, Hanlon?' asked Corrigan. He gestured expansively towards the darkened bar area, the ranks of serried bottles. 'The place is ours.'

She shook her head. 'I'm driving, sir, and I have things to do when I get home.'

Instead she told Corrigan a carefully edited version of the whole business from the start. She left out anything connected with Anderson. She no longer cared what happened to her, but that might hurt Whiteside and he had been hurt enough.

Corrigan said little while she briefed him. He drank some more Scotch, but mainly contented himself with swirling the pale liquor around in his glass. It was a Laphroaig, a west coast malt from Islay. Corrigan could taste the peat from the water it was made from; its smell reminded him of a childhood long ago. Of a burning fire in a cottage when he'd been a boy on holiday.

He knew Hanlon was leaving great chunks out. But let her, he thought. If it wasn't for her, well – he didn't deal in ifs, but he was profoundly grateful.

'Mawson was a shock, sir. I was expecting Edward Li or even Serg to be the Russians' man in the government, never him.'

'You should never trust likeable bosses, Hanlon,' said Corrigan. 'You're better off with old bastards like me.' He sighed. 'He was my friend. I've known him since I was, what, seventeen. But now we know what we know. . . Well, he gave up being a firearms officer after he killed an armed suspect. He was exonerated and he said he couldn't go on doing that job after that, but it did look suspiciously like he'd shot him for fun. But because he was who he was, Mr Nice Guy, well, we never thought anything of it. We thought, it's Mawson, it can't be. His wife died unexpectedly too, come to think of it. I have a horrible feeling that if we started looking into his past. . . *Straw dogs*, eh, Hanlon.'

He fell silent, frowning. He hadn't imagined Mawson capable of anything like this. He certainly wouldn't be making any of that public. All Mawson's cases gone over, floods of litigation and appeals. God knows what the press would make of it. Mawson could take all of this to the grave with him.

Let Mawson become one of his own statistics. Let DC McIntyre, or whatever she was called, put photos of Mawson out on social media and the Internet. Hanlon could start the investigation into his disappearance.

'I got your email, Hanlon.'

'My resignation, sir.'

He nodded. 'What was it Surikov said to you about duty?'

'He said, sir, "If I left I would feel a traitor."'

'Well,' said Corrigan, 'you care about people, Hanlon. Surikov has Russia. You've got London and an abstract sense of fair play. If you left you'd regret it. You're not even going to face an inquiry over this. Nothing, technically, has happened.'

Hanlon felt a surge of affection laced with irritation towards Corrigan.

'I may have arranged an operation for Mark Whiteside,' she said. 'I need to concentrate on that, sir.'

Corrigan brightened. He poured himself a massive Scotch.

'Six months' compassionate leave, Hanlon, effective in a fortnight. We can put it down to post-traumatic stress from your last case, followed by six months' unpaid leave but your job open if you want it. Think of it as your gap year, Hanlon. Deal?'

Despite herself, she smiled. Corrigan thought, I've hardly ever seen her do that. It transformed Hanlon's sombre face. He suddenly thought sadly, I wish I wasn't so old. Oh, well. I suppose I'd better look wise and avuncular.

A gap year, she thought. She leaned forward and shook his hand. 'Deal. So what are you going to do about the Russians, sir?'

'Nothing, nothing at all,' said Corrigan. 'The only witness of tonight is this Arkady Belanov and he won't be coming forward. God knows what will happen to Myasnikov's businesses but that's not my concern. Enver and Huss can forget the whole thing happened and you tell me that Joad will seek early retirement. Mawson's gone.'

'Well, Hanlon, you're still in Missing Persons,' he said, draining his Scotch. 'In a couple of days you can add Mawson to the list. I doubt he'll be turning up.'

Hanlon thought of the Edmonton Waste Incinerator near Anderson's pub.

'No, sir, I don't think he will.'

It was four a.m by the time Hanlon wearily opened the door to her studio flat. In the east she could see the darkness beginning to lift.

Like Huss earlier, she stripped off her clothes. Like Huss, she bundled them into a bin bag for disposal later. Like Huss, she showered with intense concentration.

She wrapped a towel round her wet hair and stood naked by the window, looking out at the Thames far below, her face inscrutable. She picked up her phone.

Oksana's number appeared and Hanlon tapped in: *A life for a life*. Five words. She pressed send. She hoped it would bring Oksana some measure of solace. That was the past dealt with as best she could. Her obligation discharged.

She selected another number and this time she hesitated. This was the future. She reached a decision.

Serg answered immediately. 'Hello, Hanlon.' His voice was full of suppressed elation.

For the second time in an hour she smiled. She knew that she'd said goodbye once; she'd hardly be phoning to confirm. 'You're not the only one with father issues, Serg. I'm in Berlin next month, the twenty-eighth is a Friday. I'll be at the Neue National Galerie at eleven a.m., by the Beuys gallery.'

Serg's response was coolly matter of fact. 'Potsdamer Straße.'

'I thought you'd know it.'

'I'll be there,' he said.

'I know you will,' said Hanlon.

ACKNOWLEDGEMENTS

I received a great deal of help from various people but I would particularly like to thank the following: Narine Jordan for her invaluable assistance in translating Russian expressions and vocabulary. Roger Prior for help with what stripped down Landrovers look like.

The following are recommended to anyone remotely interested in Russian crime:

Putin's Russia by Anna Politkovskaya

Angel of Grozny by Asne Seierstad

Investigating the Russian Mafia by Joseph di Serio

Mafia State by Luke Harding

And also of interest, *Stasiland* by Anna Funder